"SMACK-DAB, IN THE MIDDLE OF NOWHERE"

By Duncan P. Pacey

By Duncan P. Pacey

Copyright © 2017 by Duncan P. Pacey

ISBN 978-0-473-41720-8 (paperback)
ISBN 978-0-473-41721-5 (digital)

All characters in this book are fictitious.
Any similarity to real persons, living or dead, is coincidental and not intended by the author.

Published by SillyGoose in Auckland, New Zealand

First edition, 2017

Cover design, Calum Beck
Cover Illustration, Duncan P. Pacey

www.duncanppacey.com

This dedication page is dedicated to:
Dedication pages
Without which this page would have been blank.

By Duncan P. Pacey

Introduction

A Bloody Wall Falls

This is the Waste.

It scratches out an existence upon the ruins of the Old World: a forgotten home to an advanced civilisation, where miracles of science were as commonplace as unexplained fungal diseases are now.

We soar over the landscape and we see a vast, undulating dusty plain stretching to the horizon both north and south. A dominating mountain range blockades the western flank, cramming the denizens of this tired place against the wild grey ocean to the east. There are no trees, for they have long stood up and left for greener pastures, but the dishevelled relics of Old World infrastructure persevere. Crumbled roads wind through the rolling landscape like chunky, rotten veins.

And then we arrive here...

...here where a battle is taking place.

Beneath a dismal sky smothered by thick cloud, the din of gunfire now echoes across these shallow hills. The sun hasn't come out in decades, if not centuries. Some suspect it will never come out again. Others build religious cults around the prospect, and burn anyone who doesn't join. There are ... two kinds of people.

But back at the battle, we see an enormous walled settlement under assault by a horde of foot soldiers. They swarm against the south gate like radioactive ants trying to find a way into a home. A river beneath the bridge at their feet runs red with blood.

This battle will one day live on in legend. Folks will talk about it like their favourite sports team; they'll debate the politics, they'll get drunk and yell about who was right, who was wrong. But today?

Mostly people are screaming.

The bandit lord known as Ash knew his end was near.

He ducked instinctively as a hailstorm of bullets scoured the paint off his fort's walls, its defenders leaping wildly for cover nearby - lest they discover what their insides look like. He cursed loudly, the spray clattering behind where he now sat in an angry slump, gripping his old hunting rifle tight in blood-stained hands. The roar was utterly deafening; it drowned the cries of fallen bandit soldiers all along the metal wall, and more so the moans of his enemies dying slowly in the river at the foot of it.

Let them sob, he grunted to himself. They could cry until the river's acid dissolved them, for all Lord Ash cared. They didn't deserve a swift death for the menace they had caused.

His slender fingers tightened around the cracked wooden stock of his aged rifle. The mob of southerners who now laid siege to his precious fort had come out of ruddy nowhere. Yesterday Lord Ash was a glorious bandit king, lord of the Ash Fort, and ruler of Can't Be Buried - the great Waste plains upon which his mighty walls stood as a beacon of power.

Now? He was fairly certain he'd shat himself.

"Lord Ash!" a voice called, somewhere beneath him.

The bandit lord grunted, shifting his weight forwards so that he could peer down to the lower rampart. He placed a hand firmly on the floor, but slipped on a pool of fresh blood. His, presumably.

He had been shot, possibly twice, but his body had given up sending pain signals from specific areas and was now blaring vague alerts from just about everywhere. His best cape, a pleasant shade of blue, was now a less-than-pleasant shade of red. His manicured, pointed beard was now ragged with filth, his patchwork metal armour even more so - not like it was much use, anyway. Couldn't even stop a bullet or two.

The Ash Fort's walls were towering bloody things, built from layer upon layer of iron, steel, and anything else vaguely solid that could be patched on in a hurry. The upper rampart, crammed with defenders, ran in a staggeringly large square the entire perimeter of the fort. It took Lord Ash an hour just to walk the length of one side - an impressive barrier keeping out the Waste's many perils, until today anyway.

The lower rampart, which Lord Ash was crawling over to investigate, was about halfway down and acted as a storage space for additional supplies, manpower, or, in one small section on the eastern wall, a pleasant little coffee stall. It hadn't sold actual coffee in years, but that never stopped anyone from drinking the tarry black mess.

Lord Ash glared over the side of the upper rampart, spying a skinny wretch of a soldier clutching a boxy radio to his breast. "Tell me some good news!" Ash called down.

The skinny soldier shuffled awkwardly from one foot to the other, staring up at his leader. "Erm," he stammered back.

"Well? Out with it, man! By jing by jove, I haven't got all day."

Then, another storm of bullets pounded the length of the wall, ripping up twisted metal and spewing it across the ramparts, deadly shards spilling onto the cowering bandit soldiers. Lord Ash rolled to his right and gritted his teeth, pointing towards the Waste side of the wall.

"Will one of you blow that bloody truck up?" he bellowed, sporadic rifle fire filling the void between hailstorms. "I just had this wall repainted!"

Not waiting for a response, he rolled back onto his stomach and gazed down at the soldier with the radio. "Good news, Gordon! Or you'll be scrubbing my toilet for a month!"

Gordon, knuckles white around his radio, stared at Lord Ash. "We jus' got word from Lady Gertrude's party in Behinds, sir."

Ash scowled. Behinds was a small, derelict Old World town about three hours walking south of the Ash Fort. "Well she jolly well better be lining up for a flanking assault, Gordon m'boy! I'm getting tired of bleeding all over my fort!"

Gordon seemed to visibly shrink. "I ... I'm sorry, sir. She called to say the southerners 'ave reinforcements on the way, and then I think she died, sir."

"You *think* she died, Gordon?" Lord Ash's face, already a poster of what stress does to a person, wrinkled further.

The lad nodded hurriedly. "Aye, sir. Not sure what else, 'Oh shit, oh shit, my insides, oh shit,' could mean, sir."

Lord Ash sighed deeply. Still lying stretched out on his stomach, a tripping hazard if there ever was one, he waved at the boy to go away, words failing him. Slowly he dragged himself back away from the edge and, wincing with pain, propped himself against the outer defences. His eyes, heavy and dark-rimmed from a day of non-stop madness, swept across the scene. And what a sad, sad affair it was.

The truck somewhere below, assuredly un-blown-up (despite his request), had reloaded and was letting loose on the wall once again. A smattering of small arms fire accompanied it from below, all to the percussive bass of angry southerners trying to cave in the south gate. Lord Ash's bandit army, proud defenders of the Ash Fort, were dying all along the southern wall. He watched a man crumple to his knees, clutching at

7

his stomach before anything could fall out. Then a woman lost her face, tipping drunkenly forwards, over the wall, and into the icy, acidic river below.

By jing by jove indeed, Ash thought to himself, shaking his head in dismay. It truly was over.

Amidst another thundering storm of machine-gun fire, one of Ash's captains rushed over to his side, kneeling low to keep beneath the wall's metal plating. It was Sir Robert, his favourite captain, and a man who had repeatedly won the Ash Fort moustache competition. By goodness was his majestic lip companion a legend. And his abilities as a bandit captain weren't shabby, either.

"Lord Ash," the man spoke, visibly out of breath. His normally pristine face was drenched in sweat, spattered by blood stains. Behind him was his lieutenant, Doris, clutching a bloodied hunting knife in her small hands. They both looked worried.

"My Lord," the man spoke again, fear wavering at the edge of his voice. "We just came from the south gate. Good golly, but this southern horde has nearly broken through. We've got men stabbing through the cracks to keep them off, but they jolly well won't let up. What are your orders? Is Gerty coming up from Behinds to give these ruffians the old what-for in their, well, their behinds?"

The bandit lord didn't speak for a few moments, his eyes shut. He breathed deeply, frowned, then stared up into the pleading face of Sir Robert. "I'm sorry, my old friend. But the day is lost. Those southerners have reinforcements coming, and ours are spent bloodying the ramparts."

Sir Robert and Doris frowned in unison, inching closer. It was Doris who spoke first. "But sir, if we can't hold 'em off, wassat mean for us?"

"Doris, my dear, it means we need to evacuate henceforth and immediately. Live to fight another day, what-ho and all that." Lord Ash knew it was the right thing to do, but the low, soft tone of his voice betrayed his inner lack of confidence.

And then the robot appeared.

Servos whirring noisily, its glimmering, smooth metal skull appeared first atop the Waste side of the wall, quickly panning left and right with a cyclopean, glowing red eye. Sir Robert and Doris both gasped, taking a step back, their hands instantly bringing forwards weapons.

"What the fu-?" Doris cried.

"Lord Ash," Sir Robert shouted, stepping between his lord and the skeletal figure now reaching with a clawed hand to pull itself over the defences. "Lord Ash, if we're fleeing, we need to flee, now!"

But Lord Ash didn't move. Even as Sir Robert and Doris moved to help him up, he pushed his wooden rifle into Sir Robert's hands. He shook his head, glancing briefly at the machine. It was flopping over the wall now, standing to its full, terrifying height. Two soldiers on the other side moved rapidly to intercept it, axes raised in their hands.

"DO NOT ATTEMPT VIOLENCE, FLESHY HUMANS," it roared, synthetic vocal chords sounding hollow, lifeless - a being with no desire to sound human. "ORGANIC BEINGS ARE DESIGNED ONLY TO DIE. I AM HERE TO SPEED UP YOUR PURPOSE."

Lord Ash pushed again with his rifle until Sir Robert finally grasped it. "My old friend, take this and fly. Fly with whoever you can find. Go north, leave the fort. Survive!"

"Sir, I can't just jolly well leave you here to die!" the captain protested, shouting over the noise of the battle, trying to push the rifle back.

Behind them, the robot's red eye cast an eerie, almost-prophetic glow on the face of a terrified, wriggling soldier it now held firmly in its claw. Blood oozed out from beneath the man's clothing, then the thing grasped him hard by the face with its other claw and tossed him over the side like a child bored with its new toy. The robot then stepped towards the second soldier, who was understandably reconsidering his decisions in life.

"Go you damned fool!" Lord Ash boomed. "Go, thrive, and then come back to seek revenge! By jing by jove, I will haunt you if you don't honour my memory!"

Doris gripped Sir Robert's arm and pulled urgently. Sir Robert growled loudly, teeth bared beneath his moustache, but he submitted. In tense hands he took the old rifle, stared hard into his lord's eyes for a long moment, and then allowed Doris to pull him hurriedly away.

Lord Ash listened sadly as his favourite captain's footsteps dissolved into the background ruckus of gunfire, screams and a robot's taunts. He took a deep breath, his chest hurting in places he never knew could hurt, his breath coming out in ragged rasps. With teeth grinding together, he pushed himself further against the wall, propping himself up higher. His fingers explored the bloodied metal floor until they came across a discarded axe, the hand of its previous user still gripping for dear life.

The robot, drenched in streaks of sticky blood and standing between two fresh halves of a human form, swivelled its soulless red eye to stare at Lord Ash.

"Alright, you bastard," he muttered. "I don't know why you're here, what those southern menaces did to buy your allegiance, or why you give two tosses about my fort."

It cocked its head at him.

"But by jing and bloody well by jove, you will not win this day without feeling the blade of my axe deep within your shiny metal skull."

Then the head of his axe fell off, clattering to the floor.

He stared at it.

He looked back at the robot.

Well ... it turns out the end was nearer than he thought.

Part One

Smack-dab, in the Middle of Nowhere

Bert, her blue eyes narrow and fixed on the dusty wooden rafters above, finally let out a slow breath. It had been raining for the past three hours, and at times, raining like there was no tomorrow. Which, as Bert had been concerned of at one point, there may not have been. A significant portion of the roof had dissolved in the storm, and a number of small leaks were poking through to the ground floor. And she reckoned it would be a hell of a lot worse up on the second floor, where her guest rooms were presumably evaporating.

Southerly rain storms were a regular facet of Waste life in Can't Be Buried, and a great way for folks to get rid of deceased family members. And between low pressure systems, travellers were concerned with wind and dust. Since all the damned trees had wandered west, there was very little to hold dust down. Huge, cascading dust storms killed hundreds every year, and beasties or bandits tended to kill the rest.

There was a small cheer and a scattered applause around Bert. She was standing behind the bar counter in a large, tavern-like wooden room filled with a small number of dishevelled customers at shabby round tables. Behind her was a row of shelves, each bearing a veritable science lab of delightful, albeit unlabelled, glass bottles. The great secret of Waste bar ownership, Bert had found, is that no traveller, trader or nomad of any kind cares what they drink, so long as it's cheap, it burns, and it takes away the bad memories (which tends to be every memory).

The kitchen hummed away through a small window behind the drinks, Bert's adventurer-turned-handyman and chef, Phoenix, hard at work on the day's meals. Or at least, Bert thought, he better be hard at work. One time she had found him snoozing in the corner, a rabbit-like creature he had caught to slaughter tucked asleep into his lap and dressed in a little paper hat. She didn't know where the hat came from, but they'd had to let the creature go. Neither had the heart to cut it open while it wore that stupid hat.

Giant wooden letters atop this two-storey building, one of the few intact structures from the Old World still standing, spelled out "Smack-dab. Bar. Food. Room." To some, this fine establishment was considered the jewel of Can't Be Buried, a haven for traders and other innocent folk the Waste over. Except the problem was, that Smack-dab's greatest asset

- it being the nearest shelter for hours in both directions - was also its greatest problem.

Smack-dab was inconveniently located along the Trader's Back Road, a lengthy trail that linked the trader's village of Second Thought in the north with the farming village of Gerald, south. By using the back road, you could skip the Great Highway along the coast, which although faster, took you straight through rather murdery bandit country (and the Ash Fort).

Well, Bert frowned, it probably wasn't the Ash Fort anymore, not now that those southerners had come up and toppled it. First a horde of bandits, then a cold front - what next, a forest of man-eating trees? She shook her head at the thought. That would be just what she needed on a day like today. A day when there was actual paying customers, for once.

Her sapphire-coloured stare fell to the dusty windows at the front of the room. Smacks had a little garden between it and the road, although nothing had grown there since the Old World. It was mostly just some tidy dirt, a few weeds, and a gravel pathway that wound up to Smack-dab's wooden porch. But standing there, in the middle of the tidiest patch of dirt, was a statue. It was a woman, an adventurer, who wore a crude, wide-brimmed hat that looked like two hats sewn together, and a long, patchy trench coat flowing down her body, blowing in a breeze that would never fade. She grimaced at the world, pointing forwards with one stony arm that clutched a finely carved revolver. There was a plaque at her feet, which read:

The Woman With No Name
Founder and Original Owner
RIP

And then below that, in smaller letters...

If you deface this statue,
I will come out there and cut your balls off
- Bert, current owner

And then below *that*, in a newer plaque that looked tacked on more recently:

PS. To those who have no balls,
we will work something else out.

Bert let out another slow breath, her brow melting slowly into a frown. She often wondered what The Woman would do in her situation, dealing with modern problems. Like the fort being toppled basically once a year, or Can't Be Buried's growing population of Things - you now, the ones that go bump in the night (and also eat you). The Woman didn't have to deal with any of that back when she was running the place. No, she just had to fight off the occasional Waste Beast, and struggle to find suppliers for her grog. Oh, and also die horribly in a vicious gun battle.

Bert's frown soured, lines of sadness creasing at the edge of her eyes. The Woman was the mother that didn't sell her to slavery - the one that actually gave a damn. But, like all of the Waste's great ironies, she died because of Bert, to protect Smack-dab. And now? Bert'd be damned if this bar did anything other than thrive. Smack-dab would prosper, or she'd shoot folk until it did.

Above Smack-dab, a strong gust was swirling up and over the mountains, carrying away the rain. Somewhere, a wandering trader was shot in the head for what looked like a delicious sandwich. Elsewhere, a cannibal was gnawing on her victim's rib cage, blissfully unaware that a slobbering Waste Beast was about to gnaw on her's.

All in all, it was a pretty quiet day.

But three figures were approaching the bar, and they weren't known to be quiet...

* * *

"Cor," said the young lad known as Orsen, "It ain't half big, is it, Jeb?"

Jeb smiled, folds of leathery dark skin wrinkling as his lips moved. "Aye, an' thas' just the relic of it, too. Back in th' Old World, that city woulda been huge! With buildings made o' glass - clean glass, Orsen, imagin' that! - an' towers stretchin' all th' way into th' clouds. So tall ya couldn't see th' top if ya stared from th' bottom. Not like the rickety ol' towers up in the Orcklands."

Orsen's mouth hung open, his youthful, teenage face soaking in as much of the view as possible. But something struck his mind, and he turned to face his travelling companion, brow furrowing. "So ... if there was towers an' that, where they all gone? I don't see anythin' taller than a few storeys."

Jeb nodded slowly, a veritable sage of a man. Or so he liked to pretend. "Well, m'boy, they ... fell over."

"They fell over, Jeb?"

"Aye, lad, they fell over. Just goes t' show, don't it?"

"What's that?"

"Ya shouldn't make a tower outta glass."

Orsen pondered that for a moment, nodded with satisfaction, then turned back to look at the view.

Jeb was a haggard old man, so long as nobody said that to his face. He wouldn't get violent at them, but if they didn't want to hear a lecture about how age is nonsense, a man can be anything he wants regardless of age, and that a person shouldn't insult strangers who could secretly be hiding claws in their gloves, they kept their mouths shut.

He scratched at the rough stubble on his weather-beaten face, leaning back in his puffy coat against his large trader's backpack. It clunked with various metallic sounds as it took his weight. Orsen, meanwhile, couldn't take his eyes off the view before them.

They were sitting together in a watchtower, built from bits of corrugated tin and planks of wood at the top of an Old World power pylon. Their feet dangled off the edge, the sound of waves lapping hungrily at a beach blowing in on the wind from just a mile or so away. It was a cold day, especially up in the tower, but they'd both shivered through worse.

Jeb and Orsen were staring at the Dead Church: a city, or rather, what was left of one. Most of this aged, decrepit place had been consumed when the ocean rose to swallow it, but its sprawling outskirts lay in an eerie dormancy on the shore. In a time long forgotten, this place was a bustling metropolis, filled with beautiful gardens, buzzing industry and, according to Jeb, gorgeous women who would not only take their clothes off at the drop of a hat, but who had little-to-no physical mutation (Jeb had, of course, embellished some of his story). He'd tried to convince Orsen that it was also home to robots that served humanity, working in their shops and that, but Orsen didn't believe it. The Overlords, as robots were known in this place, kicked humans in the ribs, they didn't serve them ribs. Overlords didn't work for humans, end of story.

A few moments into their silence, the lad eagerly fished into his thick, tattered coat and revealed a well-loved notebook. Jeb watched him find a blank page and scribble hastily into the book, and he couldn't help but smile.

Orsen loved himself some Old World history. Anything still standing from the time it all went tits up was like pure gold to the boy. He'd ask a million and one questions, then scribble everything he'd seen and learned into his diary. In fact, the duo were using that love as an excuse to travel around the Waste, walking from town to town selling whatever they picked up to fund their next adventure. The boy got to see what the world was like before, and Jeb taught him about modern life along the way.

Shortly, they heard some clattering behind them, followed by the grunting of voices. Both Orsen and Jeb turned to see in the other direction, spying what appeared to be some kind of construction going on just outside of Rangi's Aura, the nearby town. Actually, it looked more like *de*struction, thought Jeb. A bunch of burly sorts in matching blue dungarees seemed to be sledgehammering some hovels down on the fringes of Rangi.

"What do you think they're doing, Jeb?" Orsen asked, wriggling away from the edge of the tower to sit on the other side.

Jeb pulled his legs up as well and slowly swivelled around, feeling his old bones creak from having sat still too long. He watched a particularly large-looking woman get frustrated with her hammer and start prying the wood and metal away with her bare fingers.

"Looks like they're tearin' down homes, m'boy," he replied, scratching at his stubble again. "A new development goin' in, mus' be."

Orsen stayed silent for a moment again, gazing out at the work below. It wasn't too far away, but nobody seemed to be bothered by two shabby traders sitting in a tower.

The boy finally made a noise. "Hmm. Do you think th' folk that live there are in on it?"

They watched in curiosity as a well-dressed local waved his arms at the large woman, his mouth flapping non-stop, but the words only reaching their ears as muffled swears. Before Jeb could respond, the burly woman pushed the well-dressed man hard, picked up her sledgehammer and drove it clean through his skull. Jeb and Orsen both sat upright with a jolt. Hell, Jeb hadn't seen a skull explode like that since his last wife died.

"Err," the old man said, a little uncertainly. "Looks like they're bein' consulted now, lad."

Faced with the images before him, Jeb's face lost its smile. This strange construction work was something he hadn't seen before, and he wasn't sure what it was. His brow furrowed, deep frown lines forming crevices across his forehead. With a grubby elbow he nudged Orsen in the side. "Why don't ya finish yer notes, lad, then we'll get on the road, eh? Doesn't look like we wanna hang around Rangi much longer."

Orsen stared at the sparkling red splotch now occupying where the man's head should be, while the burly woman went straight back to her task of pulling the home apart. He nodded slowly, then curled his legs under himself and continued his scribblings cross-legged, leaning back on his pack.

It was then that Jeb spotted something metal moving between the folks with dungarees. He squinted hard, following the bobbing motion of the glare before it vanished behind a house. There was a whole horde of these strange new folk amassing outside Rangi, with what looked like more pouring through the town in a steady stream. Many pushed or pulled carts laden with what appeared to be building supplies. Rocks, mud - they'd even scrounged some wood, though Jeb suspected they acquired it nearby (rather than brave the Western Forests to fight the man-eaters for it).

There! He saw the glint again, appearing behind a throng of dungarees-wearing folk that were huddled together, having some sort of meeting. One of them even had an old plastic hardhat. Jeb's old eyes, despite being sluggish from a well-used life, jumped open at light speed, his body arching forwards as if to zoom in on the picture. The glinting, bobbing metal was a bloody Overlord, something Jeb wouldn't have expected to see this far out of a major population centre. It was stomping along with one of the strangers. But Jeb couldn't figure out where it fitted into all this. By all accounts, and the old man knew plenty of accounts, that Overlord should either be treating humans with a distant but very clear disgust, or stomping on their necks (so, less-distant, but still very clear disgust).

What the hell were these people doing? Some pulled down homes, others cleared debris, the rest seemed to be repairing the road, or digging up fields. Was this a good thing or a bad thing? And then there was the robot following one of them around...

He shook his head, feeling tired again. Good or bad, it didn't matter. His Waste senses were telling him it was time to go.

"Hey, Jeb, look there!" Orsen suddenly cried, giving the old man a little jump scare.

Orsen was pointing to a group of two men standing over what looked like an animal. A wolfcat pup, maybe. They were fairly close to the tower, away from the hustle and bustle of ... well, of whatever this whole mess was.

"What? Wassat? I don't see anythin'," Jeb stated, squinting at the small huddle.

"Don't ya see the wolfcat, Jeb? It looks jus' like Mr. Tinkles!"

Jeb frowned. "Have you been in the bonkerberries again, Orsen? I tolds ya not t' touch th' stuff."

Orsen practically leapt on the old man, gripping his sleeves tight, his young face aghast. "No, I swear! I haven't touched one. Not since last time, I swears to ya. Mr. Tinkles was my friend back at the commune."

Oh, thought Jeb, the bloody commune.

The commune is where Jeb met Orsen a number of years back, way up north in the Orcklands. He was a sheriff at the time, one of the few in the area who braved being on the, in his unpopular opinion, correct side of the law. He and a few local folk had decided to bust open one of the Orck communes, which was basically a cattle farm but with humans instead of pigcows. They were bred, raised, fed, and then eventually eaten by the

Orcks, the cannibalistic bandits who reckoned they ruled the place. Jeb's job was to make sure they knew this wasn't the case.

But though his partners had evaporated during the break-in, Jeb had managed to get one soul out of there, one soul at least who wouldn't perish in that awful place: Orsen. And now he'd taken the lad almost as far away as he could get.

"Oh no!" Orsen squealed, scrabbling to the edge of the tower, and to Jeb's horror, almost falling off it. "They're kickin' him!"

"Who?"

"Mr. Tinkles!"

"But it's not Mr. Tinkles, lad. Now come on, grab yer things. We gotta get movin' before it gets too late. We don't wanna be out walkin' after dark, not this close t' th' Church."

Jeb tried to grasp Orsen's shoulder gently but the boy shrugged him off. "No!" he cried again. "I have to go save Mr. Tinkles!"

"Stay out of it, boy! That's rule number one, wadda I keep tellin' ya? Trouble finds ya enough in life, so don't go lookin' for it."

Jeb reached for Orsen's sleeves again but the boy was already moving. Orsen grabbed his pack and had his feet on the ladder down before Jeb could so much as fart.

The boy hesitated, meeting the eyes of his mentor. "I can't stay out of it, Jeb. Mr. Tinkles needs help."

"But it's not Mr. Tinkles!"

"But it looks like him, Jeb. An' he's bein' hurt real bad."

Then his worried face disappeared, leaving Jeb scrambling to gather his belongings and pursue. Bloody hell, he muttered quickly to himself, putting his arms through the leather straps of his pack. Always stay outta trouble, it's so simple. Never get in a fight, never start a fight, and run away if it looks like there could *be* a fight. What wasn't clear about that?

As quick as he could, Jeb forced his tired old bones onto the ladder and clambered down as fast as he dared to. When his thick boots hit the dust at the bottom, Orsen was already running towards the strangers. Head-first into the Waste Beast's cave.

Orsen had a good heart, to be sure. He was always trying to help people, or animals. Jeb saw that, he was proud of it. No doubts there.

But other folk ate good hearts for breakfast.
...sometimes literally.

* * *

"Phoenix!" Bert called, noticing that the couple of traders at table three were sitting without food. "Where's table three's order?"

Smack-dab was mercifully busy today, or at least busy by Smack-dab's standards. That is to say, there were customers today, and they weren't asshole bandits just looking for a quick bit of thieving. A group of traders had wandered in an hour ago, and all of them were thirsty, hungry and most importantly, armed with money. Money Bert needed to keep the place from falling over (literally, one side desperately needed shoring up).

She turned and reached out with a chunky robotic left fist to grip the kitchen service window, her human right fist pressing firmly into her loose-fitting white shirt, which was covered by a dark-coloured, slightly tattered pigcow-leather vest. There was a dull thud as her belt knocked against the wooden wall, revealing that she carried an ammo pouch, money bag, and finely carved revolver at her waist. The creamy bone handle of the weapon glimmered gently in the light.

"Table three..." Phoenix muttered slowly, sliding up to the other side of the window. His rough beard had bits of food stuck in it, and his chef's hat had deflated, again. "Two steaks and some bread?" he asked, wiping his hands on a blood-stained apron.

Bert's brow twitched, but she swallowed her frustration. Smacks was busy, mistakes would be made - or at least that's what she reminded herself. "No, dammit Phoenix. One steak and the salad of the day."

She glanced over her shoulder quickly at the traders of table three, who looked up in return and smiled awkwardly. Bert smiled back, if only to look confident.

"But Bert," Phoenix mewed, putting down the rusty meat carver he was holding, his body shifting closer to the window and his voice lowering. "We don't have any salads. The last batch I caught ran away before I could boil it."

Oh great, Bert thought, so that's what was next, then. Fort gets toppled, roof dissolves in the rain, and now the only customers who are actually willing to pay anything were going to miss out on an opportunity to do so.

Bert scratched at her short-cropped hair with her human hand, the servos in her robotic fingers whirring quietly as they curled into a fist. "What about our vegetables? We could throw something together."

"I'd love to, Bert," replied Phoenix, his stressy face now expanding into an awkward, slightly frightened grin. "Except, err, I used up the last good ones for table five. The rest exploded."

Her other brow twitched. "They exploded?"

"Um, yeah. Not really sure why. They just sort of exploded into mist, then I got this rash on my arm."

He pushed his lanky, muscular arm through the window, sliding the sleeve back on his dirty brown shirt. The forearm was red, little bumps forming all over beneath long, luminous scratch marks.

At the back of Bert's mind, she felt The Woman's voice talking to her, echoing forwards from some far-off memory of a better time. Adapt, she had always said. The key to surviving in the Waste was to prepare for a lack of preparation, to keep your knees bent, your feet moving, and your mind alert. Because the one sure thing about the Waste, from the Orcklands in the north all the way down to Stewart's Island in the south, was that you truly had no idea what was coming. Even in Smack-dab, The Woman always maintained that the rules applied.

Except even she wasn't ready for the day it ended. But then, maybe she knew and just didn't tell Bert. She could never tell with those broody, silent types. She preferred her adventurers loud and stupid, like Phoenix.

* * *

Terrance Leeland lifted his shiny black boot off the ground before the fresh streamlet of gooey blood could cause a stain. It was bad enough that he'd gotten someone's entrails smeared all over his leather coat, he didn't need it on his damn shoes as well.

A half-hearted wind blew past, whistling through the metal trailer that now lay abandoned in the middle of the Back Road. Terrance narrowed his dark eyes as he took a wide step around the mutilated corpse at his feet. His black-gloved hands held a scuffed automatic rifle, the barrel still cooling, its ammo half-spent.

He scanned over the scene, pausing his steps every now and then to better see if there was movement nearby. After a short moment, he'd begin taking another step, his heavy soles grinding against the Back Road's crumbling, rain-soaked tarmac. His eyes carefully scanned across each of the four corpses, checking for breathing, signs of eye movement, finger twitches - anything that might suggest one them was going to spring up and attack.

But they were quite assuredly dead.

The trailer was a fairly standard scavenged Old World model, with two basic wheels and a shallow metal box to store goods in. This one had a roofless cage around the sides, with enough metal bars and handles at the front for two or three people to pull. It was stacked with goods, and that was the only way to describe them. There was no order, they were of no particular category, it was just a random assortment of things both big and small thrown haphazardly into the cage.

Terrance didn't know who these bandits were, or where they had come from. But he did know that the dungarees-wearing fools didn't know who *he* was, and that was a problem. More fool them, and even *more* more fool whoever gave them a pitiful education in famous Waste heroes, such as Terrance.

He sneered, his stubbled upper lip curling to reveal stained teeth. With a face of contempt, he squatted next to one of the corpses and yanked hard on a rusty metal canteen hanging by rope from its belt. The bastards had caught his own bottle with an arrow - a fucking arrow! - so he needed a new one before dehydration got its claws in his throat.

The bottle unclipped easy enough, but he recoiled at the contents. Whatever it was, it certainly wasn't water. And to the tune of muttered grumbles, Terrance discovered that each of the bandits was the same - water that tasted foul. He'd have to go clean up and fill somewhere else.

Gerald was probably closest, but after what he did to the innkeeper there, he'd probably be run out of town with pitchforks. Well, the uneducated bastard had it coming. These Can't Be Buried folks had no respect for their veterans. And to think they owed some of their happiness to his sacrifices.

Bastards. All of them.

So where else could he go? If he went off-road he could probably bypass Behinds and make the Ash Fort by nightfall, but rumour had it Lord Ash was six feet under, and in more than one location. A bandit city was a dangerous place for a famous adventurer like Terrance, not without a pre-existing relationship with the lord.

So, Smack-dab it was, then.

Once more Terrance looked at the scene of death around him, his teeth bared to the world. Someone really ought to have educated these morons better.

* * *

The three hooded figures were close, now. They marched in a tight group, eyes locked on the approaching silhouette of a two-storey wooden structure sitting in the middle of nowhere.

One of them revealed a long spear.

Another drew a pistol.

The last drew a bugle.

Adapt.

"Alright..." Bert said.

Customer wants the salad of the day, check. Customer has money to pay for it, double check. But ... customer won't know what a salad of the day is, because the menu is really quite vague and nobody ever serves salads. The answer, then, was an easy one. She nodded to herself.

"Grab that steak over there," she said firmly, pointing with her human hand past Phoenix, "and then peel off some really thin slices. I don't care how, just do it. I reckon it'll look like red leaves, so the customer won't know any different. Top it with something that looks vaguely like a vegetable and serve it up. We'll give them a couple of free drinks to hide the flavour."

Phoenix nodded a "Yes, boss" and vanished back into the bowels of the kitchen, leaving Bert alone by the window. She turned away from it, letting go of the frame to...

...come face-to-chest with a hulking monstrosity of a creature. Bert stepped back suddenly, gazing up the beast's monumental chest. It was somewhere between six and seven feet, that was for sure. It wore a patchwork set of clothes, a disfigured, lumpy face with one eye gazing intently down at Bert, the other ... would get the message later. It had a tiny, skinny left arm tucked up by its chest, but its right arm was easily the size and girth of a small human - a terrifying limb with muscles that looked like they had been stolen straight from a Waste Beast.

The beast, chest labouring with heavy breaths, stared hard down at Bert, who stared back.

Then they both burst into wide, childish grins.

"Good morning, Meatsack," Bert said warmly, reaching forwards to rub the creature's skinny arm gently. Being a woman of small stature, her hand looked pitifully small next to his titanic form. "Ready for the day's work?"

Meatsack, lips widening into a large, happy grin, nodded quickly.

"Alright, big guy. I want you to start by taking table three some drinks, OK? Their food is delayed."

He nodded again, taking an enthusiastic step around Bert to the shelves, but then hesitated, foot in the air and arm half outstretched. One of his eyes was gazing at the bottles, all different shapes, sizes and colours.

Bert followed his stare after figuring out which eye had his brain's attention, and patted him on the arm again. "Doesn't matter which one, bud. They won't know the difference, anyway."

His happy head turned to her, smiled widely once more, and then he moved forwards to fulfil his task.

Few people knew the full story of Meatsack, only that one day, after The Woman was already gone and Phoenix had appeared, a giant, grey mutant with the naive, innocent mind of a child turned up at Smack-dab and started working there. That is to say, he had the mind of a naive, innocent Old World child - most modern kiddies matured pretty quick. It was hard not to when they'd nearly died six or seven times before so much as taking their first step.

But despite Meatsack's intelligence, or the lack thereof, Bert treated the creature almost as a pseudo-child, helping him learn about the Waste, about running a bar, and about who not to trust (e.g. bandits). And if anyone so much as swung a fist at him, they found their hands exploding before the punch even got close.

Bert watched Meatsack fret about picking bottles and glasses, her angry blue stare having softened to almost a motherly smile at the big lug. He picked up every glass at the bar, inspecting them all against the daylight to find what he perceived to be the cleanest. Little did he know that none of them were truly clean, and they likely never would be again.

It was then, at the edge of hearing, she heard what sounded like ... music?

The disjointed notes were wafting in from far away, carried on the wind from somewhere south. Although muffled, Bert could hear an upbeat, jolly tune, something with regular notes almost to the pace of soldier's marching. The bar owner's face dropped.

She placed her robotic fist on the counter, her right hand dangling loosely by her side, fingers poised instinctively by the glittering bone handle of her revolver.

Bert knew exactly what the noise was.

The tune was growing closer, and had quickened its pace, now beeping and bopping to the gait of humans running - charging, even. It was angrier, too, harsher tones interrupting the noise. You couldn't exactly call it music, for the wielder of the instrument likely hadn't even heard the word, but Bert suspected that wasn't the point.

Some of the customers were turning their heads now, uncertainty spreading on their tired, dusty faces. Phoenix, too, placing a steamy plate of shredded steak and misc. other foodstuffs on the kitchen window ledge, poked his head through, bushy eyebrow raised.

"Hey, that sounds like the bugle you told me about," he said, cocking his head at the noise, which had grown louder.

Bert didn't nod in response, but stared at Smack-dab's front door, fingertips now dancing on her pistol's hammer.

25

"Didn't you sign a treaty or something to stop this from happening again? What is this, the fourth time?"

"Fifth," Bert stated bluntly. These assholes hadn't returned in years. Why today of all days? The day she actually had customers. Bloody hell.

Meatsack stepped back towards Bert and the bar, having delivered his drinks to table three. The strange tune outside was very loud, now, and getting closer with each rasping, breathy note. The giant mutant stared hard at the front door with one eye, his fingers tangling and untangling from each other, feet tapping the floor.

Bert pried her eyes off the door to see his worried face. "Meatsack, go hide in your room, OK? You can come out again when it's over."

Meatsack was never allowed to fight - when he got angry, well, let's just say that the last time, it got messier than expected. He glanced quickly at Bert, fingers still dancing, then nodded hurriedly and withdrew. He scampered away down a hall near the bar, the noise of a door opening and *almost* shutting squeaking out from somewhere within.

Bert turned her head the other way, to speak sideways back at Phoenix. The music was almost at Smack-dab. Footsteps could be heard running in the dust, the sound of muffled voices crying out unintelligible words.

"Phoenix, you got your rifle back there?" she asked, her face firm.

The adventurer shook his head. "Sorry, Bertio, it's upstairs in my room. I got plenty knives, though! And I learned some sweet carroty chops from a travelling guru a couple months back, so I mean, my arms are basically like guns now." The man grinned, showing a neat row of surprisingly intact teeth while he moved his arms vaguely in a carroty-chop-like manner.

Bert swivelled her body to glance properly backwards, meeting Phoenix with a straight face. "Maybe just the knives," she stated.

Her head was glaring forwards again before she saw Phoenix's sad little eyes turn downwards.

The footsteps, yells, and those strange, incoherent bugle noises were now practically upon the bar. Bert heard the familiar crunch of boots meeting Smack's gravel pathway, heard the pace quicken to a full-on sprint.

Someone outside screamed a battle cry.

Bert's fingers tensed around her pistol.

The footsteps sprinted for the front door and...

...it thudded loudly, dust scrambling off the surface in fright. But it remained, quite noticeably, shut.

Bert felt the beginnings of a headache, stemming from grinding her teeth together. Her fingers remained tight around her pistol, while Phoenix moved in next to her cradling a whole pile of knives in his arms. He dumped them on the bar counter with a loud clatter and picked up the biggest - a very, very bloody meat cleaver.

The door thudded again, louder this time. Voices muttered behind it as Smack-dab's customers hopped their seats inch by inch away from the front area. A general murmur of panic was rippling through their poor, wealthy ranks, wide-eyed heads swivelling like Old World carnival clown machines to find someone who seemed confident. Of course, this meant all eyes fell on Bert. Bert, whose blue eyes bore holes in the door frame.

Smack-dab's front door thudded a third time. Someone behind it cursed loudly.

"Bloody stars, what's this thing made out of?" he said.

"Just'th open it normally, Roger," a second voice cried.

"I want to make'th an entrance."

"Thee can make an entrance normally, though!"

"But I want to make'th a dramatic entrance!"

"Yeah, but thee can't make a dramatic entrance if you - thee - can't kick'th it down."

The bugle ceased suddenly.

"Why don't you turn'th the handle, then kick it in?" a third voice chimed in.

"That's a great idea!"

"Thank you."

"Alright, you play'th forth the Battle Tune, you turn'th the handle, and I'll kick it in."

For the third time in barely as many minutes, Bert let out a slow, careful breath. Somehow she could just feel the stress like a little, irradiated pixie sitting on her shoulders, sandpapering her lifespan down with each headache.

The first time these weird-talking nutters appeared at Smack-dab, Bert was terrified. She thought a swarm of bandits - her sworn enemies - was seizing the opportunity of The Woman's death and moving in for a quick kill. It was her first bar invasion on her own, and to this day she still regretted the amount of ammo she wasted on their small, hooded warband. It took days to clean up all the giblets.

The fourth time it happened, she followed the buggers back to their village in the mountains and demanded the madness to stop. There were threats, sure, and she had shot some folk, OK maybe, but she was under the impression that the treaty was sound. It had worked for the past couple years, anyway.

But now?

Bert drew her pistol angrily and placed it, under her human hand, on the bar counter. She didn't need this, not today.

The bugle outside began again. The Battle Tune.

A muffled voice spoke confidently. "On the count of three..."

Phoenix practiced swinging his cleaver a couple times, blood specks flinging off and hitting him in the mouth.

"One..."

He spat in disgust, wiping his arms on his face but only smearing the blood across more of his face.

"Two..."

Customers all around the bar were beginning to notice Bert's lack of terror. She wasn't cowering, or ducking for cover, or fleeing and screaming (like they would be). Some took it as a good sign and turned their chairs - drinks in hand - to face the action.

Bert gripped her pistol.

"Three!"

The door thudded again.

"Sorry Roger, I thought we were going, one, two, three, *then* kick."

The handle turned in its socket. "Alright, try'th now."

With a mighty bang, the wooden door burst inward, joyriding on its hinges and slamming against the wall in a dusty cloud. Three figures poured into the bar along with their ridiculous music, all clad in long, black robes speckled with little white stars. Their robes were noticeably burned, large holes having been singed all over, particularly the shoulders and hoods. Bert wondered if there were just three in the group before the storm swept in...

"Bear witness!" cried the one in the front, who was waving a well-kept pistol in the air quite irresponsibly. "The Stars hath sent us to relinquish thine heathen establishment of the Burny Drink!"

Bert, carefully, thumbed back the hammer on her weapon, eyes focused on the guy with the gun. His colleague in the back was of little threat – he'd brought a spear to a Bert fight.

The lead invader turned his wild eyes on Bert, pointing at her with his weapon. "You! Devil Woman! Release thine Burny Drink, in the name of the Constellator!"

"CONSTELLATOOOOOR!" screamed the other two.

Bert gritted her teeth. "No."

"CONSTELLAT- oi wait, what did you say?" The leader cocked his head to one side, his weapon dropping to his side.

"I said no. Now what the hell happened to Fred? Why have you come back here?" Bert's face was filling with red.

Phoenix, noticing the colour of Bert's face, inched away from his boss nervously.

Obviously the lead figure was back on solid ground with Fred. His eyes lit up once more, his arms lifting from his sides to wave about in the air, his mouth revealing rotten teeth. "Fred! PAH!" he spat. "Fred was marked with thine Itchy Red Spots. The Stars made him Unworthy with their pox, and he was sacrificed to their glory ... 'th. There is a new Constellator!"

"CONSTELLATOOOOOR!" cried the ones in the back.

"Shut up!" Bert roared. "Who is your new Constellator-"

"CONSTELLATOOOOOR!"

"I said shut the hell up! Who is the new Cons- the new leader? I had a treaty with Fred and I will damn well see your end of the bargain held up." Bert, now positively crimson, slammed her robotic fist on the bar counter, startling the bottles behind her – not to mention the nearby onlookers enjoying the show. Table three, though, was watching a little plate of salad going cold in the service window.

"Your pathetic alliance with'th Fred the Unworthy hath been torn asunder, foul Devil Woman!" the lead figure continued to scream. He took a step forwards towards the bar, brandishing his pistol in wiry fingers. "You will never have an alliance with the Starry Place again - never!"

"Never!" cried his colleagues.

Phoenix was now shuffling slowly back towards the kitchen, away from where things might get messy. He hesitated, thinking maybe he should collect his precious pile of knives, but thought better of it. Too close to ground zero. Bert was about to explode.

Bert opened her mouth to shout back, but the hooded figure cut her off...

"No, speak'th no more, Devil! If you will not give us thine Burny Drink, you shall'th die for it!"

...and a little dial that measured the pressure of Bert's rage ticked over into the red zone. Pipes started to whistle quietly.

The leader from the Starry Place raised his weapon in the air, clenching his other hand into a fist. "Kill the non-believers! Relinquish the Burny Drink! For the Constellatoooooor!"

"CONSTELLATOOOOOOR!"

And then his arm exploded.

* * *

"You leave Mr. Tinkles alone!" Orsen screamed, his voice hammered by his pounding footsteps.

Jeb was doing his best to catch up, but if you could say one thing and one thing only about Orsen, he was bloody quick for a skinny teenager. The old sheriff wheezed loudly, forcing himself forwards in pursuit. He saw a small irony in the situation - running straight towards the very thing he was trying to run away from - but it didn't seem funny yet. Maybe it would in a few weeks, once the bruises and open wounds healed up. Assuming they ever did, of course.

The folks with the dungarees finally stopped kicking the wolfcat, noticing Orsen's gangly, teenage battle charge. The creature lay bloodied at their feet, its chest rising and falling gently, but otherwise totally devoid of motion. One of the attackers was an older wiry fellow with messy hair and no teeth, and the other a young buck with a decent set of muscles, but a dim-witted stare to suggest nothing decent going on anywhere else. Quite frankly, Jeb reckoned they looked like an alternate-universe version of himself and Orsen. Except with dungarees.

"Stop hurting Mr. Tinkles!" Orsen screamed again.

"For cryin' out loud, Orsen, it's not bloody Mr. Tinkles!" Jeb called desperately from behind.

"But he still needs help!"

The pair he was charging at looked truly lost, much to Jeb's relief. Namely, because he was also completely lost. He figured he'd come up with a plan on the fly, but most of his brainpower seemed to have diverted to swearing, wheezing and feeling pain.

The wolfcat kickers, whom Jeb decided to call Bob and Rob, met each other's eyes for a moment, then turned back to Orsen. Then Rob, who was the tall fellah with the muscles, walked out to meet the boy.

"Leave. Him. Alooooone!" Orsen cried a third time, dragging out the final word all the way to...

...a fist. Rob, without speaking, planted his foot and threw a flying fist of fury straight to Orsen's squishy, surprised face. The boy flopped back like he'd been bitten by a paralytic bitefly – a real bugger in swampier areas of the Waste – and landed in an ungainly heap on the dusty plains.

And that was it. They just sort of stood there after that, both Rob and Bob. Rob looked back at Bob, presumably for assurance, but Bob shrugged with eyebrows raised and pointed at Jeb, who was still doing his very best to be of any assistance whatsoever. Then Rob pointed down at Orsen, where the lights were definitely on, but quite clearly nobody was home.

Bob shrugged again, moved away from the wolfcat over to the prone lad, and laid a boot into his ribcage.

"Oi!" Jeb shouted, albeit hoarsely. "You leave that lad alone! He's jus' a boy; he don't know what he's doin'!"

Look, it wasn't an ideal situation, but at least Jeb now had Bob and Rob's full attention. They watched in uncertain silence as the old man closed the distance to them. Rob stepped forwards again, flexing and unflexing his fingers, but Bob held out his hand and stopped the younger man.

"What the fuck is goin' on, eh?" Bob asked, his voice coarse.

Jeb slowed to a wheezy, puffy stop, finally arriving at the battleground. He placed his hands on his knees and bent forwards, eyes examining the prone figure of Orsen, who was now floundering like some kind of lanky fish.

"Don't hurt us," Jeb asked, swallowing some sticky spit while his lungs cried for mercy. "Please, we's jus' humble folk, don't mean ya no harm."

Bob held out his arms, one solitary eyebrow raised (Jeb didn't know where the other one was, but he could swear it was there earlier). "Wad'ya mean? It was you's that attacked us."

Just behind them, Orsen was woozily getting his feet beneath him, a grubby hand checking his face. It was still there, but maybe a bit flatter than before.

"Look," Jeb said, the fire in his lungs slowly diminishing with each rattling breath, "Jus' let us go, alright? We'll be on our way. The lad doesn't know what he's doin', is all."

Bob, mouth agape, looked at Rob, who looked similarly gapeful. The older of the pair turned back to Jeb. "But ... but it was you's that attacked us!"

Orsen seemed stable now, or at the very least, upright. His eyes, squinting, fell on the backs of Rob and Bob, then on Jeb, then on the wolfcat, now curled up in the dust not far from where the peace negotiations were taking place. He lingered on the wolfcat.

"It's alright, don't ya worry about it," Jeb said, holding out his hands in a pleading motion while showing off various types of innocent grin. "We're jus' gonna be on our way and thas that, eh? No harm done ... except to the lad, o' course. But between you an' me he deserved that one, eh?" He shuffled a foot forwards through the dust.

"Now look, mate," scowled Bob, now lacking both eyebrows. "Me an' me son are jus' out 'ere teachin' our pet wolfcat 'ow t' behave, and in yer come as happy as ya like screamin' yer lungs off about tinklin' an' attack us!"

Rob nodded, matching Bob's scowl.

32

"*Now* yer tellin' me ya mean no harm, she'll be right no worries off yer be on yer way? Well I've 'ad enough o' this. Yer takin' me for a ride, mate."

Bob stepped forwards, his knobbly fingers curling into tight fists. Rob stepped up with him, bearing his teeth. Though Jeb felt "fangs" might have been a better descriptor.

The old man sighed in defeat. This is why he always tried to keep Orsen out of trouble. Because if you got into trouble, well, you were in bloody trouble, weren't you? And all you had then was broken dreams, and probably broken bones. And probably broken plenty else, because trouble was like that. It caused trouble.

While Bob and Rob, whom Jeb had now forgotten who was which, stepped forwards to show Jeb what being pulp felt like, Orsen was kneeling down next to the injured animal. It had started to wriggle gently in the dust, but didn't try to escape when Orsen leaned in to scoop it into his arms. In fact, the battered creature nuzzled into the nook of his elbow.

Bob and Rob were now close enough to smell, which was never a good place to be. Especially if they smelled like Bob and Rob.

"I reckons," sneered Bob, or was it Rob? Whichever one was the older one. "I reckons we're gonna teach ya a lesson, so we will. Ya don't attack men o' the Farm an' expect t' live. We're out 'ere makin' th' Waste a better place, an' ya scream at us? Uh uh, not on our watch, eh Maddison?"

The dumb one nodded again. Jeb refused to call him Maddison.

Orsen was now standing moderately firmly, wolfcat curled in his arms. He seemed to have gained some semblance of normal consciousness. Jeb flexed his fingers, shook his knees and took a deep breath.

"Look, I appreciate th' situation here, but let's come t' an arrangeme- RUN, LAD, RUN!" he screamed, swinging his pack off his shoulders in a heavy arc and leaping into a sprint.

The dungarees duo didn't need to jump far to get out of the way before the pack clobbered them, but it was space enough for a skinny old man to hop through. Jeb launched himself between them and ploughed straight ahead towards the fleeing figure of Orsen, shouldering his pack again.

They ran as though a Waste Beast were chasing them, the fear of death motivation enough for Jeb's old bones to give him a last hurrah. Jeb vaguely heard a voice crying behind him about a pet wolfcat, but there was no turning back now.

Rob and Bob would never catch up, nor would they ever truly know what the hell happened, why they were attacked, and why two random, grubby traders offed with their wolfcat in broad daylight.

So at least it wasn't a bad day just for Jeb.

* * *

Smoke dribbled out of Bert's pistol almost as fast as blood gushed from the lead cultist's new arm stump. Her face glowed with a dangerous tinge of crimson, the skin between her eyebrows knotted tight in a glare. The sound of her shot ricocheted around the dusty wooden room, rattling windows and one old customer's square glass eye (he didn't know how to carve a sphere). Phoenix was frozen in place, meat cleaver in hand, his wide eyes darting between Bert's weapon, her blazing sapphire glare, and the shocked O-shaped lips on the leader's face.

In seconds the echoes died out, and for a moment there was no sound but the wind whistling loudly through cracks in Smack's weatherboards. Then...

"This ends right fucking now," Bert growled, gritting her teeth. "The only way you're getting any grog is if you pay for the stuff. And you can be damn sure you're going to deliver a message to this new Const- this leader of yours about what happened today."

The man in front, staring at where his arm used to be, blinked twice. His mouth slowly drooped lower, and he glanced back at his companions. Phoenix clutched his cleaver close to his breast and took a further step back.

But Bert was still mid-rant. She waved her gun at the door. "Out there, you do whatever the hell you like. But in here?" She stamped her foot hard on the floorboards. "In here you play by my rules, and I'll floor any one of you who disagrees."

A little pool of blood was forming at the armless leader's feet as the colour drained from his face straight out the new hole...

"Hey, assholes," Bert shouted, "are you listening to me?"

...and then he clutched his stump with his remaining hand, collapsed to his knees and started screaming.

And the flimsy illusion of peace shattered into a thousand itty-bitty pieces.

The guy's buddy with the spear howled and leapt into action, literally. Tipping the polished blade of his long weapon forwards, he pounced over his colleague's kneeling figure roaring with energy, pushing forwards to the bar.

Bert hammered back her pistol to unleash another shot, but a bloodied meat cleaver spiralled in out of nowhere and caught the attacker in his shoulder. It spun him in an arc sideways, swear words escaping from his lips as though he couldn't get enough out in just once sentence. Then the man with the bugle also moved, spinning his instrument to grasp it like a club with both hands. He sprinted for Phoenix by the kitchen entrance while the spear-wielder stumbled in a drunken circle.

This is where Bert started to lose control of the situation.

The man with the spear was stumbling, his friend with the bugle was charging. Phoenix was weaponless and preparing to use his carroty moves, while Bert was picking a target. The guy who lost his arm was still screaming, but the noises had morphed from a high-pitched squeal of pain to a mad howl of rage.

Phoenix stepped forwards to meet the guy with the bugle, but his opponent hefted the small metal instrument straight at Phoenix's face. The adventurer was too close to properly combat roll out the way, and so took the instrument fully on the nose. He went down with a squeak that he would one day deny, landing on his back with his hands over his bleeding nostrils. The instrument clattered down next to him.

At the same time, the guy with the spear had fished the cleaver from his flesh and was back on the offensive, thrusting his spear forwards towards Bert as one arm dangled loosely at his side, cleaver dropping to the floor. His leader was still howling, but now he scrambled madly in his own blood for the pistol - which still had fingers clinging to it.

Bert lined up a shot as urgently as she could and squeezed the trigger, the force slamming into her right shoulder as a fresh new bullet went to say hello to the cultist with the spear. As the deafening bang bounced once more into Smack's customers, who were now laughing at the unfolding scene, the bullet tore a gash in the spear-wielder's ribs and disappeared through the front door. The man coughed out an "Oh bloody hell" and spun once more, his spear whistling through the air to catch the armless man in his leg.

On the other side of the room, Phoenix was beating off the musician with his fists, who was doing an admirable job of beating Phoenix with his. Now, though, the leader, who had shaken the fingers from his pistol, was crying a second time, flopping over onto his side. He let the pistol go in order to clutch at the spear protruding from his thigh, only for the thing to land in the pool of blood, bounce from the impact and let out a shot of its own.

Bert dove beneath the bar as the bullet whizzed past where her torso would have been, hitting the floor hard and grunting with frustration. Above her, the bullet shattered one of her bottles, bore through the kitchen wall, bounced off a rusting iron pot and flung itself back into the front area, where it embedded itself in the skull of the musician, who promptly fell over.

So now the man with the spear was wriggling on the ground with blood coming from his ribs, his leader could not clutch at both his thigh and his stump, and the musician had exploded all over Phoenix - who was spitting out brain particles from his teeth.

Having not seen this new development, Bert sprang up to her feet, droplets of booze and shards of glass catapulting off of her back. Instinctively she brought up her pistol, hammered and ready, to defend against whatever the hell would happen next. Her eyes quickly scanned for the most immediate threat.

But nobody seemed to be paying her any attention anymore.

And the traders, oh how they applauded.

Cautiously and ignoring the traders, Bert stepped around the wooden bar, exploring the scene with her gaze. One headless cultist, one armless, all three bleeding on her more-or-less (particularly less) clean floor. She kept her weapon forwards, finger on the trigger, ready to respond at the slightest of changes. To her side, Phoenix was sliding away from the corpse and futilely wiping his face with his bloodied sleeve. Little did he know that he'd be tasting brain matter for hours.

Bert was above the cultists' leader, now, the barrel of her gun casting its hollow eye on his forehead. He was squirming, writhing on the ground with moans of pain interrupting his heavy breathing. The spear hadn't completely gone through his leg, so the point was embedded somewhere in his thigh, with nearly two metres of wooden shaft flopping on the ground. That's not to mention his stump, which was now foaming green. Bert didn't know why it was foamy, but she didn't want that crap on her floor, that was for sure.

She cast a quick sideways glance to the least-injured invader, who had managed to sit himself up to inspect the bullet graze. He didn't seem like he was going to attack, namely because his attention was quite firmly fixated on the fact that he could see his skeleton through his robes.

"Meatsack!" she called behind her, "bring out the first-aid kit!"

The armless man glared at her as she squatted down next to him, her gun still trained on his head. "Now you listen close," she said through gritted teeth. "You go back to whoever replaced Fred and you tell them, you tell them that unless he, she, whoever, is willing to pay for grog, it's gonna end the same way every time." She grimaced openly at the man while a door creaked in the background. Heavy footsteps padded towards the front room. "And it ends with you bleeding on the floor, and me telling you to get the fuck outta my bar. You hear me?"

The man's lips set in a grim line, his brows twitching with barely contained contempt. "Thee..." he said, his voice cracking, "...will never have'th an a ... an alliance with the Starry Place again, Devil Woman..."

Bert's eyes narrowed as Meatsack's overbearing shadow passed above the pair.

"We ... we will return. We will return with an ... an army the likes of which thee hath never seen."

Behind them, Meatsack knelt down nervously and held out the first-aid kit: a little wooden box with a crude white cross scrawled on the top of the lid. Bert, nostril's flaring, pulled her gaze away from the injured invader and forced a smile at Meatsack, gently taking the box from his thick fingers. "Thanks, bud. Now I need you to go get your mop, OK?"

He nodded hastily and vanished backwards.

She brought the box forwards, opened the lid and pulled out a roll of bandages and a splint. Then she placed the box to one side, gripped what she'd revealed from it, and stared down at the man. Her face was still glowing, and she could feel sweat forming on her forehead from the sheer heat of her blood.

"Take these," she said, pushing them into his grip, "and get the fuck out of my bar."

* * *

Later in Smack-dab, the cultists who had survived were but silhouettes limping over a hill in the distance. Phoenix and Bert had moved the corpse outside to be taken by whatever came crawling around at night, and Meatsack was now in the front area swooshing his mop around. He would never be able to clean up the blood and gory bits such as they were, but he had learned that with enough swooshing, you could spread it out so thin that nobody noticed it was there.

Bert now leaned against the bar, feeling exhausted. It was barely even late-morning and she felt like night was falling, that she'd worked a full day and it was time to either shoo customers out, or get them to buy a room. And she could always convince people to buy a room, because nobody wanted to be out at night this close to the Dead Church.

Phoenix was sitting on the bar next to her, watching Meatsack move the blood about. He had just returned from table three, taking a tepid (at best) plate of salad to their table, and reminding them that salads could be served either hot or cold – so the fact that it was somewhere in between was just the best of both worlds.

Bert rubbed her tired face with her human hand, leaning on her left. "Fuck me, what a day," she said, quietly.

Phoenix turned to look at her and grinned. "Well, I would if you'd only let me."

She looked up and smiled wryly at the man in the sad chef's hat. "I told you what you'd have to do to get that."

He pouted. "But how am I supposed to kill a Waste Beast with my arms tied behind my back?"

Bert shrugged, but her smile felt more genuine. Giving Phoenix crap always cheered her up. It was like playing with a baby wolfcat, only Phoenix wouldn't grow up to maul and eat her innards.

As a gentle silence fell over them both, Phoenix turned back to look at the blood stain. There were still chunks of exploded arm lying on the floor, which Meatsack was actively avoiding.

The adventurer shook his head. "You sure love this bar, huh?"

"Phoenix," Bert said, her smile fading. "If anyone walks in here and tries to take what don't belong to them, it will always end the same way."

"You're gonna get yourself hurt one day. Some big boulderfrog you can't intimidate."

"I've already been hurt," she replied, her eyes falling on her robotic prosthetic. Little servos whirred in the silence as her fingers curled into a fist. "This bar is my home. We'll see if this big boulderfrog of yours has the balls to take it from me."

By Duncan P. Pacey

Part Two

A Taxing Problem

It was a bright new day in the Waste, and Can't Be Buried was looking as lovely and green as ever. The sun was shining, the birds were singing, and the little pixies were all holding hands and singing whilst they toiled away on the day's glorious work.

...

...

...and then whoever dreamt that woke up.

It was indeed a new day in the Waste, but to say Can't Be Buried was looking as lovely as ever would be like telling a Waste Beast it had a pretty smile. The sun was *maybe* shining, but the greasy, roiling smog still had it in a permanent chokehold. And if a sparkly little ray ever broke through, the smog would power slam it back into submission. Mind you, one might argue that the birds were singing, and some of the more intelligent gullpidgeons were actually very good at Puccini's Nessun Dorma (not that anyone knew what that was anymore, except maybe the gullpidgeons). However, the vast majority of the Waste's bird species - almost all carnivorous man-eaters - hung about the air in complete silence, waiting for an unwitting traveller to tie their shoelaces.

Now, near the bottom of a thick, towering mountain range, a little bar called Smack-dab was preparing for a brand new day.

"Phoenix!" Bert shouted, calling to the adventurer-turned-chef she knew would be milling about the kitchen at this time of morning. This yell was a very common way the day at Smack-dab began.

It took a few moments, but shortly Phoenix rested his arms and chin against the service window and peered through at Bert. His eyes were still groggy from sleep, his rough-cut hair sticking out at defiant angles. There was a bit of luminous green eye gunk clinging to one of his tear ducts, but when Bert glanced at it, it scuttled back into Phoenix's eye.

"Wassamattaboss?" Phoenix sighed, his voice still begging for five more minutes.

Bert pried her gaze off the man's tear duct and looked him in the eyes, frowning. "Why is table three still at table three?"

Phoenix cocked his head. "You lost me."

Bert sighed and shook her head, beckoning for the man to come into the room. He let out an audible grunt of dissatisfaction, but didn't dare say no to Bert. Shuffling on tired feet and wearing home-made fluffy slippers, the adventurer grumbled his way to stand next to his boss by the bar counter.

"Present and 'counted for, boss," he said, slapping his forehead in tired salute.

"Right," she replied. She spun him to face table three and pointed with her human hand. "Why is table three still at table three?"

She was asking because, sure enough, the two traders at table three were still sitting there. Now, this might not seem like that big a deal, it's a bar and eatery, right? People come to drink and eat, and then sometimes sleep, and then sometimes have breakfast. But the issue was, and Bert could not make this clearer to Phoenix, that table three had literally not moved a muscle since finishing their meal and drinks the night before. Literally. They were stalk-still, frozen in place in an upright position, their faces locked in a twisted look of confusion and minor aches and pains.

"Oh," said Phoenix.

"When I went to bed, Phoenix," Bert said, sighing once again, "I asked you to clear the bar. Surely you noticed them?"

"Weeell..." the man replied, scratching at his scraggly beard, still bearing dried brain matter from the day prior. "I saw them of course, but I reckoned they looked as happy as can be. I told them just to find their way to bed when they were finished, and then I went to sleep."

"And you didn't think that ... *this*, was weird?"

Phoenix shrugged. "One day we had a customer made entirely out of bees, you know?"

And once again Bert found that her only responses could be to grit her teeth, sigh openly, or rub her face. She decided to cycle through all three. "What the hell did you put on that salad?"

"Umm ... I just grabbed anything vaguely organic from my Bits 'n' Bobs box."

"But that's been sitting there for months."

He shrugged again. "All the mould fled deeper into the box when I opened it, so I reckoned that meant the stuff on top was clean."

Bloody hell, thought Bert. Look, Phoenix certainly had his uses around the place, especially when push came to gun violence. She didn't regret taking him on board, but sometimes ... sometimes he pushed it. "Go get Meatsack," she said, defeated, "and move them both outside. Bury the plates."

The man's face dropped. "But Bert, I don't wanna work with Meatsack," he cried. "He smells weird, and I never know where he's looking."

Bert glared at him warningly. "You work with Meatsack or you move them both yourself. Then you're scrubbing toilets for a week because you fucked up."

Phoenix considered this for a moment. "Actually Meatsack doesn't smell too bad, when you really think about it. Relative to the toilets and that."

The man shuffled off to go find his overgrown, potentially smelly colleague, while Bert stared at the frozen customers. But before Phoenix disappeared down the hall at the back of Smack's seating area, Bert called out again.

"And Phoenix?"

He turned to look.

"Just ... check their pockets, OK? Maybe we'll, you know, find a next of kin. And, um, be sure to keep their money, you know..."

"Safe?"

"That's the one."

He nodded and vanished.

At this point, the front door creaked open and a gust of wind blew in around Bert's feet. She pried her gaze away from The Mystery at Table Three to greet the newcomer.

"Howdy, welcome to Smack-dab. Kitchen isn't open yet, but if you grab a table I can ... I can..." and then her voice trailed off. The man was tall, muscular, but ageing. The skin around his eyes was folding in on itself, his hair, where it hadn't receded, was turning a dull shade of grey. But that didn't seem nearly as prominent as the fact that he not only carried a large automatic rifle on a sling, but that his black leather coat was smeared with ... was it entrails?

Her welcoming Hi Please Buy Things face evaporated almost in an instant, melting down into a suspicious stare. The man had stopped just inside the door, eyes narrowing right back at Bert. "Look, stranger," she stated, her human hand moving down to her hip, where a glittering bone-handled pistol lay in wait. "You walked into the wrong bar if you're here to cause trouble."

The man sneered openly, revealing yellowed teeth. He spoke in a coarse voice, rusty with dehydration. "You don't know who I am?"

Bert's finger twitched, scraping her weapon's smooth handle. "Should I?"

He continued to sneer, his dark gaze fizzling against her sapphire fire. "You young fuckers are all the same."

"Excuse me?" Twitch, twitch.

The man shook his head. "No respect, no education. Everything's the way it is because it's the way it was when you were born, right?"

"Listen, pal-"

"A drink will be fine," he cut in, before Bert could finish her statement. "And a place to wash once I've wet my throat."

She stared at him in silence a moment longer, the wind outside whistling and rattling around the walls. It was almost as if it screamed a warning of danger, but a warning to whom? The wind didn't care, it just liked whistling.

Then Bert submitted, something she'd fume about later. She waved the angry, messy stranger over to an empty table. "You got cash to pay for that drink?"

He nodded silently and sat down.

"Fine. And you can wash through there once you're done," she said, pointing to a door marked 'Bog' just off the side of the seating area.

The room fell to a tense silence immediately, with the man brooding in his own grubby thoughts while Bert set about getting a drink. She hated backing down, but she was a professional, and professionals needed folks to spend money so that professionals could keep being professionals. Bert smiled an evil smile, at least, when she spiked his drink with her secret stash of, well, she didn't know what it was, but by heck was it strong. And drunk people always spent more money, in her experience.

Phoenix reappeared as Bert was delivering a stout glass tumbler filled with a sparkling brown liquid to the stranger's table. She placed it down firmly in front of him and was about to say something when, suddenly, he sat upright and locked eyes on her chef.

"You," he stated coldly.

Bert looked back. Phoenix's mouth was hanging open and he was pointing straight at the stranger. Meatsack was just behind him, looking between Bert and Phoenix with a growing, desperate look of uncertainty.

The big lug always knew when trouble was afoot.

* * *

Dawn should be charged with crimes against humanity, thought Jeb groggily as a ray of light slapped him in the eyeballs. It was breaking and entering, not to mention aggravated assault with intent to wake. He rolled away from the rusting, mouldy tin wall that had more holes in it than Lord Ash's last radio play. Alas, comfort was not to be had on this bitter Can't Be Buried morning. Jeb just couldn't find a good position on his bed of stony rubble.

Jeb and Orsen had spent the night in a cramped Old World tin shed, with battered old walls, a roof that could barely be constituted as such, and a timber frame so eaten away by rot that these days it was the tin sheeting holding the support framing up. It had been a fairly typical night in the Waste, with two people attempting to sleep by a fire while all sorts of shuffling, groaning and bumping went on outside. Smart folk always slept indoors in Can't Be Buried, and even smarter folk had a fire, or better yet, a highly advanced automatic sensor lighting grid and a constant source of electricity. The smartest folk had a highly advanced automatic sensor lighting grid, a constant source of electricity, and automated drone defence turrets set to kill anything that so as much as tiptoed in the night, let alone went bump.

Jeb, though, had a little electric lantern that he made himself, and sometimes a fire - when he could get one going. Hey, life wasn't perfect, but at least he was alive to say it wasn't perfect.

Slowly, the old man propped himself upright and blinked the sleepiness from his eyes. "Orsen," he grumbled, "do ya want hot water for breakfast, or the last o' th' mouldy bread?"

Silence responded.

"Orsen?"

Jeb looked around the shed. Orsen wasn't there.

"Orsen!" he called out, jumping to his feet, knees cracking like gunshots. "Orsen, m'boy!"

Jeb battered open the shed's door with a thick-soled boot and stumbled out into the morning smoglight. An icy wind bit into him with chilly fangs, blowing up and around to sneak into his clothing. He shuffled a panicked two steps forwards, clutching his puffy jacket tight to his body. "Orsen!" he cried, his eyes darting all around.

"Mornin' Jeb!" a cheerful voice called out behind him.

The old man spun to see Orsen sitting by the side of the road, stroking the wolfcat pup. Jeb's breath spiralled out of his mouth in thick wisps, his heart hammering like it was trying to beat up his other organs. That boy'll be the death o' me, thought Jeb. The bloody death.

"What're ya doin' out here?" he said aloud, walking over to the lad.

"Couldn't sleep 'cause I was worried 'bout Mr Tinkles, Jeb," Orsen replied. The animal purred softly under the boy's red fingers. "When mornin' hit, I thought I'd take him for a wee walk. See how his strength was."

Jeb looked down at the skinny, bruised creature. It was sitting on its hind legs, nuzzling its small face into the boy's hands. "Looks alive t' me," he stated.

"You wanna pat him, Jeb?" Orsen asked, looking up with wide, innocent eyes. "He's only bitten a couple o' times."

The wolfcat cast an eye at the old man, and gave just a hint of fang. Hint enough to know that those teeth were large enough to put a good hole in Jeb's arm, and the pup knew it. "Err, maybe not today, Orsen."

Orsen nodded and turned back to his pal, scratching it gently under the chin.

Jeb shivered, his boots crunching on the gravel beneath him. It certainly was a cold day today, make no mistake. The smog above, normally a cottony white (a dirty cotton, that is), was all congested with dark, slimy grey. Jeb wondered if that meant another rainstorm was on the way. He sure hoped not - most of the leftover sheds around these parts would be as much use in the rain as a bra on a Waste Beast, and the intact buildings weren't safe to enter. Too much of a risk - could be Things hiding in there. Jeb and Orsen needed to get moving as soon as possible, to reach Second Thought where it was safer.

"Jeb," Orsen piped up all of a sudden.

"Aye lad?"

The boy nodded down the road, to where two Old World street signs clung to the very last dregs of their life. They flanked the cracked, weedy road on either side. "Wassat mean?"

Jeb squinted, reading the signs. One was illegible, too rusted and acid-beaten. The other one was a little more defiant, but had taken a few gunshots for its troubles. It might have once been green, with a number in a big red circle with a rough, faded word beneath it:

80

Cu t

"Well, lad," Jeb started, squinting again, "I reckons it means … err … that there were 80 cun- I mean, folk, livin' 'ere back in the Old World."

Orsen stared thoughtfully at the signs, his skinny fingers dancing in Mr Tinkle's wiry fur. "Think there's anyone still there?"

Jeb's eyes peered off down the straight, dishevelled road. There were derelict Old World buildings all along either side. Burnt-out vehicles of sorts were littered between them, rubble strewn between those. Most of the buildings were shells; carcasses of once-charming houses that the dust storms and acid rain hadn't managed to topple yet. But there were some with four walls and a roof, with dark, shadowy interiors that Jeb couldn't see into. It was these that he was worried about. The ones where something, or rather, some Thing, could creep into and wait for you until twilight.

The old man nodded slowly. "Aye lad, but I don't think they're the friendly human sort they once were."

* * *

"Holy shit," Phoenix exclaimed. "I oughta blow your head off right here, Leeland. And I'd be doing the world a favour, you ugly bastard."

The stranger's eyes narrowed again. "Like you shot that Overlord Primarch down in Second Eden?"

"Hey, that wasn't some fancy-pants Primarch, that was just a dumb soldier. It was barely even that, too!"

"The Overlords don't seem to agree." The stranger leaned back in his chair, rocking it onto two legs. A sly smirk was spreading over his face. "Is that why you're here, eh Phoenix? Hiding away in backwater fucking nowhere while real adventurers do all the work?"

Phoenix balled his hands into fists.

"You know, there's a bounty on you down in Oughta-Go. The Overlords want your head."

"Why don't you come and take it, Terrance?"

"Alright enough!" Bert growled, standing between them. She pointed at Terrance. "You, shut the fuck up and drink." Then she glared at Phoenix. "You, explain."

"He's a grubby old adventurer that thinks the world owes him the world," Phoenix said, his eyes still locked on the stranger called Terrance Leeland. Bert had never seen him act so serious. Even when they went out to cull bandits on the Back Road, or clear a Waste Beast out of a cave, Phoenix never, ever, acted serious.

"The world does owe me, you bastard!" roared Leeland, leaping up and downing his drink in one. "I'm the damn Hero of Bank Island. I was at the battle of Da Big Fort! *I* fought on the One Acre Wall." He was standing now, his face red with rage. "What have *you* done, Phoenix? Except shoot an Overlord and flee with your tail between your legs."

Bert somewhat regretted giving Leeland a stronger drink, but it was too late now. She had played with fire, and now she would have to either put the fire out, or have the bigger fire. Meatsack, meanwhile, was shuffling over to Bert, hunched low as if it would make him invisible. While the two adventurers growled at each other, she placed a reassuring hand on the giant's arm, stroking it gently. But her face didn't soften.

"Will you two stop measuring your dicks in my bar?" she said.

Phoenix snorted. "Why are you here, Leeland? The Highway's where all the action is."

Leeland beckoned to himself. "Don't you see? I've had plenty action already. In fact, you should be thanking me, and I don't reckon I'll be paying for this drink."

Something burst on Bert's forehead. The pipes were beginning to whistle again. "Excuse me?"

"Yeah, fuck you, and fuck that. There was a gang of dungarees-wearing bandit a-holes on their way here with a trailer, and I gutted them on the road." Terrance was visibly swaying now, his speech starting to slur.

Boy, thought Bert, that stuff acts fast. Definitely a big mistake, in hindsight. But then, hindsight was always a bitch.

Swaying didn't seem to stop Terrance. "Yeah, they wanted me to pay them Tax, can you believe that? Me, the Hero of Bank Island, of Da Big Fort, toppler of man-eating trees at One Acre. And they wanted me to pay them a fucking Tax. It's like they didn't even know who I wash ... was. Hiccup."

Bert stepped forwards, Meatsack scuttling away slightly into the background (not realising that there was never truly a background when you're seven feet tall). "Woah woah woah," Bert said. "Slow down, there. What's this about Tax?"

Phoenix's knuckles had gone white.

"Yeah, Taxss," said Terrance, the Hero With Many Titles, now swaying like a leaky boat. "They ssaid that they, they were collecting Tax for the new lord of Can't ... of Canb'burred. He's 'Making the Waste a better plaste', and wanted me to pay for it? Cany'believethat?"

A couple of traders who had stayed the night muttered in agreement. Bert hadn't even seen them come in - traders could be sneaky like that.

Then again, she supposed you had to be quick and quiet to be a trader, because you never knew what would try to eat you out on the road. It could be a Waste Beast, it could be a tree, it could be the guy you thought was your best friend and lover.

"He's right, ya know," said one of them.

"You heard about this, too, Derick?" Bert replied.

"Aye," said the man. He was an older trader, with droopy frown lines on his head, and cheeks that hung almost past his chin. He wore multiple layers of ragged coats, with a thick woolly beanie covering his bald scalp. He sat next to a woman of a similar age and, quite frankly, similar appearance. Old traders all sort of looked the same after a while. "This new guy, Farmer Brown he calls hisself - but don't ask me what it means - is spouting all sorta rubbish 'bout fixin' things up. But he's just a bully."

"Hiccup," Terrance said.

The old woman nodded. "Picks on traders and the like, so he does. Sends out gangs with trailers t' steal yer goods, then lectures ya about how yer helpin' folk." She shook her old head, cheeks getting the message just a few seconds after.

Phoenix and Bert looked at each other, then back at the group. Neither had heard of this before, but at least it seemed to be distracting Phoenix. His fingers had uncurled ever so slightly, but he hadn't moved from his position, and he hadn't taken his eyes off the unstable figure of Terrance bloody Leeland.

Who now spoke. "Fuck that bandit bashtard," he growled. "I oughta march in ... into hiss fort and throw him off the wall."

The older man raised his eyebrow. "You know, it's not a half bad idea, eh Hilda?"

"Aye, love. We gut the bugger an' then its traders who own the fort!" She smiled, revealing a complete lack of teeth.

Terrance found Meatsack in his wandering gaze. "Hey, you, big guy. Get meanutherdrink."

Meatsack stepped away from him and hunched lower.

Derick scratched his chin, a thought seeming to pass before his eyes. Sometimes it took old traders a few run ups to truly get their sentences in order. "You know, Bert, you got a decent bit o' firepower in this bar." His droopy frown lines attempted to shift upwards into a more hopeful expression, but didn't quite get organised enough. "I mean, Phoenix used to be an adventurer, right? He easily counts for what, five bandits?"

"I'd say ten to be safe," muttered Phoenix, glancing between Derick and Terrance.

Terrance stepped around his table, the conversation having veered away from him. Not that he noticed anymore, anyway. "Oi, you grey bashtard. I wannannutherdrink. Go get it."

Meatsack looked between the bar and the drunken adventurer, and with his eyes the way they were, did so at the same time.

Derick was on a roll, now, and it would be a while before his brain knew to stop. "An' then you got the giant, Meatsack. Why I reckons he could cave a man's skull in with his bare hands, eh? Put a club in his hands an' who knows, you know?"

Hilda leaned forwards, a flash of understanding in her mischievous old eyes. "Ooooh aye, I get ya Derick. An' you, Berty, how many folks've ya kicked out o' this place with a few extra holes in their coat? Ain't no one tougher'n you."

Bert raised her robotic hand to stop them. Her attention was focused on the two traders, while Terrance stumbled towards Meatsack somewhere off to the side. "No, stop there," she said.

Their wrinkly old raisin faces dropped.

"I'm sorry, but Smack-dab isn't going to get involved in some battle for the fort. We're three people who run a bar in the middle of nowhere, do you know why we haven't been burned down yet?"

They shook their heads.

Bert shook hers as well. The pressure gauge in her head had come down, the pipes quieting. Bert was quick to anger, make no mistake. What she lacked in physical presence, she made up for in sheer, unadulterated Bertrage. She had to be that way, because how else was one small woman with a tiny pistol supposed to run a business in the middle of Can't Be Buried? Hell, they didn't even have a sheriff. But her customers were also many of her friends, and there were plenty she knew from back in The Woman's day. She understood their plight, she felt for it. But she felt more for her home.

"It's because we don't get involved," she continued, finally pulling a chair and perching next to Derick and Hilda. "This is a neutral place, and the only time it ever wasn't was when The Woman was running things..." her voice wavered with a sort of human radio static, "...and you can just look outside to see how that ended up."

Behind them all, Terrance was in Meatsack's chunky face, prodding a finger into his chest. "Do you even know who I am? Do you even know who I fucking am?! I'mm a damn hero! I've bled for asshholesh like you!"

"Look," Bert continued, seeing the hope dissolve off her friends' faces, "I respect that you're having trouble, but being Taxed is still better than dying, right?"

Reluctantly, they agreed.

"Aye, I thought so. I'm sorry, I am, but Smack-dab can't fight. We're pacifists, and we need to stay that way. And pacifists don't fight."

And then Terrance Leeland, a true hero, swung a fist at Meatsack.

* * *

Deep within the town formerly known as the Ash Fort, a skinny bandit wearing tidy dungarees was holding a clipboard. More specifically, he was clutching it - a much more frightened style of holding objects in one's hands, and a descriptor key to understanding how this man currently felt. To be even more specific, he was clutching it tightly, knuckles going white, in front of his breast. His chest was motionless, the breath within currently on pause.

"Missin', ya say?" rumbled a deep, vocal earthquake in front of the man.

"Aye, erm, yessir," he replied, feeling smaller now than he ever had before. He'd heard that people sometimes said you shouldn't shoot the messenger, but he wondered how many times that had actually helped said messenger at times of shootiness. "Never checked in at th' construction site," he continued, voice wavering, "an' nobody saw 'em at Second Thought, so's they never even made it that far."

Silence replied, and it was the loudest silence he'd ever heard.

The skinny man with the clipboard was standing in a large, well-kept wooden office on the second floor of the Manor. This building, built long after the Old World fell away, was the lavish palace of the late Lord Ash, and now the command centre for the new lord. The front courtyard was damn good for public executions, too. Nice and wide, with plenty of space for a gallows or three.

"So what yer tellin' me," the titanic voice said, "is that somewhere 'tween Geral' an' Second Thought we lost a whole trailer load o' Tax? Jus' like that?"

The skinny man nodded.

"Well?" the voice boomed.

"Uh, um, err, um, yessir. Gone, sir."

"Hmm..." the floor vibrated.

Silence again. Fingers clenched and unclenched around the clipboard.

"An' what exactly is between Geral' and Second Thought?"

The man gulped. "Well, err, s' far as we know, umm, that is to say, nothin'."

"Nothin'?"

"Some derelict houses, sir, an' a river. But again s' far as we know, there ain't a thing out there."

"So why're we puttin' trailers on it, eh? Walkin' up a road with nobody there."

The skinny man shuffled his feet nervously. "Well, err, traders use it."

"Traders?"

"Uh, yessir. Traders that don't want t' walk the Highway an' risk gettin' caught by, well sir, by us. They calls it th' Back Road."

The man's eyes lifted upwards as the Being, for that was the only word he could use to describe such a creature, stood to its full height and took a few ponderous steps to the Manor's window. The floor shook as though it might collapse with each step, until finally the Being halted and stared down into the busy streets below.

The skinny man waited, his muscles hurting from the tension.

Then the Being spoke once more. "I can't have murd'rous folk gettin' in the way of me plans. We're gonna make this place bett'r, whether they likes it or not, so we will." The window vibrated gently with every syllable.

"Um, yessir."

"If there be traders usin' sum back road, there mus' be somethin' out there. Nobody'd walk s' far without a place t' stop."

"Yessir."

"Well." The Being turned its gaze on the man with the clipboard, staring down at him with a dangerous, frightening glare. "I wants yer t' walk out there, so I does. An' if ya sees the folk responsible f'r murderin' our folk an' stealin' from us, you come right back 'ere an' tell me."

The skinny man stood straight upright, to attention. "Yessir, right away. But err ... am I going, ya know, alone?"

Something heavy, that sent little vibrations fleeing through the floorboards, slithered out of the Being's throat. It was laughing, a low and menacing sound.

"Oh, ya won't be alone, so ya won't."

And then a singular red lightbulb inside a boxy, metal skull clicked on in the shadows.

* * *

Smack-dab moved in slow motion.

Phoenix, still standing where he had stopped, opened his mouth in shock and, at snail-like-speed, bent his knees to move.

Hilda and Derick rocked back in their seats, their wrinkly foreheads catapulting upwards with the force of a slight breeze.

Terrance's face was contorted in a drunken rage, finally having given up on discussing anything with poor, gentle Meatsack. His right hand closed in on the giant as though it had all the time in the world.

And Bert? She moved quickest of all. She watched the shadow of Terrance Leeland recoil backwards to lead into a punch, and was on her feet, chair exploding out behind her, as his fist launched forwards. Her weapon was in her fingers while he was mid-way to the attack.

And his hand was exploding before it ever had a chance.

Time reset.

The floorboards shook, dust cascading off the walls as yet another shot rang out in Smack-dab. Terrance's hand burst like a grenade had gone off inside it, chunks of blood and bone spraying over Meatsack in the worst fireworks display ever. The big giant flinched backwards, nearly tripping over a nearby chair. Phoenix was crouched, about to pounce. Derick and Hilda were pushing their chairs back, ready to get under the table at the drop of a hat (or, in this case, the drop of a hand).

Bert, a pacifist remember, was squeezing the handle of her weapon, face glowing red.

Terrance screamed with a ferocity Bert had never heard before in a person, despite all the years she spent with bandits. A cold tingle ran down her spine, the hairs on her arms and legs pricking up. The man's automatic rifle fell from his shoulder, banging against the floor. Nobody in the room made any noise, except for, you know, the spine-tingling screams of pain and horror.

"You apologise to Meatsack right now, you arrogant son of a bitch," Bert snarled. She forced down the primitive caveman instinct that said 'Maybe don't push your luck with this one, he seems a bit angry,' and cautiously approached Terrance - a Waste Beast ready to finish the job. "Nobody hurts my staff."

"Aww," cooed Phoenix.

She glanced back. "Not you, Phoenix."

"Aww..."

Terrance, hunched over on himself and tucking his arm up in his stomach, looked up at Bert. His face was twisted, almost unrecognisable. "Fuck you, you damned ... ugh ... bitch!"

And then the wounded man of many titles launched himself forwards, a wolfcat unleashed. His hand (the intact one, obviously) went for his belt, where it revealed a colossal knife made of what looked like a Waste Beast's tooth. Something deep in the stranger's throat boiled and gurgled with a wild berserker rage, his stub hand hanging loosely by his side and spraying flecks of gore all over the show.

Bert the Holy Pacifist tensed and stepped backwards as the knife careened for her chest cavity. She was too close to fire another shot, instead sidestepping to the left in an effort to create more room. But with the chairs all scattered about, there was too much clutter on the floor for easy manoeuvring. The wild figure of Terrance Leeland missed her, but he caught her arm with the edge of the blade. Bert flinched at the sudden sting, grabbing hold of a chair to get her balance. Then she growled and swung her robotic left fist as hard as she could.

One of the major benefits of having a prosthetic hand was that, when times were tough, Bert always had a weapon. You might have said she had the ... *upper hand*. But Terrance was like trying to catch a naughty child (that was covered in blood). He half-rolled, half-stumbled his way out of her fist's arc, roaring all the while with words too ghastly to think about.

Without a moment's hesitation Bert pulled her weapon up, hammered it back and fired a shot. But again, Terrance drunken-mastered himself out of the way at the last minute, the bullet zipping unobstructed into the floorboards. Adventurers were always a bastard to fight. You could argue (and boy would they) that they were the most skilled folks in the Waste, at pretty much everything you can imagine - even if you had to admit that, rather begrudgingly, about an arrogant bugger like Terrance Leeland.

Speaking of whom, he launched himself back at Bert, who ducked sideways and swung her fist again. Terrance caught her hand, a menacing, evil grin splitting open his blood-stained face. He roared a "Die, bitch!" and lifted his knife to finish the fight once and for all. Bert held her breath.

The knife ploughed through the air.

Then a blur from left-field slammed into Terrance and he tumbled to the floor, caught by surprise.

Phoenix, also a pacifist, let's not forget that, was on Terrance's back, coiling around him like a two-headed python going for the kill. Bert fell back against a table to recover her breath. She watched Phoenix visibly increase the pressure on Terrance's neck, muscles bulging beneath his shirt and veins popping in his neck.

The pair of adventurers flopped around on the floor like two drunkards play-wrestling, Terrance attempting to gain his footing enough to lever Phoenix off. But every time he employed some of his close-quarters expertise, he found again and again that his right hand was missing from the equation. Of course, this only made him angrier.

Terrance flailed as best he could, but the mad thrashing was beginning to ebb, becoming dozier, softer. Phoenix locked his legs around the man's waist, trying to contain his stabby stabby arms before the Waste Beast tooth knife did any real damage.

They rolled, Terrance thrashed, Phoenix tightened.

Leeland's fuel gauge ran lower.

The orange light flickered on.

In just a few more tense moments, the thrashing died out completely, and Terrance went quiet.

Slowly, very slowly, Phoenix released his grip and shuffled out from under the man, his clothing now covered in blood.

Bert stepped forwards, gun trained on Terrance's prone figure. The adventurer was still alive, even conscious, and wheezing softly on the floor. He coughed something about Bank Island, and maybe man-eating trees. It was hard to tell through all the quiet swears.

"You OK?" she asked Phoenix, who stayed crouched near Terrance.

He looked up and smiled, but he looked out of breath, rattled. "All in a day's work, eh?"

She half-smiled at him, and then turned to look at Meatsack. The grey giant had blood all over his front, with narrow streamlets drawing down his face as tears fled his eyes. "How about you, bud?"

He sniffled loudly.

"C'mere," she said, smiling reassuringly at him and opening her arms.

Meatsack padded over softly and let Bert hug him tight. She rubbed him on the back, or as much of it as she could actually reach, anyway, and spoke softly up at him. "You're OK, bud, you're OK. Thank you for not getting angry, I appreciate that."

He nodded quietly, tears still falling from his face. But his eyes, or eye, rather, was staring at the squirming figure of Terrance Leeland.

Bert followed it back and, still half-hugging Meatsack, called out to her chef. "Phoenix, get rid of this asshole."

He nodded without a word and pushed himself upright, reaching down to grasp Terrance's dishevelled coat. The man was still woozy, his eyes far away.

Then Bert remembered table three.

"Phoenix," she said.

He looked at her.

"Get us some more salad while you're out there."
Pacifists the lot of them, eh? Couldn't hurt a fly.

* * *

Jeb and Orsen crept down the main road of 80 Cu t in absolute, nervous silence. A moderate wind danced through the corpselike structures around them, blowing through the duo's coats and straight into their bones. Nothing but the wind stirred in this place. There were no other sounds except those of two humans breathing cautiously, a wolfcat's claws padding against the ground, and the grinding, rolling crunch of trader's boots on broken asphalt. But as quiet as Jeb and Orsen tried to be, every boot crunch seemed caught in its own echo chamber, amplified to the level of a bloody scream. They may as well have been banging pots and pans together singing classic Waste songs like, 'Oh My Darling Clementine, Please Don't Cut Me Anymore.'

A short ways past the two signs, Jeb and Orsen passed a decrepit old power station, or at least what was left after locals had stolen most of the parts. Further down, on their left, an Old World machine of sorts lay in rust-coloured dormancy. The remains of a giant, metal arm lay at its foot, with a kind of shovel-like claw half-buried in the dust beside it.

"Wassat, Jeb?" Orsen said in a loud whisper.

Jeb gazed at the machine as they walked past. "Hmm," he whispered back after a while. "I reckons it was to defend against Things back in the day."

"But I thought they weren't no Things in the Old World?"

Jeb thought for a moment longer, considering the point. "Well, lad, it's that kinda thinkin' what probably got the 80 folks here killed, eh?"

And that was that.

The duo walked on.

They were in the heart of 80 Cu t now, no turning back except to flee in a mad hurry (should it come to that). A tall building, somehow still standing, was rotting off to their right. It had a high roof, with a pointy tower at one end. Jeb and Orsen both stared at it intently as they passed, instinctively keeping a wide berth. There was an old sign hanging in one window, big, black lettering still bold against the clouds of mould that ate the poster piece by piece each year.

> *REPENT!*
> *You can run from the bombs,*
> *You can run from the plague,*
> *You can run from the quakes,*
> *But you cannot run from God.*
> *REPENT!*

"Who's God, Jeb?" asked Orsen, his voice lifting from a whisper as curiosity overcame intelligence. "He sounds like a right bastard."

Jeb put a hand on the lad's back and urged him forwards, away from the place. His eyes were glued to the window. It might have been a trick of the light, but he could have sworn he saw something move within the shadows of the place.

"He's nobody that helped this place, lad."

And the duo walked on.

About ten tense minutes further into 80 Cu t, Jeb could see the housing density beginning to relax. The tight-knit maze of burnt-out, broken structures was giving way to straight, open road and rolling, barren plains. Finally, Jeb thought, they were coming to the end of this bloody town.

And then something rattled in a building to their left.

Jeb practically jumped out of his boots, a wrinkled hand shooting for Orsen's shoulder. His right foot stepped sideways onto a piece of loose rubble, the rock flipping over on impact and turning Jeb's ankle painfully. The old man stumbled backwards with a curse, gripping Orsen's shoulder tightly and pulling the lad with him.

They fell in a heap of puffy jackets and weighty packs. Orsen hit his ass on the pockmarked asphalt, a gasp of pain blowing out his mouth in the opposite direction. Jeb went down straight on top of Mr Tinkles - a soft landing for Jeb, but nothing too pleasant for the wolfcat.

The creature yelped loudly with pain and shot out from under the man, sprinting away from the duo towards a solitary, two-storey structure not too dissimilar to Smack-dab in shape. It was old, wooden weatherboards rotten, scoured by dust and acid, warped by time. It had a porch all along the front facade, but the roof had collapsed along most of it, leaving only a splintered, gaping hole in the wall for entry.

But perhaps more importantly, skeletal remains and half-eaten scraps of meat were scattered in piles all around the building. Blood stained every inch of what was once a neat garden, with splashes painted across the wood of the building mixed with long, streaking handprints.

It was nice that the occupants gave so stark a warning.

Mr Tinkles yelped all the way to the edge of the road, and then halfway up the garden towards the building.

"Mr Tinkles!" Orsen cried, scrabbling to his feet to give chase. "Mr Tinkles, wait!"

"No!" Jeb shouted, lashing out and grabbing the boy by his ankles.

The old man was pulled forwards with a jerk as his fingers gripped tight, and his face scraped against the road. Orsen gasped as he fell forwards, his feet pulled from under him.

Something stirred within the building.

"Jeb, what are you doing?" sobbed Orsen. "Let me go!"

But Jeb held firm, despite the boy's wriggling and kicking. "Don't be a fool, boy! You can't go near that place."

Orsen struggled again, waggling his legs back and forwards to shake the old man's vice grip. Jeb thanked every god he'd heard of that he was a sheriff in his past life. If Jeb gripped someone, they'd have more luck prying the gun from a statue's hands; they weren't going nowhere.

"Let me go, Jeb! I gotta go get Mr Tinkles."

"No, lad, I can't let you." Fear touched the edge of Jeb's voice, cracking it like puberty. With one hand still clamped down on Orsen's ankle, he brought his other forward to manhandle the boy's backpack. Now Orsen was definitely going nowhere, Jeb slowly crawling up him, his fingers always tight, holding the lad down.

Mr Tinkles watched with caution, his body tense and low, ready to flee should the humans attack again.

Tears welled in Orsen's eyes. "We can't leave without Mr Tinkles, Jeb, we've been through so much together."

Jeb sighed openly, moving his body so that he was sitting on top of Orsen's back. "I've been good to ya, lad, I have. I've not said a word since we got th' thing, but it's not Mr Tinkles and ya know it."

"But it looks like 'im, Jeb. It looks like my Mr Tinkles. Sniffle."

Something inside the building fell over, banging against ancient floorboards.

Jeb stared at the structure, then down at the small wolfcat staring from by a particularly green meat pile. He shook his head sadly, expression grim. "No, Orsen, we're leaving."

He stood carefully, his eyes fixed on hole at the front of the building. But the moment the pressure was released, Orsen lurched forwards, hands outstretched to pull himself away while boots scrabbled for purchase on the dusty ground. Jeb launched himself after the boy but missed his legs, instead landing on his stomach in the cloud left by Orsen's sudden take-off.

When he looked up, Orsen was inching up the garden, crouched low, offering his hand forwards.

"Cummon, Mr Tinkles," he cooed softly. "I ain't gonna hurt ya..."

Jeb's eyes were frozen as wide as they could go. "Orsen!" he whispered, as loud as he dared.

"Cummon, puppypup. Come t' Orsen..."

Jeb crept forwards with quick, soft footsteps, his eyes still glued to the torn hole at the building's front. He let his pack slide gently to the dust as he moved. He needed speed, now, not clobbering power.

Orsen approached Mr Tinkles.

Jeb approached Orsen.

Mr Tinkles growled quietly.

...and bolted into the building.

"Mr Tinkles!" Orsen wailed.

Ah shit, thought Jeb.

Without a moment's hesitation, or any remote cousin to what might be called intelligent forethought, Orsen took off after the small creature. Jeb pushed his feet under him and lurched forwards as well, swearing loudly at the boy. The porch boards creaked in pain as Orsen stomped across them, and they screamed their discontent as Jeb followed closely in pursuit.

In a moment, a loud, high-pitched yelp burst out of the structure. It repeated and repeated, undeniably the frightened cry of a wolfcat pup. There was another sound, too, a strangled, phlegmy growl.

"No, Orsen!" Jeb roared, launching himself once again as the boy slowed to step into the structure's open hole.

With a flying tackle, Jeb slammed into the boy, taking them both swearing through one of the porch's rotten pillars. It cracked loudly as their bodies struck it, and tore in half as they passed through it. They toppled to the gravel beneath and rolled to a halt some ways away. Then the rest of the porch roof finally caved in, piling in on itself with a deafening crash and a mighty cloud of dust. The hole in the wall vanished behind splintered wood and clouds of dust.

The squealing, helpless cry of the wolfcat continued and then...

...then it suddenly stopped.

Silence swarmed in all around Jeb and Orsen as they lay on the ground, dust sweeping over them from the crash. Orsen was sobbing, repeating the name of his beloved friend over and over. Jeb breathed heavily on top of him, sweat pouring off his face despite the bitter cold.

"I'm sorry lad," he whispered between laboured breaths. "I'm so sorry."

Part Three

Meet the Farmers

Phoenix stood alone upon the ruins of what civilisation had grown to call the Back Road.

He was having a moral conundrum of sorts. You see, someone once asked him, if a man-eating tree tripped over in a forest and nobody saw it, did it truly happen? This sounded philosophical enough, but Phoenix couldn't help but think that of course it happened, and all the tree's friends probably pointed and laughed. "Have a nice trip," they would say. "See you next fall."

Now, though, Phoenix was wondering: If somebody were to sucker punch a wounded, drunken man, but nobody was there to see it, did it truly happen? Great heroes were never supposed to kick a man while he was down, no matter how much of a bastard he was. It would be unethical. Damn near immoral. At least bloody rude. But, standing on the broken asphalt as little wisps of dust rolled past his boots, Phoenix couldn't help but grin and look at the blood on his knuckles.

Fuck it, he was retired.

The distant figure of Terrance Leeland was fading to brown in the murky horizon to the north. His ragged silhouette limped and staggered all down the way, leaving a little trail of breadcrumbs ... made of blood. He had sworn revenge. He had sworn he would return. He had sworn an awful lot. Well, at least he had learned some manners before he left. Right to the face.

Smack's adventurer felt proud in his full adventuring gear, a man finally back in his own skin (not that he was ever in someone else's skin, which should be clarified. There are plenty in the Waste who have found human skin makes a nice coat, especially when it's fresh). He tapped out a gentle rhythm on his thick, plated body armour and began strolling in the opposite direction to Terrance. His long, brown trench coat billowed out behind him like a muddy waterfall of fabric, a large Waste Beast tooth knife (acquired *very* recently) dangling by rifle magazines, grenades and myriad pouches at his belt.

He shrugged his shoulder to push the strap of a large automatic rifle into a more comfortable position, preparing himself for a long march into nowhere. The weapon was heavily customised, even compared to other Waste weaponry (that was often measured not on weight or balance, but use of duct tape and spikes). It had enough slots for two or three magazines, an additional grip at the front, a bloody great scope on the top, a slot for a bayonet (which Phoenix had lost), a laser sight that never worked, and plenty more that Phoenix had forgotten the use of.

Phoenix considered himself Smack-dab's resident badass. He understood that Bert and The Woman were close, but she really had to admit that The Woman's adventuring gear was not up to modern standards (or, considering her demise, not up to historic standards, either). She didn't have bandit-tackling shoulder plates like Phoenix, or punchy punchy metal knuckles, or steel-capped boots. Hell, she didn't even have theoretically bulletproof armour, which was armour that you were told is bulletproof, but you haven't had tested yet. All she had was a bone-handled peashooter and a grimace. Oh, and a statue.

Not that he'd tell Bert any of this, of course. Especially at the moment, as she appeared to be particularly shooty. And so, gently humming the Starry Place's Battle Tune - which had been stuck in his head since the attack - Phoenix pushed down his thoughts of superiority and went to go do Bert's dirty work.

So, Phoenix thought to himself, if I were a salad, where would I be?

He stopped walking and narrowed his eyes. Through dirty, well-worn goggles he saw the big ol' Waste, and rather dismayingly, not a whole lot else. The last salad Phoenix had caught was half way up a mountain, clinging to a rock on a sheer cliff and gnawing on the bones of some long-dead creature. A *big* long-dead creature. Boy had that turned into a shitshow. He'd wasted a tonne of ammo, a precious and very limited commodity, and then the little bastard had the gall to escape!

The nerve of some food, Phoenix grumbled quietly. Every salad that escaped meant he'd have to kill another rabbit thing, and he hated killing them. They were so cute, and innocent. And quick.

And that was how the bottle holding Phoenix's feelings shattered open.

On the note of salads, he harrumphed with pouting lips, why was there even salad on the menu? Who does Bert think she is? Oh yeah, let's just put a damn salad on the menu. That sounds fancy. That will draw the customers. That'll make the moneys. Nyer nyer nyah nyer nyer, I'm Bert, and I put salad on menus then ask other people to catch the sneaky little bastards. I don't think about work health and safety.

Yeah well, screw you, he yelled (silently, where Bert could never hear he was complaining). Screw you and your, your stupid ... ass.

The gentle sound of laughter met Phoenix's grubby ears, carried on the dulcet tones of a small, fierce bar fight. He heard the sharpness of a woman's voice rebuking someone, followed by a bigger, bassier thump. The laughter only increased, but the thumps and bumps ceased. Phoenix shook his head and started walking again.

That woman, his thoughts continued, pouring through his brain like green foam from an open wound. That ludicrous, red-faced, angry, stupid, blue-eyed goddess of a woman. That, that blasted, no-good, tight-assed, short-tempered, sexy bar owner of a, a bloody woman. That's what she damn well was. Yeah. A bloody woman.

And you know what the worst part is? his mind continued, a veritable flamethrower of emotion. You know, the worst part, really, is ... is ... Gah! He threw his arms up and kicked at the dirt, which hadn't done anything to him except make the mistake of being dirt that was kickable. Phoenix could barely get a good rant going. Every time the motor in his brain worked up to a good speed, he'd see a mirage of Bert's ass swaying across his eyes and the motor would stall and spit out smoke. It was like that story he was told by a trader, about an Old World bus that couldn't slow down without being blown up by bandits. Except the opposite. Curse that stupid, perfect, awful, down-right spectacularly bloody beautiful piece of human backside. It was a weapon of mass destruction, and the Overlords ought to be told so they could confiscate it.

He walked on, a little stompier than before. Behind him, a patch of dirt swore that it was done with big-Waste life, and would return to the humble Old World garden where its family was worried sick to death.

The wind was picking up around Phoenix, grabbing clumps of dust and throwing them into his face. It blew in unobstructed from the coast; an icy gust that bit through his body armour and coat, gnawing at his bones. He shivered and hunkered down into his coat, pulling it tighter across his chest and crossing his arms.

But the sudden wintery blast had doused the flames of his mind.

Bert had taken Phoenix in when nobody else would, then resisted his advances like nobody else could. Or at least, he had thought that nobody could. Oh lovely, terrifying Bert. She was a bitch, quite honestly - though he would never be so honest where she could hear. But she was the good kind of bitch. The kind of bitch that was at her bitchiest when she was protecting what she cared about. Like Meatsack, and even Phoenix. And that stupid bar.

He didn't really understand why Smack-dab was so important to Bert, but he had of course seen the statue out front and heard some of the stories. To Phoenix, home was wherever you collapsed, either wounded or exhausted or, typically, both. He'd never felt the same passion Bert had for Smacks. It represented history, or rather, History. She was willing to die for that place in the same way that someone would be willing to die for their loved ones, or to die for some promise they had made to a dead loved one. Or ... something about dying loved ones, anyway.

But then, death was all that would ever happen unless Bert made some more friends. She was too much of an isolationist, if you asked Phoenix. The Woman had been quite the relationship builder, and tried to act as a political entity in Can't Be Buried. But when she passed away (or rather, when bullets passed through her), Bert closed right up. Open for business only. No politics, no friends, and definitely no bandits.

Oh goodness, and Phoenix couldn't even get started on Bert's hatred for bandits. He'd never heard so many insults before.

A mischievous gust of wind drove dust through Phoenix's thought bubble with a comedic pop. A feint, sweet smell wafted through the air in front of him with beckoning arms, curling into his surprised nostrils with little smoky fingers. Phoenix recognised it instantly, and eagerly traced the smell back to a tiny little bush just off the road, momentarily distracted from being distracted. The adventurer grinned widely and pulled out his Waste Beast tooth knife.

This was one of the few remaining fruit bushes that hadn't decided to fight back. It was a bonkerberry bush, and when the sweet little red fruit was chewed, juiced or taken as a suppository, the user would be in for ... well, Phoenix would be using it this evening, that was for certain.

But as he was gently cutting berries from the bush...

By Duncan P. Pacey

"Ho there!" a surprise voice sung out. It cut through the quiet, shifting air like a vocal machete.

Phoenix almost fell over the bush, spinning with a fright. His weapon was in his hands even before his conscious thoughts had decided that would be a good idea, his body dropping low, ready to spring.

Two figures were approaching from the south, walking along the road. Phoenix hadn't noticed them in his dream state. Stupid! he roared at himself. Stupid, stupid! That's how you get killed out here.

With a tense hand he pulled the cocking mechanism back on his rifle, and an ominous *kachunk* echoed across the Waste. He peered through the scope to get a better look at the approaching bogies. The hazy air was getting all up in his line of sight, thick clumps of dust drifting in and out of view, but he could tell that one of the figures was a short fellow with neat hair and a patchwork, though very tidy, set of dungarees. Oddly enough, though, the short man had no discernible firearm or clobbering implement – just a small clipboard clutched in his skinny little fingers. But as odd as a clipboard might seem in the middle of a barren, clipboardless environment like the Waste, it didn't quite have the same oomph to Phoenix as the man's travelling companion.

Phoenix's face grew tight, alarmed, and the blood drained right out of it. The great sea of haze had parted enough for him to see a humanoid robot keeping pace with the short-arse. Its polished metal shell gleamed gently in the smoglight, a cyclopean red eye fixed in the middle of its boxy skull. Some type of massive, flashy Overlord cannony thing was mounted to its back, not like it probably needed a large-calibre weapon for most fleshy little human victims.

"Shit," whispered Phoenix. "Shit shit shit shit."

They had found him! His mind started panicking. Sweat broke out in a riot on his forehead, and the police of his sleeve only made the crowd angrier. He had travelled into the ass of the Waste just to escape the Overlord's creepy claw-hands of wrath. There were no major population centres here, there shouldn't be any Overlord activity. The Ash Fort wasn't big or dangerous enough, was it? No, it fucking wasn't.

They were walking straight towards Phoenix, approaching from the direction of the fort. But why was an Overlord with a human? Now

68

Phoenix's adventurer instincts were kicking down the doors of panic and arresting any thoughts that might stir up trouble. His brow creased and his fingers tensed around his weapon. Overlords didn't work with humans, they tried to restrict and control their population. When the Old World moved out and the neighbourhood got a little rougher, the Overlords decided, for some inexplicable reason, that it was humanity's fault. They took it upon themselves to wrangle the human population into relative peace – so folks couldn't keep nuking themselves. But their numbers dwindled without the resources to build more units. They stuck to the big cities, and never went into the countryside without a good reason, let alone with a human. So why was an Overlord walking with this guy? It didn't make any sense.

"Howdy, stranger!" the short man shouted again. The duo was close.

Phoenix kept his weapon trained on the robot. Too close. It was decision time. Kill or be killed. Now or never.

The little man waved with an innocent smile on his face, stopping a number of metres away. If he seemed bothered by the rifle trained on his menacing companion, he didn't show it. The robot didn't seem to care, either. But then, there wasn't a whole lot of emotion that a singular light bulb could display.

"Mind if ya put down that there weapon an' come over t' have a wee chat with us?" the man called.

Phoenix's finger danced on the trigger. "What do you want?" he called back, feet sliding into a wider stance.

Dammit, Phoenix, his thoughts yelled at him. Just shoot the both of them! Snap the clipboard in half and beat him to death with it. Those are dungarees. *That's an Overlord!* But the man seemed so calm, so pleasant. Phoenix hesitated.

"We'd like t' talk, if ya don't mind. No need f'r violence, just lower yer weapon."

Then the short man's smile lost its realism, as though his face had glitched. It was a worried smile. "Please, unless ya want my ... friend, t' get nervous."

On cue, the Overlord reached back and unhooked the cannon, bringing it forwards. Its arms, although no bigger than your average human's,

By Duncan P. Pacey

supported what must have been an immense weight like it were plastic and shot foam darts.

"MAKE A SMART MOVE, STRANGER," it stated through hollow-sounding synthetic vocal chords. The voice had no emotion, couldn't comprehend inflection, but somehow still dripped with a poisonous malice.

Phoenix gripped his weapon tight, but he knew that an Overlord holding its gun diminished his survival chances from <insert maths here> to <insert lower maths here>. He didn't need the specific numbers, just the adrenalin.

"It doesn't look very nervous," he replied, though he wasn't sure why. His brain didn't catch the words in time before he said something antagonistic. To an Overlord. *A fucking Overlord.* Oh for the love of...

"Well I assure ya, sir," replied the human, his face a forgery of pleasantness, "yer'll make it that way. Now put yer gun away and let's have us a chinwag, eh? Before this gets worse than it needs t' be." He raised his hands to simulate peace.

Phoenix only tightened his grip further. He wondered silently how many bandits a single Overlord might be worth.

Hopefully it was less than ten.

* * *

Jeb and Orsen had continued along the Highway for some time, now, with not a word spoken between them.

Silence was not a healthy thing, Jeb felt. It gave weary travellers too much time to think. For instance, maybe that weed over there was a man-eater? Or what if those Old World ruins hid a Waste Beast? And worse still, what if none of this was real, and everyone was actually locked inside some kind of giant Overlord computer, waiting to be turned into goop for the Overlords to fuel their bodies with?

Thinking would be the death of a man, Jeb reckoned.

But he couldn't stop.

It was weird, he thought, how stress always made you think about more stress. How you'd have a thousand little arguments inside your head with

70

people who couldn't argue back, or you'd think back to some of the worst moments of your life. Jeb often thought about his time as a sheriff, foiling the Orcks day by day, and fleeing from them night by night. And he thought of his string of ex-wives, four of which had been Orcks in disguise, two of which died of infectious diseases (which Jeb swore he didn't give them), and the most recent of whom exploded - particularly in the cranial region.

He trudged along glumly, mind whirling, Orsen a step behind with his eyes fixed on the dusty road at their boots. Jeb's feet ached from all the day's action. His body felt weak and tired. But 80 Cu t had his brain in a little noose, and the flashes of memory that flickered before his eyes only tightened it.

Somebody had to say something. The silence was too much to bear.

Jeb finally opened his mouth to speak, but Orsen cut in.

"Look, Jeb ... I'm real sorry," he said miserably. His eyes never left the road, and the pair never stopped walking. "Mr Tinkles ... he was my best friend at the commune..."

Jeb watched his young protégé as the misery leaked from his lips. He knew he was about to have to say something encouraging and thoughtful, but wasn't sure what that would be just yet. He marked it TBD and let the boy keep speaking.

"He was my only friend, really," Orsen continued, his voice barely audible above the ambient gusting of the Waste plains. "I just ... I couldn't let another Mr Tinkles get got. He needed savin', Jeb. The whole Waste needs savin', I reckon."

Jeb stayed silent for a moment longer, staring at the boy. "How'd the last Mr Tinkles go, lad?"

Orsen's head sunk lower. "Orcks."

"Ah."

This, Jeb knew, was the moment to speak. To give a short speech that would lift the boy's head, and not to mention his spirits. They'd be back to their old selves, putting the day's horrors behind them. Hopefully forever, but you never really knew what horrors would catch up in the Waste.

But Jeb wasn't very good at this sort of thing. The only feelings he had much experience with were the manic passions wild Orcks raved about before opening up someone's belly like a can of beans. And those were pretty easy to deal with, relatively. They opened their mouths, they said something stupid, he shot them in the head. He could arrest the corpse afterwards, but it was usually easier on his back to just leave it there and let something take it in the night.

Real feelings were much trickier. If Orcks were Waste Beasts or man-eaters, real human feelings were more like boulderfrogs - you'd never know a boulderfrog was there until you sat on it, and then not only would you quite suddenly know it was there, but you would get the grand tour of its mouth and stomach, too.

Yep, just like feelings.

Jeb's mouth floundered like a fish out of water, but he couldn't figure out what to say. So he went with what he knew instead (except not the shooty guns bit. He went with other stuff he knew. People can know more than one thing, don't you know).

"Orsen," he said.

The boy finally looked at him. His eyes were all filmy and sparkly, his cheeks red. Damn if he didn't look utterly devastated.

"How 'bout we go visit Smack-dab, eh? We're not too far, maybe a couple o' days at most. Ya can play with Meatsack, an' we can sleep in real beds. How 'bout that?"

Orsen smiled weakly and nodded. "That sounds a'right, Jeb. I'd like that."

Jeb smiled back, a big fatherly grin. "Well OK then. To Smack-dab we go!"

* * *

Phoenix stood in a stare-off with the dungarees-wearing short man and his frighteningly static Overlord companion.

"My name's Ernest," said the man whose name was Ernest. He was interrupting what was becoming a very tense silence. "And this 'ere is H2-149. What's your name?"

Phoenix lowered the tip of his weapon to see what would happen. "Phoenix."

H2-149 lowered its cannon precisely the same degree.

So it was an H-unit, eh? Phoenix thought. That meant it was just a soldier - the lower in the alphabet the bot, the dumber it was. But that made even less sense. He could understand a robo-human partnership if a political body was involved, maybe a C-unit or something, but some dumb-ass soldier? That made about as much sense as Phoenix's growing love of Bert and Meatsack, but mostly Bert. Meatsack needed some work before he could be fully likeable. A bath would help. And a brain.

"There," said Ernest, earnestly, "now ain't that better?"

Phoenix's face turned to a grimace. No, it wasn't better. If anything, it was a little worse. "What do you want?" he asked, deciding to try get this over with. "I'm a busy guy."

"O' course, o' course!" the shorty exclaimed, a little flash of warmth sparking somewhere behind his faux-smile. "Let it not be known that a man o' the Farm was one t' hold up a good day's work!"

"HIGH PRODUCTIVITY IS IMPORTANT IN A TRADER'S LIFE, PATHETIC HUMAN," the tin-man added. "WE SALUTE YOU."

"Trader?" Phoenix said, lowering his rifle entirely. "Hell no, not this guy. I'm out here hunting for Smack-dab." He beckoned the rifle to prove the point.

Idiots, he thought, thinking he was a trader. What trader wanders without a pack? Maybe these two weren't so dangerous after all.

Ernest glanced very briefly at his companion, as though something had just connected in his brain. H2-149 did not look back.

"Smack-dab, huh?" Ernest finally replied, scratching his tidy hair. "Can't say I know what a Smack-dab is. That a new town or somethin'?"

"Town?" Phoenix frowned. "What kind of rock is your farm planted under? It's the Back Road bar, up thataways." Phoenix shrugged in the direction of Smacks.

Short McClipboard spoke a little "Huh", and brought his board up. He scribbled on it hastily with a well-used pencil, mouthing the words 'Smack-dab' and 'Back Road bar' as he wrote.

"What kind of farmer has Overlord bodyguards, anyway?" Phoenix asked, gently scratching his balls and looking at H2.

Ernest glanced quickly up from his work. "Farmer? Oh no, sir. We're 'ere representin' the Farm - it's the new name f'r the town down the road. Ya know, with the big walls an' that. One of our smart lads, 'fore he was decapitated that is, captured an' reprogrammed H2 for the boss. Pretty neat, eh?"

Flush, and the blood swirled out of Phoenix's face. His metal-plated glove paused mid-ball-scratch.

The robot's eye didn't move, but by golly did it see. "DETECTING EMOTIONAL CHANGE: NERVOUSNESS INCREASING. BE AT EASE, COWARDLY FLESH BAG."

Ernest fully put his clipboard down now, letting it dangle from a bit of string on his belt. He rubbed his hands together, fingers red from the cold. "Woah there, friend, no need t' get all frightened. Farmer Brown don't mean ya no harm. We're just out 'ere doin' some inves'gative work, an' then we'll be on our way." He paused, picking the clipboard up again to briefly re-scan the words. Then his beady eyes looked back up at Phoenix. "Don't suppose ya heard anythin' about a group o' fine folk with a trailer gettin' murdered recently?"

At this point, two thoughts happened simultaneously in Phoenix's brain.

The first came from a little horned demon, who was red and farted smoke. It told Phoenix that he ought to go get Bert, so she could handle this so-called investigative pair. The dungarees people must have been out here looking for the companions that Terrance killed, and Phoenix wasn't sure what to tell them that wouldn't get Smack-dab further ... investigated.

The second thought came from a tiny little pixie, clad in white and glowing gently as though it were soaked in radiation. If Phoenix had heard of angels, he'd have called it one. Its voice sounded a little more like this: Kill them, Phoenix. *Kill them now.* No more talking. Kill. Kill. Kill. Kill. *Kill. Kill...*

Someone had once told him that the personalities of these little voices were the wrong way round, but they found it hard to convince a man of anything logical once he'd seen little pixies screaming on his shoulders.

"Uhh..." was the awkward noise that finally escaped his mouth.

"HEARTRATE INCREASING," the robot noticed. "SKINBAG KNOWN AS ERNEST, THE SKINBAG KNOWN AS PHOENIX KNOWS SOMETHING."

"Uhrm...."

And there it was again: Ernest's weird, glitching face. His smile didn't move, it was still at all the same angles, but something inside it died. In this case, something inside it died violently. "Please, Phoenix, if ya knows somethin', ya gotta tell us. We're out 'ere makin' the Waste a better place, ya know? Fixin' roads, buildin' farms - we're just claimin' a little Tax is all. Now if it were up t' me I'd leave ya in peace, so I would, but I'm afraid we gots t' know what 'appened to our trailer. Got no choice."

In Phoenix's mind, he carefully (but quickly) weighed up the options. If he attacked now, the robot would almost undoubtedly see it coming. Insert Bullets A into Torso B. The way to avoid a conflict, then, was to tell Shorty McClipboard all about Smack-dab, the trailer, and presumably, Smack-dab's money. But if Bert found out he'd told a dangerous group of bandits not only where Smack-dab was located, but that it also had money and very few staff, she'd probably pull out his insides. He was confident her robotic hand was capable of such a feat.

So he decided to mix it up a little. It wouldn't be lying, it would just be not telling them everything.

He smiled widely, innocently, and relaxed his stance. "Well, it just so happens that I *do* know what happened to your trailer."

The robot's head tilted to the side - the first movement it had made since lowering its weapon. There was something creepy about a thing that moved suddenly, but subtly, after being as still as a statue. Something in the back of Phoenix's head worried he might start to have nightmares about The Woman's statue coming to life. That would be just what he needed. *More* angry women attacking him in his dreams.

"TELL US WHAT YOU KNOW."

"Oh I'll tell you, tin-man."

"THEN TELL US."

"I'm going to."

"NOW."

"OK, let's do this telling thing."

Silence.

More silence.

"Oh, right," Phoenix awkwardly chuckled, "I'll be doing the talking. So, umm, your trailer was attacked by a stranger. An adventurer with, like, big guns and an ugly face. Yeah, real ugly face. Write that one down. He just murdered all your folk because they asked him for Tax, and because he's meant to be famous but they didn't know who he was. Probably on account of his ugly face. Who wants to make that famous, you know? That's it, that's the whole story. Bandits ask stranger for Tax. Stranger realises he's not famous and he's ugly and he sucks. Stranger takes it out on bandits. What a bastard, right?"

Phoenix smiled openly and widely, emanating pure goodness from the bottom of his very soul. Right? ...right?

Ernest looked between the robot and Phoenix.

The robot stared straight through Phoenix.

"I DO NOT BELIEVE YOU."

Phoenix pouted. "But I'm a believable kinda guy!"

" 'e seems like a believable kinda folk t' me, H2."

"I DO NOT BELIEVE HIM."

"I think that's on you, not me."

"The story seemed plaus'ble t' me. Ya can't trust a man with an ugly face an' big guns."

"I FOUND IT LACKED BELIEVABILITY."

"Well that's just rude."

"YOU ARE RUDE."

"Your lightbulb is rude."

"TELL US THE TRUTH."

"I told you the truth!"

" 'e told us the truth, H2."

"HE DID NOT TELL US THE WHOLE TRUTH."

"I don't know what you mean."

" 'e don't know what we mean."

The robot stepped forwards, its legs whirring noisily. The cannon in its hands hummed all of a sudden, little twinkling lights flashing on all down the shiny casing. "I WISH TO KNOW WHY THE PATHETIC BAG OF MEAT KNOWN AS PHOENIX HAS NOT TOLD US HOW HE IS SO SURE THE

TRAILER WAS ATTACKED BY A STRANGER. A STRANGER THAT HAS BEEN DESCRIBED ALMOST IDENTICALLY TO THE PATHETIC BAG OF MEAT KNOWN AS PHOENIX."

"Hey," Phoenix frowned, fingers tightening once again on his rifle, "that's just hurtful."

Ernest scratched at his chin, face in thought. "I gotta admit, I'm a little unsure o' that meself now that it's mentioned. 'ow are ya so sure our trailer was attacked?"

"Because he told us."

" 'e told ya? Where?"

"At Smack-dab."

Then Phoenix's eyes grew wide. "Oh wait! I mean, he told me personally. One on one. Mano-a, um, -uglo. Whilst I was out here doing my solo thing. You know, alone."

"YOU ARE NOT DOING A SOLO THING."

"Yes I am."

"NO YOU ARE NOT."

Phoenix scowled. "Who are you to tell me what I am or ain't doing?"

"YOU TOLD US YOU ARE OUT HUNTING FOR A SMACK-DAB."

...

"No I didn't."

"Aye, ya did, I think."

"YOU TOLD US THIS INFORMATION AT PRECISELY A406 dash 43 dash 453439."

Nobody really understands how Overlords track time.

Phoenix shuffled his feet nervously, fingers wrapping and unwrapping from his weapon. He'd dug himself into a right old hole, this time. Bert was gonna be real pissed. She'd probably yell at him about his mouth or something, then stomp around and flex her fists. She liked having fists, Phoenix had noticed. She was always, you know, fisting. Oh, but not in, like, a weird way. Just having fists. Not fisting. Fisting was the wrong word. Unless she did that in her spare time, which was cool if she did because that's her business, but it's not what Phoenix meant.

Yeah.

"TELL US EVERYTHING YOU KNOW ABOUT THE DEATH OF OUR TRAILER. THEN TELL US WHERE SMACK-DAB IS. YOU OWE TAX TO-" the robot twitched, as if being forced to change its words, "<lord and protector of the Farm, Farmer Brown, long may he reign>."

"Please tell us what ya know, Phoenix. If ya don't, it's gon' get real ugly for ya." Ernest looked genuinely concerned. He obviously knew what 'ugly' meant.

OK, enough was enough. Phoenix had to either piss or get out of the bog. It was showtime, for the greatest show of all. A little show called Life. Phoenix's Life. Phoenix's Life Which He Enjoyed Living and Quite Wanted to Keep Living. It was gonna be a damn good show.

And at this point, Phoenix felt that it should involve a little bit of adventurer's strategy. He was an adventurer, after all. A hero. He knew every trick in the book. He could escape any situation. Tie him up over a burning fire? He'd get out. Strap him to a weird altar and try to sacrifice him to your gods? Good luck, he hadn't been sacrificed so far.

It was just an H-unit soldier. Phoenix felt pretty confident that he could outwit that. Hell, he'd even done it before, right before he shot it. Or was that an A-unit Primarch like Terrance had said? Naw, pretty sure it was just a soldier. A soldier they were real mad about losing for some reason...

Anyway, it was time to employ one of the greatest heroic tactics the Waste has to offer. A time-honoured tradition of heroism that had been practiced for generations, probably dating back to the Old World.

First, he looked past the duo before him and frowned.

Second, his eyes opened wide and he pointed urgently.

Third, "Holy shit! What's that behind you?"

* * *

Not too far away, a rabbit was wearing a hat. Although, explaining that it's a rabbit is technically a disservice, for it's no more a rabbit than a hamster is an octopus. But it was small and fluffy, and through an absence of any competition, had become known as a rabbit-like creature around these parts.

At this point, the rabbit-like creature wearing a hat was observing three figures. The first was a man it recognised as the Bringer of the Hat, and he was fleeing wildly and making a loud, high-pitched sound. Fleeing and screaming was something the rabbit-like creature understood, and so he quietly rooted for his large human friend.

Right behind the running figure was a shiny human with only one grentuputron eye (rabbit-like creatures have their own colours). It was shouting as well, and gaining quite quickly on the first figure.

The third figure was in the back, trying to keep up. The rabbit-like creature with the hat knew he would be the first to die if a Waste Beast was chasing them. You never had to be a fast runner in the Waste, only faster than the creatures you were with.

As the wind picked up around it, the rabbit-like creature observed the shiny human tackling the friendly human to the ground. Then it caught the scent of something tasty nearby, and decided that it had seen enough of the show.

It hopped away.

* * *

Now it was no longer now, it was later. And later, which is now known as now, Bert was pissed.

Phoenix groaned loudly, holding a defrosted slab of bloody meat to his swollen forehead. It was a few hours later, to be precise. Phoenix was in Smack-dab, having only just returned. Stumbling home had been more unconsciousy than he predicted.

"And you just ... told them?!" Bert growled, huffing and puffing, pacing angrily on the spot. The situation had just been explained to her, and she wasn't taking it well.

Meatsack hovered nearby, the trusty first aid box held tightly in his fingers. He'd already mummified Phoenix with bandages, and wasn't sure what to do next other than fret. He was very good at fretting.

Phoenix himself was covered head to boots in mud, dust and blood. His own blood, mostly. And a little steak juice, on account of the defrosting. He was bruised all to hell, and every time someone plugged up one of the holes in his skin, another one burst open and leaked just as much. It was like trying to save a sinking ship, which, coincidentally, is similar to how Bert currently viewed the man. Except it was a ship she wasn't going to go down with.

"In my defence, Bert, there was an Overlord stomping on my skull at the time," Phoenix mewed weakly, scrounging for some semblance of redemption. "That's prolly why I passed out for so long."

Her sapphire fire bore holes into his eyes. "Phoenix, how could you be so *stupid*? They didn't know about us, and now they do. *And* they think we murdered their trailer folk. We're supposed to be staying out of all this!"

Phoenix involuntarily flinched as she paced past him. The heat of her anger could have scraped paint off the walls (if there was any). "Look, I said already, I told them about Terrance and what he did."

"They just didn't believe you."

"Err ... no."

"And now they think there's some piss-weak bar with no defences, killing their folk."

"Yes." Phoenix was visibly shrinking.

"And an H-unit can run almost as fast as a vehicle, so they've probably already reached the Fort by now."

"...yes."

"And we know this new bandit lord has a truck to come back with."

"...yes..."

"So he's going to get here within the hour."

Phoenix didn't respond this time. He hung his head. Which is fine, because it saved Bert the trouble of doing it to him.

Bert finally stopped pacing, her fingers curling and uncurling (fisting, you might call it), her dangerous glare unleashing itself on a window, staring out to the depths of the Waste. Her human hand twitched unnervingly close to the bone-handled pistol at her hip.

All around her, customers waited in an understandably nervous silence. Most of the traders from the night before were still sitting around consuming a drink or six, "working themselves up" for going out in the cold. But Bert knew they'd be staying another night at this rate. And in fact, she counted on it. Her prices had mysteriously, but encouragingly, dropped.

But first they'd have to survive whatever was about to happen.

She turned her head to cast a gaze across her customers' myriad grubby, uncertain faces...

...and hoped like hell some of them had guns.

* * *

The rabbit-like creature with the hat had lost track of its enemy. It had been trailing a smaller rabbit-like creature (no hat), who was known to rabbit-like society as an upstart, a wannabe king. But just before the rabbit-like creature with the hat could pounce and end the rebellion before it began, a gritty, wheezing noise startled the smaller animal and it bolted.

And now the rabbit-like creature with a hat watched with the pure naivety that only animals can achieve as a large, loud object rumbled towards it on the human's road. Whatever it was, it was huge, and it belched a thick, black cloud of smoke as it approached. It was spiky, and growled like nothing else. The rabbit-like creature with a hat pondered if it might be some type of new Waste Beast.

It knew that it should flee, but something about this large creature was mesmerising. The behatted rabbit-like creature couldn't take its eyes off the thing's dirty red colour, the glittering scales plating its nose and flanks, and most of all, its two glowing yellow eyes.

The large, rumbling spiky creature spewed out another cloud of smoke, its growling growing in volume.

The rabbit-like creature with a hat cocked its head.

The spiky thing got closer.

It squished the rabbit-like creature, and its hat.

* * *

"Bert," Phoenix pleaded, "the Tax folk might have come here anyway. If Terrance hadn't murdered the trailer gang, they might have walked all the way up the Back Road. We couldn't hide forever."

Bert locked eyes on Phoenix. "But they also might not have. If they didn't even know we were out here, they had no reason to come up this road."

"That we know of."

She gritted her teeth. "Yeah, that we know of."

"So," Phoenix continued, feeling emboldened by his slight victory, "what I'm saying is, we can't just stay isolated forever. The Waste doesn't work that way. At some point you're going to have to come out of this, this *shell* and build relationships, alliances! Or else we're always gonna be someone's bitch. If not this farmer guy, then the next lord. Or the one after that."

Bert raised her hand to cut him off. "No! Building relationships is what got Smack-dab messed up the last time. What got The Woman killed."

Phoenix frowned. "Not making any friends is going to get *us* killed!"

Pipes whistled. Bert thrust her chunky robotic finger towards the man. "No, Phoenix, *you've* gotten us killed!" she growled. "You and your damn big-ass mouth."

Phoenix was struck by a shockwave. As in, a wave of shock. He was shocked. And it hit him in a wave-like manner. The wave continued past him, sweeping over the bar. Smack-dab's light background chatter was snuffed out. All eyes rotated to Bert. Phoenix opened his mouth to say something else, then his eyebrows turned upwards and he looked hurt. Bert breathed heavily for a moment, her face stuck on full burn. Blood boiled in her cheeks.

Then she felt a large hand weigh her shoulder down, and turned to see Meatsack standing there. His eyes were lightly covered in tears, his lip quivering. Bert looked up into at least one of those little eyes and swallowed hard. She couldn't stay mad with that face staring at her. Slowly, the harsh edge of her face softened and she reached up to put her hand on his, letting out a long breath.

"I'm sorry, Phoenix," she said, quietly. "I shouldn't have said that."

Phoenix looked at the floor. "You really think we're gonna die?"

Another silence permeated the air.

Then Bert spoke. Her voice was low, but it was edged with something sharp. Something determined, that wouldn't back down. Something ... something very *Bert*. "Not a chance. Not if I can help it."

Phoenix looked up. "So what do we do? Farmer Brown will be on his way here. He's prolly already close."

Bert's brow furrowed with thought. She paced around the front of the bar quietly, tapping her face with a human finger. Farmer Brown was on his way to either claim Tax, seek revenge for the murdered bandits, or a mix of both. Possibly a mix of both. ...probably a mix of both.

But then, just how many troops would a bandit lord bring to some backwater bar in the middle of nowhere? If the stories were true, his soldiers were spread all over Can't Be Buried, even as far north as Rangi's. It would be stupid to bring an army to a bar fight, so surely he'd just bring a regular, run o' the Waste horde? And most bandit hordes weren't too scary once you got past their leader.

Adapt.

Back in the day, just two angry women and a handful of weapons fended off one of the fort's most infamous historic leaders. They did it by themselves, and Bert had only gotten better with a pistol since then. And, arguably, quite a bit angrier. So maybe all she had to do was look tough enough to make this Farmer Whatshisface think twice about assaulting Smack-dab and instead sit down for a civil chat. Or at least as civil as a bandit lord can be when all he really wants is to rip your head off your neck.

Bert's eyes fell upon the statue at the front of Smack-dab. She slowed to a halt, unable to take her gaze elsewhere. Sure, her and The Woman had fended off the horde, but at what cost? And what would the cost be this time?

"Bert," said a croaky voice, one of the traders. She looked like a mad old hag, sitting by a dusty window gazing out with a wrinkled face. "Ya got people comin' this way."

Bert tore her stare from the statue and bounded over to the window with the trader. "What kind of people, Maggie?"

"Too far t' tell, Bertie. They's kickin' up a dust storm an' a half, though. I reckons you got an engine incoming."

Sure enough, not too far down the Back Road to the south, a large, boxy silhouette was bouncing closer to Smack-dab. It was decked out with what looked like spikes and billowing flags, and it coughed noxious black fumes into the air. A dust cloud trailed behind it like a loyal hound.

Learn to adapt, The Woman's voice echoed, *and you'll be ready for anything.*

The fine-tuned cogs in Bert's brain grinded into overdrive. There wasn't any time left to doubt, to pussy out. Maybe this encounter would cost her, but at least then it would be over. Either way, there was no backing out. Now it was time for some cold, hard staunching.

She pulled back from the window, took two steps away and looked swiftly around the room.

"Listen up!" she shouted.

They listened in an upwards direction.

"Who here has guns?"

The traders all looked at each other for a moment, a murmur rippling through the crowd. There were maybe ten or so traders in Smack-dab today, and about half put their hands up.

Bert narrowed her eyes. "Who here has guns that actually work?"

A few put their hands down.

Alright, she thought to herself. There was no way in hell some big-thinking bandit lord was going to waltz into her place and demand so much as a place to piss without paying the proper dues. This was Bert's home, this was her love, her reason for existing: To run Smack-dab, keep the dream alive, and keep it out of filthy bandit hands. And all the bizarre gods in the Waste wouldn't be able to help this farming asshole if he so much as laid a finger on it. Or Meatsack. Or Phoenix, for that matter. Well, or Phoenix a second time.

"OK, here's what's going to happen," she stated, loud enough that everyone could hear whether they wanted to or not. Nobody was going to slack off defending the bar. If they wanted a drink, they'd bloody earn it.

"I need your help defending Smack-dab, and I'm willing to offer free grog, food and lodgings to anyone willing to pitch in."

This got an approving mutter from the crowd.

"Good. Alright. Everyone in this room is going to arm themselves and take up defensive positions in a ring around this door." She thumbed to the front door. "I want tables flipped up, and anyone who's got a gun in the front row. Phoenix."

The man stood up, wincing.

"I need you on your rifle behind the bar."

He grinned wide, clearly relieved the punishment and yelling was over. "Yes, boss." He limped off behind Bert to get his weapon set up.

One of the customers put up her hand nervously.

Bert took one glance and knew what the question would be. Traders were simple folk. "Yes, you can take your drinks with you while you work."

The customer cheered along with her peers and everyone in the room started moving. Just like the famous Waste battle of Da Big Fort, a whole load of nothing was being pushed, shoved and grunted at until it became a something. Hopefully a fortressy something. Tables became walls, traders became soldiers, and one old man, who had fallen asleep despite the excitement, became a tripping hazard. Soon, spiky things poked through gaps between tables, and anyone with a gun was checking it was actually clean enough to shoot like they'd promised.

Bert stood with her fists on her waist amidst the chaos, Meatsack hunched and trembling by her side. She gave the guy a wide smile and put a comforting hand on his small arm. "Meatsack," she said quietly, "I need you to go hide in your room again, OK? I can't risk you getting mad and upsetting our new guests. You can come out when the bad men are gone, and you might need your mop."

She paused and thought about this for a second. "...you'll probably need your mop."

The giant mutant nodded anxiously and then vanished into the bowels of the building.

And a wheezing, grunting engine could be heard coming closer outside.

"Nobody," Bert shouted, "and I mean *nobody*, fire a shot or so much as say a word until I order it, you hear?"

A loud silence yelled back.

"Alright. I'm going to try to solve this with words, like civilised folk ought to."

Bert flexed her robotic hand and rested the palm of her human one on her pistol grip, standing firmly in the middle of the room, right in front of the main entrance. She spread her legs a little ways apart, hip jutting to one side, face set hard in a glare. Sassy, but dangerous. Her sapphire eyes bore holes into the front door. Let them just try to take something from this bar.

Let them fucking try.

* * *

Inside the truck, a radio crackled.

First thinhssh first ya gotta put your gloves onhssshause this could get real messy.

Like this, Bobhsssh?

Yeah you got it. It's a bit of a hashhsle, but safety's imporhssshant.

The figure driving, a skinny bandit known as Ernest, peered out through the dusty windshield. He hunched forwards in his seat as the truck bounced and rocked on the cracked asphalt, eyes squinting as the wind sneezed dust across his field of vision. Something was smudging into view ahead.

Now what, Bob?

Hssshkay, grab the salad by the bottohssh, but keep your hand away from the stalks hssssssssh.

That's the deadly part.

Aye, Hilary, hssssshat's the deadly part.

Something was there, by the side of the road. And as dilapidated as it might look from the outside, it most assuredly wasn't another Old World ruin. This building had some love in it. Which, from what Ernest could determine, meant that it had more than three walls and at least the better part of a roof. It looked a little ... slanty, though. Like the building was drunk. Ernest glanced to his left to check if the man, no, the Being, in the passenger seat was awake.

It was, and its titanic head, crammed like the rest of its giant form inside the small cabin, was staring at the same structure Ernest was.

Now what hsshwe'll do is turn it upside down to point the stalks away, then with one swifhssh motion, cut it in half with our machete.

Right. I'm grabbing it hsssh the bottom.

Good, that's it.

I'm lifting it up, slowly.

Yes, hssheep going.

And - ARGH! Oh sweet hsshercy, it's all over me. hssssssh I'm burning! I'm fucking meltinhssh

hsssssssh

My arm, argh! My arm fell off. Somebody call the docthssh, the fucking doctor!

"Turn it off," the Being rumbled.

Ernest reached for the truck's centre panel and pressed a switch next to some pick 'n' mix dials. He didn't know what half of them did, but the mechanic had at least shown him which one was the radio. Pity there was only ever one broadcast at a time. And true to its Old World heritage, it was always talking or ad breaks.

He tightened his grip on the steering wrench as the truck tumbled through another particularly deep crack in the road. The building ahead was clearly visible, having coalesced from a vague brown lump into a less vague brown lump. It was a two-storey wooden structure, technically, with a statue out the front. There were big wooden letters on the roof, one of which looked to be peering over the edge and contemplating its existence.

The Being leaned forwards as best it physically could, and Ernest felt the weight of the truck tip forwards.

"This th' place?" it asked, vibrating the cabin.

Ernest nodded. "Um, yessir. Right where 'e told us."

"Good," it said, leaning back. With a hand the size of two hands mashed together, it plucked a small metal box from the cabin roof. A wire cord connected the box to the truck. The Being lifted it up to his gargantuan lips and pressed in a small button on the side.

By Duncan P. Pacey

"This is Brown," he spoke, slow and clear, his voice transmitting to an Old World shipping container hinged to the back of the truck. "Prepare to dismount. We're here."

* * *

Bert felt the ground thud with pondering, Waste Beast footsteps. Her body tensed, her fingers danced on her pistol. Outside, gravel crunched, rolled, and, at one point, swore. Then Smack-dab's wooden porch screeched under an immense weight.

The noises stopped outside the front door.

Bert prepared her glare.

Phoenix cocked his weapon and hunkered down behind it.

The traders whispered nervously to themselves.

And then Smack-dab's front opened inwards.

Gently.

However the man who followed looked anything but.

A thick, chunky hand was attached to the door handle, with a tree trunk arm jutting out of it and fitting somewhere into the torso of someone who presumably was always described by their size - never their profession or their personality, just a man with a size. He had to retract his head into his mountain range shoulders just to fit under the door, and each long step shook the floorboards with miniature earthquakes.

Without realising it, Bert took a nervous step backwards.

The troll finally got his skull under the doorframe and extended to his full height, buzz-cut hair practically scraping the roof. He'd probably knock the lighting fixtures around if he moved too much. More fool him, though, because the dust up there knocked back. His body looked as though some mad god had reduced three men to putty and haphazardly slapped them together again. Then the god, wild with a mad glee, coated the Being in heavily scarred metal armour and leather, a pair of knee-high rubber boots (with spikes), and a flowing blue cape. Oh, and to top it all off, the god handed him a colossal great bloody hammer made from an anvil and said, "Here you go. Now you have fun, dear. Don't forget your lunch," before fading into smoke, cackling.

Bert's feet debated the consequences of fleeing in terror, but she nailed them to the floor. She tightened her expression into something hopefully resembling contempt, but which might have looked constipated. So long as she didn't look afraid.

The man before her, if you could call him that, swung his heavy glare around the room. Bert gritted her teeth, feeling almost naked as this invader judged her life's work. I've shown you mine, she thought, now you show me yours.

And he did. A small swarm of bandits oozed in after him, each armed mostly with clubbing sticks and leg breakers - no guns, so far as she could tell. There were about six all totalled, forming an aggressive arc behind their leader. Most worryingly, though, was the Overlord standing behind and to the left of the titan in front. It wasn't growling or shaking weapons like its human companions. No, far more disconcertingly, it just sort of occupied the space. Like a placeholder for something far more horrifying, but which hadn't been designed yet.

Six bandits total wasn't bad, though. Bert had more manpower behind her, and more guns. But then, should it come to a fight, her folks would most likely surrender at the first sign of trouble. And then the Overlord would probably kill them anyway. At least she had Phoenix. He was the right mix of stupid and skilled to at least put up some resistance, though his performance recently left much to be desired.

The titan's gratuitous eyes landed on Bert. With a face chiselled (crudely) from granite, he stared at her, almost expressionless. His lips, suffering from a sizable underbite, twitched hungrily. And all Bert could think at the time was how pitiful her pistol seemed against a monster like this. Would he even feel a bullet? Or would the pain message take so long to travel that he'd have ripped her in half before knowing he was dead?

The monster opened his cavernous mouth. Presumably there were teeth inside it somewhere, but he seemed the kind of man to swallow things whole, and thus, not require them.

"So..." he spoke, dragging out the word. His voice was thicker than Smack-dab's pathway. "This be th' Back Road bar my man has been tellin' me 'bout, huh? Wouldn't have guess'd there be somethin' like this 'round these parts. Yer a bit out o' th' way."

The noise swept over Bert, blowing at her short, sweaty hair. She shot a few more nails into her feet, just to be sure they wouldn't try anything stupid. "We like it that way. Means bandits can't find us." Her fingers twitched.

The man's eyes narrowed. "Yer've done a grand job there, then, have-"

"You must be the new lord," she stated, interrupting him.

He frowned momentarily. Then his grotesque neck muscles squirmed up and down. It might have been a nod. "Aye, that be m'self. Brown, ya can call me. Farmer Brown."

"Well, *Brown*," she said, emphasising his name, "what's it going to take to make you go away? Your filthy bandit horde is tracking mud all into my place."

Farmer Brown again swept his gaze slowly around the room, the edge of his lips suffering slight continental drift. He was either smiling, or having a stroke. Bert hoped for the latter.

"Dun't look like we could make it much worse," he said. Lipland ground further up into Cheek.

Bert's brain was quickly becoming a dangerous chemical cocktail that lingered somewhere between blood boiling anger and pants-wetting fear. The pipes rattled, pressure gauges spinning wildly, and the little mechanics of common sense and rationalism ran around her mind with wrenches, banging things and generally not being helpful. She didn't know what to feel, and to Bert, that defaulted her state to Bertrage.

"How about we cut the bullshit and you tell me what you want?" she demanded, face filling with crimson. She realised that her hand had clamped around her pistol.

The continents on Brown's face drifted apart. A flash of anger trekked across the landmass of his skull, but it was gone as soon as it appeared. Did Bert just hit a nerve by refusing to play his game of banter, or did she see the true Farmer Brown, if only for a moment? No doubt a few more prods of this particular Waste Beast and she'd find out for herself. Front row seats, even.

"Alright," he said, the vocal equivalent of a deep growl from a dark cave, "business 'tis then. I bin hearin' stories, so I has." He started pacing, each step a threat to put a hole in the floor. "Stories o' a little piece o' shit bar in the middle o' nowhere darin' not jus' t' refuse the Tax they rightfully owe, but t' slaughter innocent collect'rs, too. Jus' folk out there tryin' t' make the Waste a better place, an' they had t' die f'r it."

Bert opened her mouth to retort, but one of his megahands shot up to stop her.

Phoenix hunched behind his rifle, staring through the scope, his finger already on the trigger and dreaming of squeezing. Through his scope reticule, he saw the close-up image of a red lightbulb.

The traders all around Smack-dab watched in fascinated horror as the scene unfolded. Most had forgotten they were supposed to be playing a role, and were just enjoying their drinks and a show.

Meatsack, pressed his ear against the door of his room, straining to hear at least a flutter of sound – something to tell him Berty Bert was OK, and the bad men were leaving. Don't get mad, he repeated to himself. Don't get mad.

And Farmer Brown continued to pace. "I'm a reas'nable man, *Bert*," he continued, flashing her another angry look. "Maybe ya didn't realise who me lads were. Maybe ya thought, these are some bandits pretendin' to be somethin' better, eh? An' out o' fear, ya shot 'em dead before they could take what yer reckon is yours."

He stopped suddenly and brought his heat-ray stare back to Bert. She stood with muscles as solid as The Woman outside, her teeth grinding together. If her mouth were any dryer, she'd be spitting fire. Bert kind of hoped that would happen – breathing fire and smoke would certainly emphasise her points. The pain was a future problem.

"Maybe ya got no friends, *Bert*, and ya shoot first to protect yerself. Tell me, d' ya have any friends? Allies? Anyone that gives a shit about ya, who'd actually wanna help?"

Bert's knuckles went white. She knew the answer, and she knew he knew. And she knew that he knew that she knew he knew, which made her knowing that he knew a whole lot more annoying. And she knew that, too.

If snakes were seven foot tall and cared to laugh, it would sound identical to what was slithering out of Brown's mouth at this point. "I didn't think so," he cackled. "So here's what's gonna happ'n. Despite ya killin' my folk, denyin' what ya owe, I'm gonna be good t' ya, Bert. We're here t' make the Waste a better place, after all. But yer in no position t' be bargainin', so ye can take yer hand away from that pistol, as much good as it would do ya. I'm here t' make ya an offer ya can't refuse."

* * *

"*That* disgusting old road?" said a harsh woman's voice. "Why would anyone want to go down there? You'd be killed for sure."

The voice belonged to an equally harsh woman. She was tall and elegant, with cheek bones so sharp you'd cut your finger on them, assuming she so much as let you near her face. She wore a long, shiny red robe beneath a heavy leather travelling coat, with jewellery of every shape and size adorning her ears, nose, fingers, neck, forehead, eyebrows and, if you believed the stories, a few more private places too.

"Nah, Lorry, ya got it all wrong!" replied Jeb, taking another swig from his pint of frothy grog.

They were seated in the Second Thought, a tavern at the heart of its eponymous trader's village that, quite to the original tavern owner's pleasure, seemed to have sprung up around it over the years. A thick crowd thronged outside the grubby tavern windows as locals and travellers alike wove their way through the myriad stalls and stores of Second Thought looking for a bargain (in order to fob the same product off at twice the price over in the next town).

Orsen smiled widely in a seat next to his travelling companion, his fingers wrapped around a pint glass of the same frothy liquid, but a steaming hot version. He didn't order it hot, but when the tavern owner poured his drink, it seemed to come out hot. Jeb had offered to swap for his cold one, but Orsen decided that a nice hot drink would be good on a chilly day like this, even if nobody knew quite why was hot in the first place.

"There aren't no bandits on the Back Road, Lorry," the boy smiled. "That's why we all use it. None of the tribes can be bothered trailing along it when there's better traffic along the Highway."

The gaunt woman seemed unconvinced. "So if there isn't enough traffic, where exactly do you expect me to be able to pass on the Great Word of Gachook, our Lord and Saviour?"

Jeb and Orsen exchanged a sly glance. The horrors of 80 Cu t were being drowned in the same mental catacombs as all the other horrors they had witnessed in life. Jeb winked knowingly at the woman. "Well ya see, ain't that just th' trick. We're headed t' a secret bar a ways down the Back Road. Smack-dab, it's called, an' ya won't find no bandits there. Bert hates the buggers."

Lorry's pale face frowned. She had what could only be described as piercing eyes. The kind of eyes that could bring back all sorts of awful childhood memories with just the slightest of rebuke. These eyes glanced around the Second Thought, making some of the other patrons duck out of the way in terror. Then the eyes fell back on Jeb, and his grinning, wrinkled face.

"A bar," she stated.

Jeb nodded. "Aye, best in the Waste if ya ask me."

"But we're already in a bar." She waved one of her elegant, bejewelled hands.

Orsen leaned forwards. "But it's a different bar!"

"Aye," said Jeb, "An' one ya ain't banned from preachin' in."

"So you wish me to pay you to take me to this ... secret bar, where you are confident there are individuals receptive to the Great Word of Gachook, our Lord and Saviour?" She drummed her long fingernails on the scrap-metal table.

"Err," said Jeb, briefly glancing at Orsen. The boy smiled back. "Aye," he continued. "They's plenty receptive. I've always thought, ain't that Bert receptive t' other people's ideas in her bar? Very welcomin' environment, if ya ask me."

Lorry stared at them both, showing clear disdain at the very notion of travelling together.

Jeb and Orsen grinned back innocently.

Her fingers drummed more on the table, then stopped.

"Fine, I shall take your word that this *Smack-dab* shall receive the Word of Gachook. Perhaps my Lord and Saviour is simply testing me."

"Excellent, excellent!" Jeb said gleefully, slopping his grog around with a wave of his arm. "Then all that we needs is for ya t' pay our advance fee for expenses an' that. We leave first thing tomorrow mornin'!"

* * *

"An offer I can't refuse?" Bert repeated, her brows knitting themselves together.

"Aye," Brown replied. He loomed above her, whatever constituted for a grin pricking at his whale mouth.

Bert narrowed her eyes. The little mechanics in her mind had given up now. They sat in a gloomy silence as steam poured around them. They wished that it was dry enough to eat a sandwich, but the steam was only getting worse. And it was turning black.

Phoenix smiled to himself. This was it, he thought. The crosshairs in his scope centred on that stupid red lightbulb head.

The traders sweated at various levels of profusity.

Meatsack trembled nervously, thinking about whether or not he should grab his favourite club and go help. But Berty told him not to. Don't get mad.

Brown's bandit horde readied their weapons and tried to look menacing. Some of them were even successful.

H2-149 didn't move.

"Why can't I refuse it?" Bert asked angrily.

Brown's head tilted to one side. "Because it can't be refused."

Now her upper lip twitched. Everything was twitching without her consent. She'd make a terrible poker player. "So what if I do refuse?"

"Well, ya can't." His voice was deepening, all niceties gently throwing themselves off the balcony.

"You said that, but what will you do if I do?"

"I don't think that'll happ'n."

"I'll refuse on principle alone if you tell me I can't," she said.

If rationalism, common sense and calming down could scream, they'd be red in the face by now. They'd go home to their wives, husbands or communal families later and complain about their short-tempered boss, and how she never listened to their good ideas. Their partners would say something comforting, and quietly suggest they look for new jobs. But they'd keep going back to the same job, scream at their boss, and probably be ignored. Because though Bert was certainly intelligent, the moment somebody threatened her bar or her folks, something burst. Maybe she wouldn't win the poker game of life, but with enough force of Bertrage, she'd make damn sure her opponents didn't win, either.

And this made something new flash across Brown's face. A momentary look of concern nearly made it to the stage, but a bouncer must have caught it first. The mass of his face went serious.

"Ernest!" he bellowed. And it truly was a bellow.

The bandit crowd parted to reveal a skinny, timid-looking man clutching a clipboard in his hands. Bert assumed this to be Ernest, the figure that Phoenix encountered along the Back Road. He didn't look so tough in real life. He didn't even have fangs, or claws, or muscles the size of your skull - which Phoenix had described him with. But what did this less-than threatening person have to do with the situation?

Ernest skidded to a halt by his lord's side.

"Ernest," Brown said. "What d' these people owe?"

The man raised his eyebrows and scratched at his chin. "Owe? Well, where t' start, sir?" He looked down at his clipboard with a frown, then at the ceiling, as though answers might rain down upon him from the gods of maths (who, in certain Waste circles, were known to be some of the most unforgiving and ruthlessly boring of masters). He licked the tip of his pencil and started scribbling. "First ya gots the gen'ral Income Tax, I reckons. Aye, aye thass a big one -scribble scribble- Then there's the new Road Levy so's we can repair the road out here and up t' Second Thought -scribble scribble- There's the gen'ral Protection Fee -scribble- which ya gotta have, ain't nobody who'd not want that -scribble scribble- An' I s'pose we should charge int'rest f'r havin' t' come all this way t' be threatenin' an' that -scribble scribble- We'll call that one 'Consultation' -scribble scribble- Then finally there be a Fine f'r the deaths o' our lads -scribble- either that o' someone goes t' jail -scribble scribble- Or I guess we throw 'em in the river -scribble- Cheaper than th' gallows, anyway."

Farmer Brown's throat rumbled. Or perhaps there was a thunderstorm brewing somewhere. One of those two things happened, anyway.

Bert stood listening to the man's ramblings. She didn't know what a Levy was, but it sounded like this lot weren't just here for a keg or two of grog. She angrily hoped that they would accept bullets as payment - and Bert knew a convenient way to deliver them. Why, she had a tool just for it.

"All in all..." Ernest continued, underlining something on his clipboard, "we're lookin' at about sixty-five per cents o' everythin' this bar made f'r the last fish-call year."

Bert, Phoenix and anyone else in the bar who understood that a percentage wasn't food gasped in horror - the type of horror that only Tax statements can bring.

"Sixty-five!" she roared, stepping forwards. "That's daylight robbery, that is."

Farmer Brown's evil grin stretched onto his face once again. "We're bandits, woman. Best ya not f'rget that."

They locked stares, causing a small high pressure system to fizzle between them. A trader once told Bert that it was probably two gods glaring at each other that caused the start of the universe so many millennia ago. They were probably married, too. You had to be married to have a proper glare off. That way you knew enough dark little secrets that you could cripple your opponen- err, your partner in an argument. But you also knew that they knew all of yours, so you kept your mouth shut and let the incredibly hot cold war continue. And then, at some point, planets happened. It wasn't a very good story.

Bert tried to formulate a response that wasn't just pulling a gun and emptying it into Brown's big ol' face as the bandit lord's smile condensed into a snarl.

"Now," he said, slowly, carefully, "send one o' yer lads out back t' fetch yer sixty-five fish-calls, woman, 'cause I'm not havin' some bar in the middle o' nowhere ruin me plans t' make this bit o' Waste something worth a damn." His body hunched over, lowering his head closer to Bert's height. His voice dropped in volume, from a bellowing comic-book villain to parents who are disappointed (not angry).

"Yer gonna cough up what ya owe, and yer gonna smile an' be nice about it, 'cause if ya don't, I'm gonna tear this place apart and use th' planks to' make me own bar next door." He paused, leaning closer. "An' I c'n use yer ground-up bones f'r the cement. So pay up or dare t' refuse me offer, woman. Either way I win."

As if on cue, Brown's retinue waved their various implements of killiness and growled like wild animals. Bert's robotic fingers couldn't physically tighten any further, and her pistol grip was squeezed so hard in her human palm, it would probably be bruised by tomorrow.

Phoenix, behind, took the cue to apply a feathery pressure to his rifle's trigger. In his head, he begged for the shooting to start. Pop, pop, pop, no more robot. The world would be a better place. Phoenix the hero, they'd say.

Maggie and the other traders were glued to the scene, unable to take their eyes away from it. This was better than one of Lord Ash's old radio plays, and felt a lot more realistic. And if the shooting started, they'd feel just how realistic it was.

H2-149 didn't move.

* * *

While all of this tomfoolery was going on in Smack-dab, further south along the Back Road, the corpse of a rabbit-like creature lay pancaked on the ruined asphalt. A team of small ants had gathered on the dirt-stained meat - local miners from the nearby colony. They'd been hired by Corpse Co. to pick at this corpse with their miniature axes for the next three days, leaving no scrap behind. It was good work for an ant, if you could get it.

But something approached.

It was a smaller rabbit-like creature. Or at least, it *was* a smaller rabbit-like creature, but now was technically bigger considering the rather horizontal nature of its one-time nemesis. The smaller-but-now-larger rabbit-like creature, which was known as Randolf the Conqueror, Ruiner of Worlds and Bringer of Shadows, eyed up the situation with deep suspicion. Was this a trick? Some devious ploy by Randolf the Conqueror,

Ruiner of Worlds and Bringer of Shadows's arch nemesis to get him to lower his guard?

But when he saw a squished little hat jammed between two chunks of road, he knew that this was not so. The Great Behatted Enemy, Lord of Rabbit-Like Kind, had been defeated.

Randolf the Conqueror, Ruiner of Worlds and Bringer of Shadows slowly picked up the flattened hat in his paws and stared at it.

With some careful unfolding, he gave it shape again.

And put it on.

Now he was Randolf the Conqueror, Ruiner of Worlds, Bringer of Shadows, and Lord of Rabbit-Like Kind. He towered over the corpse of his fallen foe, and the future stretched out before him. There would be change to come, and great battles to be fought. But first, he needed to snack.

He looked down at the ants.

* * *

Bert's blue eyes were sparkling supernovas of anger, her face radiating their heat. Any last vestige of fear was washing away under the red floods of sheer, unadulterated Bertrage. Out in the Waste, she didn't care who did what. New bandit leader? So be it. Someone trying to play god? Fine with her, so long as it stayed out there. Because inside Smack-dab, there was only one god. And she sure as hell wasn't merciful. Not when you refused to pay for your grog, and especially not if you made threats.

"I hear your irrefusable offer, you bandit piece of shit," she stated, standing tall to meet his eye level, "and I refuse it."

Silence fizzled between their eyes.

Then noises happened. Noises and expressions. Particularly expressions.

Farmer Brown looked taken aback, as though nobody had ever defied him before. Which, considering his immense size, was quite likely true. But then his throat vibrated with a deep, ominous hum. It seeped out through the cracks in his lips as he stood back to full height, a sound that rattled out slowly but somehow still felt like it was booming. His ears started to glow like Old World lava lamps, his weight shifting onto his front foot - ready to pounce.

Bert and Brown were now in the most volatile phase of a Waste negotiation. Anger was long past safe human levels, and anybody present with any semblance of self-preservation would be finding an excuse to leave quietly. This was generally the moment where terms were sorted out the quickest, either because one person would cave or, more often than not, one person would cave ... the other person's skull in.

Seeing Brown's posture shifting to an aggressive stance, Bert finally drew her weapon. Brown's bandit entourage flinched and scowled in response, with the obvious exception of H2-149.

Phoenix sucked in a breath.

Meatsack trembled.

The traders leaned forwards.

...H2-149 did nothing.

Baring teeth the size of fingernails, Brown reached back with a meaty hand, going for his anvilhammer. But Bert straightened her arm, pistol highlighting the lord's skull.

"If you so much as fondle that hammer of yours, I'll give the word and everyone in this building will open fire. Play it smart, big boy, or I'll shoot you dead." She smiled grimly, finger on the trigger. "Either way, I win."

Brown glared at her, the rumbling of his throat silencing. "Ya wanna start a fight, woman?" he growled. "I think ya need t' look in a mirror, 'cause ya ain't half as tough as ya thinks ye are."

Bert snorted back. "Maybe I ain't so tough-looking, but I'm the one with the guns. Take a step, asshole, and see if you're faster than a wall of bullets. There are more than a few folk here who I reckon'd love to show you what happens when you steal from the good folk of the Waste."

Brown did nothing but glare, nostrils flaring. Then his hand slowly moved away from his hammer. The beast didn't step forwards.

Good, Bert thought to herself triumphantly. At least she was getting somewhere a little safer. "Here's my counter-offer, and do you know what? I think you'd be smart not to refuse it."

His eyes narrowed.

By Duncan P. Pacey

"How about you take your half-wit, dungarees-wearing bandit scum back to the truck you parked on my lawn and you *fuck off* back to where you came from. Or buy a drink, then fuck off."

The wind howled outside Smack-dab, rattling windows and whistling through cracks in the weatherboards as though it were quivering with fear. Bert couldn't hear it, anyway, with the blood rushing so loudly past her ear drums. All she could see was the hulking great bastard in front of her, and all she could feel was the pistol in her hands, aiming straight at his head.

Farmer Brown, seven feet tall, built like a Waste Beast, the bandit whose army just massacred the fort, lifted one of his Yeti feet to step forwards, but hesitated. His eyes were locked on the small-statured, robo-fisted bar owner before him - who is, supposedly, a pacifist, let's not forget - who clenched her bone-handled pistol like her life depended on it (and, to be fair, it did). The room around the duo was muggy with anticipation. Would a volcano explode in Brown's head and set him off on a smashy-smashy hammer spree, or would everyone get to wake up the next morning? The nervousness was so thick you could have stitched it together and worn it as armour. Bert's pistol could have balanced a feather.

A miniature cyclone swirled in and out of existence in front of Farmer Brown as he let out a long, slow breath. His stance relaxed, if only slightly, and he lowered his boot to the floor. "Alright," he said slowly. His eyes never left Bert's. "We c'n play it yer way, so we c'n."

Bert glared at him in silence.

"Keep yer fish-calls t'day, woman, but know this: I got an entire army all around ya, an' it'll only take a week t' bring 'em together. An' what will ya do then, eh? When *all* me boys come down on ya. Ya got no friends, woman, but I got plenty. An' we won't just be comin' f'r no measly sixty-five next time. It'll be yer pretty lil' head, then."

He paused for a moment, as if about to explode and say something else, but then a growl bubbled up from the pits of his gullet and he snarled, waving at the front door. His retinue began to file out, stomping on the floor in a final show of toughness. The lord himself paused as he ducked under the doorway, dust rolling past his feet. He turned and looked over his shoulder to stare down Bert one last time.

"Yer've made a powerful enemy today, woman," he said.

Bert sneered back. "It wouldn't be the first time, but here I stand."

Farmer Brown snorted and pushed through the entranceway, marching down the gravel path after his followers. Bert watched as, halfway down the garden, Brown stopped, looked back up at her, and then booted The Woman's statue with his thick, rubber sole. The statue toppled out of site, a grim, serious look on Brown's planetoid head.

Then the truck outside coughed to life, Brown squeezed into the cabin, and, with quite incredible disagreement, the machine rolled away.

Silence resumed inside Smack-dab.

Nobody moved.

The front door swung loosely open and shut in the wind.

Bert, finally, breathed out.

"Shit."

Her pistol began to tremble.

By Duncan P. Pacey

Part Four

The Acquiring of the Three

Maggie, a well-respected trader in nick-nacks and small souvenirs, watched the truck as it trundled out of sight. Around her, the bar was silent. Bertie was still standing in front of the door holding her weapon, and none of the other traders had the balls to do or say anything. Well, Maggie reckoned she had balls enough for the lot of them. She had four pairs at least tucked in her backpack. Old boyfriends, you know how it is. Keepsakes and that.

A wide grin spread over her leathery face, her quite unfathomably unclean breath staining the window brown. Hee hee, she thought, a dry cackle escaping her throat. We showed them, didn't we? A bunch of traders and wanderers up against the big bad Farmer Brown and his silly little bandits.

She looked back at the fortress, at the upturned tables and ramshackle soldiers. Just like Da Big Fort, she thought, only more interesting. And the good guys actually won.

She smacked her dry, chapped lips together. Yep, sure tasted like victory.

She threw her arms in the air.

And cheered.

* * *

Bert flinched as a sudden roar of applause gobbled up the silence she was busy wallowing in. Her customers were cheering, slapping each other on the backs and swapping over-exaggerated stories about who did and did not piss themselves. By the sounds of things it was about fifty-fifty. But Bert hadn't moved since Farmer Brown left. Her robotic hand was still balled into a fist, her pistol hanging tightly in her human hand by her side. The Bertrage was subsiding fast, and like most people after they'd been on a major high, she was realising that the things she had just said and done in the past ten minutes were, perhaps, if you really thought hard about it, not quite as good an idea as they were at the time.

Farmer Brown's final utterings lingered in her brain like a mental bad smell. Powerful enemies were the worst kind of enemies - they were the ones who followed through on their threats. They had that perfect blend of pride, reputation and raw firepower.

"WOOO!" cried Phoenix's voice from behind.

The adventurer appeared in Bert's peripheral to the left. He was dancing forwards towards the front door, gesturing wildly at where Farmer Brown would never see him gesture wildly. His face was ecstatic.

"Let that be a lesson to ya, you overgrown bastard!"

Meatsack appeared next, shuffling quietly out of his room and into the bar, smiling widely at Phoenix's antics. He laughed nervously, clapping his hands awkwardly together and dancing on the spot.

Bert seemed to be the only one who didn't feel the buzz of the room. But that was to be expected. They weren't the ones who just threatened a terrifying monster with a tiny little pistol. She had gotten herself out of the frying pan, oh yeah, there was no mistaking that. It was a frying-pan-free zone up in here. But when she hopped out the frying pan, where did that leave her? On the rest of the stove, that's where. Where all sorts of other pots and pans awaited you. Like griddles. She didn't want to be on a griddle.

Phoenix was now running around high-fiving some of the traders, hugging those that shared his excitement and picking up anybody smaller than him. Meatsack followed closely behind, but the lumbering giant managed only to knock people to the floor rather than hug them. He hadn't quite figured out the depth perception required for glomping.

"Phoenix," Bert stated. Her words, quiet, scythed through the mood.

Phoenix froze, a particularly tiny trader dangling from his arms.

"Take Meatsack and go pick up The Woman's statue outside." Her face was serious.

Her chef glanced quickly between Bert, the other traders and Meatsack. Nobody was moving.

"Now."

The tiny trader hit the floor.

Bert now surveyed the rest of the room with a distant gaze. She could see it as it was, long ago, *a gout of flame enshrouding the front door, bullets pouring through the woodwork, bandits streaming through any entrance they could find. Bert and The Woman were pulling back from their fortress setup not dissimilar to the one in the present. Bullets zipped past their heads like little hyperactive bees, a grenade having just torn through the main entrance. They started running, Bert in front, The Woman screaming at her to get up the stairs, quick. Bert turned to look back, saw The Woman's determined face, and felt like she actually might survive. How could she not with such a powerful human behind her? One nameless woman who had done and would do anything to keep Bert safe, to make her happy. Then she watched in shock as The Woman convulsed suddenly and a splash of red hit Bert in the eyes.*

"Bert...?"

She scowled quickly and shook her head, snapping back to reality. The tiny trader from before had picked himself up, brushed himself off and presented himself in front of Bert, gazing up at her nervously, hat in hands. Bert hadn't noticed the room was deathly silent, all eyes upon her.

She quickly wiped her eyes. "Manfred, hello, sorry. What can I do for you?"

"Um, well," the small man replied, fingering his hat slowly as he spoke. "We was just wonderin' what to do next, is all."

Bert nodded and forced a smile on her face, if only a small one. He was asking one question, but she knew he had meant another one. There was promise of free grog, after all. No trader would forget that in a hurry.

"Well," Bert began, "first things first we need to get these tables righted, don't you think?"

The man looked crestfallen, a disappointed murmur dribbling out of his mouth.

Bert smiled again, a little more genuinely this time. "Then I think everyone deserves a drink, don't you?"

His little face lit up. "Aye, that sounds like a fine plan!"

The crowd nodded with approval and started moving about. Around Bert, her Big Fort was picked up, dragged and shoved back into it's good ol' Smack-dabby self. Tables were stood up, chairs placed neatly under them, and one old man was poked rudely to the tune of "Oi, you dead, mistah?" until he awoke.

Bert finally released the tension in her robotic fist, holstering her pistol at the same time. She was going to lose her bar and die horribly, but you know, it could have been worse.

She could lose her bar and live to see it.

* * *

Outside in the cold and the wind and the dust, Phoenix groaned loudly, struggling to lift The Woman. With bent knees and cheeks puffing out, he gripped the statue's skull and pulled as hard as he could. Being a man of unparalleled strength and ability, he successfully managed to lift the heavy stone maybe a half-foot into the air before the weight of it threatened to pull his shoulders out of their sockets. In but a few seconds it was flumping into the dust again, this time accompanied by an impressive lexicon of swears dedicated to pain in one's arms, back and knees.

Meatsack lingered awkwardly behind the fiasco, switching weight from his left to right foot and back again, one of his eyes fixed on Phoenix. The adventurer stood up to an orchestra of joints popping, one hand clutching his spine to check it was still intact. He shot the giant an angry look.

"Well you gonna help or what?" he said, grumpily.

Meatsack reeled back a step, then nodded anxiously and pattered forwards. He shuffled quickly past Phoenix and leaned down towards The Woman's statue, finding her head with his chunky fingers. He delicately changed grip more than a few times, treating the statue as though it were some highly sacred religious icon, and that merely touching it the wrong way would be an immediate death sentence and the rest of eternity in Freckle (the particularly nasty underworld where Gachook sends you).

"Honestly," grumbled Phoenix, shaking his hands out, "I don't know why she bothered sending you out here, too. It's not like I need you to help lift this statue. Could easily do it on my own. Just gotta stretch first. There you go, there's a free piece of advice, ya big dumb lug. Always stretch before you do any heavy lifting."

Meatsack glanced nervously between the statue and Phoenix (and was able to do so at the same time), then smiled innocently and tensed his arm. The statue raised out of the ground easily, Meatsack seemingly having no trouble propping up its immense weight. Phoenix watched with his jaw hanging open in disgust as The Woman rose like a feather from her dirty grave and regained her footing in the dust. Myriad little streamlets of dirt escaped out through the delicately carved folds in her frozen clothing, and though she wobbled for a moment, she soon stood as inspiring as ever.

Meatsack smiled widely, proud of what he'd done. He looked back at Phoenix for acknowledgement, positively beaming.

But Phoenix was scowling.

"How come you're so strong, anyhow?" Phoenix probed. "I never see you eat anything nutritious."

Meatsack cocked his misshapen head to one side, his smile faltering.

"Ah fugeddaboudit," Phoenix sighed, waving his hand at the creature. He wasn't sure why Bert treated Meatsack like some weird surrogate child, but at least he knew how to mop a floor. Maybe that's what he was for? It certainly wasn't for his conversational skills, or his attractive good looks.

Not like Phoenix.

Then he heard the big lug whimper.

"Wassat? What've you done now?"

Meatsack was staring at the ground again, his tiny, skinny arm over his mouth. Phoenix followed the gaze to see a stony object still lying in the dirt, a wee ways from The Woman's feet. It was an arm, clutching at a bone-handled pistol, hammered back and ready to shoot at whatever dangers may threaten Bert and her beloved bar. It also seemed rather ... amputated.

"Ah."

Phoenix and Meatsack met each other's eyes for a long, tense moment. Even the wind seemed to die down. The last person who vandalised The Woman's statue found out quite exceptionally quickly that Bert wasn't making empty threats on the plaque at the statue's feet. And you know, in Phoenix's heart of hearts, where all the warmth and fuzzies lay, he felt it would be unjust - cruel, even - to stress Bert out any more than she was right at that moment.

And, in his heart of his heart of hearts, he really didn't want to see what she'd do to Brown if she found out he'd broken The Woman. Even after a life of adventuring, there was some things a man - especially a man - just couldn't stomach.

"Well," he finally said, coming to a decision, "I didn't see that if you didn't."

* * *

Bert was halfway through a strong one when Phoenix flopped down in a chair opposite her at the table. Around them, Smack-dab's moderate group of customers had gotten back to their business, either departing Smack-dab to escape impending doom, or enjoying free booze and food before departing Smack-dab to escape impending doom. Now all that was left were a couple stragglers with big stomachs and, with a distant expression on her face, Bert.

"We've got one hell of a problem," she stated.

Phoenix started, jumping a little too quickly into a nervous grin and awkward laugh. "Problem, ha ha ha, what problem?" A bead of sweat abseiled down his forehead.

Bert looked up from her drink, eyebrow raised. "The fact that I just threatened the lord of Can't Be Buried, or can you think of something else I should be worried about?"

"Oh!" Phoenix replied, awash with relief. "Ha ha, yes yes, what a conundrum. Mmm, indeed. Tricky little number, that."

Bert eyed him up for a moment longer, uncertain what stupidity was on her chef's mind this time. But, she decided it couldn't nearly be half as bad as what just happened.

She took a deep breath. "I think I might have just said some things I shouldn't have, Phoenix."

The adventurer visibly relaxed, leaning forwards in his chair. His face, for once, looked like it might actually understand the gravity of the situation it was in. Now if only it could do that all the time, hell, maybe Smack-dab wouldn't have been in this mess.

"Look, if we could go back in time, maybe there were a couple of lines that we could take out," Phoenix replied. "But that was insane! Standing up to him, I mean. He was what, like, three times your size? Four?"

Bert felt a smirk prick the edge of her lips, the burning liquid pouring through her veins sufficient to start making the bad ideas good again. "I could have taken him. It was you and the others I had to worry about."

Phoenix smiled back. "It's nice to know you care enough to worry about me."

"Well, who's gonna do the cooking if you're gone, right? And you won't catch me out there hunting."

He laughed softly, and even though that laugh usually meant something stupid was about to happen, it at least made her start to feel better. A little better, anyway. Like, a fraction. A small fraction, anyway. Still, however minute the betterness, it was most assuredly more than zero betters. And in the Waste, folks got to cling to what they can.

Silence resumed between the pair, each staring into the other's eyes. Bert contemplated what to say next as she swirled the contents of her glass tumbler in her fingers - contemplating what to *do* next was still miles away, and quite a few more drinks. And then Phoenix started leaning in, his eyes slowly closing over. She felt his hot man breath wash over her face and suddenly, quite suddenly, she realised what the hell was about to happen.

Bert rocked back in her chair, slapping Phoenix across the face with her metal hand. It clanged loudly against his cheek, and he spun out of his chair in shock, clattering to the floorboards as Bert took to her feet. Her face flushed red, eyebrows closing in tight on each other.

"What in the fucking hell, Phoenix?" she growled, but more shocked than angry.

Phoenix scrabbled on the floor, clutching at his face and looking up pitifully at his boss. Tears welled in the eye above what was now becoming quite the red splodge on his face. It made a nice contrast to the black and blue from his earlier encounter. "I thought we were having a moment!"

"We *were* having a moment!"

"Nooo, I thought we were having a *moment* moment!"

"A *moment* moment?"

"A *moment* moment! You know." he mewed.

"Oh come on, Phoenix!" she said. "Why do you always have to be such a man?"

"I am a man..."

"Not every moment is a *moment* moment."

"But some moments become *moment* moments when you're not expecting *moment* moments," he cried.

"That moment was just a moment, not a *moment* moment. It was just a regular moment."

"It felt really *moment* moment to me, Bert. We were staring into each other's eyes and everything!"

"It was just a normal moment, Phoenix, of two friends. One of whom works for the other. That's it."

"Are we just plain old friends?"

"We're good friends, Phoenix. But don't get all *momenty* on me for saying it. I won't admit it again if you do."

He paused.

"I feel weird saying the word moment, now. I've said it too many times in a row."

"Oh for the love of-" Bert sighed, finally relaxing and stepping back towards her prone chef. "Get off the ground, you ass."

"Moment," Phoenix repeated, shakily finding the floorboards beneath his feet. "Mooooment."

Bert reached down with her human hand and yanked him ungracefully up, resetting his fallen chair so that he could sit down and be stable for a while.

Phoenix rubbed his face softly, wincing at the pressure. "Did you have to hit me with your metal hand?"

Bert smiled, a snort of a laugh coming out of nowhere up her throat. "I'm sorry, Phoenix. You really took me by surprise."

He mocked a frown. "Are you laughing at me, now?"

"Hey," Bert said, the snort rolling into a giggle. "It's pretty funny. I mean, I just hit you. Right in the face."

"It really hurts."

She started laughing fully now, all the shock and anger and fear of the day finally coming uncorked and spraying like an out of control fizzy grog. Phoenix started smiling too, then he too couldn't contain it any longer. He burst out laughing as well, systematically bellowing, then wincing, then laughing at the pain, then wincing again. Bert's cheeks were starting to hurt from the smiling, but presumably not as much as Phoenix's were gonna hurt tomorrow.

Meatsack, obviously hearing people laughing, came running over to join in, sitting down in a chair at the table and chuckling happily despite having no idea why anyone was doing it, or what was funny in the first place. He just liked it when people laughed, and he liked being a part of it.

The three of them laughed like the world was actually happy and they weren't all going to die horribly, even as the last of Smack-dab's customers found their way to the front door and out into the Waste. Soon, though, as was inevitable, the laughter ebbed and eventually died, leaving only an empty, quiet Smack-dab and the chittering wind that shook it.

Bert and Phoenix held each other's eyes again in neither a moment nor a *moment* moment. This was a moment of knowing, and understanding, but of wordlessness. What could they say to each other, when they were both haunted by the image of a towering great bloody bandit and his stupid, shiny lightbulb-faced companion? Meatsack was present, of course, but he wasn't a part of the moment. He was just happy to be there.

Bert finally did something to break the static. She placed her glass down, her elbows onto the table and her head into her hands, sighing deeply into them. The laughter had truly faded now, leaving only a dark hole behind. "What the hell now, Phoenix?" she said.

Phoenix and Meatsack looked on, worry moving across both their faces. Though Meatsack mostly without knowing what to worry about.

Bert kept her head down, speaking through her hands. "If we're here in a week, there's no way we can fight off Brown's army. We'll lose everything."

"And be ground into concrete," added Phoenix, if a little unhelpfully.

Bert looked briefly up at him with an angry glare. "Yeah, thanks. And ground into concrete." She pressed her face back into the relative safety of her hands.

Phoenix stared at her.

Meatsack stared at both her and Phoenix.

The wind wailed.

"Let's run away," Phoenix finally said, shuffling forwards towards her.

Bert looked up, confused. "Run away? What about Smack-dab?"

"Err," Phoenix replied, "we leave it behind. You need to let it go, Bert. Let all of this pain go. We'll run south to Second Edin or Crumble or something. Somewhere where there's no Farmer Brown. I'll grow a moustache so the Overlords don't recognis-."

Bert brought her hands down on the table hard, giving Meatsack a fright. "Absolutely not! -sorryMeatsack- We're not leaving Smack-dab alone to be torn apart by the likes of Farmer fucking Brown."

"What's the use in fighting? He has an army! You only have me, and this thing." He thumbed at Meatsack, who was trying to correct the balance of his chair after nearly toppling over at the fright. "Now, I could take down a fair chunk of his army by myself, but it's still too much even for me to handle."

Bert scowled, but it wasn't a scowl of her usual Bertrage. It was a scowl carefully painted over despair, over desperation. "We can't just leave Smack-dab, Phoenix. This bar is my life's work! If we let some arrogant bandit lord lay his filthy fingers all over it, what was the whole point in being alive? The Woman will have died for nothing - for a dream that we'd be shitting all over. This is our home! You can't just let anyone walk in and take your home. Or else, what do you have in life?"

"Well what are you going to do, Bert?" Phoenix was starting to lean over the table, ass above the chair rather than on it. "Who's pissed off enough at Farmer Brown to help you fight him, huh?"

"I don't know, Phoenix. The Second Thought militia, maybe? Highway bandit tribes?"

Phoenix shook his head, still leaning on the table. "First off, the Second Thought militia consists of about six retired sheriffs who just sit around and smoke all day. Yeah, great army. And bandit tribes, Bert? Really? You hate bandits!"

Bert shot to her feet, her chair flying out from underneath her, startling Phoenix and Meatsack once again. "You're right, Phoenix - sorryMeatsack- I hate bandits. Yeah, I want to find every one of the bastards and do to them so much worse than they've ever done to me. I want to cut bits off their bodies they've never even heard of. But you know what? You said it yourself, what choice do I have? Do *we* have? If we could convince them to help us, maybe we've got half a chance of putting a dent in Brown's numbers - making him think twice about messing with Smack-dab."

"A couple of bandit tribes won't be enough to beat Brown, Bert..."

"Well I don't know. We'll make another alliance at the same time. You can go up to the Starry Place and offer free grog in return for soldiers. The Woman did that sometimes back in the day and it occasionally even worked."

"Bert..."

But Bert was already moving away from the table, storming behind the bar reaching for a thick coat and a grubby pint glass full of bullets. "We're doing this, Phoenix. Pick up your rifle and get some food for the road."

"Bert," he repeated, softly this time. Phoenix stepped away from the table, around Meatsack, towards the bar where Bert now stood, threading her small arms into the sleeves of a long trench coat. It was clearly too big for her, but it had been tucked at the hem and tightened around the waist to fit more snugly to her slight figure. The coat, most noticeably, had a patchwork front, new scraps of random material sewn over bullet holes from a time long-passed. A time where a different woman wore this coat.

"Bert," Phoenix said again, close to her now. "Think about what you're doing. It's just a bar."

She froze while clasping up the coat. Something burned behind her eyes, and her human hand visibly trembled. She brought her gaze slowly up to meet Phoenix's, the whites of her eyes sparkling with a film of water. "It's not just a bar, Phoenix," she said, forcing her volume to remain level. "You know this is more than a bar. This is home. This is life! Smack-dab keeps us safe from the Waste, and now we have to keep her safe in return."

Phoenix said nothing back. Even he had to admit when he was defeated. Arguing with Bert was like bashing his skull against an old brick wall. Except if he bashed his head against an old brick wall, he might actually break it down one day. So, really, arguing with Bert was worse than bashing his head against an old brick wall.

Bert started moving again, finishing the clasps on her coat and filling pouches on her belt with fresh bullets. Or at least bullets as fresh as can be in the Waste. They weren't exactly common, and most folk had forgotten how to make them. "You're going up the mountain, I'm going to the Highway. And Meatsack?"

The mutant stood up quickly and saluted, a clumsy gesture with a hand practically too wretched to even reach his forehead.

"Meatsack, you're locking up behind us and watching the bar, OK? Don't let anybody in while Berty and Phoenix are out."

He nodded quickly and smiled.

Phoenix was still on the same spot, staring at his boss with his bearded jaw hanging slack. Finally he shook his head. "You're nuts."

"We're all nuts," Bert snapped back. "This is the Waste."

And with that, it was time to go recruit a little firepower.

* * *

A seven-hour walk, plus a fair old chilly night later...

The fresh, crisp dawn hit Bert like a hammer. Then it hit her again out of malice, and kicked her in the lungs with its boots. Bert was waking up, groggily to say the least, inside a decrepit Old World structure along the Back Road, having slept there overnight. She was hiding in a cupboard, where the Things couldn't find her - but nobody would ever need to know that. If they asked, she had chased the Things off singlehandedly with her pistol, guffawed at their cowardice, then slept out in the open in a mark of defiance. Of course, the reality was in fact that she had been ambushed quite suddenly by Things just down the road, punched one in the face, fled for her life, then hid in the aforementioned cupboard for what semblance of safety it could offer.

Now, the morning's dismal little rays leaked through deep gouges and bullet holes in the cupboard's aged, rotten door, splashing a murky, chickenpox light on Bert's grumpy face. She pushed gently at the door handle, but found that it wouldn't budge. The door then bowed almost soggily outwards upon a firm second test with her shoulder, but seemed intent in remaining fixed rudely shut. Bert scowled for a moment, then drew back her robotic fist.

A blanket of dull, shadowless light enveloped Bert like a hug from a Thing as a cascade of door splinters scattered about the dusty, pockmarked floorboards. Next came a stinging slap in the nostrils from a dead Thing nearby, the sheer sticky sweetness of the awful smell threatening to reach inside her stomach and yank out the breakfast she hadn't even eaten yet.

Bert covered her mouth with the large collar of her trench coat, hoping the musty old fabric would help keep out any airborne nasties that might threaten to turn her into one of those ... those Things. Nobody was quite sure whether Thing disease spread via blood or air, but it never hurt to be careful. Especially because it would hurt a whole lot more to not be careful, particularly when the disease made your bones start growing into claws right where they had no business growing, let alone into claws. So, rather than brave stepping around the lifeless, twisted corpse that had the gall to die at the front door and bleed its filthy green ichor all over the entranceway, Bert took up the mantel of adulterous lovers the world over, and climbed out the window.

It looked like it was going to be a beautiful day, which is to say that the noxious sky wasn't as greasy as it was yesterday or the day before, suggesting the worst of the acid had moved on to ruin someone else's property. A moderate wind gusted past in thick, quick blasts, carrying dust from one location to another for its own nefarious purposes. Bert pulled her coat tighter around her waist and allowed her head to sink into it, stuffing her hands into deep pockets.

As her boots crunched quietly on the gravel driveway, heading down back to the Back Road, a gentle chorus of birds twittered around her, except they didn't because this is the Waste and they were all dead. But the few survivors let out a squawk every now and then to remind the world that they were still here, and occasionally a gullpidgeon would fly past twittering opera.

Bert was at a junction in her life, both metaphorically and quite literally. A few feet from her lay the end of the Back Road, where it finally intersected with the Highway. An ancient, warped, rusting street sign stood meekly on her left, pointing out the various Old World towns you could see along the Highway's northern arm to the left. All the words had long become illegible, but some do-gooding travellers from who knows how long ago had painted new letters on:

Second Thought (not far, mate)
Rangi's Aura (Pretty far - pack snacks)
Wipe Arr (Bloody ages)
If you see Trader Bill, tell him he owes me an arm anna leg. Thieving bastard.
I don't owe you shit. I paid for these limbs an I'll keep them. Greedy prick.
Stop writing on the sign, you're both assholes.

But Bert had no business in Second Thought today, and especially not the supposedly Farmer-occupied township of Rangi's. She would be taking the arm that curved away to the right, down to the coast and, if you were particularly brave, the Ash Fort - or Farm, whatever.

Bert came to a halt before she reached the intersection. She stared hard in a silence that stretched on for eternity, or maybe five or so minutes, her eyes flicking between the southern arm of the Highway and the Back Road behind her - back to the safety of Smack-dab. But it wasn't safe now, was it? And that's why she was here.

She swallowed a slow breath of icy air, her cold sapphire eyes at once gazing down the road and also deep, deep into time. Bert thought she'd never march this stretch of broken road again. She knew every twist, turn and gallows for miles between here and Gerald to the south. She could tell which town she was closest to just from the smell. But however popular the Highway, however convenient it was for traders, despite the immense and quite unparalleled risk of being murdered, for Bert, this was a miserable, rotten road, walking upon which was less appealing even than being shot repeatedly in the face, or torn to itty-bitty shreds by a pack of Things. She'd nuke the whole damn place if she could, but that would attract too much attention from the Overlords, not to mention what the fallout would probably do to her bar. The last thing Bert needed was a local Overlord government trying to regulate Can't Be Buried. No business owner in their right mind wanted regulations.

She felt a cool prick on the palm of her human hand and flinched before realising it was just her pistol. Her hand had gone to it by itself for comfort, unbuttoning the holster quietly and lying in wait on the grip. Bert's enthusiasm for this brilliant plan was a distant memory, fading away just like the rest of the Waste. Her idea now seemed like it had more holes than Lord Ash's last radio play - literally his last, thought Bert. And possibly her last brilliant idea, too. Wonderful.

The very notion of begging for help from bandits - the scummiest of the Earth in an Earth full of scum - made bile form at the back of Bert's throat. She'd rather make a deal with the horde of Things spreading further and further from the Dead Church with whatever passed for a day here in Can't Be Buried. At least with Things, you knew where you stood. You didn't stand, you lay down, dying, your insides being clawed out by grotesque hands that had long since turned into bony, discoloured claws. It was an arrangement you could trust. But bandits? Filth, the lot of them. Disgusting perverts, shameless thieves, murderers, loiterers - and worse. They'd smile at you today, then pilfer your wallet in the night, then smile at you again and help you look for it, then pilfer your kidneys the next night. Only certain few bandits would anaesthetise you before they did it, too. The rest would just ask you to stop screaming, then make you stop screaming if you were having trouble.

Fucking bandits, grumbled Bert.

Fucking Farmer Brown.

But this, all of this, was for Smack-dab. To keep the dream alive, protect her home; to give her, Meatsack and Phoenix a life that was worth a damn. Especially Meatsack, the poor bastard. Without Smack-dab, he was just another big dumb mutant born from an in-bred cannibal family. Nobody else would care about him. They'd probably kill him for sport, because what else would people do along the Back Road with no Smack-dab to drink the pain away in?

Fucking Farmer Brown.

Bert gritted her teeth to steel her resolve and took her first steps along the southern arm of the Highway. The sooner this was all over, she felt, the better.

In her determined, whirlwind of a daydream, she totally missed the next street sign - one a little further down, and made long after the Old World disappeared.

Welcome to the Highway
Please have your wallets open and ready

* * *

You know, escorting Lorry was making Jeb and Orsen a good bit of cash, but the experience wasn't going quite as expected. But then, a false expectation, really, is the beholder's problem, so it was their own damn fault. When you assume, you make an ass out of you and me, or so they say. And Jeb felt like an ass right now.

He was beginning to wonder how painful it might be to cut his own ears off. And more complicated than that, would cutting his own ears off ruin his ability to hear like he wanted, needed, or would the sound still find a way into his brain? Like a parasitic worm. A parasitic worm that couldn't stop preaching the word of Gachook, Our Lord and Saviour.

"And that's how the Old World disappeared, you see," the parasite known as Lorry continued, now moving into the second mind-numbing hour of sermon. "The Old Ones couldn't stop fighting each other – shooting, bombing, stealing each other's faces for their books, you name it – so Gachook, in His Infinite Wisdom, called forth the Seven Deadly Chickens to clean up the whole mess. Now, the Sev-"

"Stabbin'?" Orsen asked, out of nowhere, his eyes so wide it looked like his head was more eye than face. The boy seemed to follow a strange personal principle that, the wider you open your eyes and mouth while someone is speaking, the more knowledge you're likely to take in. But really, all Jeb reckoned it let him take in was dirt. And sometimes passing insects. Oh well, at least he was enjoying the conversation. Unlike Jeb.

"Stabbing, young one?" Lorry replied, her gaunt face rotating perfectly straight on her slim neck as though she were a statue. But, like, a creepy one. That turns its head to follow you as you walk. Oh man did that bring back some of Jeb's memories. Some of the Orcks sure loved theatrics. And torture, unfortunately.

"Yeah..." said Orsen, putting a lot of thought into this. "You said 'you name it', so I was thinkin' o' other things t' name. Like stabbin'. You

118

know, with knives an' that. An', um, axes. An' maybe pencils. I got stabbed with a pencil once an' it was pretty sore. Still got th' scar in my left eye from it."

Jeb, who followed the other two from as far behind as he felt manners would allow, snickered quietly to himself. Lorry had clearly never spoken to a starry-eyed lad like Orsen before. You always had to prepare more conversations than you expected to have, because the lad would stumble from one to another to another without necessarily explaining. Talking to him was often simply an elongated act of catching up.

"Well," said Lorry after a moment's uncertainty, "I think they probably stabbed each other, too, yes."

The boy nodded, satisfied.

"So as I was saying, Gachook sent his Seven Deadly Chickens to destroy the chosen Ninety-Nine Per cent. This sounds harsh, I know, but do not be afraid child, for it was all part of His master plan. If only a small lump of humanity survived, they would have to learn to live differently in order to keep surviving, you see? Like germs, child. *That*, is the brilliance of Gachook, Our Lord and Saviour.

"The first Chicken he sent was that of Carnage, the Chicken of One-Thousand Flaming Missiles. It is said that Carnage rode on the back of the very first missile, and that you could hear his disgust for humanity as the mighty bomb struck the Old Wor-"

"What about fists, Lorry?" Orsen interrupted, though not out of rudeness. The thought simply struck him quite suddenly, and the motion continued out of his mouth without slowing down.

"Wha-, whe- ... excuse me, child?"

Jeb grinned.

"Yeah, you know ... fists. Did the Old Ones fight with their fists, too? Or were they too old? Only I see a lot o' fist fightin' these days, but mostly the old timers stay out o' it. Their backs an' that, you know?"

"Oh, um," Lorry stuttered, her sharp cheeks filling with the colour of blood. Her mouth formed a number of unsaid words as it struggled to get traction on this rather sudden new track.

"No, the Old Ones wouldn't fight with their fists," she said finally, wheels starting to spin properly on the slippery conversation. "They had technology to fight for them."

"Ah," Orsen said, happily accepting this profound new piece of information.

Lorry took a breath and pondered for a moment before continuing. "So, if that's that then, the second Deadly Chicken of Gachook was that of Rot. Rot came up from the ground, child, and pecked out the true, ugly, barbaric nature of the Old Ones, creating the first Children of Rot - who you would call Things. But Rot was rather afraid of the sun, unfortunately, and his children couldn't handle the light - a grievous oversight if you ask me, but who am I to question Gachook, Our Lord and Saviour? So by day the Old Ones feared Carnage, and by night they suffered Rot. Oh and child, oh my child, those were only the first two of Seven Deadly Chick-"

"Did they carroty chop each other?"

Lorry's face twitched. Even from behind, Jeb could tell it was a good twitch, with plenty of eyebrow and bottom lid.

"Carroty chop, child?" she responded, bless her, as politely as one can respond politely through the gritting of one's teeth.

"Yeah, Jeb taught me carroty chops once. I don't much see the point, mind, when ya could just punch someone, but Jeb says there use' t' be folk who were masters at carroty choppin', an' would, like, chop right through folk's skulls with one hand."

"Yes, fine," said Lorry, a little too quick and a little too loud. "They carroty chopped each other all the time."

"Oh, neat."

"So the third Deadly Chicken was that of Winter, Carnage's lover. It is said that Winter always followed behind Carna-"

"And carroty kicks, too?"

Lorry shuddered, her whole body quivering from head to toe with almost cartoon exaggeration. "Yes! Yes they kicked each other as well."

"No," said Orsen, frowning, "not normal kicks. Like, carroty kicks. Kickin' through people's skulls."

"OK, yes! They did that, too."

"Wow."

"Can I continue?"

Orsen nodded, smiling happily. He'd have plenty to write down later.

"OK, right. OK. So it is said that Winter always follows behind Carna-"

"What about flame throwers?"

Jeb smiled happily to himself, his gait taking on a bouncier, satisfied step. Lorry was practically roaring now, desperately trying to find somewhere in the chaos of Orsen's young mind to find a place to lodge the word of Gachook, Our Lord and Saviour. She kept flipping bits around, reshaping them, and forcing harder to put them in a hole that would actually stick. But alas, his mind was more circle than square, and the word of Gachook, our Lord and Saviour, was quite a bit more pomple (a bizarre, multi-sided shape used exclusively by members of Gachook's order) than circle. Every so often Lorry would look around to Jeb to plead with her eyes for assistance, but he would just smile silently in a maliciously not-listening fashion, then suddenly see something very interesting elsewhere and allow it to capture his full, unwavering attention.

And so the madness and the yelling and, now, the waving of arms continued, even as they passed the junction to the Back Road. Maybe bringing Lorry on the trip to Smack-dab would be worth the money after all, Jeb grinned to himself.

* * *

Meanwhile elsewhere, after a night camped hiding in a large bush, and then a morning spent untangling from a large bush...

A sticky body suit of sweat clung to Phoenix like the slimy, detonated entrails of his last adventuring partner. It slithered down his face in gloopy streams, poking at his eyeballs with salty fingers, then oozed all down his back, each warm streamlet sending little shivers up his spine as they made their tickly migration to his ass. And his balls? He didn't even want to think about his balls. But the words 'wet sponge' were coming to mind. Phoenix's entire body ached to some degree or another, but it was his feet and legs that were suffering the worst. If you shot him, then punched the bullet holes, then stuck something in them, twisted it, and then released burning acid into his veins, it still, in Phoenix's mind, wouldn't be nearly as uncomfortable as what he suffered now in his poor little legs and feet.

On the bright side to all this, though, Phoenix no longer felt the stinging, icy cold from the day and night before that had rolled up the bottom of his coat and lodged itself into his nervous system. In fact, right now, at this very moment in time, Phoenix was prepared to strip completely naked so long as it meant the pain and the sweat and the awful, rasping sandpapery noise from his lungs would have mercy on him.

Needless to say, and right now Phoenix couldn't really say a whole lot without sounding like someone was standing on his windpipe, it had been a long time since the heroic, brave and mighty adventurer had climbed a mountain. But that's exactly what his mission called for, and so here he was. Climbing some dumb-ass mountain. But for a good cause, at least.

Well, for a cause, anyway.

The mad, often in all senses of the word, star-worshipping cult known as the Star Gazers lived in some crappy little village at the top of Mount Butt - or at least that's what Phoenix thought it was called. It may also have been Hutt, or Futt, or something -utt, anyway. It was said that they had formed the Starry Place - the name of the village - at the point where their original members, no doubt mutants and inbreds and idiots the lot of them, first saw the stars however many years ago. Folks say that in a stroke of sheer luck, the greasy smog had dissolved a hole in itself that fateful night, if only for a moment, and the very sight of what lay beyond drove the group quite startlingly insane. Successfully insane, albeit. They must have made a killing on cult entry fees.

Now? To the descendants of those wealthy bastards, the fatty layer of gristle coating what constituted for a sky in these parts was considered a great wall, separating the land of man and his many, many sins with that of the Stars, and all their godly goodness. Phoenix always assumed they were naked and bonking up there, because why else would they want privacy? And what else were gods of the Waste meant to do? Repair the land and free mankind from the toils and perils that lay in the night to brutally murder him? HAH! As if. Naked and bonking, that was for damn sure. And there'd be little three-eyed cherubs floating between the orgies with drinks of water, keeping everyone hydrated. Sometimes the gods would spill something, and that's why it rained. And, more importantly, that's why the rain was of inconsistent textures.

The trail Phoenix now climbed was an unsealed Old World road that had fallen largely into disrepair, literally. Whole sections had slipped away, ripped from the mountainside by whatever natural or man-made disaster was occurring at the time, to tumble off down the slope. One moment, Phoenix would be clambering over an ancient mound of fallen dirt, rocks and tree corpses (quite assuredly dead, Phoenix checked), then the trail would then narrow to barely a man's width, and each footstep would get the cliché crumbling of rocks and one foot slipping, just to keep things dramatic for anyone watching.

The landscape itself, in Phoenix's critical eye, was as boringly, unyieldingly brown as brown could be, beginning in the brown foothills of the slope and winding up through brown ridges, brown saddles, brown gulleys and some seriously brown-ass florpadorps (the little wrinkles that mountains sometimes have, or so Phoenix was told by a trader once). A small amount of dry shrubbery clung here and there unmoving and so far not man-eating, and yep, they were akin to the colour of one's shit.

Phoenix slowed to an exhausted halt, let out a hoarse huff and scratched at his beard. Then he furrowed his brow in disappointment, for he had intended to let out a deliberately long, slow huff, but what came out was more a little wheezy puff, like that of a dying old man who had nothing good to say for last words. With grumpiness mounting, Phoenix stared up the winding mountain road before him, which had once again widened into an acceptable road-like shape. Somewhere up there, near the smog and the stars and the idiocy, was a village. And in that village was a leader.

And that leader had no idea just how awesome a hero was coming their way.

He shook his head and began pushing himself up the slope once again. Bert sure better be grateful after all of this. Damn grateful, with clothes flinging to the floor faster than he could say "Let's do it, you gorgeous monster."

If she wasn't, or didn't, well, well ... he'd ... he'd quit!

Hmm. Well, maybe he'd threaten to quit, but then he'd see her shocked, sad face and he'd pretend to give her a second chance. That was bound to work.

Yeah.

* * *

Meatsack shuffled back into Smack-dab's main room, where he had set up one of the chairs near the front door, but facing back into the bar. He had just come from the bar's generator room down the hall, where, repeating Bert's strict orders over and over in his head, he was performing his daily morning task of switching off Smack's perimeter of electric lights - which helped create a Thing barrier around the building so guests didn't have to worry about anything other than sneaky lovers climbing into their windows.

Although it took some degree of strategy and contortionism, Meatsack managed somehow to scrunch his bulky frame just enough so that he could curl up on the chair, knees by his head, one huge arm wrapping around his shins all the way to his other side, and the other arm making an effort at the same, but not quite achieving as identical nor as functional an effect.

He was alone, except for his long-time friend Windy blowing through gaps in the weatherboards. He and Windy often played together as children, but now that he was an adult and had a serious career, he just didn't have the same amount of time to give Windy the attention it deserved. But, much to his delight, his sheer and complete loneliness made for the perfect opportunity to grab a pretend drink and have a thorough conversation about what everyone had been up to.

Meatsack had plenty to tell Windy about Bert and Smack-dab and Phoenix, and all the many adventures they had been up to. Like that time they had served customers together, and when Berty had yelled at a trader who was delivering the grog late, or that one day Meatsack had joined Phoenix for a hunting trip but, oh what a laugh it had been, had come back with a giant fang stuck in his big arm. It had truly been the best of times for Meatsack, a fact he was delighted to share with Windy.

Windy hadn't been sitting about, though. In fact, it had become a highly successful entrepreneur in the dust business. Windy was a travelling salesman and dust expert all rolled into one little gust. It'd scour the Waste for only the very best dust, then with the utmost speed and efficiency – as Meatsack would expect from his long-time pal, who had always been the leader of the duo – it would transport the dust through Can't Be Buried to be delivered on time, on budget and in the right place.

But then Windy had to go, which wasn't great but was OK. Windy was far too busy to hang around Smack-dab pretending to drink and having long, thoughtful conversations, as much as Windy assured Meatsack that it would prefer to be doing. There was simply too much dust to be transported, and Windy had a family now. It had to provide. Meatsack understood, and let his friend seep out back through the cracks in the walls.

His friend disappearing down the road, Meatsack swept his gaze, or at least half of it, around Smack-dab. He was asked to Watch the Bar, and there was no way he was going to let Berty Bert down.

And so he sat alone.

And so he watched.

* * *

Further south along the highway, the ocean could be seen ravaging Can't Be Buried's coastline in a show of quite extraordinary aggression. Giant, angry waves puffed their chests out as they stormed forwards, frothing at the mouth, before piling onto the beach and dragging whatever they could back into their watery domain. The sand and rocks made a bold defence, adopting their regular tactic of going all slimy and difficult to move, sacrificing a small number of their army to be relinquished into the dismal depths, but at the same time grabbing as many of their allies back as possible. It was a constant tug of war, and it had been going on for billions of years – ever since the land dared to challenge its enemy, to fight back against the oppression of the deep blue, and rise up out of the ocean to form its own air-dwelling dirt nation.

Their war was long and brutal, and piece by piece, the ocean sought to reclaim its territory. But after thousands of years and very little erosion to speak of, in the larger scheme of things, all seemed lost for the watery warriors. That was, however, until strange lifeforms atop the land suddenly allied with the ocean in a last-minute change of politics. Within the past two or so centuries, these lifeforms began doing everything in their worldly power to poison the world's atmosphere and free the ocean's additional reinforcements that had been encased in ice since what seemed like the beginning of time. Each passing decade, more reinforcements were released from the ice caps and the ocean grew in strength. It pushed further into the land's territory, engulfing the pitiful attempt by beaches to blockade this onslaught.

With victory after victory racking up for the ocean, its army was rejuvenated, and though the lifeforms had done their fair share of poisoning the water, too, this was the moment the politicians and warmongers of Ocean had been waiting for. No amount of acid would stop their conquest, no amount of nuclear fallout. And so, the waves rose, they frothed, they roared and they crashed. And this time, they were winning.

But the civilisation of these strange lifeforms persevered, despite their over-eager oceanic ally destroying much of their coastal cities, towns and roads – including large chunks of what is now known as the Dead Church. It was on land, on the other side of the highway, that a shadow, unseen behind a cadaverous Old World shed, crouched low and watched intently as an angry-looking woman stomped down the coast road, her head looking hither and thither, and then a bunch of other directions. She appeared to be what one could only assume was a deeply troubled mix of intense disgust and hyper suspicion; her eyes threatened death, but her jittery head movements and the tension in her body seemed like, perhaps, the parliament in her brain was trying hard to pass a vote of no confidence.

The shadow narrowed its equally shadowy eyes and beckoned to a second shadow, which was hovering nearby. The second shadow stooped down to peep through a hole that had been eaten through the corrugated metal of the shed, saw the approaching woman, and gave a quick, professional nod of understanding. The second shadow then hastily beckoned to a third shadow, which immediately started whistling like a bird (species undetermined) over its shoulder towards a giant, rotten tree that hadn't survived Gachook's wrath. Straight away, a garbled whistle sung back.

Now, the second shadow leaned in close to the first shadow. "She looks a little angry, sir," a female voice whispered hesitantly.

The first shadow nodded slowly and twitched its quite incredibly luscious, if a little worse for wear, moustache. "She does, my dear," the male voice whispered in response, "but look at that fine weapon at her hip. I bet we could fetch a jolly price for it, wouldn't you say? Or perhaps we could use the extra firepower if we are to thwart that mad farmer and his robotic companion."

There was a moment of silence between them as the female shadow pondered this. "Is that the weapon she's gripping tight, sir?"

"The very same."

Another moment of thoughtful pause.

"The weapon she looks intent on using, sir? Potentially on those who would try to steal it, sir."

"Err, yes. We are talking about the same weapon."

The woman was getting closer, but no less angry or suspicious. Angspicious, you might say, particularly of the sudden warbling of local birds which, as far as the woman was concerned, had gone extinct decades ago.

The female figure nodded in agreement. "Yes sir, it's definitely a pretty gun."

Now the third shadow, the one which made the original if undefined birdcall, shuffled over awkwardly, trying to keep low and its footsteps light. "She's gettin' close, sir. We doin' this or what?"

The female shadow glanced back at him. "I think we're just deciding that now."

The moustachioed shadow fingered an old wooden hunting rifle in his hands, his gaze transfixed by this angspicious stranger and her gleaming bone-handled revolver pistol. "It certainly is a very lovely weapon," he said.

Another silence loitered awkwardly between the trio, kicking its feet and checking its watch impatiently.

Then: "I'm sure it only carries six or so shots, sir, assuming it's loaded," offered the woman.

"That size of weapon? Yes, sounds about right, Doris my dear."

Another pause.

"Well, sir, there's a good few more of us than that."

"Excuse me?"

"There are a few more than six of us, sir, if you understand my meaning."

His moustache twitched, indeed both hither and quite thither. "Ah," he said slowly, "I think I see your point. Indeed, the odds would seem in our favour, despite our rather miserable state of strength."

The woman's stomping was now audible through the roaring of the waves. The shadows could see that her face was red from the constant salty spray whipping up all around her, but as far as stature went, she was not an impressive being. Not physically, anyway. Her face, though, seemed to have that "I dare you" quality about it, which suggested that physical prowess meant little to a woman with a robotic fist, a pistol, and blue eyes so intense, the shadows uncomfortably tried to avoid them even from back here.

"She does look quite ready for a fight, though, sir."

"Oh yes, terrifying face indeed. The stuff of nightmares, really."

"If our nightmares weren't already full, sir."

"Yes, quite right, Doris. Quite right indeed."

"She's almost on top of us, sir, gettin' a bit close for comfort. What're your orders?"

"Hmm."

After a moment he nodded, the confident nod of a leader who was making a confident decision, whether they were genuinely confident in its confidence or not. "Well," he finally said, "I rather think we can handle a few bullet wounds, can't we? Henry certainly took plenty for the team last time, didn't he?"

The lady shadow smiled warmly. "He did, sir. A real gentleman and scholar, may he rest in peace."

"Right, well, I think I'll jolly well start us of, shall I?"

A *kachunk* echoed out from behind the shed and bounced excitedly across the road.

Part Five

More Acquiring, But Still Only Three

Bert gasped with fright and threw herself into a crouch as a rifle shot lanced through the tumbling ambience of Can't Be Buried's coastline. The bullet screamed "Weee!" past where her face would have been had she kept walking, and then lodged itself with a mighty clang in an old burnt-out vehicle by the side of the road. Bert swore loudly as she dropped, whipping up her pistol and sprinting, low, for the car.

A second shot burst into the scene just as she was sliding behind the vehicle's skeletal bonnet, digging up a spray of dust in the ground not far behind her. It would be a while before Bert calmed down enough to realise there was a brand new hole in her coat.

When the second shot missed, a voice muttered a swear from behind a nearby tin shed. A small, muffled discussion erupted thereafter, but Bert couldn't make out what they were saying. Extinct birds chirped frantically at each other

Behind the car, Bert shuffled, heart pounding, practically rolling in the dirt, further into cover so that it offered at least the illusion of protection. Its four rusted doors were hanging loose, but they were present nonetheless. As was the driver, or rather, what was left of the driver's ancient skeleton. The thudding in Bert's chest felt like a mutant insect battering at her insides to get out.

That was way too close, she thought, suplexing her lungs to bring them into submission. If she hadn't heard the cocking of the rifle, she'd be done for, no questions asked. Just another corpse for some creature to eat. Bert growled at herself. She thought she'd been cautious, alert, prepared for anything, but then, how prepared can you possibly be along somewhere so inherently chaotic as the Highway?

She hoped the spirit of The Woman wasn't shaking her head with disappointment.

Then a third shot rang out, slicing the salty air, and with similar ease, a large chunk of the metal that was supposed to be Bert's cover. Shards of door curled back like a dead spider at the impact, leaving a shredded little hole near Bert's chest cavity - which, coincidentally, was precisely somewhere she didn't want a shredded little hole.

In response, she ground her teeth together, gripped her weapon tight and flung herself up, pistol finding its way through the empty car

131

windows for a clear, but semi-protected, shot. She spotted a couple of bedraggled figures creeping out from behind a tree in the background, but the moment they saw she was up, they made a frightened "Oh shit" face and threw themselves back in a hurry.

Bert had the perfect shot, but hesitated. Her finger dwindled on the trigger, applying the lightest touch. She couldn't squeeze, could she? It might have been a little while since Bert was amongst scumbags like Highway bandits, but unless politics had drastically changed over the years, they certainly wouldn't take kindly to having their various limbs blown off (even if they were trying to do the same to her...). And limbless bandits would not only make for particularly ineffective bargaining partners, they probably wouldn't be much use in a fight against Farmer Brown. Except to nip at his ankles with their teeth.

So, Bert needed to get these assholes talking, not shooting. Especially not shooting. She puffed out her cheeks and hid again behind the car, needing some protection to think for a minute. Instantly a panicked bird chirped again, and she heard footsteps shuffling cautiously somewhere over the road. She'd need to surrender somehow, but popping up with her hands up might still catch her a bullet to the face, and she sure liked having one of those. No, she couldn't risk startling whoever had the rifle, so she'd need to warn them first. Offer the white flag before the face, as it were.

"Hey, assholes!" she shouted.

The footsteps stopped.

Waves crashed into the beach, then hissed as they retreated.

"What?" shouted a voice back.

"I surrender!"

Crash. Hiss.

"...what?"

"I'm coming out, don't shoot!"

Bert cautiously popped the top of her head up first, in case she needed to duck very suddenly. She flinched back down the moment she spotted a large number of bandits hesitating on the road, but nobody pulled a trigger. Slowly, with her ears straining to catch just a whiff of imminent doom, Bert inched herself up with her weapon stowed and her hands where folks could see them.

This was it, she thought. This is where I find out whether I'm gonna live...

...or die trying.

* * *

"Stupid Bert," Phoenix wheezed, his breaths now coming out more like sparks than air. "Stupid Bert and her stupid, stupid-ass plan."

Phoenix was what he felt must surely be most of the way up the mountain by now. He'd been walking for two, maybe three hours straight up, winding all the way: trudging up a steep slope, around a corner, down into a saddle, up the other side. Repeat. Repeat. Change the order. Repeat. His legs burned so hard he reckoned they must surely be about to fall off, and it felt like he'd worn his feet down to little bloody stubs about two florpadorps ago. He had Terrance Leeland's arm for feet, now. What a disaster.

It was in this moment of painful lucidity, far up into the sky and hours from Smack-dab, that he wondered whether the little cushion forming on his belly was in fact not a biological evolution that he was developing and thus making him superior and more comfortable than other humans, but in fact stomach fat from not exercising enough. It certainly had the various properties of fat, but he wasn't willing to submit to it just yet. He needed to run some more tests before coming to a well-reasoned, logical scientific conclusion.

But where would he even get a bone saw? Ah well, that was a future problem.

His now problem was, as it usually was, Bert. He didn't even remotely agree with this mission, but what could he say in the face of such raw power? Such determination. And even worse, the somewhat regrettable cocktail of hormones that was permanently jammed in his brain. It wouldn't be so bad if he had been given a better task, maybe if him and Bert had swapped. Pretty much anything but storming up a steep mountain to talk with some nut job cultists who hated Smack-dab and

By Duncan P. Pacey

literally, *literally*, days before came in to shoot the place up. Worse still, somewhere right at this moment Bert was off gallivanting and having a blast with bandits, probably swashbuckling - whatever that was - and fighting single-combat style.

Damn he was jealous. The only buckle Phoenix was swashing was that of his belt, which he had to loosen because it had somehow magically shrunk these past few years.

"Stupid Bert," he mumbled again, just to make sure the world had gotten the message.

In a swooping flurry of grumps, he spun on the spot, swirled his coat, produced a water bottle, and flumped unhappily down on the nearest boulder. Bugger it, if he was going to talk to a bunch of Wacko McSchmackos, he would at least be rested.

With begloved fingers he unscrewed the cap of his canteen and took a deep swig, relishing in the cool liquid putting out the raging forest fire that was his respiratory system.

Then the ground moved. Or rather, his seat moved.

Phoenix jumped up with a high-pitched yelp as a massive set of jaws opened up in his trusty boulder and snapped at his backside. He hopped and stumbled away back onto the road, fumbling with his canteen and dropping it straight into the surprise maw.

Two rows of sharp, long fangs snapped shut in a flash to the sound of crunching metal. The boulder writhed and bulged as it chewed on the bottle, then belched loudly, catapulting a particularly tough bit of canteen back out the jaws and straight into Phoenix's eye.

"Ouch," he complained, clutching his face and stepping back again.

He glowered openly at the rock and kicked a little pebble at it in his distaste. "Well excuse you," he said, pouting.

"Excuse you, sir," the rock replied, with a voice as deep as the sea.

Phoenix froze and his face went pale. He started backing away very slowly, hand hovering on the sling of his rifle.

"Ribbit," the rock croaked.

* * *

Meatsack stared at the bar.

It hadn't moved.

Good job, Meatsack.

* * *

Phoenix slogged on, looking over his shoulder regularly to make sure the boulderfrog wasn't following him. A small wooden sign was flapping in the wind not too far ahead of Phoenix, who was feeling extra dehydrated simply because the stupid frog ate his water bottle. The sign was your classic three planks nailed sideways to one plank contraption, with what was hopefully red paint scrawled into tidy letters along the front face.

Phoenix stood in front of it and stared thoughtfully at the words. Not only were they quite incredibly neat and tidy for a Waste sign most of the way up a mountain, but the content itself was very helpful. It so kindly reminded Phoenix that he was entering a sacred and holy place and, as you would expect, he should turn back immediately lest he face ... face ... Hmm. He wasn't entirely sure what the Excruciating and Mercilessly Swift Castigation of Six Million Stars was, but it had sufficient emotional impact behind it to leave the reader feeling threatened, which was presumably the idea.

He considered the threat for a moment longer, then with all the respect in the world, strolled right past it with a happy little tune on his lips. Six Million Stars was for other people - Phoenix was a VIP.

About twenty minutes further up the slope, Phoenix rounded an exceptionally crumbly corner and finally saw it. Saw something, anyway. Something that wasn't fucking brown.

A large, rusting metal gate, moulded into what appeared to be a spiky circle - oh, it was a star, duh, it was a star - blockaded the rest of the path up the hill. More importantly, though, Phoenix could make out buildings, houses mostly, lathered across Mount Butt's florpadorps and growing like black mould further up the hill, towards the peak where the housing density seemed to increase. The gate was connected to a similarly imposing fence that was determined to defy whatever Mount Butt could throw at it, twisting and turning in any particular direction it felt was required so that it created a precarious perimeter around the entire village – or at least what Phoenix could see of the entire village.

Phoenix whistled. This place was a *lot* bigger than he expected.

"Oi!" cried a voice.

Phoenix cocked his head.

There were two robed figured next to the gate, both of whom were now running towards Phoenix. He could make out that they wore the typical regalia of Starry folk, which entailed black robes with white speckles all over them, and not a whole lot else that was of much interest. These guys additionally, however, carried long, ornate spears (in the sense that they were regular spears with colourful tassels stuck to both ends), tipped with glinting metal blades that were also shaped like stars.

Phoenix stopped walking and watched with interest as the duo charged at full speed towards him. Their robes flapped wildly in the wind, but to their credit, and to Phoenix's admiration, somehow their hoods stayed on with what appeared to be minimal effort. These guys were clearly professionals.

When the pair arrived in front of Phoenix, both tipped their spears uncomfortably close towards him. Phoenix smiled warmly and waved.

"Hi there," he said, ensuring each individual got an equal share of his charming smile.

"Halt ... stranger!" one of the hooded figures shouted, his breathing at a level of harshness Phoenix could readily sympathise with. The figure was the figure of a man, mostly because it *was* a man, a man whose face was chubby and misshapen, and awash with sweat. He abruptly propped the end of his spear in the dirt and leaned on it for support, doubling over as gasps fell out of his mouth. The other figure tried to remain composed and fearsome, but it just seemed embarrassing for them both.

The doubled-over figure glanced up at Phoenix, glaring between ragged breaths. "You have ... hath, I mean ... strayed unto the Starry Place, heathen traveller. Thus, I, Abbelous, and ... bloody Stars I'm unfit ... I, Abbelous, and my fellow gatekeeper Fabbelous, shalt render, woo boy, render unto you the Merciless and Supremely Painful Castigation of Seven

Million Stars. Prepare ... prepare yoursel- thineself - Stars it, you know what I mean!"

Phoenix smiled as sweetly as he could, which is to say, sweet enough to rot the teeth right out of someone's mouth. And if that didn't work, metal-plated fists always finished the job. "Six million."

The guard apparently known as Abbelous stood more upright and squinted at Phoenix. "Eh?"

"Six million. And I think it's meant to be Excruciating and Mercilessly Swift, or at least that's what your sign says down thataways."

Fabbelous spoke up next, a woman with a tiny and highly un-guard-like voice. But, the type of tiny voice where there's a lot of passion behind it, and nobody has the heart to tell her that she's not as intimidating a guard as she perceives herself. But, self-perception is more important than what other people think, so, here they all were. "Oh, we upgraded thine Castigation since then," she said.

Abbelous nodded. "Aye, got a brand new'th one. Not even used yet."

"Oh," replied Phoenix, still smiling. "Well isn't that lovely. I'm glad to hear you're developing. That's really nice to see, in this day and age. Anyway, before this whole Castigation business, I'd like to quickly see the Constellator-"

"CONSTELLATOOOOOR!"

"Yeah, that person," Phoenix said, maintaining his smile at all times despite getting a little fright from the sudden outburst. "They're expecting me, I believe."

Abbelous, regaining his breath finally, squinted again. "She expect'th you?"

"Yessir, spot on the money."

"Oh," he said, before glancing at Fabbelous.

Fabbelous reached up to pull down her hood, revealing she had two noses and a Picasso mouth. Not that anybody here knew who the hell Picasso was, and that it was even a person - not a type of nut.

"Is thee Trader Bill?" she asked.

"Nope."

"Johnny Lentil?" Abbelous added.

"Negative."

"Starry Petunia Sara?"

"Negamundo, ma'am."

"Then who are you? Thine are the only three names on'th the list."

"I'm Phoenix."

"Who?"

"Phoenix."

"Phoenix," Fabsy repeated.

"Phoenix," replied Phoenix, whose name was Phoenix.

"Like'th the bird?" asked Abbelous.

"What bird?"

"You know, the phoenix."

"Don't know any phoenix bird, me buckaroo. Just a Phoenix me."

"Well who is thee, then?"

"Phoenix, I just said."

"Yeah, but who is thee in relation to the Constellator-"

"CONSTELLATOOOOOOR!"

"-in relation to the Constellator expecting thee?"

"I've got an appointment," Phoenix lied.

"An appointment, eh?" said Abbelous.

"Thassaone, sir."

"When'th is thine appointment?" Fabbelous chimed in, examining Phoenix intently. She moved a step closer, her head zooming in slowly, eyes sweeping across Phoenix's many fine features.

"Oh, it's right now," Phoenix said, his smile wavering as he tried to edge politely away from this invasion of his personal bubble.

"Well then thee is late, isn't thee?" said Abbelous, clearly getting grouchier. "The Constellator-"

"CONSTELLATOOOOOR!"

"-the Constellator's hut is still going take thee a good twenty minutes to get to."

"Is that right?" Phoenix said, scratching his beard. "Well, it's in twenty minutes then."

"What?"

"Yeah, it's in twenty minutes."

"No it isn't."

"Well it isn't anymore."

"Then when is it?"

"About nineteen minutes and thirty seconds."

Abbelous, having only just flushed the red of exhaustion out of his wobbly face, now found himself floundering in a sea of crimson exasperation. *"But you just said it was now!"*

"Did I?" Phoenix replied, practically dripping with innocence. Slimy, slimy innocence. "I must have been rounding."

Fabbelous stepped back, snapping her fingers as her face widened open. It turned out there was a second mouth kicking around unseen just next to her left ear, and it revealed itself with a little O of realisation along with the rest of the orifices. "Hey! Thee is the Grubby Chef from the Place of the Burny Drink, right?"

"Excuse me?"

"You know, the chef that is grubby, and works for the Devil Woman at the Place of the Burny Drink."

"Never heard of him."

"No, it is thee, I know it's thee. I'm a real big fan of thine work."

This caught Phoenix's attention, and so the first little crack in his facade snuck its way into the conversation. "Oh you are? Well, would you like me to sign something? One of your three fine breasts, perhaps?"

"Five, actually, and no that's OK. Because ahah!"

"Ahah?"

"Ahah?" repeated Abbelous, who wasn't keeping up.

"Ahah!" restated Fabbelous. "Because thee just admitted to being the Grubby Chef!"

Phoenix's face froze. "Err, no I didn't."

"Oh shit ... 'th," exclaimed Abbelous, his angry expression wobbling open with horror like a shocked flan. He quickly picked his spear off the dust and lowered the blade to threaten Phoenix's torso.

Now the both of them had their starry spears almost pressed into Phoenix's armour and clothing, and their faces suddenly seemed a whole lot less accommodating than just before.

"Thee is lucky, for thine Grubby Chef *is* someone who has an appointment with our mighty Constellator."

139

"CONSTELLATOOOOOOR!"

Phoenix smiled grimly, taking a step back. "Is that right?"

Fabbelous sneered. "Oh yeah, thee is most wanted, you might'th say. In fact, we're going to have to insist that thee come'th with us right now."

"Oh, err, right now?"

They narrowed their eyes.

Phoenix took another step backwards. "You know, I just remembered I actually have this, you know, appointment somewhere else. Argh, foolish, double-booked myself. You know how it is. Ha ha."

And the last thing he remembered hearing was the shuffling of feet he didn't realise were behind him. Then something heavy struck him on the back of the head, and the last thing he remembered *seeing* was the ground.

And it was coming closer than it normally would be.

* * *

Bert stared at her pistol.

It was not a happy stare, nor was it even remotely a contented casual glance. It was an unblinking gaze. Importantly, she stared at her pistol clutched in the filthy bandit hands of somebody that, most assuredly, wasn't her.

Minutes before, after Bert had stood up behind the dishevelled car, she shuffled around the front of it and the bandits had swarmed out of their hidey holes to surround her completely. Weapons were waggled, and growls were growled.

"I mean you no harm," she had said rather stupidly, in hindsight.

"Oh but dear," their leader had replied, a rifle in his hands, "we most certainly *do*."

But it had all gone well, you see. Bert had survived the crucial first moments of any Waste encounter (the shooty bit), and had the opportunity to, well, make this pack of bandits an offer they couldn't refuse. And you know what?

They had refused. But they were at least willing to talk, so long as she handed over her beloved pistol.

So maybe things weren't going quite as well as she had hoped...

Windy bellowed like an angry child suffering its first mutation, slapping at the corrugated tin walls of the Old World shed Bert and the bandits had moved to after her surrender. She was sitting cross-legged on the mouldy wooden floor, her hands bound behind her back with a rope she hoped was meant to be black. She had vocally disagreed with the need for such measures, but when a horde of armed, seasoned bandits ties you up for their own safety, the best way to take it is to be flattered.

Most of the small horde waited outside, but before her sat one of the most finely dressed bandits she had seen since the days before Smack-dab, and long before Lord Ash or this Farmer Brown mother fu-

"It really does sound like a load of fisticuffs we needn't be a part of," spoke the man. He had a truly spectacular moustache on his grubby, weather-beaten face - the kind that women he'd been close to probably either passionately loved or deeply hated, for it was not a mouthpiece for anything other than extremes - and his outfit looked as though, in a distant past life, it had been a three-piece, pin-striped suit. Now it was a three-piece, pin-striped, muddy, bloody, torn and altogether bedraggled ensemble, but relative to what bandits usually wore, which consisted of far too much leather for Bert's taste, the man may as well have been royalty. Bert had learned his name was Sir Robert, the ex-captain from Lord Ash's private guard, and a man who was not a man, but rather a chap. Or a lad. An old boy would also be an acceptable reference. These were the Polite Bandits, apparently. Though it seemed an oxymoron to Bert.

Inside the shed were two other individuals: one a slender, nervous-looking man called Toddrick whom Bert had found out was behind the bird calls, but who would not accept that the species had gone extinct years back (and who Bert suspected simply couldn't do any other bird calls); and the other was a woman. Now, this was not unsurprising in and of itself - women bandits were not uncommon after all, and some of the worst packs Bert had met were women-only - but the disconcerting thing about the woman known as Doris was the ease with which she could at once eagerly grip the most rusted, most well-used hunting knife Bert had ever seen, whilst at the same time smiling as sweetly innocent as someone who had never been out in the Waste before. She was the type of person who, upon seeing their face for the first time, you'd immediately wish to be friends with. Best of friends. For to be anything other than allies would be terrifying.

"But don't you want the fort back, Sir Robert? It's rightfully owned by the Polite Bandits, you said so yourself," Bert responded, tearing her gaze from the bone-handled weapon.

"Well, Bert," replied the man carefully. His eyebrows rose and fell in majestic, thoughtful waves. They would be considered finely manicured and superbly presented were they not up against the competition of his fuzzy upper lip. "If you feel my jolly band here could siege the fort, and I'm not saying I particularly agree with you there, but if you think we can, why don't we just, if I do say, siege the fort, eh? I rather think that getting involved in this Smack-dab business puts us," he stopped, snortled a chortle, and then grinned proudly, "...smack-dab in the middle of trouble."

"Top word play, sir," said Doris, smiling that sweet, sugary smile. Except it wasn't sugar, it was probably anthrax.

"Thank you, Doris. Would have been a good one for Lord Ash's radio plays, eh?"

"Absolutely, sir, a fine bit of banter."

Sir Robert turned on Bert. "Did you know our Doris here used to be an actress in those plays? She was quite the rising star, if I might say so."

"Oh stop, sir, you'll make me blush."

"No no, I simply must brag. I'm sure you heard them, Berty, everybody listened in."

Bert had. But now wasn't the time to voice her true opinion about the *Lord Ash Chronicles*, which she had angrily told Phoenix once that she felt were utter, complete tripe - particularly the acting, which again, she would fail to mention at this very moment.

Sir Robert was still smiling, and talking. "Quite the emotional journey, I felt. If you weren't laughing, you were crying."

" 'cept the one about the duck," muttered Toddrick, who was leaning against the outer wall.

A darkness fell over the group's faces - even Doris.

"Ah yes, that was poor taste. My apologies, Doris, but it was a terrible choice of script."

"Almost a career killer, sir, no need to apologise. We learned our lesson."

"Indeed, indeed, and speaking of lessons learned," Sir Robert said, returning his attention to Bert, "we've had our fill of death at the walls of the fort, Berty, and I rather think now is not the time to do it all again. So, if you won't mind, my dear, I'm going to kill you now and rob you of all your belongings."

Kachunk. The echo was loud in the small shed.

Sir Robert levelled his rifle while Toddrick sidled behind Bert in the background, the glint of metal sparkling in his hands.

"Wait!" Bert gasped, a quite drastic surge of adrenalin exploding into her brain. Internally, the spirit of Bert wrestled with the spirit of Rage, trying desperately to hold it down and to keep this conversation as polite as can be. An outburst of Bertrage would probably do poorly until her hands were free. Pipes rattled with the stress, but it seemed, at least for the moment, that the spirit of Bert was winning for once.

Sir Robert frowned at her with open disappointment, a harrumph of impatience juddering out from beneath his furry lip companion. "I'm sorry Berty, but it's cold today and I'd really rather be popping back south to our HQ in Burnt Ham for some tea right now. So make it quick."

Bert breathed out slowly, letting the steam in her system vent out her mouth. It curled in angry little wisps, shaking its misty fists at the rest of the room. "Look," she said, her voice trembling with calm, "how much has Farmer Brown taken from you, Sir Robert? How much money? How many men? And your home. He's trying to take my home, too - take my family. But if we can unite enough people against him, we can stop this madness before it goes any further."

Sir Robert eyed her with a deep suspicion. "And how are we going to get that many men, hmm? I barely have enough survivors to defend Burnt Ham, and our town is minutely small. We wouldn't fair too well against an army that has already toppled us once, behind a fort no less, now would we? It's tough just finding fighters fit enough to meet our weekly theft quota. I've had to adjust them down twice this month already. We're starting to let traders through Burnt Ham without harming them, would you believe it? It pays more to just toll the buggers, me oh my what a disaster."

Doris and Toddrick shook their heads.

A few muscles in Bert's upper lip attempted a mutiny on her face, pulling into a slight curl at the very thought of bandits robbing traders and other folk along the Highway. And here was Bert sitting with them, practically begging them for help. And worst of all, they actually seemed kinda nice – except the part where they wanted to kill her, but then, that was mutual. Bastards. Utter bastards. Mentally, she punched her upper lip in the face until it came back down again. Now was not the time for open contempt.

"As we speak I have men trolling Can't Be Buried for allies," she said, forcing the tone of her words into some semblance of civility. And it wasn't a *complete* lie, either. A little embellishment of truth never hurt between bargaining partners. Mostly. "I'm building an army of my own, Sir Robert, and I want to hand you the grand prize. You help me defeat Farmer Brown, help me put an end to his reign of Taxation, and you can take the fort in his place. Reclaim your home, and your honour."

And then I'll deal with whatever mess you create later, she added in her mind.

"Hmm," said Sir Robert.

The man stroked at his moustache with long, twirling motions. His fingers grasped thoughtfully at strands beneath his nose, gently meandered their way along the soft, greying river of his facial hair, and flicked into a neat curl right at the end. The oil and grit in the hairs helped them stick in place, too, giving him that classy, cultured curly look. If he wasn't a barbarian in a waistcoat, an up-tight son of a bitch, and, not to mention, a bandit, he might even be attractive. He'd probably only be a three-drinker – Bert's measurement of attractiveness in men. She was yet to meet anyone who came close to even being a one-drinker (and she couldn't imagine a no-drinker even existed).

"No," he finally said, shaking his head apologetically.

"No?" Bert replied, aghast.

"Quite," he said back. "Too many variables, you understand. No real guarantee for me and my own. It really would just be smarter for me to shoot you now, take your things, and start our own little uprising should we feel slighted in the future. But in the meantime, it's back to road tolls and rebuilding. So, on that note, goodbye, Bert. It has been a pleasure."

Bert swore in her head. She tensed her crossed legs and pushed at the ground with her feet, trying to spring off to the side. She was just achieving lift-off when she, in the kind of horrific, salt-in-the-wounds slow motion that seems to occur mostly for people about to die, giving them a perfect opportunity to watch their own demise in glorious detail, watched Sir Robert squeeze the trigger of his rifle.

Her eyes closed.

The shot fired.

...

...

...

...

...

...

...

Bert opened one eye.

She was still in the shed, but now she was prone on the ground. Her left shoulder bloomed with pain from the impact on the floorboards, which despite how soft they felt from rot, turned out to be a less than ideal place to land. Her ears were trying out tinnitus for size, but perhaps most noticeable of all was her ability to notice.

She was still alive.

Bert opened her other eye and absorbed the room, feeling out of breath from the expectation of being, well, permanently out of breath. Sir Robert was clutching the hunting rifle in his mitts, but the barrel was pointing at the far wall. To what appeared to be Sir Robert's mutual surprise, Doris had a firm grip on the barrel and had yanked it towards herself, thus directing the shot conveniently away from Bert's internal organs. Toddrick was looming above her prone figure, a machete raised in anticipation.

"Doris," Sir Robert said, finding his voice in the sticky silence. "Would you care to explain what just happened?"

The woman named Doris promptly let go of the rifle, allowing it to drop lifelessly to Sir Robert's lap. A little streamlet of smoke drooled out of the barrel.

"I'm sorry, sir, I'm out of line, sir, but if I may, sir?" Doris replied, her words anxious.

Sir Robert glowered up at her. "I rather expect that you might, Doris, for there is a great deal of explaining needing done."

Bert wriggled like a worm on the ground to curl her legs up to her stomach so she could sort-of fall upwards into a seated position. The rope sawed at her wrists, much to her discomfort, but so long as her skin held firm, she wasn't at risk of an infection.

Doris nodded quickly. "Yes sir, sorry again sir, but sir, our honour, sir."

"Our honour, Doris?"

Bert propped herself up, and Toddrick plopped himself down. They sat side by side, shrugging at each other, equally not a part of the goings on. It was almost as if one of them wasn't just about to machete the bullet-ridden body of the other.

"Our honour, sir, yes, sir. It's true that Bert's deal isn't perfect, but our honour, sir, if I may, we need to think about that. Remember what that Brown did to Lord Ash and the lads? Horrible, it was."

Toddrick, silent until now, murmured low in agreement, his head bowing low. Sir Robert narrowed his eyes.

"If I may speak above my status, sir, I would say we owe it to Lord Ash, and to Henry after him, and to all the rest who died at the Ash Fort, to honour their memory and show that Farmer what good manners looks like. And, if I may be so bold again, sir, what the impolite end of an axe looks like while we're at it."

Toddrick grumbled a "Here, here."

Bert stared deep into Sir Robert's soul, or at least her best guess as to where it might be. She always figured most bandits were just big, black voids filled with devilish goop that sought only to steal and burn, and sometimes fuck, but mostly the first two. So far her perceptions had never been challenged. Not until Doris, anyway.

Something resembling a grumble oozed out of Sir Robert's magnificent moustache. "You're suggesting I risk our entire tribe for dead men, Doris? Men who, might I add, are well and truly gone? We didn't even find all the bits of Henry."

"Exactly, sir, that's what I'm saying. Our own Henry, bless him wherever he might be now, wasn't even buried whole. He's off to whatever afterlife he believed in without both his feet, some of his organs and only three of his eyes. He used to need all five, sir - he'll be blind wherever he is. And Lord Ash begged us for vengeance, sir."

Toddrick sunk lower, giving the impression of one removing one's figurative hat.

"So it's not just for Henry, sir, or Lord Ash. It's for our honour. A chap can't be a chap without his honour."

Sir Robert stared at his lieutenant for a long while, his fuzzy caterpillar (which, in certain parts of the waste, is a highly dangerous insect) twitching back and forth. His fingers drummed on the cracked wooden stock of the rifle, his brow creasing slowly. Then his eyes darted to Toddrick, still sitting in a glum minute of silence.

"Do you agree, Toddrick?"

The man mumbled out a "Yes."

"Hmm."

Sir Robert's gaze fell back on Bert.

He sniffed.

"Do you really believe we could teach that Brown a lesson?"

Bert nodded, for it was the only logical response for self-preservation whether she truly believed it or not. "I do."

"And this new army of yours will be a match for Brown?"

"We'll make sure it is."

"And his truck?"

She felt her eyelid twitch. "Not a problem."

"Well then," Sir Robert replied, gazing once again around the room. "For Lord Ash. For our honor."

Toddrick looked up, and he and Doris responded as one. "For our honor."

Then, a quiet sigh escaped through the dense forest that was Sir Robert's mouth. "So, what next?" His eyebrow arched.

The slightest smile of satisfaction played on Bert's lips, despite her general misgivings about bandits. Bandits or not, this was still a victory - and Bert liked to win. Mind you, her eyelid still trembled, and her upper lip tried curling again at the thought of spending more time in the company of Highway bandits. But her smile was to win the war of facial expressions.

"Well, I need more bandit tribes, if you know of any."

Sir Robert nodded after a moment. "Indeed I do. There's a strong old group down in Dunce Town - moved in after Gren and his Catchfires caught fire. But this new group are, how should I say, less ... polite, than us."

Bert's smile pulled a Catchfires and fizzled off her face. "Less polite?"

"Yes, they have quite the tendency to mutilate, I'm afraid. Bit of a bad habit, I understand. Not quite our style, but then Lord Ash always trained his tribe better than most."

The words 'Breaking News: This is a bad idea, awooga awooga' scrolled past at the bottom of Bert's vision as the war of expressions broke out once again on her face. Her eyebrows put her lids into a chokehold and her lips fought bravely in an all-out brawl against her cheeks, but somehow her voice managed to squirm its way through the throng and croak some level of response before finding itself under a pile of fighting emotions.

"That'll do," it managed. "Let's go get them."

* * *

Another day had passed, and Meatsack still sat hunched in an awkward ball upon his chair. The bar had behaved today, and Meatsack was proud of it. A few hours ago he'd found a giant spider in the bar, but after he pried its fourteen hairy legs off his neck, it had scuttled away into the shadows - sadly, with one fewer leg. All up, though, it had been quite a successfully uneventful day. Berty Bert would be happy. She'd say, "Good job, Meatsack," and it would be true, for he had done a good job, and he was Meatsack.

Now, the big lug rubbed gently at the thick bruises on his grey neck, tapping his feet on the floor nervously. The warm fuzzies of a day's job well done were slipping away as each hour passed, sliding along the floor with the rest of the natural, shadowless daylight. Night was seeping in fast, circling Smack-dab before deciding how to pounce. Darkness bubbled out of dusty corners and snuck its way under chairs and tables, hiding and making angry hissing noises.

Meatsack tapped his feet, vibrations bouncing through the woodwork from the weight. He didn't like the night time, for that was the scariest of all the times. Morning was a good one, but that was when Berty Bert Bert was usually at her grumpiest, and Phoenix was meanest. Meatsack liked mid-afternoon, when everyone was happy, busy and being nice(r) to each other. It was a good time.

Not like right now.

Outside, the sun - behind its wall of clouds - crept silently behind Mount Butt as if slinking out before anybody noticed it. A blanket of shadow inched across the Waste.

Meatsack tapped his feet.

He wished Berty was home. She always made him feel better. She was so nice and kind and loving.

He drummed his fingers on his lap.
It was time to turn the lights on.

* * *

Down the road, Randolf the Conqueror, Ruiner of Worlds, Bringer of Shadows, Lord of Rabbit-Like Kind, was sitting on his furry hind legs sniffing the wind, observing a group of wanderers doing the thing that wanderers tended to do, that is to say, wander. A group of sneep (or 'three' in human language) humans was hasting along, and had noticeably increased in speed somewhere between an hour ago and now, when daylight had quite rudely gone from being a commodity you could take for granted, to being rarer than good personal hygiene. He did not blame them for their frantic pace, for the night was dark and terrible, and not to mention bloody cold.

Randolf the Conqueror, Ruiner of Worlds, Bringer of Shadows, Lord of Rabbit-Like Kind, had been observing the strange human pack for some time, quietly bouncing along the Waste in parallel to them, debating all the while whether or not to strike. He figured his size would be a disadvantage, but one of the humans was old and ragged, one was young and unseasoned, and the final looked like a twig in garish robes. His ferocity could far outmatch any of theirs, but then, there were sneep of them and only snip of him. The numbers were the numbers, and Randolf the Conqueror, Ruiner of Worlds, Bringer of Shadows, Lord of Rabbit-Like Kind simply couldn't deny that, no matter how confident he felt.

So he had simply observed, waiting to see if they would leave the old man behind, as most human packs tended to do eventually. That was when he would close in, and the human's decrepit corpse would be a feast to remember, not to mention a magnificent trophy to take home. Human feet were highly valued in rabbit-like society - they brought good luck, or so it was said.

But it never happened, for despite his extensive years on this planet, the old man seemed determined to keep up with the pack, who must surely have been tired of his age and smell and wrinkliness by now. Or at least that's how it appeared to Randolf the Conqueror, Ruiner of Worlds,

Bringer of Shadows, Lord of Rabbit-Like Kind, anyway, who admittedly was not an expert in human society. His fifteenth sister, Freydis, was far better at that sort of thing, and he silently wished he hadn't eaten her years before. She'd be quite useful now that he was a Conqueror, Ruiner of Worlds, Bringer of Shadows and a Lord. But anyway, that was another matter, and there was no time for regret in the Waste.

A chill wind washed in from the ocean, bringing with it a significant drop in temperature. Randolf the Conqueror, Ruiner of Worlds, Bringer of Shadows, Lord of Rabbit-Like Kind, hunkered down into the folds of his fur, shivering to himself as he observed the group grow closer to the rickety human structure, which now lit up in a brilliant spectacle of ugly yellow light. It appeared that his prey was going to go inside, which meant they would be temporarily unavailable for feasting. A disappointing result, to be sure, but there were always ants and other unlucky creatures around to consume in the meantime.

Randolf the Conqueror, Ruiner of Worlds, Bringer of Shadows, Lord of Rabbit-Like Kind, could wait.

And wait he would.

* * *

Finally, Jeb took the trio's lead and walked through Orsen and Lorry to be out front. Three triumphant heroes were returning after a long adventure, and Jeb felt he was the triumphantest. At the very least, he was the one with all the money, which was essentially the same thing.

Smack-dab rose above them like a brilliant wooden totem, a precious holy icon dedicated to the god of grog. It was a little sad that the icon of Smack-dab was so slanty, but then it was said that some of the humans in the Old World built towers made of pizza, and that those towers were never straight. So who knew when it came to Old World structures - most traders, Jeb included, just accepted that dems da facts, and Smack-dab is as Smack-dab leans.

All around the group, night was circling in. Small, rolling hills were growing into towering, ominous bulges, tiny shrubs and grasses morphed into vicious spike pits in the dust, and any movement that could not be immediately identified as either Jeb, Orsen or Lorry was filed under "Run Away From". The Back Road was swiftly becoming a dark and most foreboding of places, and only the very brave, very foolish, or very, very unlucky would be caught out without a light or shelter.

But here stood Smack-dab, a veritable beacon of sanctuary for hungry, thirsty, frightened travellers. Its hideous yellow lights could be seen spilling ungainly over the horizon for miles around, and although they flickered and threatened to explode almost every night, the bar's floodlight system regularly, if not confidently, provided a magnificent barrier of light between food, grog, and sleep, and the Things that lay beyond.

And now three weary travellers - the teacher, the pupil, and the one that paid to be there - were enveloped in this glorious bastion of sickly yellow. Jeb took point to blaze a trail up Smack's gravel pathway, with Orsen in the middle and Lorry in the back, eyeing up the two-storey building with open cynicism. As Jeb mounted the first creaking planks of the front porch, he turned back over his shoulder and grinned wide.

"Wait til' ya get a load o' this, Lorry," he announced cheerfully. "Best bar in the Waste."

Lorry sneered in response, distrust apparent over her frowning, narrow-eyed expression. "Is it always this quiet?"

"Huh?" Jeb replied, his happiness faltering. He glanced back at the bar, which, quite noticeably, was devoid of any of the more classic Smack-dab noises, such as laughing, fighting, or Bert yelling. He scratched at his travel-weary face and pondered for a moment. "I, uh, I'm sure it's just one o' those quiet nights. It'll prolly pick up soon."

"In the middle of the night?" An eyebrow, one of two dangerous blades on Lorry's face that, coincidentally, was also pierced with dangerous blades, rose sharply.

Jeb laughed nervously. "Aye, well, maybe not soon soon, but ya know, soon. Like, soonish. Hey, you alright, Orsen?"

This last comment was directed at the young lad, who was staring in horror at the tall statue of a woman loitering in the middle of Smack's lawn. She grimaced openly at the Waste, long coat billowing out behind her, wide-brimmed hat blocking Smack-dab's embrace of light so that her face was cast in a dark shadow. But she looked ... different, to what Jeb remembered. Orsen carefully crouched down and fondled a disembodied arm at The Woman's feet, touching it with the delicacy normally reserved for things you expect to touch back.

"Oh no," Jeb whispered, the significance of this amputation dawning on his face at about the speed of, well, of dawn, actually. "Did ya break Th' Woman's statue, Orsen? Oh my sweet mercy, what 'ave I told ya about touchin' it?!" He started towards the boy.

Orsen looked up suddenly. "I didn't break it, I swears, Jeb! It was like this when I got here."

Jeb was practically leaping off the porch, now, moving to intercept Orsen before he could cause any more damage. "Don't lie t' me, lad! That statue is never anythin' other than pristin– *bloody hell don't pick it up!*"

The boy squeaked with the sudden rebuke, releasing the long arm from his skinny fingers. Pistol in hand, the arm fell quickly to The Woman's feet and promptly slammed into the dirt in a little cloud of shadowy dust. Orsen's face was bleached white.

"Oh for the love of–" Jeb said, flinching wildly back as gravity had its way. "You can't just drop The Woman's arm like that!"

Orsen gasped an "Oh no" and stooped to pick it up again.

"Oh mercy *don't pick it up again!*"

He dropped it out of his fingers.

"*And stop dropping it!*" Jeb's voice was quickly ascending in both pitch and panic.

Behind them, one hand on her narrow hips, Lorry shook her head with a *Tch* noise and scowled at the pair. Sometimes, although she would rarely openly admit it, but sometimes she questioned the choices of Gachook, Our Lord and Saviour. She understood that humans were like germs and had to be almost eradicated in order to evolve, but the one per cent that survived the initial wrath of His Seven Deadly Chickens was at times ... odd. It felt like the Gachookian theory of only the strongest and the smartest surviving was put to the test far too often in this horrible, dusty land. But then, who was she, just a simple human mortal - one of the germs - to question the will and the word of Gachook, Our Lord and Saviour? It was blasphemy of the highest order.

No, Jeb and Orsen, however stupid they might seem on the surface, and quite possibly deeper beneath as well if Lorry was to be the judge, must have had some kind of redeeming feature, or else Gachook, Our Lord and Saviour, would not have ordained to let their ancestors live. Maybe they were particularly skilled at, at, oh Lorry didn't know, probably whistling, or something like that.

Well anyway, she decided that, regardless of their suspected whistling prowess, it was time to leave them to their pointless bickering over a false stone idol – that Gachook, Our Lord and Saviour, would probably crush soon anyway – and go spread His word to whatever backwater scum inhabited this particular establishment. So, she spun on her heels, marched straight up the path onto the porch, and reached for the front door. Her face composed itself, and she prepared the opening dialogue to one of her favourite sermons, simply titled: *"Have you got a minute? Oh good, well let me tell you about your salvation, your holy protector, and the answer to all your problems, Gachook, Our Lord and Saviour"*.

Lorry turned the door handle and sucked in a confident breath.

"Praise be to Gachook, Our Lord and Saviour, for He has sent His follower to– hang on a second..." Lorry paused, turning the handle again and again and pushing gently at the door.

It wouldn't budge.

She scowled at this sudden trial from Gachook, Our Lord and Saviour, but steeled herself. No mere door would undo the great work she was yet to do, but soon would do, and would do extraordinarily well so long as the ruddy door opened. Her fingers grasped at the handle again, turned it appropriately, and then she put a little shoulder into the action.

Still, the door wouldn't budge.

"Oh you've got to be fu–"

"Havin' trouble?" Jeb asked, springing in out of nowhere. The debate about the arm seemed to have ended precisely where it started, except now the faces were a little paler and the arm a little dirtier.

Lorry turned on him like a Waste Beast suddenly noticing someone is there at the same time it suddenly noticed it was hungry. Her tall, spear-like figure towered over the shorter, hunched man, her many piercings sparkling yellow in the barrier of light.

"You damn old fool!" she roared, seeming even taller and angrier and more pierced. "It's locked!"

Jeb blinked. "Locked?

"Locked! You dragged me all this way to preach at a bar that isn't even open!"

"But ... but," Jeb stammered in disbelief. Smack-dab was never shut! Open all hours, that's what was written on the big roof sign. Jeb glanced quickly upwards for reassurance, but was met with no such sign. OK, he quickly thought, maybe that's not what's written on the roof, but it's what's *unwritten*, just like all the best Waste laws. Like 'Don't get caught at night without a light or shelter', or 'Don't pick a fight with the Overlords', and 'Don't trust when a man-shaped figure made entirely of bees comes to your door.'

Lorry was storming off back down the path when Jeb managed to fight his way through the immense confusion and back into Nowland. With her long, leggy stride - like a pissed-off giraffe, an animal that somehow still existed, but not in Can't Be Buried - she was hurriedly approaching the end of the yellow barrier.

"I followed you for two fucking days!" she screamed.

"Wait, Lorry!" cried Orsen, skipping down the path after her. "You can't go out into the night!"

"Piss off you stupid little boy," Lorry yelled back, her feet breaching the invisible yellow wall that separated certain death from Smack-dab's less-certain death.

Jeb shuffled after Orsen, who had already arrived at the edge of safety but hesitated at the precipice. "Lorry, wait!" Jeb shouted. "It's too dangerous out there! Smacks bein' shut is prolly just a misunderstandin', it'll open up soon!"

Lorry's figure was hungrily enveloped in the Waste's nightmarish shroud of darkness. Tendrils of black eagerly wrapped themselves around her as she stormed back up the Back Road.

"Gachook will protect me!" Jeb and Orsen heard as her slender figure vanished completely. Then slightly after: "And he'll do a damn site better job than you idiots ever could."

And then she was gone. Blackness took her, and around here it rarely spat people back out.

Jeb glanced at Orsen, who glanced nervously back. Their feet perfectly lined up with the edge of the light, but neither was brave enough to step over. They just stood and stared, mouths agape, eyes perfect circles, peering into the nothingness in case somethingness peered back.

A tense moment passed with only the wind breaking up the ambience. Then, Orsen shivered.

"Will Gachook really protect her, Jeb?" he asked, his voice barely a peep.

Jeb stared hard into the night, searching for any sign that Lorry was coming to her senses and returning. When no such sign waved back, he let out a long, slow, icy breath. "If I knows anythin' 'bout them religious types," he muttered, "not a chance."

Part Six

When in Trouble, When in Doubt...

Freddy and his sister Fredina, whose three and a half parents were more imaginative with a knife than names for children, felt they were good bandits. Certainly, their outfit had all the classic bandit bells and whistles, except they had been ordered to remove most of them because it was too noisy when sneaking up on unsuspecting victims. But their prowess at standing on one spot and looking at things for hours was unmatched, and not just because Freddy and Fredina were two heads sharing a single body, either. They had practiced standing in one spot and staring at things for hours their entire life, ever since their parents had abandoned them at Dunce Town years ago. Since then, Freddy and Fredina had decided to keep an eye out for their parents' eventual, though clearly unfortunately and unintentionally delayed, return.

But, their parents had yet to do so, and so Freddy and his dear sister Fredina had taken up banditing to pass the time. They hadn't even noticed that the Catchfires were gone and some new lot had moved in, because it didn't matter. They just stood on the spot and stared at things, and occasionally attacked a trader when asked.

"Flur ehnyhlur sher?" asked Fredina, a small amount of drool pooling at the edge of her protruding tongue. She had never been the same since their triplet head, Frederous, had been forcefully removed by a trader's bodyguard not two years back.

"Not so far, sister, but I'm still looking." replied Freddy.

"Niiigh high oh."

"Yeah, lovely night. Bit chilly, though."

"Hrmm."

"Mmm."

* * *

Sir Robert, crouching low behind a ragged wooden fence, motioned for the group to stop. And they did, all coming to a halt in a similarly crouched pile stretching the length of the fence down the road a ways. Bert was second behind him, with Doris behind her and then everyone else, with Toddrick bringing up the rear (which someone had teased him about earlier, much to his embarrassment). Sir Robert's elegant face, normally the pinnacle of politeness and pleasantry, had drawn stern and still. Even his moustache had stopped waving in the wind. Bert watched intently as the man popped his head up over the fence, briefly scanned the immediate area, then popped back down to ponder, growing sterner.

They were just outside Dunce Town. The Polite Bandits had approached from the north, leaving the road a few minutes earlier to pick up a side trail that ran parallel into town. It was dark as hell without any source of light, but they couldn't afford to get spotted on the way into town – or so Bert was warned. So, she had allowed Sir Robert to lead her and the band to this small side street, where a few Old World houses still remained ... more or less.

Impatient, Bert popped up as well, peeking over the top of the rotten fence to see what was going on nearby. Not far away, a wide figure with what appeared to be two heads and one neck stump was standing in the middle of the Highway between two Old World signs marking the edge of town. The figure occasionally spoke with itself in quiet tones, but mostly just stared up the Highway. The landscape was masked in the night's thick, inky black, but a distinct orange glow hovered above Dunce Town somewhere deeper in the settlement, and smaller yellow lights pockmarked the perimeter, including where the wide figure with the heads and stump now stood. Dunce Town didn't look like it was too different to when Bert had last passed through years before, but then, she couldn't really make much out to particularly tell.

Bert peered over the fence and stared into the black. "So if we're attacking these guys at night, at what point will they stop and join the fight against Brown?"

Sir Robert, barely visible in the darkness, looked as though his lips creased upwards. "Quite frankly, my dear, that's why we're attacking them."

"Eh?" Bert did not have the patience or the trust in Sir Robert to get messed around. Her human hand felt its way towards the chill handle of her pistol, which they had quite ungraciously handed back to her. It only took a fist fight and some yelling. "Explain."

He did. Sir Robert explained how relations between the Polite Bandits and their Dunce Town counterparts had, well, "broken down" was the term he used rather carefully. The "Impolite Bandits" were notoriously violent and their leader infamously short-tempered, not to mention hideously ugly - like a rotten apple with one misshapen eye carved out the front of it, or that's how Sir Robert described him. To simply march into town and demand a parlay, though it would work for the Polite Bandits, in this particular case would likely result in Bert and Co. getting assailed on all sides by ravenous madmen with axes and whatnot who were both curious and enthusiastic to see what human internal organs looked like. Indeed, negotiating for peace, as simple as it may seem, was so far off the table, it was out the door, down the road, getting on a boat to sail across the ocean and then being eaten by a carnivorous blue whale as a light snack. All in all, it was not going to happen.

"So what are we here for, then?" Bert asked with a harsh whisper. She had to put all her emotion into her voice, because she wasn't sure if Sir Robert would see her glare. "I need allies, not corpses."

"Ah you see, Berty, that brings me to the brilliant scheme I have devised." He sounded cocky, which Bert wasn't comfortable with. She just needed this nightmare to be over. To be back at Smack-dab, kicking Farmer Brown in the face so that she could open up business again, forget he ever existed, and go back to surviving. Was that so much to ask?

"We're going to use an unwritten bandit law, Berty," Sir Robert continued. "You see, everybody knows that should someone challenge a bandit chief to a singular and most bloody of combats, he or she, or it - I won't assume, Gren wasn't human after all."

"That's probably why he caught fire," added Doris.

"Yes indeed, quite probably, Doris. Anyway, he or she or it must accept the combat immediately and see it through to the finish, which might I expand on, is typically death. Should the challenger win, then to the victor go the spoils, however spoiled they may be. And so you see, with just a moderate amount of violence to which we are all accustomed anyway, one can easily assume control of the Dunce Town bandits and save our energy on words. Which, might I remind you, will not work on this occasion."

Bert flexed her robotic fingers slowly as she dissected the information. "So you're saying, all we need to do is kill the leader and then the rest of the tribe will follow us?"

"Almost, Berty," Sir Robert chuckled patronisingly. "One individual from our side must officially challenge him first, *then* we can kill him and take his tribe."

Well, Bert thought, I've certainly heard *worse* plans. And violence wasn't exactly something foreign to a pacifist like Bert. You didn't get to call yourself a pacifist without understanding how to fight and shoot and yell, because usually you needed one or more of those in order to remind someone just how much of a pacifist you really were. And considering the amount of stragglers, hagglers and other distasteful sorts she'd had to throw out of Smack-dab (literally), what was one more little fight?

"Of course," Sir Robert said again, "a volunteer will need to challenge the chief. And it won't be a, err, civil fight, shall we say."

Bert curled her robotic hand into a tight fist now, staring at it. She listened for the satisfying sound of whirring motors functioning as whirring motors should. "I'll do it."

"Are you sure?" Sir Robert's eyebrows looked raised, or maybe it was just his general forehead wrinkles, it was hard to tell in amongst all the black. "He's a little, hmm. How would you describe him, Doris?"

"Meaty, sir," she replied, smiling sweetly (presumably).

"Yes, wonderful little word. He's meaty, Bert. I think it would be best if someone like myself were to give it a right old go. I've got a bit more experience in both combat and leadership, you understand."

Bert frowned as the haunting figure of Farmer Brown stomped across her brain. Now there was a man who you could describe as meaty. Hell, there was a man who you could describe as the entire bloody cattle farm. She'd never truly consider someone else meaty again, not after an encounter with Farmer Brown.

Her pistol felt cool and comforting in her human hand. Bert knew she was small, especially compared to the hulking great giants that plagued Can't Be Buried. She was toned, sure, even a little muscular, but small of stature. She couldn't tower or loom; her physical presence didn't impose or intimidate. If she walked into a room full of strangers, nobody would so much as notice she was there. That is, not until she opened her mouth and let it be known that Bert had arrived. For if she had one thing, it was her brains. She was sharp, sharper than any axe or whatnot. And quick, too.

161

Maybe not ludicrously so, but quick enough. You only ever needed to be quick enough in the Waste. Never the best, only better. And, most importantly, Bert had one thing that nobody else in the Waste had. She was fuelled on some deep, primal level by sheer, unbridled, terrifying Bertrage. In her mind, that was far superior to any slab of steely muscle slapped onto a dim-witted giant.

"It's my bar," she stated firmly, "and I'll be the one to challenge this chief."

Doris and Sir Robert exchanged a look that suggested they didn't wholly agree. But it was nowhere near as powerful as the determined expression etched into Bert's face.

"Err, are you sure, my dear? I really would advise that you let me take the bullet, as it were," Sir Robert tried. "Not literally of course, because I intend to win."

Bert swung her chilling sapphire stare at Sir Robert and hoped that the darkness wouldn't dare block it. Her blood was already filling with the adrenalin necessary for a full-on Bertrage, and her mind raced with potential strategies for taking down a monster. Hell, it might even be good practice for killing Brown.

Sir Robert opened his mouth to say something else, but awkwardly shut it under the pressure of the gaze. Not even the Waste night could stop Bert's sapphire fire.

Bert wasn't allowing herself to trust Sir Robert just yet. Especially not with the keys to a whole new tribe. The relationship had gotten off to a bad start, and not just because he was a bandit. No matter how good their manners seemed on the outside, Bert had to remember that if Sir Robert's diminished horde were suddenly bolstered by fresh, violent "madmen", there was no telling what he might do, particularly if he felt he had sufficient numbers to challenge Brown head-on without the need for Smack-dab to be involved. She'd lose her army, Sir Robert would probably still get crushed, and she'd be back to square one - which, she most definitely didn't need to remind herself, involved her pretty little head ending up somewhere it shouldn't.

No, she would be the one to defeat the meaty chief. It would be her tribe, her battalion. Bert's Battalion. Hey, that had a nice ring to it...

Bert drew her pistol and clutched it tight. "What are we waiting for? Let's get this over with."

* * *

Phoenix smiled widely as the unicorn approached him. He was relaxing, sitting casually in a vast field of emerald green grass, its millions of dewy blades gently swaying to inaudible funky beats as waves of wind wafted gently through the scene. Phoenix's adventuring gear lay strewn care-free across the lawn, the man himself bare-naked, feeling the cool, wet blades on his tired skin. Mr Pumpernickel had just left to go get some fizzy drinking water from the magic stream up the hill a ways, which was absolutely fine with Phoenix – more unicorn for him.

It was the most perfect of perfect days. The smog was a brilliant, luminous blue above him, stretching to infinity in all directions, and the birds were twittering in perfect harmony, singing one of his favourite Waste tunes, '*Why Does Radiation Do This To Me?*'. But Phoenix had to admit that, despite the sheer perfectivity of the day, it was somewhat mired by the incessant thumping in his head.

The ache had started as a dull pressure in the back of his skull, but while Mr Pumpernickel was discussing his theories on particle physics and how to repair the Waste with an army of pixies – which, Phoenix felt, was quite probably the very cause of the ache – it had grown into a significant throbbing. Now it held an almost tribal rhythm, booming and clattering through his skull like, well, like an army of pixies.

Boom.

Boom boom.

Phoenix twitched. But he wasn't about to let this terrific day go to waste. Pain be damned! He reached out calmly with his muscular, hairy arm and gently beckoned for the unicorn to come closer. It was such a splendid beast, he couldn't help but want to stroke its glorious white scales, and feel one of its four muzzles nuzzle his palm in that adorable unicorny way.

Boom boom.

Boom.

Its mane was a glittering star field, streaking out behind the unicorn's long, snake-like necks as though it were the tail of a spectacular, interstellar comet. Its duck-like webbed feet trotted almost silently on the fresh grass as the beast moved towards Phoenix on its six insect legs.

Boom.

Boom boom.

Phoenix thought he could hear chanting now; the voices of many people gathered in one place. It was a distant echo, almost insignificant, except for the fact that it was growing louder, and coming from the unicorn's many nostrils.

Boom boom.

Boom.

The beast was close, now. Phoenix could feel its perfumed breath wafting over him with each of its slow, hot breaths. He leaned forwards to place a hand on its nearest head, but the unicorn hesitated.

"It's OK, buddy," Phoenix cooed softly, letting it sniff him first. "I won't hurt ya."

Its heads all looked at him with the innocent scrutiny of an animal contemplating bite or flight, then it whinnied, and its voice was an orchestra of cosmic sounds swirling around Phoenix's head in the voice of a thousand microscopic bagpipes. And the bagpipes all produced the same words.

"Constellator. Constellator. Constellator."

Boom.

Boom boom.

Suddenly Phoenix was on an altar, bound by rope at his hands, ankles, torso and even neck. Sweat formed on his naked flesh as he struggled and panicked, desperately trying to free himself from this insufferable bondage so he could stroke the unicorn, which was now standing on its hind legs some distance away. He saw it fold its insect arms across its chiselled, muscular chest, reaching down with its second set of arms to scratch at … oh, what was that dangling by its knees?

…oh.

Phoenix woke up.

Immediately, his senses were ambushed by booming and chanting, ramping the pain in his head from feeling like being hit with a hammer to a searing atomic explosion. His vision swam in front of his eyes, but it didn't know any good techniques so mostly it just splashed about unfocused and crying for help. It seemed pitch-black, but Phoenix could make out vague orange-tinted waves above him as the smog continued to fight amongst itself. Groaning, Phoenix tried to reach up with his hand to massage the battlefield that was his skull, but his arms wouldn't move. For that matter, none of his body was free.

The bondage wasn't a dream.

He was on an altar, so that too wasn't a dream. It was a giant concrete slab of a thing, bitterly cold on whatever bare skin touched it, but brilliantly smooth - as though someone had kept it polished, which was unusual in the Waste. Keeping things was not as easy as acquiring them. Phoenix took a few long, deep breaths and pushed away thoughts of what goes between a unicorn's legs, wracking his brain to do something useful. He tried to think like an adventurer.

Every hero ended up in a position like this some time or another. It just went with the territory. Sometimes it was an altar, other times it was a roasting spit above a fire. One time it was even a leather and chain swing hanging in the bedroom of a- actually, you know what? Phoenix had opted into that one, so it didn't count. Anyway, after some careful, scientific wriggle checks, he determined that his ankles, hands, torso and neck were all bound. His hands and neck already burned from the constant rubbing of old, wet, bacterial rope on bare skin, and his back and ass were debating between feeling either completely numb or excruciatingly painful. Phoenix had apparently being lying here some time. This, to the initiated, possibly meant that the evening was going to be one of those ceremonial drags-out-for-ages type of ordeals, or else he'd be dead already. To the uninitiated, of course, it just meant, "Oh, my back and butt are a bit more painful than usual. I wonder if someone will free me soon..."

The booming and chanting continued to wheel around Phoenix's head, a vicious noise that seemed more intent to punch his brain through his ears than to maintain any semblance of musical timing. It was a drum

165

beat, of this he could determine now, or at least it was many drum beats all happening in a vaguely similar time frame, but not quite all at once as was presumably the idea. At least the chanting was doing well - everyone seemed to have the knack for saying the name of their lord in a perfect, creepy unison.

"Constellator. Constellator. Constellator."

Boom

Boom boom

Phoenix flinched as a particularly loud thump passed through his ear drum with all the grace of a brick to the face. "Hey," he yelled, "could you guys keep it down? I'm trying to come back from unconsciousness here."

Nobody heard him.

Blah, he thought. Visual check next.

He tried turning his neck as best he could, pushing through the nauseating dizziness that threatened to drown him in his own vomit. He realised that he had some limited side-to-side motion available. With great pain and effort, he rolled his head to the right.

Cultists. Everywhere. All over the damn place. They were in some kind of hilltop square at the peak of Mount Butt, or what at least appeared to be the peak in amongst the crushing blackness that was the Waste night. White-speckled cultists were crammed together in a wide arc surrounding him to the right, and through the bobbing, hooded heads he could see that the thick throng continued a ways down the hill, too. The Starry Place lay beyond, with a veritable skyscape of twinkling lights marking the winding little streets of the cramped town. They were electric lights, Phoenix could discern, but they were dim, perhaps meant only for discouraging Things more so than for navigation. That was fairly common, particularly in Can't Be Buried where electric infrastructure was as limited as humans that lived past fifty years. It was easier at night to bump into objects hazardously placed at shin height (as was always the case) than to find the means to run high-power street lights for an entire town. None of the house lights were on as far as Phoenix could make out, which suggested that the whole starry population was up here at the square. But then, Phoenix thought the entire mountain was writhing and rolling like a fuzzy caterpillar on an unstable boat, so who knows what was going on. His woozy head clearly didn't.

To his left was the more interesting stuff. Phoenix could make out a tall, long building built around some kind of metal Old World structure; a veritable mansion compared to the small-statured huts present in the rest of the Starry Place. Thick wisps of pale smoke dribbled out of the gaps around its ornately decorated double-doored entrance, and an avenue of star-shaped flaming lanterns guarded a cobble-stone path from there to where Phoenix now lay. Interestingly, out of the right-hand side of this large structure came two cables higher than a man's height, each of which slinked off into the Starry Place below. Chairs hung precariously from the thick metal cables at regular intervals, some of which seemed cushioned and designed with safety in mind, and the rest ... well, you'd be clinging for dear life if you sat on one, let's just say that.

Standing either side of the star-covered double doors were cultists with similarly tassled spears as the gate guardians, their faces shrouded in shadow. Nearer Phoenix, a small group of robed cultists had split off from the main mass. One he recognised as a perpetrator from Smack-dab, whose face was grumpy and his arm missing. In his other hand he clutched a long wooden bat, a stain of blood still congealing on its wider end. Blood that Phoenix thought might have come from his beautiful head.

There were two other figures next to the one-armed Batty McHitsYouFromBehindLikeaCoward. One was a slender woman who grasped a metal bugle tightly in her fingers and tapped her feet anxiously. The final figure, standing next to a tall stone table upon which was a small, shiny wooden box, was an older man, hunched at the shoulders and tattooed extraordinarily heavily with stars, comets and wavy lines. The lines might once have been connected, indicating whooshy little movements, but the onslaught of age on the man's face and driven vast faults through the art. He was, most assuredly, the human equivalent of a sultana.

BOOM BOOM.

BOOM BOOM BOOM.

The thumping clamour of drumming increased in enthusiasm (but not skill), and the crowd started to lose its perfect harmony. Excitement washed quickly through the buzz and folks appeared no longer able to quietly chant, instead screaming wildly the name of their lord, whistling and hollering. They may as well have sawed off the top of Phoenix's skull and yelled straight into his brain goop, for what it was doing to his head. Phoenix writhed on the altar, eyes tight shut, begging whatever gods he could think of for the noise to end. Somehow, though, he didn't think Gachook had jurisdiction in this town.

Then, smoke around the ornate closed doorway started sputtering out in thicker clumps, clawing its way quicker through the gaps and spilling into the sky to join the roiling smog above, which must have been like Valhalla to smoke.

BOOM BOOM.

BOOM BOOM BOOM.

BOOM.

...

...

The drumming had stopped.

The crowd followed suit.

An eager hush fell upon the landscape, with barely a murmur escaping into the bitter night air. All eyes were glued to the wafts of white smoke pouring out this strange door. More importantly, though, Phoenix watched as the shrivelled old man near the altar carefully opened the wooden box next to him and produced what could only be described as a dagger - not a knife, but a bloody dagger. Its gilded handle was brilliantly polished, with perfect star shapes carved into the glittering metal. The blade itself rose plump from the hilt, as though it had seen a long, happy life of consuming many an altar victim. It sparkled as a mixture of electric and fire light danced off the flat blade. The decrepit old man held it with barely a withered finger and thumb in each hand, a satisfied smile playing between the deep wrinkles of his crusty face. This was a man who knew his duty was important, and relished in every second.

Phoenix was glued to the blade, his mouth forming an O and his eyes wide open.

Sometimes, he thought to himself, I hate it when I'm right.

* * *

Terrance Leeland wandered alone, cold, and in a seething fury. His stump arm ached with every throb of his pulsating, dark heart, and his mind raced with the brutal images of just how he'd enact his bloody revenge on Bert and that hideous grey mutant. Oh how he'd tear them apart, both figuratively and literally. He'd savour every moment, enjoy it till the last drop fell to the floorboards and Smack-dab was no more.

Night had swooped in quickly, leaving Terrance alone and with minimal protection along the darkened Back Road to Smack-dab. After his insufferable defeat at the hands of the obnoxious, incompetent Phoenix, he had departed east, off the road, and wandered aimlessly into the Waste, considering suicide. To many it might seem an extreme measure, but Terrance was supposed to be a hero, a veteran adventurer who had saved the day more times than half the population of Can't Be Buried had even seen fucking days. But yet, everywhere he turned, not only did people not know who he was, they didn't care. They didn't care that the Sandcastle was gone, because another fort had sprung up in its place. They didn't care about how he quelled the riots on Bank Island, because Bank Island was just a place where mountains grew and sometimes people with money went - it didn't affect their daily lives. All of Terrance's stories were other people's problems, not theirs. And now, to top off years of misery and a complete lack of the fame he deserved, he had lost a battle to the most ridiculous bar in the entire Waste.

Bastards.

But as he staggered along the unkempt, winding trails that networked between the Back Road and the Highway, he came upon a young land seal bathing on a large, flat rock. It had glanced up at him, jet-black eyes searching him for signs of threat. Well, they had certainly found one, and after Terrance had disembowelled the blubberous, stumpy-legged creature for its fat, meat, and skin, an older land seal had sprung out of the nearby weeds and assailed him from behind.

The battle was long, vicious, and would have been a total embarrassment had anyone been watching. The land seal fought bravely, but clumsily, using its rows of sharp fangs and the bulbous fat claws of its square legs to slash and tear at Terrance's skin and clothing. But there's only so graceful a fat, inelegant creature once designed for aquatic combat can fight on land. Terrance, despite having lost a significant amount of blood and having only one hand, wrestled the beast to the floor and strangled the life out of it. And then as he sat, breathing hard, resting his head on its bloodied, pudgy rolls of fur and fat, it planted a seed in his brain.

A seed of revenge.

If a land seal, just a stupid Old World creature that got scared of some water, could muster up the courage to seek vengeance on those who would do its family wrong, Terrance could surely do the same to Smack-dab. Surely that was the hidden message in all of this? The sign that some Waste deity was trying to tell him. Well, whether it was a sign, luck, or just the complete unravelling of Terrance's sanity, he decided that the world was telling him to march back to Smack-dab and obliterate it. Wipe it completely from existence.

And so he had marched to Second Thought, purchased himself a new gun (one-handed, of course, but with an extended magazine and a scope, because he was still an adventurer and adventurers need big) and begun the trek back to the worst bar in Can't Be Buried.

Now it was night time, and he was climbing as best he could into the ruins of an Old World house. He had a small electric lantern dangling from his belt, casting a timid glow around most of his body to help him navigate the dangerous rubble and shards of the structure. Soon it revealed an empty, small space that may once have been a bedroom, a rotten chest of drawers still standing to one side, caving in on itself on one half. The drawers were long gone, though, so to be honest it was mostly just a chest of space.

Terrance kicked at the thing until it broke apart, giving him enough shrapnel to build a fire. He did so, but not without considerable effort on account of ... *the problem*. After some time, a small orange blaze danced to its own tune in the centre of the room, painting Terrance's face with a low-lit, dangerous shadow. He stared into it, face creasing with the deep wrinkles of anger, eyes blazing from the reflection of the flame.

And he did what all would do in his situation; a man plotting horrible murder whilst in equally horrible pain himself.

He brooded.

* * *

Freddy and his sister Fredina stopped what had now become quite a heated argument about worldly beauty, and listened. There was an insect somewhere in the darkness, a species that neither had heard before. Fredina was quite an avid entomologist and was curious about the development, though Freddy hated the horrible little beasties. His cheek was bitten by a fuzzy caterpillar once, and the scar never healed properly.

Quite unexpectedly, a metal pipe lunged out of the shadow and clocked Fredina straight in the temple, knocking her out instantly. She slumped to the side, bumping Freddy on the way down, who jumped, startled at the sudden commotion. Panic filled his mind as thoughts of losing another one of his sibling heads gusted through his imagination, while a host of armed figures materialised from the crushing black night. His panic soon curdled, souring to an intense rage. Rage that someone would try to take his family away from him while he was out here waiting for more of his family to come back.

The mass that was now just Freddy turned to face his immediate attacker: a three-armed, tall bandit wielding a bloodied metal pipe. The figure was taking cautious steps backwards, presumably realising that his efforts at knocking out Freddy and Fredina was somewhat complicated by the victim having two heads in need of knocking.

Without a second thought (literally, considering Fredina's situation), Freddy fingered a large metal horn at his belt and hurriedly unclipped it. He brought the ugly, twisted shape up to his lips and sucked in a mighty breath before something flashed in the corner of his vision and then struck him in the skull, just like his sister.

His vision swam for a moment, spots forming where spots never used to be, and spots dissolving where spots used to be. Then he saw a short, angry-looking woman with a chunky metal fist pulling back for a second swing, which came for his face.

Then everything went black for Freddy.

* * *

Bert quietly wiped her metal knuckles with a piece of her clothing as the Polite Bandits snuffed out the mutant's light and proceeded into town. The night pressed in all around them, oppressing Bert's senses as though she were standing in a small, cramped cupboard. Occasionally someone would flicker a light on and off to check the route, but mostly the Polite Bandits walked softly through the darkness.

They came in through the main road, but soon split off into multiple small groups as they approached closer to the middle of Dunce Town. Bert was partnered with three low-level bandits, each of which were far too scared of Bert to dare take command of the group - which was fine by her. Bandits were a lot more pleasant to be around when they were being crushed under her heel.

As the groups parted, skulking off between derelict houses and bedraggled streets, their members used nondescript insect noises to communicate relative positioning. From Bert's guess, she was close by to maybe two other groups, and the rest were arcing around the orange glow to flank from the other side.

The town itself would have been considered small even by Old World standards, and though Bert couldn't see much right now, she remembered bits and bobs from her prior travels through here. The houses were reasonably sized with plentiful garden space around them, and the streets were nice and wide - perhaps because neighbours didn't want to be too near each other? Bert could only guess. Except of course now it was all ruined, and only the skeletal remains of the reasonably sized houses persevered through dust storms, acid rain, and the general wear and tear that comes with existing in the Waste. The wrecks of cars littered roads and old driveways, but most of even those were gone now, long picked clean by roving bandits, scavengers, and passing scrap merchants (who were arguably all of the above).

In a deafening silence, Bert and her three lackeys crept from wall to wall, fence to fence, slowly closing in on the orange glow, which was now accompanied by the muffled sounds of laughter. An insect nearby revealed that another cell of Polite Bandits was pushing out to the left, to which Bert's insect responded by saying they were going to proceed straight into the glow from here.

Then she heard a scuffle somewhere nearby, and she hissed at her companions to stop. They froze in place, crouched low behind the corpse of an old minivan, straining to hear anything above their own breathing. Footsteps crunched dust nearby, approaching slowly from the direction of the glow. Bert narrowed her eyes and focused, trying not to let her robotic hand move for fear that the whirring might alert the passer-by. Carefully, she craned her neck up and glanced through a hollow window in the van's side, peering hard into the murk. Against the slight orange tint ahead, she could just make out a muscular shape coming closer, straight for the van. It walked with caution, taking long, slow footsteps with what might have been a weapon of some description clutched tightly in its fingers.

Bert let out a very soft, very slow breath and strained her muscles to keep from moving, sensing that the minions next to her were doing the same. The silhouette came right up next to the van, on the other side of it from Bert, and appeared to make one final glance left and right.

She narrowed her eyes.

Then heard a zipping sound.

Oh for the love of-, she thought.

The sound of liquid hitting metal filled the bitter air, a small grunt of satisfaction emanating from the shadowy figure. Bert gritted her teeth as the silhouette relieved itself on her hiding place, listening to the inconsistent stream reveal what must have been a disappointing struggle. The liquid splashed out in quick bursts, not a steady stream by any means, and the man grumbled at it to hurry up.

For a solid ten or so seconds Bert and her minions crouched in absolute stillness as events unfolded, but Bert could feel her patience wearing thin - particularly as the noxious smell of ammonia, must, and rotten pus swept up from the van and invaded her nostrils. She almost gagged from the smell.

Then, it ended. The man breathed a final sigh of relief, cursed the name of what Bert presumed was a previous sexual partner, and then zipped up.

He marched away a lot quicker than he came, half-jogging to get back to where there was better light. And silence resumed.

Bert heard three breaths released all around her, and someone snigger quietly. She turned to shoot the bandit a look, then realised he probably wouldn't see and relegated herself to reprimanding him at a later date.

And so they continued onwards.

More insect noises stated that the Polite Bandit's noose was beginning to tighten, with each group closing in on the orange glow. A chill wind whistled through the open streets, coughing up whorls of dust and discarded food scraps into Bert's wincing face. It chittered and cackled as it shook the ragged corpse buildings of Dunce Town, carrying with it the sound of hearty laughter, people fighting and the occasional echoing belch. Bert followed the sounds like a wolfcat might trail its prey, a slight flicker forming on her lips as she realised that, for once in her life, *she* was the Thing to go bump in the night.

It felt good.

Then, as she ducked around the corner of a half-crumbled brick wall, she slammed straight into the ass of some sweaty, dusty figure who was standing as a picket guard where Bert hadn't been paying attention. She fell back with surprise, swearing under her breath as she hit the ground. The figure turned around to reveal a middle-aged woman with scars all over her face clutching what appeared to be an Old World electric drill duct-taped to a stick.

"What the...?" the woman said aloud, her voice sounding like a booming thunderstorm amidst the sticky silence of the night's raid.

Bert watched as the woman held her small lantern up, her face widening in horror as Bert was cast out of the shadows. With no time to do anything else, Bert pushed herself off the ground, robotic hand reaching out for the woman's face. But the bandit stepped suddenly backwards out of the way, narrowly avoiding robotic fingers that reached to cover her mouth. She raised her drill-axe in defence, her face still an O of shock.

"Who the fuck are you?" she growled. "Wait, you're an intruder! Holy shit."

The bandit kicked out at Bert just as she was launching a second assault. Bert knocked the foot away with her arms but it threw her attack, causing her to stumble back and lose the momentum. In that backwards motion, she watched with frustration and horror as the bandit dropped her lantern and went for her horn.

But it never made it to her lips.

Arms wrapped around her from behind, smothering her nose and mouth, then coiling around her neck. The arms tightened firmly, muscles bulging beneath fraying shirt sleeves, cutting off all oxygen supply to both the bandit's lungs and brain. They staggered on the spot for a moment before a second pair of arms reached out to grab her torso, then a third to snuff her lantern. Bert stood awkwardly, not knowing whether to watch or help, as the life was squeezed out of the poor picket guard with every passing second. In an eternity that Bert would only remember as a flashing blur, the woman went limp.

Darkness closed in again. Bert heard a dull thump on the dust.

"You OK?" whispered a voice after a moment.

Bert nodded, then rolled her eyes as she remembered that they couldn't see her too well. "Yeah, I'm alright. Thanks for the save," she replied.

"No worries. Let's get moving, eh?"

"Yeah, let's."

After proceeding past the limp body of a poor picket guard whose name nobody would likely remember, at last Bert and her troop could see the campfire, blazing brightly in the middle of a courtyard teeming with a vast bandit tribe. Men, women and those somewhere in between danced, laughed and fought their way around the brilliant orange totem, drinking from huge barrels and showing off their spoils in great competitions of testosterone. The group had obviously come across a trade caravan recently, for a two-wheeled metal trailer was parked in the centre of the camp and its crates and boxes were strewn around the area. Two charred human shapes could be seen smouldering in the piercing white heart of the flame. Bert's lip curled.

A bellow of laughter exploded to her left, and she saw a man sitting on a crude throne of corrugated tin and old car parts placed upon the traders' trailer. At the sight, Bert's stomach churned and roiled like the vast, grey

By Duncan P. Pacey

ocean, a wave of nausea sweeping across her and threatening to buckle her knees. Her skin paled, her eyes widened and her fists tightened into angry balls. Especially her metal fist.

She recognised him.

He was a big man in all respects; meaty was a good word. His muscles swelled beneath leathery dark skin, with scars laced over his body like spiderwebs. He wore nothing on his exposed torso despite the harsh cold of the recent weather, instead showing off his impressive muscular abdomen and the network of injuries that tattooed his skin.

Bert's blood boiled at the very sight, and her left arm ached where flesh met metal. Insect noises jumped around the evening's festivities, but Bert no longer paid them any attention. Pipes rattled in her skull, steam whistling out through her ears and nostrils, soon turning into jet-black smoke. The sounds of laughter and fighting muddied to an indistinct thrum. The pumping of her heart filled her ears as blood filled her face, her iron gaze locked on the man on the tin throne.

Insect noises crooned again, accompanied by one ill-placed bird caw. Around the camp, Polite Bandits emerged from their hiding places with weapons raised, leaping on the Dunce Town mob and wrangling them into restraints. Fights were breaking out around the edge of the courtyard, some of the quicker mob realising they were under attack. The clash of metal rung out in the night.

Bert saw it all through a red haze. She too emerged from her hiding place, but marched straight for the bastard on the trailer. A young Dunce Town lad tried to swing an axe at her, but one of Bert's minions leapt in from behind and tackled him to the dust. Her hands and legs shook uncontrollably as she marched resolutely towards the trailer, her pistol having appeared loyally in her hand as her knuckles went white from clenching.

The bare-chested bandit on the throne was standing up, fury stretching across his ugly, angular face as he roared at the sudden ambush. A scar ran down one side of his face, starting at his bald head and winding down, through an eyepatch, to the base of his cheek. On the other side of his face, one singular brown eye was getting smothered by a patchy eyebrow above it.

And then the eye found Bert in the crowd, and it widened with sheer, genuine shock.

And Bert snarled like a wolfcat, closing in on its prey.

* * *

The double doors before Phoenix swung open with a cliché creak, a wall of smoke following behind, leaping in slow motion from its shadowy abode.

The crowd gasped in anticipation.

Phoenix wriggled in his bonds, hoping to slide his wrists out from the tangle of filthy ropes holding him to this infernal slab. But alas, if the cultists knew one thing and one thing only, it was how to tie a fool to an altar. He glanced side to side, hoping to spy something, anything, that could help him find his freedom. But it was to no avail. He was in that classic adventurer's situation, where all hope seems lost and he just had to sit and wait, playing the part of the worried victim, until his quirky group of friends rode in to save the day at the very last minute. A rag-tag group of allies would also suffice.

But Phoenix had neither, and he didn't think Bert would be slogging up Mount Butt any time soon. Not when she was on the other side of Can't Be Buried bargaining with bandits.

He wriggled again, just to make a point of it.

And then a voice did speak.

"THINE LADIES, GENTLEMEN, AND OTHER STARRY FOLK..."

And the people, they did squeal in exaltation.

It was a woman's voice, and it boomed all over the square, seemingly coming from every direction. It rattled Phoenix's ribcage and gnawed at his headache, and the wild crowd squealing that followed was the boot to the stomach while he was already down.

And the voice, it did speak again.

"PLEASE, PUT THINE HANNNDS TOGETHER..."

And the people, they did prepare thine hands.

It was loud, bloody loud. If the tribal drums were a punch to the brain, this was a mortar strike. Phoenix winced and struggled at his bonds, desperately wishing this was a less enthusiastic cult. Like those suit-wearing money people from Bank Island. They were far more brooding and grim, like a good cult ought to be. Better dressers, too.

And the voice, it did speak once more, but slightly quieter so doth to build thine excitement.

"**Forrrr ... theeeee...**"

And the people, they did suck in an excited breath.

Phoenix flinched in advance, instinct telling him what was about to happen.

Then it happened.

The voice, it did scream.

"**CONSTELLATOOOOOOOOOOOOOOOR!**"

And the people, they did go absolutely bananas.

Phoenix could only squint as the crowd exploded around him. A solitary bugle fought for supremacy above the noise. Begging disbelief, it was somehow even more tuneless than the last musician. Next, through the great double doors sprang a short, plump figure in a garish black robe. Her garb was speckled with brilliant, jewelled stars, the satiny fabric glittering in the dancing light of the lanterns. A collar hugged the back of her neck, rising up in a towering star pattern to halo her chubby face. She smiled wide at the crowd and waved, the two starry guards at either side of the door standing ruler-straight in salute.

Now, the woman hopped and danced her way to the altar, stopping every so often to wash the adoring crowd in her regal smile, ensuring that every one of them thought she was smiling at *them*, and not anyone else. She laughed modestly, like this massive crowd of screaming fans was totally unexpected and oh *my*, wasn't this a lovely welcome, oh ho ho.

Phoenix stared at her, at her womanliness, and a plan began to form in his head. A devious plan, filled with heroic banter, sly manipulation, and the subtle art of seduction. All things Phoenix was a master at. The glimmer of freedom beckoned to him at the far end of the tunnel of doubt.

The Constellator was next to the altar now, approaching the VIPs of the shrivelled sultanaman, one-armed WhateverHisNameIs, and the bugle player, who was now more sweat than human. She was still going strong on the instrument, cheeks flaring red, bashing out what Phoenix thought might be the popular Waste tune *"How Bizarre, My Foot Fell Off"*, but which was so layered beneath flat notes and poor timing that it was nearly impossible to tell.

A quiet conversation took place between the Constellator and the half-sultana/half-human creature, who was bowing low (lower than he was already naturally bowing, anyway) with the dagger held in a way that the starry people would almost definitely describe as 'aloft'. The Constellator smiled at him, waggled her fingers above his head and then lifted the dagger gracefully from his tired old bone fingers, which seemed to get a giddy little response from the old man. He inclined back to his regular ninety-degree posture as the Constellator lifted the dagger high above her head.

The crowd cheered again, and from somewhere in the middle of the horde, a pair of undies took flight. They soared like a majestic old dove, flapping and twirling through the night sky before landing in a bedraggled, ungraceful heap on Phoenix's chest. He gasped, eyes rocketing open, shaking his torso to try and dislodge the pile. It was a whole rainbow of colours, but the one it assuredly wasn't was what appeared to Phoenix to be the one it was supposed to be, which was some kind of white. It was almost as if the wearer, deciding not to clean them back to white again, had decided to combine the entire colour spectrum to try get there in the other direction. It had, at least to Phoenix, not worked.

Meanwhile, the Constellator had produced what appeared to be an old microphone, with a long, winding cord taped into the base of the handle and trailing off somewhere into the night on its own. She smiled wide and a high-pitched feedback screech silenced the crowd.

She lifted the microphone to her large lips, then paused to let a dramatic silence fill the space. "Good citizens of thine Starry Place," she spoke, her voice casting clearly over the entire square with the volume of the Big Bang. "I stand'th before you but a humble servant to the Stars, praise be Their glory."

Phoenix tried to listen, but his attention was being drawn continually in by the underwear, which was now crawling of its own accord to the edge of the altar.

"As thine great Constellations be'th witness from behind their Cloudy Wall, we gather on this beautiful night for a most momentous of occasions."

The underwear, after hesitating for a moment looking over the slab's edge, was now lowering itself down slowly, clinging to the edge as it sought for a foothold somewhere on the altar's side. Phoenix stared in utter horror as it vanished from sight moments after.

"We have before'th us thine Grubby Chef, from the Place of the Burny Drink!"

The Constellator waved her arm in a wide, slow arc above Phoenix's body, an eruption of boos and hissing meeting her from the crowd. She smiled, a proud parent of horrible children that only she knew how to love. On his altar, Phoenix strained to see over the edge to spot where the underwear scuttled off to, but it was gone, vanished somewhere into the black. Another creature to scare kiddies at night.

"We all know'th the Place of the Burny Drink, a place of *sin*!"

"BOO!"

"A place of *debauchery*!"

"HISS!"

"A place of *drunkenness*!"

An uncertain silence answered this one.

The Constellator frowned. "A place of debauched, sinful drunkenness!"

"BOO! HISS!"

She smiled again. "Tonight! On this very night. This night of nights..."

Phoenix finally re-joined the scene. He looked at the nearest cultist - the one-armed Who'sHisFace - and grinned. "She really knows how to drag out a speech, huh?" he whispered.

The one-armed man scowled. "Shut up!" he hissed back.

Phoenix shrugged, or at least tried to.

"...This night that we now'th occupy. The Starry Place and its people will have'th their revenge against the Robotically Handed She-Demon, and the Stars will bathe in the blood of her Grubbiest of Chefs.'

The crowd cheered once again, delight on each and every one of their faces. You could have injected them with liquid bonkerberries and they'd still not end up nearly as blissful as they were right at this moment.

"For on this night of night of nights, I will open the Grubby Chef so'th that thine great acidic tears of thine Stars might cleanse his insides, and spare us - but humble servants - of thy heresy that is the Place of the Burny Drink."

Phoenix made raspberry noises with his lips, staring up at the smog. "Man," he muttered, "this speech is really *starting* to drag on." He grinned childishly, rolling his head to the left to see if the one-armed Who'dYaCallHim heard such a tricky, delightful play on words. "Get it?" he asked. "*Started*? Like, stars? Eh? ...eh?"

The man quite deliberately looked away.

Phoenix frowned. "Ah fuggedaboudit, you don't get it."

And the Constellator continued. "Let us bathe, good Starry people, let us bathe for the night is filthy with the sin of sinners. Let us bathe for how can we not, knowing there are such devils in our world? In our minds? In our *homes*?"

Some of the crowd shook their heads, waving hands of "Amen" in muttered, angry breaths.

"Hey, hey you!" Phoenix shouted at the Constellator. "Over here!"

"Let not the sinner into thine home, good people. Good *Starry* people. For if he gets into your home, he, well, he gets it all grubby!"

"No, not grubby!" cried a voice.

"But I jus' cleaned m' hut last month!" cried another.

"Hey ... hey!" Phoenix continued. "Hey, listen!"

"So that is why thee are gathered here'th this evenin- oh what the hell do you *want*?!" she growled, stopping mid-sentence and glowering at the adventurer. Her stare was like that of an angry schoolteacher, lips set in a perfectly straight line of utter contempt. It was a childhood image Phoenix could relate to.

But he smiled as charmingly as he could, despite remembering Mrs. Truman and her love of cats (the nine-tailed variety). Phoenix reckoned he could disarm anyone with his suave eyes, perfect lips and rugged chin. Except Mrs. Truman. "What I want, oh lady lord, who is so beautiful and intelligent," he started, staring straight into her soul, "is a mere fleeting moment of your most precious and important of time. I have come to your village with a divine purpose, and did I mention that you are oh so talented and your village so prosperous and beautiful and quaint, but in a good way, not a sarcastic way?"

She glared back. She could have chiselled stone with that glare.

"Yes, oh Wise One who is the most supreme of supremes. I, eternally in your shadow of greatness and beauty and masterness, have come from the Place of the Smack-dab, err, Drink, to trade with you, oh beloved ruler of the people on this mountain, which is a nice mountain. It is my most humble and innocent and, um, gratitudious pleasure to beg of you for a one-one-one consultation in your chambers, gorgeous and intelligent Const- err, leader of the Starry Folk. For you see, not only am I a renowned and gentle lover, famed for his tenderness and great skill with womeny bits, but I am also here to make you an offer that, I most humbly assure you in no way maliciously, just FYI letting you know in advance, that you simply cannot refuse."

The Constellator raised an eyebrow.

Phoenix grinned in what he believed was a confident, charming manner. He put on his best mesmerising eyes. Mesmereyes.

She continued to stare. "An offer I cannot doth refuse?"

Phoenix nodded calmly. "Yes indeed, oh sweet and loving and almighty lord. A tender, passionate and explosive consultation, then an offer you cannot refuse."

She slowly brought her gaze to the one-armed ThingamePerson. "Roger, hun, can you please gag him?"

And soth, the hero was gagged.

A sly smirk flickered on the Constellator's stupid pudgy face as Phoenix tried not to taste the years of built-up filth on the rope now invading his mouth. He had heard what contamination can do to a person. He spat at the rope and tried pushing it out of his mouth with his tongue, letting saliva pool at the front of his mouth and dribble out, rather than swallow it.

He was not having a good time.

"Let the sin wash away!" cried the Constellator, raising the dagger. "Let us bathe, together! Begin the ceremony!"

* * *

Smack-dab wasn't quiet anymore, and Meatsack was starting to get upset. He hunched as tightly as he could in such a small chair, hoping desperately that the noises would go away. But every time he ignored them, they would come back louder and louder than before.

Bang bang bang, went the front door.

Bang bang bang bang.

Meatsack dared to glance behind him, his youthful curiosity temporarily overpowering his utter dread at what the noise might be. Many a young Waste adventurer throughout time had died in precisely the same manner. But in Smack-dab on this night, Meatsack spied a young figure, face pressed up against the dirty brown glass, spying back at him. The figure's eyes lit up when they made contact with Meatsack's, and the figure jumped enthusiastically out of sight. Meatsack shot back around, eyes forwards, hoping that maybe, just maybe, the figure was jumping out the way for something else, and not because they made eye contact. He wished he hadn't recognised the boy outside. He liked him. He was nice. He liked Meatsack back.

Bang bang bang.

"Come on, Meatsack! Please open up! It's bloody freezin' out here."

Oh no, the Voice was back. He had heard it a number of moments before, back when it was yelling with the Other Voice. There was some kind of argument, which Meatsack tried very hard not to eavesdrop on because dropping eaves was rude, or so Berty said. But there was an argument with or without Meatsack's understanding it, and the Other Voice seemed to have disappeared since. Now it was just the Voice remaining - that of an old man, one that Meatsack vaguely remembered as being kind and friendly, but who was definitely not allowed in the bar at this moment. Berty Bert said to let nobody in. Not even buddies or pals. Nobody. Nobody in.

Berty Bert.

He wished Bert was here.

By Duncan P. Pacey

Part Seven

...Run in Circles, Scream and Shout

A thick-fingered, well-worn hand gripped her arm tight. Roberta was being led through a maze of wooden corridors to one of the Mayor's guest rooms. The air was stuffy and close, swirling with brown dust as she was dragged violently by the arm. Her skin felt like more bruise than not bruise right now. She thought one of her ribs might be cracked for the pain it was causing with each shallow breath.

The chunky hand jerked her suddenly and she stumbled, falling sideways towards the wood-panelled wall to her left. Instinctively, Roberta reached out with her arm to stop her from slapping against the wall, but instead slammed her still-healing arm stump into the wood. Blood started to soak through her filthy bandages as her body tumbled to the side. Agony burned through her brain, drowning out the bruising elsewhere.

The hand jerked her forwards again, ignorant of her pain. She was taking too long. Roberta thought she could smell the skin rotting beneath her stained bandages, but it didn't make her sick; it made her mad.

She had arrived about a month earlier, maybe less - it was hard to tell the time when you were kept indoors most of the day, and beaten into unconsciousness if you got too smart. Which, considering how much more intelligent Roberta was to the majority of her captors, was almost impossible to avoid.

Prior to being a prisoner of this arrogant wooden mansion at the heart of a bustling, heavily defended Can't Be Buried fort, Roberta was, unfortunately, still a prisoner - but of other people. A bandit tribe known as the Awesome Squad, operating out of the derelict town of Burnt Ham maybe two, three days walking north of the fort, were the fuckers who purchased Roberta from her starving bastard parents. She had been kept as a dancer, nurse and maid, held in a cage until she was needed to either dance, stich, clean, or a mixture of all the above. Dancing while cleaning was becoming a bit of a specialty, but she was still working on how to dance while stitching a wound. She was lucky not to have been an 'entertainer' as well, but the Awesome Squad had a significant female population and despite being the cocky bitches that they were, they at least protected her from that.

But those days were over, now. The Awesome Squad had pissed off the local lord, Mayor Barns, and one of his death squads had sieged Burnt Ham in the middle of the night. Roberta had watched from her cage as men and women slaughtered each other with tools and utensils she didn't even know could be used to slaughter. She'd never seen real gouged eyeballs before, but it was the kidney that haunted her nightmares. Just one, sitting on its own perfectly happy in the dust. Where had it come from? Why was it there? It made her shiver just thinking about it.

But fear aside, while the sticky rivers of warm blood soaked their way through the drought-stricken dust beneath her cell, Roberta frantically worked at the lock on her cage so she could escape during the chaos. She had almost gotten the damn thing open, too, before a giant of a man (meaty, some might call him) stepped out of the madness, drenched head to toe in blood, and unlocked it for her with the key – still clutched in its previous owner's hand. But it wasn't some daring rescue by a handsome adventurer. It wasn't even a passing good-will gesture from an assailing Barnsville bandit. No, he was just another bandit looking for a new prisoner.

He pulled her out by the hair and tossed her to the ground. And, just because she was obviously a woman with the gall to try and escape, he held her left hand down and lifted a huge, bloodied axe...

Back in the wooden hall, the meaty man and Roberta arrived at a peeling, faded door and stopped. The giant turned a fierce gaze on her, gripping her tight by the shoulders with hammy fists.

"Now you listen real good, Berty," he spat. "Diz guest is import'nt t' Mayor Barns, an' you gonna treat 'er wid r'spect, hear? Give 'er an orgasm she'll remember f'r years. Dat'll make 'er easier t' do bidness wid, he he he."

Roberta glared back as the beast cackled, imagining all the things she would do to the man's ugly face if she got the opportunity. Why she reckoned she'd start with an eyeball, that'd work. But she'd leave the other, so he could watch. Fucker.

"Diz is yer last chance, Berty. If ya don't make our guest happy enuff t' talk 'bout money tomorrow, da Mayor is gon' give ya t' me as an example t' yer udder slavey bitch friends. An' ya know I don' keep my toys f'r long."

He growled with the throat of an animal, then turned sharply away to open the door. His demeanour changed dramatically as it opened, the anger melting off his face, morphing into an awkward customer service smile. There was a woman inside what turned out to be a very small room. She sat still on the lone bed, fingers steepled by her face in thought. She looked up with an offended, stern face, no fear of the meaty man apparent in her dark eyes. Roberta found herself peeping from behind her captor, trying to get a better look at the stranger. She was an adventurer, by the looks of things. She had that long adventurer's trench coat they so often wore, with a big, wide-brimmed hat on her head that looked like two hats sewn crudely together in the middle. But more importantly, adventurers always had a secret stash of weapons.

An idea was forming in Roberta's mind.

Her captor smiled a wide, rotten grin. "Wid his r'spects, ma'am, da Mayor offers ya diz gift."

Roberta was suddenly gripped harder and yanked into the room, presented to the stranger like some prized object. She lingered awkwardly in the centre of the room, not really sure how to stand. Her dress - which she was forced to wear - plunged and rose in places a dress should neither plunge nor rise, but it was better than the costume she had before she dug her thumbs into the quartermaster's eyes, which was mostly just a few strips of old cloth covering, well, not really covering anything. But this strange, dark-eyed woman did not slobber or whistle like the bandits of Barnsville. The woman stared straight into Roberta's eyes, as if searching them for something.

The meatman spoke again, smiling his horrible grin. His decrepit breath filled the still air. "Take yer time, OK? Ya gots all night if yer wants it."

The door shut gently behind Roberta, leaving the duo alone. The woman remained seated in the same position, her backpack and pistol placed tidily on a small table on the other side of the small space. Its bone handle gleamed in the dim electric light. Roberta stared at it just a moment too long.

"You could probably get it before I do," the stranger said. Her voice was deep, confident, but silky smooth compared to the rough grating of Barnsville bandits.

Roberta jumped, rapidly turning her gaze back to the stationary woman. Her face began to flush red - she could feel its heat filling up her cheeks.

The woman narrowed her eyes. "But let's say you do. What then?"

The sudden adrenalin made Roberta's stump ache; the itch was almost maddening. She controlled the urge to scratch, instead digging the nails of her intact hand into her palm. "Escape," she croaked, suddenly realising how dehydrated her throat was.

"With one pistol? Not likely, especially not in your condition. You'd need to sneak your way down to the mess before you can start shooting. A body as weak as yours looks needs at least water before you go exerting yourself."

Roberta stared at her with suspicion. Who was this person?

"You could probably steal some weapons on the way out. The guards who patrol the mezzanine looked armed with automatic rifles. Grab yourself a knife from the kitchen, slit their throats on the way out, then you've got two guns."

"Why are you telling me this?" Roberta asked, finding her voice somewhere in the depths of her uncertainty.

The woman arched an eyebrow. "Hmm. You aren't prepared, are you? The only way to survive in the Waste is to be prepared for anything. Learn to adapt."

Roberta scowled. She didn't like being condescended by some strange woman with a tacky hat. "I've survived this long," she countered.

"Yes, perhaps. But as a prisoner."

This shut Roberta up.

"Of course..." the woman continued, stroking her thin face, "you could try to recruit some assistance. Perhaps you ask me for help? Or arm your fellow prisoners."

"Why would you help me? Aren't you here to deal with the Mayor?"

She narrowed her eyes again. It was a dangerous look, Roberta felt. It sparked something buried in the human brain's animal instinct, something that suggested 'fight' might look better with an L in the word. She wondered how many people had seen that look before they died.

"I was. But he has been pressing me quite unsubtly for the secret location of my money, and I suspect he intends to betray me the moment he knows where it is."

"Prepare for anything," Roberta found herself saying. The words just tumbled out before she knew it.

"Exactly. He has told too many lies, even after a single day I've seen through them. No, I intend to leave in the night and never return, but..."

"But?"

"Hmm," the woman said, finally standing up. "But perhaps before I do, we can help each other."

Now it was Roberta's turn to narrow her eyes.

"There's a trailer with food and drink supplies out back," the woman said, now standing before Roberta. She was tall, very tall, and muscular. She wasn't a woman to pick a fight with. "It hasn't been unloaded yet, but it's guarded. I need those supplies to start my new bar, but I cannot steal them alone. And if I'm correct, neither can I purchase them."

"Start a bar? Wait, what?"

"You heard me. Help me get that trailer out of Barnsville and you can come with me. Work for me and I'll even pay you."

Roberta couldn't find the words to respond with. She stammered and stumbled, her mind racing a million miles an hour trying to comprehend the situation. *"How do I know I can trust you?"* she finally said, feeling it to be the next best question before thoughts of escape could infiltrate her mind.

The woman cocked her head. *"You can't. But you can follow along with my plan and prepare you own in case I betray you. So long as you can get a weapon, you can kill me and try escape on your own."*

Roberta and the woman stared at each other in silence for a moment, their gazes fizzling in the air between them. She felt the familiar ache in her hand stump, and the pain of something as simple as trying to breath. Every muscle she tensed, another bruise sang out in protest. The decision practically made itself, really.

"Fine, I'll help. But on one condition."

"And what's that?"

"I need to pay the man who brought me here a visit before we go."

"Ah," the woman replied. She cocked her head to the side again, pondering. *"OK, I accept your terms. We'll draw him in here and you can do what you like."*

Something strange happened to Roberta's face, next. Her lip felt like it was trying to push up at the corners, something they hadn't done in a long, long time. Meanwhile, the woman was gathering up her weapon and backpack, drawing a short, stubby knife out of a pouch.

"You'll need this," she said, handing the weapon to Roberta hilt-first. *"What do I call you?"*

Roberta, hand beginning to shake from anticipation, softly took the weapon and held it like it was sacred. She could feel her future laying out before her, a giant cavernous maw of hope finally widening its jaws after years of neglect. Roberta couldn't even remember the last time she felt ... what was the word? Oh yeah, optimistic.

"Roberta," she said. Then she paused, feeling the weight of the blade. *"But you can call me Bert."*

* * *

Bert took a deep breath. "Hurl!"

Her voice tumbled through the chaos like a drunk homing missile, bouncing from building to building until it had silenced the entire courtyard and landed somewhere near its target. Bandits paused mid-fight to stop and ogle, hands frozen around necks, feet ceasing on rib cages, and the occasional mouth drooling on its opponent's ear. Only the bonfire at the battle's heart dared to defy the trend, concerned more by its fleshy feast than trivial human matters.

"Hurl you overgrown sack of shit, I challenge you."

Bert stood, feet apart, hand on her weapon, and metal finger pointed straight at the chief. Her brows had come so far down into a glare that they were almost a single strip of hair. Her blue eyes danced with a dark, orange glow in the fire's light. Her trigger finger begged to be released, to satiate its most primal of desires, but the man on the trailer needed to accept her challenge first. Otherwise it was just straight up murder. No, a pointless bit of banter needed to take place first before murder would become politics.

The meaty bandit known as Hurl rose to his full height on top of the metal trailer, one solitary eye wide open, pupil small. What was left of his face twitched uncontrollably, the emotion behind the expression unreadable. It was a face even a mother could hate.

Bert stood and watched as the man, cyclopean eye fixated on her in its best impression of an Overlord, took a lumbering step towards the edge of the metal trailer and stepped off with a loud thud. A weapon dangled at his waist, bumping loosely off his leg as the man moved. It had a short handle made from an old wrench, maybe a foot and a bit long, with what looked like three individual Old World axe blades welded together at one end. Rust had discoloured the blade's edge, or rather, blades' edges. Bert felt intimately familiar with the weapon. Her skin started to ache beneath its metal prosthetic, and it just made her madder.

Hurl searched Bert's face, either scowling, laughing or quaking with fear – it was really hard to tell what was going on. He took his time, taking one long footstep after another towards her, lip twitching with maybe anger, but possibly also lust. It may also have been trying to smile.

Either way, the point here was that he was emoting in some fashion, and moving slowly towards Bert, who tensed, her body feeling impatient, wanting to be let loose.

But she needed the words.

The man's face twisted in on itself in what could be assumed was a frown, his lips mouthing the word "Who?" in silence. Wind wandered around in the background, hissing through the corpses of Dunce Town carrying an icy chill. Ancient wood moaned with displeasure as it fought back against the pressure, bringing the entire historic town to life with the long, slow conversation of dead houses. What they were saying to each other was anybody's guess.

Then Hurl got slapped by a wall.

More correctly, it appeared that he was slapped by a wall. His hunched, predator shape suddenly shot upright, shoulders back, feet sticking to the dirt. His one eyebrow fought its way up his head while, in a separate but equally difficult struggle, his lips clawed open into an O shape. Blood flushed into his face and threatened to pop out the seams. But it was laughter that instead broke the surface tension.

First there was a "bah", which slipped out without the body noticing. Then a "hah" followed suit, but it shattered the foundations beneath his expression and the whole face collapsed downwards. Another "hah" rolled out third, and then another, and another, and soon the bandit chief known as Hurl was locked in genuine hysterics, doubling over and slapping his knees. His face danced to the tune, but with quite an incredibly poor sense of rhythm, revealing a wide, toothless mouth.

Bert bared her teeth, while nobody else in the camp dared so much as whisper. Even Doris, her machete locked around a bandit's neck, had stopped smiling.

It was a number of seconds more before Hurl's bahaha-ing ebbed sufficiently for him to manage to sneak a word or two out at the same time. "Well, well, well," he said, a tear drooling out the edge of his bloodshot eye as the Waste Beast bellowing faded. One of his muscular arms fell onto his axe. "Ain't diz a blast from da past, eh?"

Bert bore two eye-shaped holes into his misshapen face.

"Ya know, Berty," he said, voice deepening. His smile faded, either because it was tired of fighting for supremacy or because the man was now growing deadly serious. "I've dreamed of ya."

He took another step, left, and started to circle slowly. "How long's it been? Years, I reckons. But I rememb'rs ya, Berty. Oooh don't ya bring back mem'ries, so ya do. Took me a second, eh? He he he, not so good at seein' dese days widout me eye, so's I ain't. I sees ya got a new hand, dough. Pity, eh? I dink ya looked bett'r wit' da stump – showed off me handiwor-"

"-Do you accept my challenge or not, Hurl?" Bert cut in, grinding her feet into the dust. And, at the same time, grinding her teeth into dust.

Hurl stopped circling.

Bert bent her knees ever so slightly, preparing her balance for the impending fight. He was much bigger than she, but she had a gun and he didn't. From her memory of the man, he'd be a charger – someone who cares little for strategy and wit, but knows the power of their beefy upper body and the axe that it wields. This might be trouble if Bert only had a melee weapon, but who brings an axe to an axe fight? She'd give him a bit of banter, he'd get mad because he's stupid and can't think of a comeback, he'd charge in and get shot in the face. Probably more than once. Bing, bang, wallop, fight over.

She sneered at the man. "Or do you feel scared after our last encounter at the manor?" Go go banter.

Bert saw his knuckles tighten, giving her the slightest flicker of satisfaction. "Ooh yer a brave one, Berty, dats for sure. But yer don't have da Woman with ya tonight, eh? Nobody t' save ya. Pity ... I hear she got what wus comin' for her when da Mayor came for his money. I hear she screamed till she died, tryin' t' save you."

Uh oh, thought two little mechanics in Bert's brain. They watched in trepidation as a pipe burst down the hall and steam started to pour. Sandwiches were ruined.

"He he he. Struck a nerve, eh? What, you dun like remeberin' how da Woman was shot full o' holes 'cause o' you? I guess dat's like how I dun like talkin' 'bout wut you did t' me face all dem years ago, eh? When you wuz a coward, hidin' behind da Woman. But you toughened up now, eh? Here you stand."

"Here I stand," Bert replied through her teeth. Say the damn words, she thought afterwards.

"Alright, Berty, if yer wants t' die so badly, I'll make it happen. Ye can jus' try t' take me crew from me. But nobody dun take Hurl's Crew - not you, not Farmer Brown, not anybody."

Doris looked on with bated breath, Sir Robert frozen in anticipation next to her.

The Polite Bandits clenched their collective anuses, nervous about the outcome of the coming storm - and, ultimately, about whether they'd be going to war or not.

Hurl's Crew almost forgot about the fact that they were being headlocked, half-stabbed, and held to the ground by boots, their attention instead coiled around the scene before them.

And Bert stood in the centre of them all, the two sapphire eyes of the storm. Her human hand waited in readiness atop her gleaming pistol, her left fingers curled into a tight fist, skin pulsating beneath metal. Her mind raced between images of the Mayor, Hurl's face, and the Woman's final moments: *Her determined expression when she turned around, the confidence that shone with her every fibre, the blood that seemed almost surprised to be bursting from her chest.* Bert had forgotten or repressed so many memories from the days before Smack-dab, but those were the ones that stuck out - veritable splinters nestled just beneath the skin of her brain, where she struggled to pull them out. Hurl was the last remaining link to her past, and ironically, the key to her future.

He just had to say. The damn. Words.

Next, something happened to Hurl's lips. They got a little wider, but it took a few attempts. From the look in his hungry, lonely eye, it may have been an evil grin, but then, all grins are evil when you wear an eyepatch and have a scar running the length of your face. That's just science.

"Berty," he said slowly, chewing the words on the way out. "I accept yer challenge, for what good it'll do yer."

Finally.

By Duncan P. Pacey

In the nanoseconds between Hurl's words emitting from his face and for the attack order to travel from his brain down to his axe, Bert was moving. Her breathing slowed to a freakish steadiness, her eyes trapped in blinkers, Hurl the only visible target. Her body began to tense again, feet sliding just slightly farther apart. All at the same time, her hand closed quickly around the butt of her weapon and drew it from the holster, the shiny metal of the barrel trembling in the flickering orange fire light. Her thumb fingered the weapon's hammer and pulled it down, her trigger finger slipping into place with practiced ease.

Hurl was also moving, axe coming free from its leather belt strap, his grin disappearing under the weight of momentum. His mouth started to open for a battle cry, his animal throat rumbling with a distant thunder. He took the first steps forwards, shoulders lowering down, arm drawing back for a first strike.

The pistol's hammer clicked a familiar sound as it locked into place. Bert's face looked grim, determined, as she squeezed the trigger to end this nonsensical waste of time once and for all. To tie up the last loose end of her past on a one-way train to repress-your-memories town. But more importantly, to steal Hurl's significant horde of monsters, fight back Farmer Brown, save Smack-dab, and go back to the way things ought to be: Bandits staying the hell away and dying on the Highway while Bert served drinks to good, honest folk. Or at least good folk. OK, just folk. But at least they weren't bandits.

Her finger finished curling, the trigger letting loose its hungry hammer. The hammer needed no further introduction, thrusting forwards with all its tiny might to peck at the firing pin. The primer was struck, and Bert waited for the familiar recoil as gunpowder exploded in the casing and a bullet launched from the barrel to gore through Hurl and end his life.

Except ... it didn't happen. The bullet was a dud.

Hurl roared.

* * *

Boom.
Boom boom.

The bugle screamed with renewed vigour as a fast, ominous drum beat rolled across Mount Butt's florpadorps. It wailed and howled, crying in pain as an untalented musician blew with all her might into its slobbery, metal rectum. All around, starry people hooted and hollered, praising the Stars, the Constellations, the Constellator, and in one instance, Andy Buckley's Discount Robe Warehouse, which was having a special at the moment and needed some good promotion.

Phoenix was getting nervous, now. There were too many things going on at once for him to be able to carroty chop them all. A deadly knife point examined every inch of his body - something he wished he was doing with the Constellator, funnily enough - and he felt, for the first time in a very, very long time, that he might actually have approached this quest in the wrong manner. You might even go so far as to say that mistakes were made, but Phoenix wasn't quite at that point yet. It did seem awful hopeless, though, which was a real buzzkill when it came to being hopeful. But ... adventurers didn't die on altars atop mountains and florpadorps and whatnot. They died in a blaze of glory, bullets flying all over the show, swords swinging, axes twirling, people screaming. It was the way to go. Some historic adventurers had gone to great lengths to ensure their death was as big as possible, even starting full-on wars between regions. There was a reason that the Overlords had moved in to Mal's Murderborough up north a couple years ago - it went from unthreatening wine country to craterous, irradiated battleground in less than a week! And Sandra Bulletface had gone down in history after that. She'd also gone down in a ball of flame, but then, that was the idea.

Boom boom boom.

Boom boom boom.

Boom boom boom.

Oh shit, thought Phoenix. An increase in tempo was never a good thing. Especially seen as how, at this very moment, the Constellator was making all kinds of weird whooshy noises with her mouth, waggling the dagger over the alter and speaking in what could only be described as tongues, for it was no real language.

Ideas, Phoenix panicked, think of ideas!

The Constellator's eyebrows knotted together and she stood, feet apart, in the centre of the altar's side edge. She took a deep breath and raised the dagger aloft, clutching it tightly with two clenched hands.

Boom boom boom.

Boom boom boom.

BOOM BOOM BOOM.

Phoenix desperately wished he was high. Then he could just shut his eyes, smile dopily, and go dancing with Mr Pumpernickel and the unicorn. OK, maybe not the unicorn right now, but Mr Pumpernickel was a family-friendly sort. So long as he didn't get into the grog. Phoenix wriggled once more, with feeling, hoping desperately to reach with grasping fingers into his pocket, searching for the bonkerberries.

Wait, he thought. Bonkerberries, that's it!

An idea raced through his head at the speed of flight, which in Phoenix's experience, was often very bloody fast. How did he not think of this before?

The Constellator looked at her adoring followers, her face serious. "Behold! For it begins!"

" 'ONKER'ERRIES!" cried Phoenix, thrashing madly in his restraints.

The dagger wavered.

" 'ONKER'ERRIIIEEEEES!" he yelled again, his speech cracking with sobs.

The Constellator gave her raisinous old companion an uncertain glance, but he was as much at a loss as she. One of his bony fingers scratched at the scalp under his hood, and chunky white flakes trickled past his head.

" 'ONKER'ERRIES 'OO 'ASTARD, 'ONKER'ERRIES!"

Her eyes scanned Phoenix with a mix of pure fury and complete confusion, and the Constellator carefully reached down with her dagger and unhooked the rope, now soggy with spit and tears, from Phoenix's mouth. He spat noisily, a spray of saliva fountaining in ichory globules into the air, and drew in fast, nervous breaths.

"Ifyoudon'tsacrificemeIwillgiveyousomethingbetterthanyouevercoulddream!" Phoenix cried, face red.

The Constellator frowned again, then nodded at someone out of Phoenix's field of vision. Shortly after, a hand flew in and slapped him straight across the cheek.

"Pull yourself together, man!" she growled. "It's only a bloody sacrifice. Now what in the Stars is thee babbling about? We've all got things to do and you're not the centre of the ruddy universe."

Phoenix, face stinging, gasped loudly, wrangling his breath under control. He needed to compose himself, clear his thoughts so that he could turn his witty banter back on. He needed to be an adventurer, not a pansy-ass sacrificial goat-lamb creature. A sacrificial glamb. Oh boy was Phoenix glad that Sandra Bulletface wasn't here to see all of this. Why she'd be so embarrassed for him she'd probably erupt in a fireball all over again.

"If you cut me loose, mighty Const- mighty leader of the Starry Place," Phoenix said under a few more deep, calming breaths, "I will give you something that will unleash a power like you've never experienced."

At last, the Constellator flashed an emotion that wasn't some brand of disgust, displeasure or disapproval. "What in the Stars could thee doth possibly have with such a power? You are but a Grubby Chef."

Phoenix shook his head as best he could, given the circumstances. "You have to cut me loose before I will reveal my secret, but I can tell you that it will let you talk with..." he paused for dramatic effect, "...the Stars!"

The crowd gasped.

The one-armed man apparently called Roger dropped his bat.

The old sultana collapsed in on himself like an Old World deck chair.

The Constellator looked flabbergasted. But then angry. Very, very angry. Furious, even. "How dare you speak of their name with such heathen tongues!" she screamed, pressing the ornate dagger firmly into Phoenix's neck. A bead of blood welled on the edge and fled down the length of the blade. "How can a mere mortal speak'th with thine Constellations? 'Tis lunacy!"

"Lunacy, no! Truthacy! Cut me loose and I shall show you."

"I don't believe you. The sacrifice shall continue!"

"WAAAAIT!" Phoenix squealed. "If you forego a chance to speak with your Starry godpeople, how will they ever forgive you for wasting the opportunity? You sacrifice me and you will never know if it was true or not. You cut me loose and I'll prove it.'

Silence.

The Constellator stared at him in disbelief. Her face burned with fury, but then the old man stepped forwards. Or rather, he grunted and swore until he'd managed to unfold himself again, and *then* he stepped forwards. He raised a shaking hand in a calming motion, but seemed nervous to actually come into physical contact with the Constellator. Well, no loss for Phoenix, because he had no such objections, even now after all this sacrifice business. A little one-on-one would do Smack-dab-Starry Place relations some good. Especially with Phoenix at the helm. The Constellator locked eyes with the old man, exchanging one of those looks that said a thousand words (but yet neither party really knows what the other is saying), then glanced up at the smog. The Cloudy Wall, or whatever.

Phoenix seized the moment. "If I cannot prove it, what is to stop you from knocking me out again? You have nothing to lose."

Her lips curled, her eyes still locked smogward. Then, after a moment's thought, she brought them down on Phoenix and narrowed her gaze at him, as if looking for any sign of deception that might make the decision easier. But Phoenix's face was a picture of innocence, as it so often was. Her lips curled a second time.

"Fine, you will be tested. Someone cut him loose!"

Finally! Phoenix was freed by a couple of starry nobodies and he slowly rose up, swinging his legs off the giant stone bed so that they dangled over the side. Groaning with absolute pleasure, he twisted his torso until all the bones in his back clicked and popped, then twisted in the other direction to repeat the same. When he curled back, he was face to face with an angry Constellator.

"The proof, Grubby Chef. Before you are opened to the Tears of Acid."

Phoenix smiled. "Of course, oh loveliest of lords. Of course."

He rummaged in his jacket pocket, the fear of death wandering away humming a tune as if it were never there in the first place. Fear of death? What fear of death? Pfft, the situation was under control the *entire* time, or so Phoenix would tell people one day. The tears were all for show, you see.

Smack-dab's adventurer was quick to find the berries he had so cheerfully pocketed away what felt like days ago (because it was), buried until now in the dust and lint of his pockets. He gently blew off some particularly stubborn particles and offered a juicy red morsel to the Constellator.

"This divine berry is called the bonkerberry," he began, "and it's renowned in certain parts of the Waste for transporting the user's mind to the place of the gods. A trader from a far-off land gave it to me many years ago and told me, on pain of death, never to show anybody, for its power is so great. Should it fall into the wrong hands..." He let his voice trail off, shaking his head in silence.

She frowned at him. "Doth I like like the wrong hands?"

He looked back at her, the leader of a mad cult, surrounded by hundreds of adoring, loyal servants who would be willing to walk into hellfire if it was her bidding. He remembered the wild attack on Smack-dab earlier, and the violent, frightening tales Bert had told of their history. He saw it all in a second, then said: "Of course not. I believe I can trust you, mighty and wonderful lord. Take the berry and chew on it a few times. Let the saliva flow around it. You'll be going to the Stars in seconds."

The Constellator hesitated, holding the berry in front of her eyes, twisting and turning it to see all sides. She sniffed it, then licked it, then glanced at Phoenix one last time. He smiled and beckoned her on.

Her eyes narrowed and, finally, she popped it in her mouth, chewing slowly.

"It taste'th like crap," she said.

"The taste is not the point, brave and beautiful Constellator."

Encircling them, an entire village of onlookers, straining to see what was happening, whispered, "Constellatooooor..."

Then, rather suddenly, the Constellator collapsed.

The crowd gasped.

Some people are graceful when they collapse. They fall like a carefully controlled building demolition, where first the knees go, then the waist, then the torso, shoulders, neck, and, finally, head. Each body part hits before the prior, softening the blow of the overall landing. It's graceful, elegant, the feinting drunk swan equivalent of a fall.

This was not one of those falls.

The Constellator didn't just feint. She gave the appearance that some crazy Waste surgeon had just invented a device to remove all her bones at once, activated it, and then not stepped in to catch her. She just sort of toppled, straight down, in a garish pile of satin and stars. There was even a loud slap as she hit the cobblestones, and then absolute stillness.

Phoenix paled and something vaguely resembling a croak escaped his mouth. He glanced nervously at the crowd, then at the VIPs.

They stared back at him.

"Err..." he started, "this can happen sometimes. Bit of a drastic reaction, but she'll come back soon, I promise."

From behind, the one-armed man whose name Phoenix had already forgotten ran hurriedly in and held his last remaining hand in front of her mouth. He too tried carefully not to directly touch her, but instead felt for her breath. Her face was pale, and then so was his.

"I feel'th no breath."

Phoenix smiled quickly and scanned the crowd's faces.

And then ran for his life.

* * *

Lorry was on the verge of worry when she finally noticed a small orange glow flickering in the window of a ruined Old World house ahead. The night is dark and full of terrible things, and Lorry was confident that she didn't want to meet them - even with Gachook's protection.

She approached the house cautiously, in case it might be some kind of bandit or otherwordly hell-beast trap. Gachook, Our Lord and Saviour was known for sending horrible beasts from His deadly chicken hell, Freckle, to test Gachookian followers, and see how far their resolve would go. So far, Lorry had survived every encounter, from an acid-spewing radioactive Waste Beast all the way through to a plague of drug-addicted biteflies (that is, biteflies that had bitten one too many drug addicts, and now rather fancied the taste). Lorry now knew three things: That Waste Beasts can indeed be scarier, and that is when they are radioactive and drooling acid; That biteflies high on narcotics can fly so fast they set on fire due to air friction; And finally, that her resolve is stronger than anything the Waste might throw at her.

Even in a night as arguably dark and most definitely terrible as this one...

Lorry could barely make out the house itself. The choking black of night smothered it in an impenetrable layer of nothingness, save for the one dancing light poking its head out of a solitary, desolate window. She crept towards the door to the building, which was less a door and more of a gap. OK, so she crept to the gap of the building, one of many such entrances, and slid her back up against it. She could hear nothing. Nothing except the Waste breeze flowing in its vast waves across the empty plain, and the quiet crackling of flames somewhere within the house.

She steeled herself with a slow, deep breath, filling her lungs to capacity before gently letting it out. She muttered a very quick, almost silent prayer to Gachook, Our Lord and Saviour, for his continued love and protection on a night as dark and indeed terrible as it was at this very moment in time. May he bring down the wrath of Carnage himself should there be an ambush lying in wait within this filthy structure.

Feeling somewhat more confident, but admittedly not entirely, she poked her head around the gap. And there, sitting behind a small fire made from what looked like old furniture, was a man. His face was almost so grim as to be an entirely new, as yet unnamed expression - a sort-of grim to the power of grim - and he hunched cross-legged on the floor with one handless arm tucked into his black leather coat. His other hand clutched a ridiculous pistol, with a large scope strapped to the top and an extended magazine clinging to the bottom, its ass hanging out the grip. Lorry could examine all these features in great detail, for the weapon was pointing straight at her.

She narrowed her eyes at him. "Greetings," she said, carefully.

The man inspected her for a moment, his eyes as dark as his coat, then withdrew his absurd handgun and holstered it away on his belt.

Thank you, Gachook, Lorry thought. "May I join you by the fire?" she said aloud.

"..." the figure replied.

Lorry paused for a moment, then started walking towards him. "Fine, I will take your silence as acceptance."

She strode over to the opposite side of the small fire, swooshing her robes in a big circle before plopping down on the spot. She then patted a small ember out of the bottom of her clothing, for swooshing it in a circle next to a fire was, in hindsight, rather unnecessary.

It felt good to sit, even next to a broody, menacing figure like the strange, grim man. Her feet ached with the wear of many hours walking without rest. She brought them up onto her lap one at a time to gently massage them with her boots off, paying the stranger little attention. Which seemed OK, because he didn't seem bothered by her presence. Or if he was bothered, he chose not to show it. He chose not to show anything, really. Just that same, grim stare, now pointing into the fire.

Lorry decided to spark up a conversation to pass the time, and to determine whether this dark individual might be open to the light of one Gachook, Lord and indeed Saviour.

"Have you ever been to the bar further down this infernal Back Road?" she asked.

The figure looked up at her.

"It was shut, would you believe? I paid good money for a pair of heathens to take me there so that I may spread the word of Gachook, Our Lord and Saviour - have you heard of Gachook, Our Lord and Saviour? I really ought to tell you about Him if you haven't, he's quite the entity."

"What do you mean the bar was shut?" the figure asked, his hoarse voice slicing through the word of Gachook.

Lorry looked momentarily offended, then shook it from her face. It wasn't the first time someone had cut off the word of Gachook, Our Lord and Saviour, and it wouldn't be the last. But Gachook always got the last word in the end. In that she stoutly believed.

"Excuse me?" she replied.

The figure leaned forwards, a startling blend of light and shadow playing in the crevices of his dry, dusty face. "Smack-dab, the bar. You said it was shut."

"Indeed, the door was locked and it appeared nobody was there."

"And you're sure of this?"

"Quite sure, sir. And what is it to you, anyway? Planning to travel there tomorrow?"

The figure sat back again, eyes narrowed to slits, brow knotted in a tight frown. "What else did you see?" he asked, his voice suspiciously dark, as though he were fishing for something. And what dark thoughts he might be fishing for, Lorry could only guess. "Why was it shut?"

Lorry frowned. "I wouldn't know, stranger. I care little for the trivial business goings on of such a heathenous, tragic place. I can tell you only that the door was locked, the statue outside was broken, and that the letters on the roof are bound to fall off at some point soo-"

He held up a stump hand, abruptly silencing her. "The statue was broken?"

Lorry was growing slightly mad, now. This was too many questions, and not enough Gachook. "Is your hearing as poor as your posture, *sir?* Locked door, broken statue, dangerous lettering."

A smile spread somewhere in the darkness of the stranger's face. It spread up both sides of his cheeks, a smile that would give a person nightmares for the rest of their life, if only they would survive long enough to have any. Lorry watched with caution as the man quietly rose from his seat, picking up his backpack on the way. Now completely ignoring her, the stranger gathered up his water canteen and an unopened can of food, stashing them in his pack before exiting the room through the nearest door-gap.

And then he was gone, just like that.

Lorry heard his footsteps pick up into a fast-paced run before fading to black in the distance. The wind rolled in afterwards, whistling through cracks in the walls. She shivered, but not from cold. Something about the stranger sent a tingle down her spine, and it wasn't the happy tingle of Gachook, either. Boy, she thought, was her work cut out for her. An entire region of Gachookless heathens. Lorry promised herself that she'd find an army of Gachookian missionaries and descend upon Can't Be Buried in force, bringing light to this dark, horrid place, and cleansing it of the unworthy.

But for now, she was just glad the stranger left his fire going.

By Duncan P. Pacey

* * *

Escaping the giant mob of angry cultists was not as easy as Phoenix had hoped. But then, he wasn't sure what he was expecting. The last mob he escaped from was a shambling mass of zom-bee-infected humans, who had suffered the horrific, mind-rotting sting of the zom-bee. They never ran, but just sort of moved forwards. It could only be described as movement, for no other word fitted the strange, limping, struggling surge that was a zom-bee hive.

But these cultists were different. For starters, they were alive - that was the real problem. Easily remedied in most situations, mind you, but unfortunately Phoenix had a mission here, and it didn't involve blowing up their stupid village. No, somehow he had to go from fleeing in terror to saving the day and winning the girl.

...he filed this under "Future Problem".

Cultists swarmed out of every nook and cranny imaginable, some even dropping from the sky. Phoenix ran as though his life depended on it, which was made far easier by his life depending on it. His breath detonated out of his lungs in ragged, heavy bursts, his boots pounding hard on the Starry Place's dusty roads.

The entire village had, over time, somehow coalesced on Mount Butt's rocky slopes, meaning every single street was some degree of steep and horrible. And the village huts themselves were rudimentary at best, cobbled together from scraps of whatever the hell was lying around at the time of construction. They wound down the slope in a vast network of dirty streets, all of them aiming vaguely for the entrance to the village where Phoenix first encountered Fabbelous and etc. earlier that day.

Phoenix was oddly disappointed at how normal everything looked, even as it streamed past him in a total blur. Scattered between each of the huts were streets paved with dirt and the occasional pile of shit, not the bones of the Starry People's enemies as one might expect. There were crates scattered here and there, plus plenty of cats, and wandering between two houses a bit further down, something that seemed an odd mix of both. Phoenix couldn't see any torture cages or implements of horrible star-themed death anywhere, but there was a well a little ways back up the road he now fled down. Maybe they like, you know, could throw people in there or something.

Bah, he thought. It was wishful thinking, Phoenix knew. At least they all dressed the same. You couldn't have a good cult without a uniform.

Momentarily alone, Phoenix threw himself behind a particularly dumpy hut made of multi-coloured planks and old robes, catching his breath and stuffing it back in his lungs as it tried to abandon his body for good. Sweat hung off his brow in beady, dirty clumps, and piled up in his armpits and crotch waiting for someone to dare take his clothes off. He allowed himself the simple pleasure of wheezing horrifically as he tried to think. How does one go from killing the leader of a group to having their complete, undivided adoration? And what had even happened with the Constellator?

Bert must be having a much easier time than this, he thought. Phoenix had always found bandit leaders much more agreeable.

Then he heard the myriad claps of feet that signalled impending doom, carried on the raging soundwaves of "Over here", "No, over here", "No, over here – I said it first." It was time to move, then.

Scooping up one final breath for the road, Phoenix darted out from his cover and made for down the hill. He wasn't sure where he was going, but he needed to lose these losers so that he could think properly. There was bound to be somewhere to hide in the village. The bedroom of a lusty maiden, perhaps, who would gasp in shock when she found him straddled across her bed, but quickly succumb to her deep-seeded, forbidden desires and make wild love to his tired body. Phoenix would also accept a lusty squire, or pretty much anybody. So long as they took the edge off and didn't rat him out.

"Oi, stop!" shouted a voice.

Phoenix glanced over his shoulder just in time to see a thickly built man thrusting a tassled spear at his skull. Phoenix staggered to the side in instinct, lashing out with his gloved hand to grab the weapon. He wrapped his fingers around the uneven wooden shaft and yanked hard, pulling the figure off his feet. But before he could lay into the man with a boot, three more cultists appeared from an alleyway slightly uphill and pointed at him with an accusing finger.

He turned to flee, getting only a few steps before a wailing stick of a woman landed in a mad flurry on top of his shoulders from somewhere above. The pair fell to the ground in an ungainly heap, the unhelpful bastard that is physics taking them both down the hill a few extra feet. Phoenix kicked out with his boot and caught his assailant in the face, knocking her grasping, grabby grabby hands off his trouser leg. He scrabbled in the dirt and took off downhill again, just as a spear thudded loudly in the dirt where his precious torso used to be.

"Hey, that was close!" cried the woman back at her companions.

"Sorry, dear!" replied a disappointed ex-husband, who had missed.

Phoenix, now limping slightly, ran again. He could sense the injuries of a few days earlier flaring up, unhealed entry wounds feeling like they wear tearing open with each painful footstep. He wouldn't be able to keep up this pace for long, not in this condition. Phoenix started trying a few doors on either side of the street, quickly turning the handle, pulling the rope, or squeezing the strange squishy ball (depending on the door).

The first was locked shut, and so was the second. Damn and blast, Phoenix yelled silently. He sprinted for what looked like a lucky door: another multi-coloured planks affair stuck into the side of a hut made of old car doors. The door opened by turning the handle in a panic, realising it was bloody locked like the others, and then shoving hard with a metal-plated shoulder out of desperation - not the intended method of unlocking said door, but an effective one regardless. The planks - their colourful designs long faded - flung inwards, revealing a large interior room with no other doors. Phoenix hovered at the entranceway, spying a massive, fluffy four-post double bed in the centre of the space, with leather and chains dangling from the ceiling, more leather attached to each bed post, and a table piled with what appeared to be whips, clamps, and a number of items Phoenix could not readily identify the function of. One of them appeared to be a fluffy machete, which was more than Phoenix had ever experimented with, it had to be said.

Perhaps more surprising was the small male straddled bent over forwards on a stool off to one side of the room. He was totally stark naked, chained in a kneeling position over this stool, facing towards Phoenix. He was incredibly mutated, even for a Waste town like this, with limbs and other bits sticking out of places limbs weren't originally intended.

"Err ... are you OK?" Phoenix asked, without knowing which answer would be stranger.

The man looked up suddenly with three eyes, a nose and a half, and a mouth that was not immediately visible. His eyes smiled. "Oh yes, quite fine indeed. Just waiting for my wives to come home and finish my punishment."

"Right, right," Phoenix replied standing dumbly in the doorway. "Um ... You missed the sacrifice."

At this, the man rolled his eyes. "Yes, I know. I'm ashamed not to have been there, but Lucille and Ronhilda refused to let me go until I had learned my lesson, you see. Was it a good sacrifice?"

Phoenix started backing quietly out of the door. "Um, yes, well, it was alright. You didn't miss much."

"Hey, could you be a dear and just quickly scratch my balls? By Stars do they itch. I think something is crawling on them."

"Yep, lemme just, you know, I, err," Phoenix stammered. He was now slowly closing the door. "I'll just come back in a bit, shall I? Gotta go do something important, you know, elsewhere."

"No wait, it's just a small itch. Just wave the beastie away and scratch, it'll take two seconds! Wait, please, I'm begging yo-"

The door clicked shut.

Phoenix stared.

A spear thudded in the wall next to him.

Phoenix ran.

* * *

For hours, Terrance Leeland marched, trudged and stomped along the narrow, uneven trails that most Can't Be Buried folk were too scared to travel upon. These trails snaked their way from the Back Road to the Highway, an unmapped, tangled mess of walking paths and ancient roads where beasties roamed free, unchecked by hunters and hired adventurers - who typically kept the main roads safe (relatively). The wind scoured up ragged, dusty whips all around Terrance, a cold front moving in with great haste from the south, taking with it his hat and sandpapering his skin to a fiery red mess. He grimaced tightly, frowned constantly, and swore regularly. But he didn't stop.

For he had a plan.

The only reason a place like Smack-dab would be shut is because that ugly Bert and her idiotic staff were gone. No highway bar, even along a dismal strip like the Back Road, would shut so long as somebody with at least half of half a brain was there to accept money, hand over drinks, and stop any fights before they broke a table. And the owners wouldn't shut up shop if someone was just out hunting, because only a handful of staff needed to go out on those short trips. No, the only reason it would officially close for business is if everyone was gone, and they were going far.

So Terrance did some maths.

The nearest town to Smack-dab was Second Thought, approximately two days' walking - one if you really powered through it. Other than that, Gerald was at least three days, or the Can't Be Buried fort at around one or two - although the chances of Bert daring to go there were next to nil, considering how much of a pussy coward she was. But back to the maths. She was definitely home just the day before last, because that was when Terrance had his ... encounter, with the staff. Where he lost his hand.

He grimaced to the power of grimace, his memory lingering on that particular scene. He bared his teeth to the world, feeling the unyielding itch of his missing appendage, almost as if it was still attached.

She was definitely home that day. No mistakes there. Even if she travelled out the same afternoon, it would be at least four days before she ever got back, and four days from now was still a couple days away. So, if Terrance could see this ... Farmer Brown or whatever his name was, prior to that, he might be able to create some kind of alliance and steal a few bandits. Anyone will hire out their minions for the right price, and almost any minion can hold a flaming torch and throw it on a wooden structure. Hell, you'd barely have to pay someone to do it - you'd get volunteers sticking their hands up just for the fun of it.

That same, dark smile from earlier spread over his lips again. Oh yeah, this was gonna be good.

Terrance marched a little faster, knowing that the back trails could take him to the fort's gate by mid-morning, so long as he could fight off the Things and other nasties that lived along them. And in Terrance's current heightened state of rage, he was confident he was the most dangerous thing out here.

What he didn't realise, of course, is just how truly interested Farmer Brown would be in Smack-dab's current ... availability.

But he was about to find out.

* * *

Hurl brought his three-headed axe down in a wide, heavy swing, thick blue veins popping beneath his leathery skin as muscles roiled and inflated. Bert cursed at her weapon and flung herself backwards, feeling the cool hiss of air as the blades narrowly avoided kissing her forehead goodnight. She rolled skillfully in the food-littered dust, toppling over her right shoulder to land in a low kneeling position. Meanwhile, Hurl was already moving in for his second attack, using the relative nimbleness of his short-handled weapon for a quick follow-up.

Bert wasn't prepared for a fight with a fast opponent. All her assumptions about Hurl told her he would be slow, lumbering, and dedicated purely to strength. He'd take a few hits, but only needed one of his own to win. But, sadly, like they say: When you assume, you make an ass out of you, me, and the bits of brain that end up draining though the dust at the victor's feet. These thoughts poured through Bert's brain as she pounced sideways a second time, an axe swing singing past her face.

Her ears fought for breath in the noise of his battle cry, a long, rumbling roar with no particular wit or catch phrase - just straight up volume. It curdled her insides even as she clicked back the hammer on her weapon to shift the dud bullet out the way and load up, hopefully, a functioning one. The noise speared through her Bertrage and felt around in the darkest recesses of her mind for old memories, ones that she didn't dare think about. She couldn't afford a flash back right now, she needed to focus.

Bert regained a decent foothold in the dust as she landed just off to the side, while Hurl closed in a third time. He lifted his axe, and his silhouette, outlined by the turbulent orange bonfire glow, looked eerily familiar to the time she was freed from the Awesome Squad's prison cell. *When Hurl had brought her out by the hair, forced her to her knees and...*

She pulled the trigger, her ears ringing equally from the blood rushing through her head, the deafening bang of her revolver, and the sheer din of Hurl's various angry cries. Instantly she felt the satisfying shudder of a bullet exploding out the barrel, the force of it rocking her arm back into her shoulder socket. But the shot was too wide, slashing through the side of Hurl's abdomen just below his ribs. His flesh was seared open and blood began to pour as he staggered a step backwards, but he remained quite noticeably upright.

Understandably, Hurl howled with pain. No longer was it only his face flushing a deep angry red, but his entire body seemed glowing with the hot crimson of a man slowly losing his tether on human decency, rational thought, and being generally calm. He swung again, but Bert was growing familiar with his style of attack. Hurl seemed to prefer wide, long swings, either cutting horizontally or striking straight down like a bladed, handheld meteor. Bert deftly stepped around the powerful strike, her thumb already pulling the hammer back on her pistol. She arced through the air and into a position just behind her opponent, who was recovering from making the dinosaurs extinct. This was it, she thought. Bert lifted her weapon, planted her feet to fire into the back of his big ol' skull, and...

...got kicked in the stomach.

Indeed a large, metal-capped boot connected with her abs, causing her to pull the trigger and send a surprised shot flying off into the dust somewhere near the bonfire. The bonfire, meanwhile, didn't seem to mind. Bert was lifted from her feet and flung briefly into the air from the sheer force of the boot, sending her reeling into the dust behind. Pain flooded her system as air struggled to find any traction in her winded lungs. She found herself lost in a sea of coughing, floundering on the filthy courtyard ground as dust clung to her clothing and exposed skin. Something felt loose in her mouth from where she landed on her face.

"Yer gon' pay for what ya did t' me face, Berty," an animal hissed somewhere above her. "I'm gon' chop yer limbs off one by one an' use ya like a toy until ya starve."

Bert gritted her teeth in frustration and went for her pistol, but it wasn't there. In alarm, she hurriedly scanned the area to see that her weapon lay near the feet of her meaty opponent, a dribble of smoke still leaking out the barrel. Shit, she thought. How would she get it out from under him? Bert glared up at the figure looming nearby, seeing how his body was glazed with blood, dirt, and sweat like one of Phoenix's unsuccessful Chef's Specials. His chest heaved up and down with heavy, deep breaths, blood pumping out of his abdomen in a steady stream, despite his best efforts to hold it in with his spare hand. His face was shrivelled up so far it might either have dried out from lack of moisture – it was flowing out below his ribs, after all – or he was pissed off beyond all recognition. Bert began to wonder if she could goad him into an over-aggressive little bit of rage, which she could try to take advantage of.

Try being a particularly important little bastard of a word in that thought...

Finally, after coming to the decision, she snorted unnecessarily loudly, a swirl of dust flicking up where her breath hit the ground. She tucked her knees under herself and pushed down, bringing her body to an upright, if not entirely steady, position. Blood trickled out the edge of her lip. "Rip my limbs off one by one, eh?" she jeered loud enough for his crew to hear, wiping the blood away.

Hurl glared back. "Oh yeah."

"Well colour me impressed, Hurl," Bert started.

He cocked his head, his expression doing its best impression of an earthquake.

"I didn't realise you could count to one."

Hurl looked stunned for a second, a few sniggers sniggering out (as sniggers are wont to do) from either very brave or very stupid bandits nearby. His solitary bloodshot eye latched on to the hushed laughter, scouring them with a look to make even a man-eating tree question its life choices. Bert knew instantly that she was successful. But would it work, or just give him super-human angry powers all the better to smoosh her with?

The man started to tremble, veins looking like they were about to burst all over his skin, and at least one vein actually bursting next to his bullet wound. The vibration raced through his meaty body from foot to head, erupting out of his mouth as a terrifying roar of fury.

Somewhere in the darkness nearby, a small group of Things heard the roar and froze. They were waiting in the shadows for the next victim to dare urinate, and decided upon hearing the noise that, perhaps, there were better brunch options somewhere else in the Waste, and this maybe just wasn't a good time to be here in Dunce Town. There was clearly an important event on, and it was a rude time to interrupt. They could come back later, it was no big thing. They'd just come back later. And so they scampered into the night.

However, were the Things to remain where they were, they would have observed the following: A large human male whom the Things would have called Om, muscle-bound all to hell, even meaty, you might say, though the word has a different meaning to Things, was charging head-first towards a slight human female whom the Things would have called Nom Nom. She was maybe half his size, if even that. Om swings his axe in a particularly wide arc, but Nom Nom sidesteps it to the left and slightly forwards, bringing her under his giant, sculpted chest. She grabs his axe and yanks it before he has finished swinging, offsetting his balance and giving her an opening. She then thrusts with her inedible left fist and it connects with the giant's cheek bone, upon which he topples over into the ground. This is, of course, where the Things would swarm in to consume Nom Nom before she has a chance to retrieve her weapon and fight back. Then they would consume Om. But they'd only swarm in this fashion were there no other humans around, of which there were many, and of course if there was no light, which was the Great Enemy. Oh, and more importantly, they'd only do so if they were still hanging around to watch, which they most assuredly weren't.

But back in the realm of humans, Bert was now standing over her prone opponent, flexing and unflexing her robotic left fist. The servos, normally chipper and sprightly, complained with a pitiful high whine, and her middle finger wouldn't flex. She swore beneath her heavy, exhausted breathing, but was glad it was at least her middle finger that had broken, not another. If there was one finger she might want not to flex, it would be that one.

Hurl, meanwhile, was writhing in the dust, chunky fingers inspecting his jaw while the gooey red ichor that should be pumping around his body instead booked a holiday to Dunce Town and travelled out his abdomen. It was a good thing he was already missing teeth, because the sudden shock to his face would have ended the last of them. Blood pooled in his mouth and he spat it out in a large, sticky globule, blowing some of it off his lips as long strands clung on for dear life.

All around, Polite Bandits and their somewhat impolite counterparts watched on with anticipation. A few of their number had sat down mid-fight to watch the duel like old friends listening to a radio play, while many more were quietly taking bets on who the victor would be. Sir Robert remained standing, posture firm and steady, gazing on nervously as the two combatants battled back and forth. Bert could see him staring intensely at her, his moustache blowing in the icy wind, but she couldn't determine what his expression meant. Doris, however, gave her a smile and a respectful nod. The man she was still threatening with a bloodied machete did not do the same.

A chill wind swirled in and around the courtyard, brawling with the bonfire at its heart. Bert sweated in her body heat despite the bitter air slicing through her jacket. She looked down at Hurl, his muscles rolling like a fleshy ocean beneath his scars as he fumbled in the dust for consciousness, and she tried to feel anything other than hate. Bert didn't expressly like killing, it just sort-of found her lots and snuck its way into her business. There was enough shit in the Waste out to get you without her being part of it, which is why she maintained the lifestyle of a pacifist. Or rather, why she *attempted* to maintain the lifestyle of a pacifist, anyway. But Hurl? He inflamed her mind, the very sound of his grating, unintelligent voice a tornado blasting through her memories, picking up pigcows, houses, and all sorts of hidden, repressed feelings. She tried to feel some kind of disgust at the idea of murdering the man, wanted to desperately, but she felt as ice-cold as the night around her.

Bert took a few steps away from Hurl and retrieved her waiting pistol, brushing some of the dust off it. She flicked open the cylinder to see if any dust had gotten in, but was satisfied to see her remaining bullets unharmed. Her bone-handled weapon clicked quietly as she flicked the cylinder shut, and clicked once again when the hammer locked into its ready position. It was time to end this, but for real this time.

She turned around, walked resolutely back towards Hurl, and angled her pistol down towards him. She'd put a bullet in his brain, or whatever dark, slimy thing he had in his skull as a replacement. She'd take his life and hopefully it was some small vengeance for the lives he had ruined. She aimed.

Then a hand jumped out and coiled around her ankle. Bert pulled the trigger quickly but was tugged off her feet at the same time. The bullet went wide, cutting through Hurl's ear and embedding itself into the dust as he launched himself towards Bert. He pulled her all the way down to the ground, clambering with speed and strength along her body, blood dripping all over her. She swore loudly and hammered back her pistol, but the bandit chief swiped it from her clutches and growled like a rabid animal.

Eyes alight with murder, Hurl lifted a huge fist and brought it down hard toward Bert's chest, connecting with her forearms as she brought them up in defence. Drool hung from his mouth, droplets flying into Bert's face as Hurl brought his fists up again and again, hammering and hammering on her forearms, using his fingernails like rakes to try and pull them apart.

Bert's heart thudded in her chest almost as hard as Hurl was pummelling her, her stomach filling with acidic little butterflies as her forearms screamed in agony. When a moment appeared between batterings she put all her strength behind her knee and thrust it into his abdomen, hoping to spark the pain in his bullet wound and shift his weight somewhere other than her chest. He shuddered from the blow and howled with pain, more spit and blood blasting from his mouth to shower Bert below. The man lifted up as he flinched from her knee, but his lower body still trapped hers. She was too weak to lever him off with strength alone, but she didn't know many close quarters techniques to dismount him some other way.

Desperate, now, Bert tried again to knee Hurl's ribs, but he countered by grabbing her thigh. His fingers wrapped around it and squeezed painfully hard, and then he brought round his other hand and grappled her shoulder. She wriggled and jiggled to get free, but the man's strength was as you might expect from all the meat stuck to his bones. He shuffled his feet apart, and started to try and lift Bert. She wriggled more, using her metal fist as a blunt weapon to his skull, punching and slapping and thumping. But he gritted his teeth, or rather, his gums, and heaved himself into the air, bringing Bert with him – clutched from thigh and shoulder.

Up into the air they rose, Hurl screaming so loud she could feel his voice vibrating all the way into her skeleton. More and more she punched him, specifically targeting his face to try and break it open, maybe drop him into unconsciousness. She felt him squeeze harder on her body, and his weight was shifting beneath her. Suddenly she became extraordinarily aware that her back was exposed, and at any moment she could be dropped onto his knee and practically cleaved in two. She'd seen him do it many times before, on insubordinate bandits, unwitting challengers to his position, and, worst of fall, the toys of his that dared talk back too many times.

Bert started to panic, her Bertrage faltering under the sheer toxicity of fear. Blindly and wildly she slapped at the man's face with her metal fist. It had worked so well the first time, but now he was madder than ever and he was just taking the hits. His nose had practically turned to dust under her blows, and his cheek, eye and jaw were clearly all broken. But still he squeezed, finding his feet in the dust for the support needed to break her back over his leg. She hammered again and again, aiming for whatever soft bits she could find – or, in this case, make. She focused on his eye, which was filling with blood and making him look like a red-eyed demon from the very pits of Gachook's Freckle.

"Fuck ... you!" he stammered, his voice disrupted by the thudding of her blows.

And, finally, he staggered. Bert was momentarily dropped as Hurl's feet slid slightly apart, but he caught both her and himself in a second. His head was swaying, rolling on the neck in a drunken manner. She punched again, and it forced Hurl a large, highly unstable step backwards.

"Die!" he growled, his voice forced through the blood and spit swirling around his mouth and throat.

He gripped hard on her thigh and shoulder and brought her down - the move she had been dreading.

This truly was it, she thought, but not the it that she was anticipating. This was the it where she failed, where she let Phoenix, Meatsack and The Woman down. This was the it where Farmer Brown rode through Smackdab like a tsunami wearing dungarees, tearing the bar to pieces and scattering its staff to the winds.

This was the it where Hurl finally got his wish and beat her to death.

Except she didn't die.

Her tired body sailed past where Hurl's knee should be and careened straight into the ground. She landed with a thud and an oof, the air bursting out of her lungs and the shock making her wish that someone would hurry up and cut off her forearms already, because they couldn't possibly be less painful than right this moment. Above her, Hurl swayed and staggered, unable to keep his footing for more than a few moments. Vague words babbled out of his face - finally no longer twitching. Shortly after, the tower that was Hurl collapsed over, and a huge cloud of dust kicked up into the air as he collided with it face-first. A bassy sound escaped his throat as he hit the ground. And nothing more.

Bert winced as she placed her arms down and pushed herself to her feet, staring at the motionless, bleeding pile of muscles that was the corpse of Hurl.

She had won. Bert's Battalion was hers.

Bandits flooded into the centre of the courtyard, congratulating her loudly and slapping her all over. Doris tried to push through the throng and fret about Bert's wounds, but the sea of cheerful faces washed her out as many times as it washed her back in again. Bandits both polite and impolite suddenly knew she was going to win, and of course there was never any doubt it about it, eh? Money exchanged hands where folks had lost the bet, and at least two or three bandits began plotting their future mutiny against the new leader, as was customary in certain unlawful circles.

Bert herself felt relieved. Maybe it was cliché to talk about huge weights lifting off one's shoulders, but it truly felt to her that the last jigsaw piece of her pre-Smack-dab life was finally shredded, and the puzzle could never again be put together. And even better, Hurl's end would mean she had the strength to have a future, to fight Farmer Brown at his own game and cast him back to whatever southern farm he grew up on.

How she was going to defeat Farmer Brown himself was of course another matter entirely, especially since she could barely defeat a man who was only half his immense, titanic size. But this seemed like one of those Future Problems, at least for now. Right at this moment Bert felt it was time to regurgitate her last meal, yell at people to stop slapping her on the sore bits, and then get Bert's Battalion mobile.

It was time to march on Smack-dab.

...but maybe after some first-aid.

And a bloody drink.

* * *

Phoenix had finally reached the base of the Starry Place, and mercifully it appeared that nobody was nearby. He half stumbled, half ran past some of the final few huts, most of which still bore the same multi-coloured, round-ended plank designs as those that were higher up Mount Butt. Bleeding beneath old bandages and feeling like he was bleeding where soon new ones would be needed, Phoenix limped further, winding his way through the steep streets to find the village gate and get the hell out of dodge, to where he could concoct an amazing plan.

He needed to somehow get back to the Constellator to see what had happened. Everybody reacted differently to their first bonkerberry, and there was a chance that she had just passed out from the sheer energy. It wasn't super common, but it was far from unknown, either. But he needed to get back to have a look, and to show everyone that he wasn't lying (about this, anyway). Phoenix was just glad the Constellator hadn't started dissolving from the inside out, which was probably the worst reaction he had ever seen - and not just because it was a fat bloke who took a long, *long* time to dissolve. Hours.

Phoenix shivered from the memory, and kept limping.

A loud humming noise hummed away to his left, and he saw a large structure with no walls catching the cables and chairs that intersected the Constellator's hut at the peak of the hill. They were moving, now, with the cables winding through a giant, rusted wheel before being cast back up the hill, chairs and all. The whole thing looked to be supported by massive pylons the entire way up the slope, but nobody rode the chairs. Phoenix watched a particularly wretched-looking specimen swing precariously in a sneaky gust of wind before snapping off and falling to its doom below, and the doom of the hut it crashed through. He swore he'd never ride that thing. Never in a million years.

A voice shouted somewhere in a parallel street and Phoenix knew it was time to limp on. He heaved his tired body forwards, focusing his mind on his destination, trying to forget about the aches and sharp pains screaming at him from just about all over. He was weaponless save for one small knife that he usually kept stashed ... well, never mind where he stashed it, it was not currently convenient. The important thing was that his prized rifle was gone, not to mention the gemstones that were his grenades, the myriad little doodads and gizmos of violence that he kept in his pouches, and, rather depressingly, his new Waste Beast tooth knife, which he'd grown incredibly fond of. All of it gone.

But still, he pushed on, for the gate was drawing near. He could see the perimeter fence in the dim village light, and there was a distinctly white glow coming from somewhere just over the next row of buildings that surely must have been the main gate. Phoenix sucked in a breath and ducked into a tight alley between two fat huts, hoping to keep ahead, and not to mention out of sight, of the wild mob nipping at his heels. He inched along, wading through old food scraps, discarded clothing, and more than one dead crate-cat, before popping out the other side to...

...to see a giant angry mob of armed cultists no more than a few feet from him.

The mob, one giant scowl, collectively barred the Starry Place main gate, which was bathed in an almost blindingly white light emanating from obese floodlights anchored to the steep slope above the Mount Butt road. Those in the mob growled audibly and gripped spears, axes, wooden bats and even one beautifully carved wooden tewhatewha - an axe-like Old World cultural weapon that was old even to the Old World, and that nobody could pronounce the name of, but which didn't matter because it was still a tewhatewha.

"Oh," Phoenix said awkwardly, coming to a stumbling, gentle halt as the realisation of the situation passed slowly through his exhausted brain. "Err, hello."

"There he is!"

"Get him!"

And to the cliché cries of mobs chasing escapees the Waste over, the mass of star-speckled angry cultists lurched forwards towards Phoenix. The throng surged like a giant ooze monster, a creature known for its particularly deadly surging. The cultists at the front were the most enthusiastic, charging off at full sprint, weapons held high and waving around irresponsibly. Those in the back followed suit row after row as the message to charge reached the cheap seats, but they had the courtesy to keep their blades and other killing implements close to their bodies so as to not chop the heads off their forward counterparts, which was awful nice of them.

Phoenix let out a squeal and ducked back through the alley, dead crate-cats and old rubbish flying up all around him like a rotten bow wave. The mob hit the same alley just behind, fighting with itself to squeeze through the tight passage that could only fit one or two pairs of shoulders at a time. The sheer mass of bodies pressed tightly into itself, desperately pushing, shoving and swearing to be the first through the alley. Some at the back, smelling an opportunity to get ahead of their companions, splintered off from the ooze monster and ran to circle around the buildings instead, hoping to cut Phoenix off somewhere ahead.

The man in question ran, finding within himself a new pool of energy with which to panic. He was always amazed at the body's ability to find new reservoirs of adrenalin, but at the same time he was grumpy at his

By Duncan P. Pacey

body for having hid it in the first place. If it had just released it all sooner, he might have beat the cultists to the damned gate and be out of this mad town. But alas, if wishes were fishes, he'd have fishes. He wouldn't know what to do with them, but he'd have them all the same.

He started towards a steep street named Bob's Knob - which he didn't remotely have the energy to laugh at - but already cultists from elsewhere in the town were pouring down it, throwing spears and howling into the night. Phoenix swore and turned, making for one of the other many roads that all connected near the gate. Everywhere, though, groups were armed, wild-eyed, and running in his direction.

And then he heard the hum. It felt quieter, now, submerged under all the screaming and shouting, but its constant, dull drone loitered just above the noise, waiting for someone to notice it. Chair after chair marched at a constant rate through the spinning disc atop the structure, before ploughing ahead up the slope to follow their companions. Another chair, tired of its old age and the constant monotony of going up and down a hill its entire life, collapsed with a loud snap and fell into the streets below.

Phoenix cursed again, but this time at himself for even thinking about thinking about the idea now being thought of in the recesses of his thoughts. His head swivelled up hill, but cultists met his gaze. He turned to face another street, but again met cultists. And each time there were too many for him to fight weaponless and exhausted. It made him angry, but out of pride more than anything else. He should be able to kill these assholes in his sleep, but here and now he was scared of just a few mad nobodies with tassled spears and stupid, flappy robes. Sweet baby Gachook, he thought, Sandra Bulletface would be rolling in her grave, if she had one.

Behind him, the mob roared. The first of its number were bursting out of the alley, and those who were smart enough to go around were circling in, delighted at the prospect of being in the front row - that's where all the stabby stuff happened, which was the best bit. Phoenix had to make a decision, and it had to be now.

His legs decided before his pride ever agreed, and pounding on the dirty Starry Place streets once again, they carried his indecisive body towards the humming. With spears and one tewhatewha close on his ass, Phoenix pounced past the spinning disc and the chairs that queued around it obediently, waiting for their turn to proceed. He aimed for one of the more intact-looking examples beginning its steady climb into the air, leaping up to grab a hold of it.

The chair was little more than a few metal bars with a cushion on top, but that was more than could be said for some of its counterparts. Phoenix's arm was almost ripped from its socket when he caught the bar, letting out an audible gasp of pain as the thing dragged his body upwards.

"Somebody grab him!"

"No, don't let him on thy lift!"

The voices came thick and loud beneath him, but they started to grow distant. Phoenix pulled himself slowly onto the chair as he was lifted into the air, taking the moment of safety to catch his breath and rest. The stickiness of sleep pestered his face, for he couldn't remember how many hours it had been since he had a decent rest, but he rubbed it away in defiance. Now was not the time.

The Starry Place slithered past far below his feet, some of the cultists who hadn't made it down the hill glancing up in horror as he sauntered upwards. The occasional spear whistled past for the sake of it, but nobody below was a skilled enough warrior to actually hit a moving target up in the air. So Phoenix continued largely unimpeded, relaxing back in a lumpy old chair that was precariously hanging on a rusting hook from a cable that must have been hundreds of years old.

It was a perfect plan.

How could it go wrong?

Then it went wrong.

Phoenix was near the top of the slope, fast-approaching the Constellator's mighty hut. But next to it, where the chairs were landing, a small group was gathered. He couldn't make out much in the bleak light, but there were distinctly pointy shapes jutting out from the silhouetted crowd, and Phoenix felt he could probably guess what those were.

He sighed loudly, wishing life could just be a little easier. That for once he could just get the girl without the effort, without all of this adventuring and fighting and just this general expending of energy.

Speaking of adventure and fighting and the expenditure of energy, the lift stopped.

Phoenix's chair got the message a second or so later, causing the entire thing to rock like a drowning boat. Phoenix's face paled to a sickly green at the motion. He clung tight to the metal bars and looked back over his shoulder to see what had happened. And lo, for there were many cultists clambering up the wires. They had little hand-held metal hooks of their own, each of which seemed to grip tight to the cable above. At some point they must have jumped on just after his chair, hanging on until someone figured out how to stop the stupid lift. Each climbed with an axe or other small bladed weapon clenched in their teeth, and though Phoenix felt holding an axe in your teeth was a horrible cliché of a thing to do, a clichéd axe could bloody you just as good as a respectable one.

Phoenix looked down, wondering if he could jump. The huts were pretty far below, but if he could aim himself for one of the sloped roofs, maybe the impact would be lessened. Hitting the ground would surely be less of a problem than being stabbed to death, right?

Or maybe it would just be slower and more painful.

He steeled himself and gritted his teeth, glancing once more over his shoulder just to make sure it wasn't a dream.

It wasn't.

Now or never, he thought. He tensed his muscles, imagining the angle of the drop and the acrobatics he'd need to perform so not to break his legs. His brain raced with mathematics he wasn't aware he could do, but just before he flung himself from the chair, it started moving again.

The entire thing lurched forwards with a spasmodic, shuddering jerk that made even it seem as surprised as he was. The cultists on the hooks close behind cursed loudly and some dropped their weapons, ceasing their climb in favour of clinging for dear life. Phoenix frowned with confusion, turning up hill to see what was happening.

And there was the Constellator, arms open wide, her face distressed, sweaty, and her eyes brimming with tears.

What the hell? Phoenix thought.

"Oh sweet Bringer of Dreams!" she cried, her voice cracking with emotion. Then her eyes turned to daggers and she stabbed the nearest guard, who visibly shrunk under the attack. "You! Get the Bringer of Dreams down from thine Lift of Chairs!"

"Uhh..." Phoenix said, or rather, Phoenix vocalised. He didn't really *say* anything, as such. But he made noises.

Soon he was at the top, sitting in stunned almost-silence as star-speckled guards swarmed up to his chair and helped him down from it, even stopping the lift so he could get off without doing an awkward little run. The Constellator was right in his face the moment he touched ground, smiling as though the very Stars themselves had come down from their Cloudy Wall and graced her with their presence. Or whatever.

"Oh Bringer of Dreams, the Stars!" she cried, tears breaking the dam and pouring openly from her face.

Phoenix grinned nervously. "Yeah, hah, the Stars, eh? Um, haha ... what?"

"The STARS!" she cried again, grasping him by the shoulders and shaking his body.

He tensed and tried to shrink away from her, spying the angry looks from other cultists nearby. She was touching him. Oh boy.

"I have spoken with thine Constellations," she wailed in his face, droplets of spittle, sweat and tears spattering on his skin. A little drool clung to the edge of her lips. "There were so many of them. I floated with them beyond the Cloudy Wall! We danced and laughed and talked. They were so beautiful, Bringer of Dreams, so soft of voice and firm of body. Their beautiful naked flesh touched me-"

The other cultists looked uncertain at this.

"-and their brilliant fingers stroked all over my body, all *through* it! I was naked, too! I have flown naked with the Stars! Don't you see? DON'T YOU SEE?"

Phoenix started to smile more genuinely, rallying from the shock of the moment to realise what was happening. The bonkerberries, they had worked! She had seen what she wanted to see, which was totally great and expected and in no way did Phoenix worry that she'd see horrible monsters and darkness and never leave her house again. Yes, it was all anticipated and carefully planned and not a spur of the moment decision.

Yes.

"I'm glad to see you awake, mighty Const– mighty leader of the Starry Place," Phoenix said, smugness creeping into his voice, still hoarse from exertion.

The Constellator peered straight through his eyes and into his mushy brain goo, where presumably his soul was hidden. Her eyes were unblinking, stained red around the edges. Her fingers were like little claws digging into his skin through his clothing, and it didn't seem the pressure was going to be released any time soon.

"You are the Bringer of Dreams, Bringer of Dreams! You are a hero to the Starry people! Where? Where can I get more of your wonderful magic?!" Her voice was manic, unable to control the pitch or volume with which it flowed out of her wet mouth.

Phoenix's smile widened to damn near a grin. Oh yeah, he thought, this was it. This shit was happening.

"I can get you more," he said, trying to keep his bubbling excitement contained.

She gripped tighter, pulling him close. But not in a sexy way. More in a scary way.

Phoenix thought about his purpose of being here, and decided that Bert wouldn't mind if he added a few more figurative cherries to the grotesque cake that was this negotiation. First he'd need his weapons, then some medical supplies. Then he reckoned he should find out about that lusty maid from earlier, and see if she knew how to use a fluffy machete. Then there was a little matter of food, drink, sleep – sweet mercy did he need some sleep – glorious riches and, of course, a massive, wild, spear-tipped army.

Oh yeah, this was gonna be good.

"Yes, I can definitely get more. But first..." he stated, in his most commanding, heroic voice. That is, a slightly deeper one than normal. "...you must listen to my irrefusable offer. And lady?"

The Constellator listened, breath held.

"I reckon you can't refuse it."

* * *

"C'mon, Meatsack! Lettus in, man!" hollered Jeb, his old fist hammering against Smack-dab's tired front door. The wood rattled loosely in its frame with every bang, presumably contemplating whether *today's the day*, or if it would just keep going a little longer to see if better things were on the horizon.

"He keeps lookin' back, Jeb, but he's not movin' off that chair," said Orsen, his face pressed flat against a nearby window, cheeks smooshed into the glass. "He's got some good balance, though. It's a ruddy small chair for a big lad like that to curl up on."

"Well balance or no," replied the older trader, "I'm so bloody cold I'm about t' start burnin' planks just t' keep warm."

"I bet that'd get Meatsack t' open up, though."

Jeb briefly paused knocking and raised an eyebrow. "Huh, yer ain't half wrong, Orsen, m'lad. Let's call that one plan B, eh?"

"Alrighty, Jeb. Plan B."

Jeb threw a few more thumps on the door, and a slight kick just for good measure. He'd never encountered Smack-dab shut before. He didn't even know this door *could* lock. And for The Woman's statue to be lying there amputated like that, her arm just littered about the place? It was almost unthinkable. And to think he was standing here thinking it right now. Thinking the unthinkable, what next? Imagining the unimaginable? The Waste was going mad, Jeb thought.

"Come on, Meatsack! We've bin out here for like, two hours! It's bloody cold, man!'

"What's plan C, Jeb?" Orsen asked, walking away from the window to stand near his mentor. He had that look on his face again - the one Jeb knew meant an Orsen moment was imminent. His eyes were too wide, too starry. They looked like they wanted to feast.

"Plan C, Orsen? We've not even gotten to plan B, yet."

"Aye sure, but what if we do an' plan B fails? Best t' be prepared, right?"

Jeb stepped away from the door, giving it a final look of offense before scratching his patchy stubble. "Well, lad, I s'pose we could break a window an' just climb in. Bert wouldn't be none too happy 'bout that, though."

"That's why it's plan C though, right?"

"Aye, lad, that's fair. So we never have to do it."

The boy nodded. He always nodded when his brain was accepting new data. Jeb sometimes wondered if it was so he could shake the other bits loose so there'd be space for something new. Goodness knows where he kept all this information – he was skinny as bloody rake, but not nearly as useful.

"Come on, Meatsack!" Jeb tried again, though with less energy. He was growing incredibly weary, having been yelling at this stupid wooden door for the past two hours. His fists hurt from all the banging, and his mouth tasted dry and hoarse. Meatsack really wasn't letting them in, and it was unfathomable as to why. Jeb and Orsen were just pleasant company to be around! "We're friends o' Bert, ya knows us!"

"Err..." said Orsen.

Jeb looked back at him.

"What about plan D, Jeb? I'm jus' worried that if we chicken out o' plan C, we'll be left up slit creek."

"Slit creek, lad?"

"Yeah, up slit creek with a paddle."

Jeb stared at him for a moment. He understood each of those words individually, but not all together like that. "Err, with a paddle, lad?"

"Yeah, a paddle."

"Ya mean like ... one o' them, ya know, sexy butt slappers like Trader Bill was sellin'?"

Orsen furrowed his brow. "I guess so, Jeb, but I dunno why anyone would want one o' those up slit creek. What is slit creek anyway?"

Jeb scratched the back of his head awkwardly. He reckoned he had an idea as to what it meant, and by the looks of how fast Orsen's cheeks were filling with a rather tellingly crimson warmth, he had made a guess, too.

"Oh," he said. "I'm not sure I know what that sayin' means anymore, Jeb."

"Aye, lad, ya got me there, too. Maybe let's just drop it, eh?"

The boy nodded.

"Alright..."

They both looked back at the door and saw, to their surprise, Meatsack was peering out from behind it with one grey eye, his chunky fingers wrapped tight around the sliver of crack that had opened. His face was glossy with tears, eyes puffy and rimmed red.

"Meatsack!" Jeb said cheerfully, smiling as wide as his face could fit. There was no time for bargaining here, Jeb was on a one-way train to guilt-trip town. He wanted inside that bar. Needed.

Meatsack stared, his fingers starting to drum lightly on the wood.

"Meatsack, buddy, pal. Please let us in. We're out 'ere starvin' and dyin' o' thirst, and that's not t' mention the cold. Oh Meatsack, it's so ruddy freezin' out here. Don't ya think ya can just let us in this once? Do ya not like us anymore, are we not welcome?"

Meatsack gasped and nodded his head quickly.

"Wait, are ya sayin' yes we're not welcome, or yes we're welcome?"

He nodded again, quicker this time.

"Ya jus' nodded yes t' both o' them."

Meatsack paused a moment, then nodded his head again.

"Is your name Meatsack?" chirped Orsen.

Meatsack nodded his head again.

Jeb raised an eyebrow, taken aback by the question. "Why are ya askin' the lad his name, Orsen?"

"I thought maybe he's broken, Jeb. Only able t' nod or somethin' like that. I was testin'."

"So ya asked him a question where the answer ya wanted is yes?"

"Err, yeah."

"Even though ya thought he could only nod?"

"...right."

"Right. Well he's not broken, lad, don't be rude. The boy's jus' lettin' us in, now, right, Meatsack?"

Meatsack retreated a step back into the room, closing the door ever so slightly so that only his fingertips and the slight gleam of an eye was visible.

"Wait, wait, wait!" Jeb shouted, stepping forwards to wedge his foot in the crack. "I thought ya said we was welcome, right, lad?"

The glittery eye nodded.

"Well!" Jeb smiled, pushing his foot further into the door. "We'll jus' be welcome then, eh? Won't be any trouble at all, I swears t' ya. We'll jus' grab our usual seat, a bit o' grog and whatever food ya got lyin' around, alright?"

Meatsack cowered further into the bar, but to Jeb's immense satisfaction, released his pressure on the door. In fact, he let it go completely and scuttled backwards into the room, leaving Jeb the opportunity to push the door all the way open. He grinned wide as he soaked in the familiar dusty sight that was Smack-dab. Bar. Food. Room. He sniffed deeply, savouring the musty smell of the damp planks, and of the old food festering somewhere in Phoenix's kitchen. It'd probably turn into a Chef's Special if he left it long enough. They'd charge double, too. Clever bastards.

Meatsack was near the bar, watching the new duo with tearful eyes. Jeb pointed Orsen to their usual spot, by one of the front windows, and smiled a friendly, trustworthy smile at the big, grey mutant.

But as they filed in, nobody locked the door again.

And that meant Smack-dab was open for business.

Part Eight

Anger Before the Storm

It was a new day. Some might have even called it a beautiful day, but that's only in the sense that those people woke up this morning, and any morning you wake up the same way you went to bed, is a beautiful day.

In reality, it was a pretty unpleasant day. The smog was feeling particularly bleak, clouds pregnant with a brooding, melancholy sort of grey snot that clogged it all up and just dared folks to travel without a raincoat. It left the landscape in a perpetual, almost shadowless tint, a black and white blanket over a world that had clearly not suffered enough. The temperature had climbed somewhat since the chill frosts of night, but this was overshadowed quite significantly by the fact that the wind was also drastically picking up. Strong gusts blasted in from the southern coasts, vandalising street signs and unstable Old World ruins, whipping up large chunks of dust along the way.

Towards the ocean side of Can't Be Buried, a vast horde of bandits was packing up camp amid the dewy landscape, and those who weren't packing up the camp were chasing the bits that weren't packed up in time. It was a rag-tag assortment of folk, to be sure, but since the violence of the night before, only minimal murder had taken place between members of the separate factions. They were superglued together, you see, with the almost literal iron fist of a solitary, small woman, who was at this moment standing ahead of the pack, gazing towards a towering mountain range that stretched as far as the eye could see both north and south. When she walked, she walked with a slight limp, and those who saw her briefly before she put on her large, flowing trench coat noticed that her arms were a brilliant rainbow of blues and purples. Her left hand, as chunky and solid as it was, seemed to have been clenched in a fist for quite some time. In fact, nobody had seen her unclench it since the fight, and it looked what you might call 'A little worse for wear'. Some had even called it 'Fucked', but they learned rather quickly that the subject was personal and their opinions were ... unwelcome.

On this same morning, high up on the slopes and indeed florpadorps of one Mount Butt, another horde stirred; one the likes of which the Waste had not seen since the destructive War of Stars many, many generations ago. An incoherent bugle beeped and bopped somewhere in the midst of this horde, which wound like a giant, black snake down a narrow mountain road. The wind howled through their ranks, channelled by the many peaks and troughs all around them. The occasional figure was lifted completely off the road and sent screaming down the slope. But nobody worried for their safety. All of these determined, black-clad, highly weaponised figures were marching down the hill anyway, and the few who took a trip off the side were just getting there faster.

Two figures strode excitedly ahead of the pack, locked in an unheard discussion. One, a moderately-built man with a billowing, armoured trench coat; the other a woman encased in a brilliantly made suit of black, white-speckled metal plating. Both kept the horde at a steady marching pace.

At the very base of the slope, a long, broken road swept past in a mad rush and stretched out for miles towards where it intersected a strip known as the Highway. It was amid the distraught rubble of this road that a rabbit-like creature with a hat sat on its haunches and stared at an approaching dust cloud. The rabbit-like creature was called Randolf, and he was a Conqueror, Ruiner of Worlds, Bringer of Shadows, and, indeed, a Lord of Rabbit-Like Kind. His black eyes shone like angry gemstones in small grey sockets, the folds of his forehead creeping down in a frown. He was on this road hunting breakfast, not to mention plotting the ultimate destruction of the human species, as well as numerous other species including but not limited to ants, wolfcats, and the sky-dwelling Devil Terrors (a type of falcon). And yet now the wandering prey he had been sniffing out for the past two hours had shat itself and fled with unfortunate haste, frightened off by the vexatious rumbling that preceded this approaching dust cloud. He began to wonder if the beast was back.

In mere moments his suspicions were brought true by sight, as he saw the beast that approached was none other than the scaly red – grentuputron, some might call it – Waste Beast that was the destruction of his predecessor. It lumbered down the road with great speed, bouncing from pot hole to pot hole all to the unending din of its constant grumbling. Randolf the Conqueror, Ruiner of Worlds, Bringer of Shadows and Lord of Rabbit-Like Kind found himself captivated by its glittering scales and its brilliant glowing eyes, but had learned the lessons of his one-time rival and superior. Reluctantly, he stepped to the side of the road and glared as the great spiked beast bounded past, roaring as great breaths of thick, black smoke burst from its rear. Dust and smoke spilled over Randolf as it passed, smothering him in filth. The Conqueror, Ruiner of Worlds, Bringer of Shadows and Lord of Rabbit-Like Kind felt his paws tremble with rage as he coughed and spluttered. This beast dared insult him? It dared?! This was of the highest insult! Nobody should so much as think about farting smoke onto a Lord of Rabbit-Like Kind without expecting some kind of rebuke. The sheer malice of the act was ... was, it was astounding! Oh how Randolf the Conqueror, Ruiner of Worlds, Bringer of Shadows and Lord of Rabbit-Like Kind seethed.

He ran for a local rabbit-like burrow, quickly moving the revenge and ruination of the great spiked beast to the very top of his to-destroy list. The beast had destroyed the previous lord and now it sought to ridicule the new one. It simply had to die - no court of Rabbit-Like Law would find total revenge anything other than appropriate.

And he'd start with where it was going - one of the human's pathetic above-ground structures, located smack-dab in the middle of nowhere.

His nowhere.

* * *

Terrance Leeland sat crushed between two figures in the seasick truck cabin. To his right was a skinny wretch of a creature, who looked more suited to administrative pencil sharpening than the stabbing of other humans in battle. This was perhaps why the man, whose name was either Ernest or who was feeling earnest at some point in the past few hours, wielded a clipboard with the same tenacity and confidence as one might wield an axe, or a shoulder-mounted tactical nuke launcher.

The other figure crushing Terrance was the one who did most of the crushing, but less of the driving. It was Farmer Brown, who could barely so much as squeeze into the front seat; his rocky shoulders forced their way into as many unoccupied spaces as possible. The complete lack of oxygen, and the horrible feeling of bones crammed into horrible positions, reminded Terrance of an old adventure, back when he was forced into strategic hiding between a rock and A Hard Place - a popular, if violent, little Waste bar to the south. Folks would flock from all over to see its famous bar fights, until the Overlords came and participated in its final, and fatal, battle. Those were the good ol' days. People knew who he was back then.

Terrance couldn't help but smile - a look that didn't suit his face. But how could he not? His plan was going better than expected so far. His power-march through the back trails last night had indeed brought him to the Farm by mid-morning, and although he had to castrate a few bandit guards to gain an audience with Farmer Brown, it had been worth the ammunition. Brown was extraordinarily receptive to his news - it seemed that the idiot fool Bert had pissed him off shortly after she had dealt with Terrance. She was denying Brown his rightful Tax as lord of the land, which he intended to use to make the Waste a better place, or whatever that meant. No matter the details, his plan sounded like it would bring more foot traffic to Can't Be Buried, and more foot traffic meant more foot problems (not the medical kind - the kind that occurs whilst walking), and more foot problems meant more jobs for a seasoned adventurer like Terrance Leeland. But more importantly, far, far more importantly, Farmer Brown himself was willing to go seize Smack-dab, and he'd brought an army with him packed into the trailer behind this decrepit vehicle.

The only way life could be better at this moment was if Bert herself appeared crying for mercy, ready to sew Terrance's hand back on so it felt good as new. But, failing that, he'd accept her complete annihilation and/or life-long misery instead.

The truck started to judder, more so than it was already, anyway. A nails-on-blackboard screech screeched out from each of the truck's five wheels, and Terrance found himself being pulled uncomfortably to the front of the cabin. His smile dissolving rapidly from his grim features, Terrance glanced out the front window to see the looming figure of Smack-dab swaying in the powerful gusts. Its lettering threatened to topple over the sides, and the window panes bowed in and out with each blast. A hiss erupted from the side of the truck and it came to a complete, merciful stop.

Doors somewhere behind Terrance squealed open with a rusty bang, and Farmer Brown's dungarees-wearing minions poured out of the trailer and into Smack's garden, taking up positions all around it, but none yet entering. A sizeable number flocked around the back to surround the place, while the rest hugged up against the front porch walls or created a line of menacing soldiers down the length of the pathway. They were an impressive sight, even for bandit scum such as themselves. Some wore patchwork scrap armour made from bits of whatever was lying around, but only a handful had guns – hunting rifles, mostly, but even those too were getting rarer by the day.

Now the front cabin door to Terrance's left squeaked open and the whole vehicle tipped to one side as Farmer Brown pushed his giant form out the small doorway. Terrance had to hold himself steady as the suspension sprung back again suddenly. The adventurer followed after him, hearing a deep, guttural laugh begin low in Brown's quarry chest and rise through his drainpipe gullet, to roll out from his chunky lips in an increasing bellow of evil laughter. The giant bandit laughed openly to himself the whole way up the path, seeming in great joy at the rickety bar before him. Terrance trailed after, the deep, dry wrinkles on his face broken by more of his sly smirking. Brown looked to be loving this, which could only mean good things for Terrance's plans.

Soon the bandit lord was stepping up onto the tired porch, pushing each plank to its absolute load limit. The doorway to Smack-dab was flapping open and shut in the strong wind, but it was dark inside to Terrance's smoglight-adjusted eyes. He watched as Farmer Brown examined the open entranceway and then beckoned for Ernest – who had the ability to appear out of nowhere – to close it over properly. Terrance arched a muddy eyebrow and swept an uncertain gaze over Brown's form. The giant crooked a slight smile as he caught Terrance's gaze.

"Life, Terrance Leelan', is all 'bout entrances," he rumbled.

"Entrances?" Terrance replied, unsure why they weren't just barging in and shooting some people.

"Aye. Nev'r just walk through a door when yer could make an entrance instead, tha's what I say. Either big an' kickin' it in, or slow an' menacin', steppin' in real slow."

Terrance scratched in confusion at the unyielding ghostly itch of his missing hand. "Could you not make an entrance normally?"

Brown shook his head disappointedly. "This'll be a dramatic entrance. Jus' watch an' learn, adventur'r."

Ernest took the cue and cowered backwards out of sight, while Brown examined the now-shut front door to Smack-dab. His planetoid eyes momentarily flashed over to Terrance before he lifted one gigantic boot and ploughed through the flimsy wooden door.

Needless to say, it was done with life anyway and gave up without much fight. A shower of splinters rode Farmer Brown's boot as it pushed through the door like it was paper, accompanied by a sudden, frightening bang and the smell of musty, damp wood. Farmer Brown continued onwards after, ducking under the top of the frame and striding slowly into the bar, Terrance following close at his heels.

The entrance had left an impression, that Terrance could tell straight away. It was dumb, but maybe there was something behind it. Smack-dab was currently serving a small assortment of wanderers and the like, each drowning their memories in the bottom of a pint glass. Well, they *were* drowning their memories in the bottom of a pint glass, but were now quite assuredly glued to the scene unfolding before them. They were scattered about various tables in small clusters, with Bert's large, disgusting grey mutant hiding behind the bar counter.

Brown surveyed the scene, his large face seeming satisfied. "Oooh Leelan'," he started, his voice low and slow, "you dun' good. You dun' reeeal good." His smile unstoppably consumed the lower portion of his face.

Terrance's boots crunched wooden shards as he positioned himself next to the bandit lord, his own eyes scanning the bar. He couldn't help but grimace at the filthy sight of the mutant, which was somehow allowed to serve food and drinks without being considered a health hazard. If you asked Terrance, the creature ought to be put down. Its life surely couldn't have been worth the pain of its own grotesque existence.

"Just like I promised," Terrance stated, still staring at the mutant.

"Oh aye, adventur'r," replied Brown, his eyes alight with mad glee. "As ye promised an' more, oh aye. Ye were right t' come get me, so ya were.

Worth rushin' for, this. I gets what I want and don't have t' shed any blood for me troubles. He he he."

The bandit lord strode slightly further into the room and peered through the kitchen passover window. Tree-branch fingers stroked at his mountainous chin. "Ernest!" he boomed suddenly.

The wretch of a man whose name Terrance could now confirm was Ernest bustled through the door with his trusty clipboard clutched in twiggy fingers. To his surprise, Terrance also saw an Overlord stride in second, its lonely red eye completely unreadable. Terrance's body tensed, fingers lightly touching his weapon. This was an unexpected surprise, but yet Brown wasn't doing anything about it. Only the traders seemed to care that there was an Overlord here, but then, they seemed to care that anybody was here, let alone an Overlord.

Terrance decided to play it out, see where it went. If nothing else, there were plenty of unnamed bandits to use as meat shields should the robot start shooting.

Ernest stood obediently next to his lord, who didn't so much as look in his direction. "Start takin' stock. I wanna know what we got 'ere, an' how much it's worth. We'll figure out wheth'r t' steal it an' blow the place up, or keep runnin' it a bit longer an' make a bit o' cash while there's stock left."

Ernest nodded quickly and disappeared down one of the bar's rear hallways, scribbling on his clipboard with a well-chewed pencil. Meanwhile, Farmer Brown stood tall on the spot and brought the full force of his presence on the traders around the room. Their frightened looks suggested they originally thought they might get away with just being background players, who could fade out at any moment.

They were wrong.

"Listen up!" Brown growled, getting a jump from some of the patrons. "This bar has had a change o' own'rship, an' yer lookin' at the new owner. Drink up an' be merry!"

He paused.

"Or else."

* * *

Jeb's face was aghast at the plate before him. Its contents steamed in gentle, meandering wisps, glistening from the oil and fat glazing its surface. Upon it was a steak, perfectly cooked, garnished with delicate curls of some type of vegetation that somehow made it a fancy steak. A pristine pint of grog sat in a clean glass next to it, bubbles excitedly rising to the surface where a thin layer of creamy head was quietly popping and crackling. The bandit who had just delivered the food and drink smiled, nodded, and departed, promising a return soon with the bill, but of course if they needed anything else they shouldn't hesitate to ask; customer service items such as bringing more food or drink, 10-minute small talk, and/or a shoulder to cry on were all available at reasonable prices, and did either Jeb or Orsen wish to see a menu of package options? They could bundle services into one to save money.

Reasonable prices. Package deals. This wasn't Smack-dab.

This was abhorrent.

"Cor, the service ain't half bad anymore, is it, Jeb?" said Orsen, whose face was almost instantly covered in steak juice and grog foam.

Jeb could only shake his weary head, eyes casting around the room. The same scene was playing out on every table: Quality products delivered on time, reasonable prices charged, and smiles on every staff member's face. That is, of course, with the exception of the many bandit soldiers who just sort of stood around, waiting for something to maim.

Sufficiently dissatisfied with the scene before him, Jeb poked at his steak with a fork - a fork, would you believe! - and much to his continued disappointment, but at this point unfortunately not against his expectation, it did not poke back.

"You're right, Orsen," he moaned, a deep sigh barging through the wisps of steam, "it sure ain't."

"Hey ... you alright, Jeb?"

"No, lad, not at all," the man replied. He shook his head again. "It ain't right. Smack-dab ain't s'posed t' have fancy food an' all this malarkey. Ya pay for what ya need, ya get somethin' that resembles it, an' then ya stay th' night or leave. Yer never asked if ya want t' pay more, or if ya want t' buy more things t' save money, but then end up spendin' more 'cause ya bought more things."

Orsen awkwardly put down the package deals menu.

"An' I bet..." Jeb narrowed his eyes, letting his voice trail off as he stabbed at the steak with his fork, lifted it whole to his chapped lips, and bit into it. Instantly he recoiled back, letting the steak fall back to his plate. He sneered openly, forcing the bite down his throat while he swilled back a mouthful of grog.

"Aye, I thought so," he muttered.

"What's wrong with th' steak, Jeb?"

"Extra salt, lad. They've salted th' bastard like there's no tomorrow. Makes ya buy more grog, ya see? Phoenix would never do that t' his food – he jus' used salt t' disguise the flavour, is all."

"An' Bert is already salty enough for the both of 'em."

"Aye, lad, yer not wrong there. What a disaster..."

He looked around the room, at all the soldiers lounging around, weapons in hand. Some stood to attention near the door and bar, and a smattering of others maintained a steady lookout outside, but mostly, they just lounged. The room had even been decorated in some of the colours from the fort: giant, heavy blue banners with the stitched face of Farmer Brown surgically attached somewhere in the middle. The material of the face looked to be almost an inch thick from the many times a new lord had sewn over the old one.

Jeb considered all the things he might do in this situation if he was back in the Orcklands – back chasing bad guys, kicking ass and, only occasionally, taking names. He'd probably be sitting here with some of the others, like Sievert or Grey, or maybe Moss and Parrot. They'd be plotting the downfall of Farmer Brown, thinking about all the ways to get out of Smacks guns blazing. Then they'd give the operation a cool name – Operation Smack Back – stand up from their tables, and kick some serious ass. Someone would round it all off with a sweet one-liner, too. "Looks like you're smack-dab ... in the middle of trouble."

But now, he had a lad to look after. He had to stay out of trouble – they both did. Life was safer that way.

Jeb sipped at his drink and quietly fumed behind his foam moustache. It would be a whole lot less frustrating if the grog didn't taste so much better, too.

Bloody Farmer Brown. Ruining everything.

* * *

Bert's army marched.

She led from the front, stomping along the Back Road with her attention firmly invested in a certain robotic fist. In particular, she was invested in the notion that she did not want it to be curled into a fist, but yet, it was resolute in its fistiness nonetheless. From the outside, it didn't look much more scratched than normal, but a few dents had wormed their way into the knuckles after the fight with Hurl. It was inside that she wanted to look at, but the flap for accessing most of the more important servos was currently buried under five stalwart fingers that were determined not to move. She needed her repair kit from Smack-dab – she'd have to pull the whole stupid hand off.

But on the bright side, she thought quietly to herself, a fist was certainly the most likely hand position she'd choose to adopt in her encounter with Farmer Brown. It's just a shame her middle finger had finally curled. That would have been a great conversation starter.

Voices flared up behind her, aggressive and posturing. Her attention distracted, she turned to see what the commotion was about. Somewhere a few ranks back, a Polite Bandit and his Bert's Battalion counterpart were having an argument over what was either a piece of cheese or something Bert most assuredly didn't want to know about. The dim smoglight glittered softly on something shiny, and suddenly there were axes waving around. Bert sighed and shook her head – a move she felt she was having to do far too often these days – and motioned for the whole group to stop. This was the third time today a fight had broken out.

Bert nodded to the three closest Battalion bandits, who promptly vanished into the bowels of the horde. She then pressed her fists into her hips and scowled into her army, foot lightly tapping at the dirt. She couldn't see much, but her ears told her that another commotion was taking place - a ruckus, some might say, or perhaps even a fracas. Shouting happened, then the distinct noise of metal hitting metal, then metal hitting something softer, then more shouting. A howl of pain pierced through the ambience of gusting winds, shuffling feet and the occasional cough, then the whole thing seemed to die down almost as sharply as it erupted.

In mere moments, the three bandits re-emerged next to Bert, one of them now slightly puffing and spattered with blood. Her axe hung loose in her fingers, droplets of crimson running their way along the edge and leaping off into the dust below. Bert looked grimly at all three.

"Juth one death thith time, Bert," said the blood-spattered woman, who spoke with a strong lisp on account of her teeth having been knocked out by an ex-boyfriend some years ago. Meanwhile, said ex-boyfriend couldn't speak at all - on account of being six feet under. Well, two feet. Six feet is a lot of hole to dig. Who's got the time?

"Good," Bert nodded in response, "we're getting better at this. Thanks for your help."

The three nodded back.

Yes, Bert's Battalion was certainly not an army to be *proud* of, necessarily, but it was still an accomplishment in a region where genuine accomplishments were as rare as clean water. Waste tribes around these parts operated in close proximity to one another, often even coming together for trade or drunken nights of rowdiness and sex, but they were far from inherent team players. You wouldn't typically find alliances long-lasting on the Highway, for sooner or later (often the former), something shiny would spark a fight and suddenly half the population of each tribe would be lying dismembered in the dirt. The absolute *differentness* of each tribe was what kept folks like Bert more or less safe from being overwhelmed by an army of madmen. So although this rag-tag group of grumpy anti-heroes could crumble into brutal civil war at any moment, the very notion that it existed at all, and that *she* was leading it, was what Bert could be proud of.

She was so proud, even, that she was beginning to like some of them, despite the filthy bandit scum that they were. Bert had discovered that there were select few within the group who seemed almost respectable, like actual human beings, until of course you asked too many questions about their past.

And so they marched on, Bert in front, not exactly smiling to herself, but at the very least not grumping quite as grimly. She was sore, she was tired, and she was sober, but she had an army to rival even that of Farmer Brown's, and Smack-dab seemed a little safer for it.

And then she saw Smack-dab, and her bubble burst with a comical pop. She stopped walking, sapphire eyes blazing alight. Her army stopped various seconds after her, those at the rear bustling into those in the front until the message to stop marching slithered its way to the very back.

Sir Robert appeared almost instantly, materialising through the throng with concern on his face. He had been leading from the rear thus far, making sure those who might take the opportunity of Hurl's death to seek another career choice were shown that there were currently none available.

"Something the matter, dearie?" he said, scanning Bert's face.

The blood-dripping bandit from earlier also stepped forwards. Her name was Sawface, and many in the Battalion saw her face as the voice of the unheard, the champion of the little guy. A union rep, you might say. "Ya look like thomeone jutht thhat in your hat," she stated.

Bert could feel the blood rising in her system, feel her face heating up, hear the blood pour past her ear drums. Someone *had* shat in her hat. Someone had dropped trou and let loose the wolfcats of war all through her wardrobe. Smack-dab, she saw, was covered in the distinct, dungarees-wearing figures of Farm bandits, with their ridiculous truck parked up on the verge. Its tyres must surely have been scoring great gouges in her lawn.

Not only that, but there were traders, too, exiting the building, meaning they had been inside it, meaning Smack-dab was not shut and locked as she requested. Meaning it was open. And people were inside it. And she wasn't there.

Her brow twitched.

Bert began marching again, a lot faster.

* * *

"Squaw, squaw!" sounded a voice from up high. It was Terry, a bandit, frantically waving his arms from his position in one of the truck's two machine gun turrets. "Squaw, ya buggers, squaw!"

Arnold, a pudgy little bandit on the ground below, scratched his bald head. "Wassat mean?" he called back.

"Ain't it th' signal f'r an incomin' enemy?"

"Naw, man, that was yesserday's. Today's signal is Tornado, tornado!"

"But what if there's a real tornado?"

"Oh, err, I dunno about that actually."

"Seems like a poor choice o' signal."

"You wanna tell that to Farmer Brown?"

"Fair, fair."

"Mmm."

"Aye.

The pair of them shuffled feet awkwardly and nodded in silence for a few moments.

Then Terry looked up suddenly. "Oh, right. Tornado! Tornado!"

Part Nine

Tornado, Tornado

Outside Smack-dab, normally a lonely place with only a handful of wanderers doing as wanderers do, trouble was brewing. Today, on this day, from the rickety porch all the way down through Smack's weedy garden and out onto the Back Road itself, two massive hordes of bandits crowded in awkward lines, glaring at each other from across a gap of barely a few feet, but which may as well have been the grandest of canyons. The hundreds of individuals now present on this soon-to-be battlefield gripped their weapons tight, showcasing a plethora of what human imagination, limited resources, and a will to either live or take life can do to a few sticks and some metal. Oh, and some duct tape. You gots to have duct tape.

Behind the more dungarees-wearing of the two hordes, a dilapidated Old World truck wobbled precariously as two heavy machine gun turrets heaved themselves around to face the new threat, squeaking loudly with that rusty, coughing sound only ancient, poorly maintained metal can achieve. The turrets were like large metal buckets drilled into the top of the truck's shipping container/troop carrier, the guns themselves built from about three or four separate weapons that seemed to fit together - more or less. The design meant that bandits could spin in all directions, but also cower in fear should the heat get too high.

Bert herself stood slightly ahead of her Battalion, one hand curled voluntarily into a fist and pressed into her waist, the other doing its own thing on the other side. The aggressive wind hadn't died down since earlier, and instead curled in thick blasts through the two hordes, billowing coats, hair, and anything not tied down properly. One bandit's favourite skull-helmet was now about a mile down the road. The day was cold, but Bert felt warm. Damn near hot. Her face burned with a fiery red, blood boiling through her system. Her pipes had stopped whistling the moment she was close enough to Smack-dab to see the true extent of its molestation, and they instead now simply screamed at a constant rate - like an angry kettle. She could see a number of traders in Smack's windows, faces pressed against the glass in anticipation, drinks in hand, mouths covered in the various juices of the kitchen pantry. She glared at them every so often, hoping to whatever gods dared listen that the money earned from those items was still somewhere inside.

She sucked in a breath to yell, but found herself cut off by a deep growl from the depths of the bar. She could hear the floorboards thud and creak as something huge came to the front door, then the hulking, monstrous figure of Farmer Brown, titanic weapon in hand, burst through the open doorway - which seemed suspiciously lacking in the 'door' part - and glared around the garden. His face was red and angry at first, but when he locked eyes with the fuming Bert, his galactic features rose up with glee. Additionally, and much to Bert's surprise and disgust, the slimy creature known as Terrance bloody Leeland oozed out after the bandit lord, trailing him like a pathetic wolfcat that couldn't lead its own pack. He looked immensely smug, and highly punchable.

The muddy, denim sea of Brown's bandit army parted as their lord barged through the ranks, Terrance in close pursuit. Brown's binary-star eyes swept across Bert's Battalion, and he didn't look particularly threatened. Brown smirked as he soaked in the sight, eventually landing on Bert herself and blossoming into a plague of a smile.

"Welcome back t' yer bar, woman," he cackled loudly, hefting his massive anvilhammer forwards and resting casually on its pommel. "I wasn't expectin' ya quite so soon."

Terrance positioned himself next to the troll, his intact hand resting on a needlessly over-upgraded pistol in such a fashion as to tell everyone, "Hey, I have a needlessly over-upgraded pistol, my penis is so big." He didn't bother looking at Bert's army, but locked eyes straight away with her. And he smiled, oh so wide, in that slimy, smug fashion. "You're looking well, bitch," he snarled. "Black and blue suits you. Oh, and I see you've ruined your hand, what a shame."

Bert snorted and moved her right hand away from her hip and down onto her weapon, mimicking Terrance's stance. The cool grip felt comfortable beneath her fingertips. "I only need one hand to slap that smirk off your face, Leeland," she snapped. "Now what the hell have you two fuck-heads done to my bar?"

Like a fissure opening in an earthquake, so too did Farmer Brown's grin split apart his face. Yellow teeth the size of pebbles glimmered with saliva in the dull smoglight. Thunder rumbled in his throat. "What, you dun like it?"

Smack-dab had more bullet holes in it than Bert remembered (she'd been counting), which meant little streamlets of dust would be filtering into the interior where Meatsack would have a hell of a time ushering them back out again. Its giant letters that acted like a beacon for thirsty travellers were still there, but one had finally fallen down and vanished somewhere behind the structure, while the others were draped in a thick blue fabric. They looked like the tattered banners from the fort, carefully pinned over 'Smack-dab' to censor it. 'Bar. Food. Roo (missing the M).' had, mercifully, been left alone, but an untidy 'or else' was scribbled on a new sign just after. In addition, a bird-pecked corpse lay off to the side of the garden, rotting and bloated under the glow of the smog, and someone had covered The Woman's statue with a towel (which may or may not have been used to mop up sick).

You could have kept Things at bay from the light and heat radiating off Bert's face.

Farmer Brown leaned further on the pommel of his gratuitous weapon, smiling in a way he probably thought was innocently. "I thought blue spiced up th' place a bit, don't ya think?"

Little mechanics fled through Bert's brain away from the cascading, unrelenting steam, deafened by a blaring alarm that screeched "Awooga, awooga, battle stations!" One by one, the pipes that maintained her composure and transferred energy from her trigger finger away to other places exploded into tiny little itty-bitty pieces. Her fingers suddenly gripped her pistol tight, muscles tensing all through her forearm and up into her shoulders. Her mouth ached from the grinding of teeth.

"Where's Meatsack?" she demanded.

Brown scratched his stony chin. "What's a meat sack?"

"She means the stupid grey thing," Terrance added.

"Ah," Brown rumbled back. "He's fine, last I saw 'im. Locked isself in a room at the first sight o' Leelan'. Haven't heard much since, mind. Could be dead f'r all we know."

Then, to the surprise of everyone present, even Bert herself, Bert took a swift few steps forwards on an angry march straight towards Farmer Brown. Her sapphire stare threatened to start a fire in his dirty face.

"I ought to gut you where you stand, Brown," she snarled, closing the gap fast. "Nobody messes with my bar and walks away without missing something. Just ask him." She waved her clenched metal fist at Terrance.

His smile faded.

Bert was nose to nose with Brown, now. Or more accurately, nose to chest. She looked pitifully small in his shadow. "Now get your ass off my property before I kick it off for you."

The bandit lord's buttery grin sizzled on the frying pan of his face. His eyebrows, warmachines in their own right, angled downwards over the tops of his eyelids. Slowly he shifted his ponderous weight off the pommel of his hammer and slipped lower, boulderous head sinking down to Bert's considerably shorter height. He stared at her, eye to eye, the reek of his rotten breath sweeping across her in a micro-hurricane. Tornado tornado, you might say. But Bert stood her ground, pistol in hand, eyes unwavering in their glare.

A Waste Beast rumbled somewhere in the shadowy pits of Farmer Brown. "I'd like t' see ya try, woman," he spoke, his words slow and careful, each syllable tipped with poison. Then his voice lowered in volume, lurching out of his voice box like a zom-bee pouncing from behind a wall. "I ain't playin' this time. Don't ya forget, I made ya a promise..."

Now he stood upright, hundreds of invisible pixie slaves pulling on the ropes necessary to heave his monumental form up into the air. His hulking great silhouette would block the sun, if there was any. "...an I intend t' keep it!"

In a flash his burly hand was wrapped around Bert's slender neck, chunky fingers curling in tight. She croaked with surprise, glare faltering, as the troll creature known as Farmer Brown lifted her bodily into the air to dangle by her neck.

A gasp followed by a call to arms bounced through the ranks behind Bert and Sir Robert brought the army a step forwards, weapons at the ready. He cried out for her to be put down in a civilised manner, but his words could not penetrate the sticky tension that formed a bubble around this duo.

In response, Brown's own army shook weapons and many of them also took a step forwards, howls and curses daring the opposing force to try something. Heavy, metallic clicks echoed over the ranks as machine guns were primed.

Terrance Leeland brought out his pistol fully now, hammering it back with a thumb.

On the front line of the Farm's bandits, H2-149 did nothing.

Bert's neck screamed at her for sweet sweet mercy as it struggled to support her body's weight without feeling like it might pop off at any moment. Her face twisted into a tight grimace of both pain and rage, her eyebrows lost for what to do with themselves. Her left fist dangled uselessly in the air, but her right hand gripped the bone handle of her weapon tight, thumb pulling back the hammer, barrel pressed firmly into Brown's chest plating. Brown glanced briefly down at the weapon, then his eyes narrowed as a lunar landscape of wrinkles and scars deepened on his face.

"You're not ... the only one with an army, Brown," Bert hissed through her teeth, trying not to choke on her words. "Go on, choke me. You'll be ... dead before I hit the ground."

Farmer Brown, holding her in the air seemingly without effort, looked back over his shoulder at the lads behind. He frowned, then turned back. Bert desperately wanted to pull the trigger and get this titan to drop her ass, but she knew that his stony fingers could do more to her than a teensy little bullet would do to him - she had to hope he didn't feel the same way. Her head sang with pain and her throat felt close to collapsing, but short of committing suicide by shooting the great lump, there wasn't anything she could do. Somehow she doubted Farmer Brown would collapse like Hurl after only a few hits to the face.

"Ernest!" he finally bellowed, a small tsunami of spit and noise washing over Bert's red face.

The little man known as Ernest appeared by his lord's side, trusty clipboard in hand. The clanking figure of H2-149 trudged alongside him. Brown glared down at them both. "Gimme sum numbers," he barked. "Tell this woman that 'er army got nuthin' on mine."

"Err, well, ya see..." replied Ernest, grinning nervously and fidgeting with his clipboard. Bert noticed that he took a slight step backwards.

Brown's throat vibrated like it was about to speak again, but H2 stepped in first. It spoke with a booming, hollow voice, singular eye shining brightly. "BASIC CALCULATIONS SUGGEST THE PUNY FEMALE SKIN-BAG'S ARMY IS SLIGHTLY SMALLER IN SIZE AND STRENGTH TO <lord and protector of the Farm, Farmer Brown, long may he reign>'S ARMY. SHOULD A BATTLE ENSUE, <lord and protector of the Farm, Farmer Brown, long may he reign> WILL WIN, BUT RECEIVE HEAVY LOSSES."

"Do ya agree with the tin can, Ernest?" Brown growled.

"ANY BEING WITH A BASIC EDUCATION COULD WORK IT OUT."

Ernest twiddled his fingers around his clipboard, flipping it this way and that. "Err ... yes. We'd be in danger o' losin' th' Farm if we get whipped too hard."

Brown remained silent for some moments, sweeping H2 and Ernest with contempt. It's likely that only one of them cared about this.

In the caverns of his gullet he muttered some unintelligible curses, then quite abruptly...

...let Bert go.

Before she could so much as squaw, Bert's body hit the dust and her legs buckled beneath her, taking her painfully to her knees. She coughed and spluttered on the ground, feeling at once the sweet reprieve of a full breath of air filling her lungs, but also the misery of choking on that very same air. She holstered her pistol and massaged her neck with the hand that actually worked, still able to feel Brown's ghostly fingers wrapped around her skin. How the hell was she supposed to topple someone as immense as Brown? She barely got through Hurl...

Meanwhile, Terrance was bounding forwards, shock apparent in his grim expression. "What the hell, Brown?!" he roared. "Numbers don't mean shit - you've got an Overlord, and me. We'd wipe the floor with these losers, let's just fucking do it already!"

At the same time, H2-149 reached back and brought its cannon off its back, easily balancing the monstrous weapon in its shiny arms. "BASED ON OVERLORD DATABASE OF SKIN-BAG PSYCHOLOGICAL PATTERNS,

FIGHTING IS INEVITABLE. DOING IT NOW WOULD BE A MORE EFFICIENT COURSE OF ACTION."

Now Sir Robert was stepping forth, placing himself above Bert with his rifle cocked and ready in his hands. "Except any fisticuffs between our two groups would result in extraordinary losses for both parties. You heard the Overlo-"

"Silence the lot o' ye!" screamed Brown, raising a mighty hand into the air. His lower jaw was sawing back and forth across his teeth, nostrils flaring wildly. He was clearly thinking, and Bert reckoned it looked difficult for him.

She rose slowly to her feet, making sure to do so steadily and with care so as not to fall over and lose whatever shred of dignity she yet clung to. Sir Robert and the robot were absolutely right. It wouldn't matter who won the battle if both sides suffered losses too extreme to keep going afterwards. Any old nut could waltz into the fort and seize it from whatever skeleton crew still remained behind, and Bert didn't need more wannabe kings stepping into the city and pretending they owned the whole damn region. Assuming she survived the battle, of course, which based on the current situation, she wasn't so sure about. Some women could pull of the damsel in distress look and get men clawing at their feet to rescue them, but to Bert it was as alien as being the sad little man at the damsel's feet. Why would she want to be a damsel when she could just shoot whatever villain was making her distressed?

No, Bert had to step in and defuse this situation before Brown, Terrance or, honestly, she, made it any worse. She had to control her rage and wait for a more opportune moment to crush Farmer Brown into a mushy little puddle and flush whatever chunky bits she could find down the toilet. Ooh just thinking it made her feel calmer.

"Brown," she stated loudly, slicing through the tense silence that was beginning to burn.

On muscles the size of four normal muscles knotted together, he spun to look at her.

"Why don't we stop posturing like a couple of hormonal teenagers and talk like good folk ought, huh?"

Glaciers moved across his eyes, or maybe it was just his eyelids narrowing over. "I reckons it was you who threaten'd me first, woman," he replied, his face stern and unreadable.

Bert responded with the same face, though less than half the size. "Aye, and I reckon it was you who invaded my property to set it all off. Twice."

Their stare-off fizzled between them like a micro-storm. A wandering bitefly, unaware of what it was getting into and just trying to get home to its family, buzzed lazily between the two and immediately exploded into sparks and smoke.

Terrance opened his mouth to speak, but caught a side glance from Brown for his efforts. He held his tongue.

Sir Roberts shuffled uneasily, fingers poised ready on his rifle, moustache wafting madly in the strong winds.

H2-149 did nothing.

* * *

Somewhere, off in the distance, things were approaching. There were two, one large and one small. Whatever the one further away was, it coursed over the landscape with all the grace of a raging pigcow bull, a hazy smudge just on the horizon foreshadowing ominous things to come. Nobody at Smack-dab had noticed this phenomenon yet, nor the feint black smudge of the second, entirely different but far smaller thing, slowly shifting along the undulating Back Road from the south.

But yet, with or without being noticed, both of these mysterious things approached nonetheless.

* * *

"So what the hell, Brown? What's it gonna take to make you go away? Everything was fine until you showed up."

"I told ya th' last time I was here. Ya owe me."

"Why?"

Brown shook his head. For a second, he almost looked taken aback by the question. "Wadda ya mean, why? I'm th' lord, woman! Ya owe me Tax."

Bert frowned. "We didn't pay Ashy any Tax, or Captain Fantastic before him. Why the hell do you need it?"

Farmer Brown seemed to think hard again, that same sawing motion moving across his square jaw. Then his look seemed change; it softened, as much as his face *could* soften. The wrinkles shallowed, his anger visibly abated, and his teeth stopped trying to pulverise each other.

"Look around ya, woman. Wadda ya see?" he asked, the gravel in his voice seeming less course than before.

Bert was uncertain what was happening, but she couldn't help but glance in two quick circles around her. She arched an eyebrow. "Two armies?"

"Naw, ya stupid bitch. Beyond that."

Bert scowled. "Fuck you, it's just the Waste."

Farmer Brown held up his finger and nodded as if this was a profound statement of great philosophical importance. "Aye, woman, the Waste. Jus' a big sea o' dirt. Nothin' to it but death an' more death, right?"

* * *

Terry the bandit was still in his position atop the truck, gazing out into the aforementioned sea o' dirt. His vision seemed fuzzier than before, and he wondered lazily if the parasites had gotten back into his eye. He blinked twice, then wiped at his eyeballs with grubby fists, then blinked again because his grubby fists made everything worse.

When he could see again, the world still seemed fuzzy. Except ... everything close by was fine and in focus. It was only the horizon that seemed fuzzy, like it just sort of blurred away as it got too far for his brain to comprehend.

"Huh," he said to himself, then rested his chin on his hand and stared out into the fuzz.

* * *

"Imagin' if someone could fix up th' roads, an' bring some proper industry t' the place," Brown continued, leaning forwards to rest on the pommel of his weapon once again. His face had lost all semblance of its sharpness and rage. It seemed almost intelligent, now, which is never what you want your opponent to seem.

"What the hell are you talking about, Brown?" Bert replied.

"Yeah what the hell, Brown?" cut in Terrance. He was visibly trembling with rage, knuckles white. "Let's just end this!"

"Shut up, both of ya! Lemme finish mah speech, damn you. If ya stop thinkin' with yer selfishness an' pay me some fuckin' Tax, woman, I c'n pay t' repair th' Waste. Bring more trav'lers, farmers an' the like. Get some real good inferstructure goin', ya hear me?"

She did hear him, loud and clear. His voice carried well, even in the howling wind. Probably because it was afraid to stop him. But, hearing wasn't the same as *hearing*. Bert was lost.

"Think about it. Farmers move in, start creatin' a bit o' product for us t' sell. More traders come so's they can take advantage o' th' new money. Bigger traders, woman, not th' pathetic lot ya got fer customers 'ere."

Bert opened her mouth to retort with something snarky, but didn't find the words fast enough to stop Brown barrelling on through the conversation.

"Those bigger traders need a place t' drink, right? So's they go t' yer bar. Or *my* bar, if ya don't pay." He revealed his yellowed teeth again, just for a moment – just to remind the world that the Brown it knew and loved wasn't gone, he was just waiting.

Speaking of the Brown that folks knew and loved, Bert had totally lost sight of him. This quiet, wistful Brown spoke words that sounded intelligent, like how a proper lord should sound. But, he was a bandit. And a particularly violent one at that, if the stories were true. She cast a look back at Sir Robert for reassurance, but he seemed as lost as she was.

"More customers means more money f'r you and yours, woman," Brown continued. "More money means ya can spend it back into me econermy. An' more money circlin' in me econermy means I can upgrade it again, bringin' in even more. Imagin' buildin' the fort into a city t' rival

Second Edin, woman. Imagin' bein' a bar close to that kinda population. Yer'd be rich, woman. Rich beyond yer wildest dreams. All ya gotta do is pay me Tax."

* * *

Terry continued to stare at the fuzz until it came close enough for him to determine what it was. It sure wasn't the parasites, he could figure that much out. And it wasn't a hallucination, or at least he didn't think it was. Most of his hallucinations involved amoebic fire blobs speaking to him with the voice of his long-dead mother, and this didn't at first outwardly appear to be an amoebic fire blob speaking to him with the voice of his long-dead mother.

The thing raging across the landscape looked like a dust storm. It was a big, brown smudge on the horizon, stretching from mountains to sea, towering up into the smog and disappearing somewhere in the clogged heavens above. If Terry was to be any judge, it looked like a fairly nasty one - the kind that tried to rip up your skin if you weren't too careful, or that deposits parasites into your eyes. Oh Gachook, Terry worried, not more parasites!

He turned to find Arnold in the crowd below, the words "Tornado, tornado" prepping themselves on his lips. But Arnold's attention was firmly fixed on the conversation taking place between Farmer Brown and the angry small woman, and it seemed like a bad time to interrupt.

And so, Terry quietly fretted to himself in his machine gun bucket and debated how and when he should mention the approaching weather.

He failed to see the second approaching thing, the one that was closer than the storm, but it didn't want his attention right now so that was fine.

* * *

Sir Robert wandered further into the gap between armies, his rifle somewhat lowered than before. He stood now, between Bert and Brown, moustache twitching uncertainly and brow firmly furrowed. "And, if I may be so bold as to jump in here, what would happen to us good dishonest folk, eh? Sounds like you're trying to betray your own kind, Mr. Brown."

Terrance wasn't about to let this go, either. He had been quietly trembling in the background for some time, his knuckles flushing red and white, face choosing between grim, grimmer, and most grim. "You're mad, Brown. You can't repair the Waste. It's beyond help, take it from me. This woman defied you! She needs to die – you have to show that you're the leader here, not some pussy who can get bossed around by this wretched barkeep."

Brown shot Terrance such a glare at these words it would have sent a lesser man into cardiac arrest. He towered over the one-handed figure of Terrance Leeland, who wasn't exactly a small man himself. "Ya better watch yer words, Leelan', before I replace yer arse with yer skull," he growled.

Terrance tensed as if about to fight back, even going so far as to stand taller, but he backed off in the end, skulking away into the background to brood.

Brown then turned his rage on Sir Robert, who had pre-empted such an action and repositioned himself strategically nearer to his lads. "An' as f'r you, ya cheap bast'rd. Ya pay as well, all of ya do. I'll Tax ya into the dirt if I have t'. Whatever it takes t' make the Waste a better place."

Sir Robert scoffed from a safe distance. "Well that's certainly not the polite answer I was looking for. And why would we pay you Tax willingly, eh? We're not farmers, nor do we care for the trade. Do we, lads?" He turned to look back at his fellows and they muttered in agreement.

"Actually," Bert said, not realising that she was speaking. "The theory works out in your favour, if you think about it."

"Excuse me, Berty?"

Bert stroked her chin for a moment. She had been mulling Farmer Brown's words over in his head, and the theory seemed solid. Better roads meant bigger trailers could come through – perhaps even more vehicles. Bigger trailers, more goods, more money, everybody wins. She explained as much to Sir Robert, more for herself to consider the concept openly than any particular desire for him to understand. More traders meant more business for bandits, which meant more business for adventurers, which meant more business for Bert. It seemed to be a cycle that fuelled itself, so long as nobody upset it by killing too many of one sub-group.

Except what was she thinking? This was Farmer Brown talking. This was a man who didn't business his way into power, didn't hold a diplomatic conference and explain his all-knowing plan to Lord Ash. He crashed into the southern fort walls like a well-armed ocean wave and brought the Ash regime tumbling down into a pool of its own blood. This was a man cunning enough to capture and reprogram an Overlord, and a bastard enough to, if the stories were true, rip down honest folk's homes to make way for ... farms, or whatever. He was a bandit, through and through. Trusting in bandits only leads to disaster. It always had.

But yet, here she stood. Contemplating the words.

* * *

Both Terry and the second machine gunner, Sarah, were staring out at the dust storm.

"Pretty big one, by the looks o' things," he said.

"Aye, that it is," she replied.

"We should warn them it's comin'."

Both Terry and Sarah looked back to the crowd, still locked in a hushed silence, gazing at the conversation taking place between leaders. It was like they were in a trance and didn't want to wake up. Terry had even thrown a couple of small rocks at Arnold's head and *still* hadn't gotten his attention.

"Definitely," Sarah said.

"Yeah."

"Yep."

They looked on in silence.

"Hey ... what's that there?" Terry asked, pointing out into the distance. He had finally noticed the second thing. It was a black shape, a mass of sorts, moving along the Back Road from the south far ahead of the storm. Light glittered off some type of little pieces of metal all through the shape, like a thousand tiny stars amidst the vastness of space. Not that either

Terry or Sarah had seen space, mind you. Or particularly knew what stars were, but regardless. Metal glittered in a star-like fashion.

Sarah squinted, leaning forwards in her bucket trying to get a better look. "Looks t' me like it could be a crowd."

"A crowd?"

"Yeah, like a big group o' people."

"I know what a crowd is."

"So why'd ya ask?"

"I didn't ask that!"

"Yes you did, you said, 'a crowd?'."

"I didn't mean it like that, I meant, like, *a crowd?*"

"How is that different?"

"I'm asking you to clarify why ya thinks it's a crowd!"

"So why didn't ya ask that, then?"

"I did!

"Alright, jeez Terry, your wife give ya eye parasites again or somethin'? You are grum-pee today."

"I don't have eye parasites again, *Sarah*! I just want t' know what th' crowd is."

"It looks like a crowd."

"What kind of crowd?"

"I dunno, like, a big one. Maybe with weapons."

"*Weapons?!*"

"Yeah, like spears an' that."

"Oh for th' love of– Why didn't you say that earlier?!"

Sarah shrugged. "Jus' a crowd, man."

Terry gripped the edges of his bucket to quell his mounting frustration. "A weaponised crowd don't mean nuthin' to ya?"

She shrugged again, clearly becoming insulted by the barrage of questions.

"Tornado!" Terry shouted, spinning around to face the armies. "Tornado, tornado!"

* * *

Phoenix screamed at the top of his lungs as he and his Starry army (his Starmy) began to charge.

His grubby face was painted black and flecked with little white dots, all of his adventurer's weapons plus plenty more items he'd picked up from Mount Butt clinging to every conceivable hook, pouch or bandolier possible. It had been a long while since he threw a proper grenade, and he was very much looking forwards to it.

A veritable swarm of cultists ran after him, weapons of all sizes (but not shapes - there was only one shape the Starry people liked) held aloft. There were ceremonial spears galore, plus plenty of star-shaped axes, maces, cudgels and morning stars, and of course a solitary tewhatewha. The Constellator herself gripped a well-crafted metal sword, with a glittering, golden star-shaped cross guard. Her armour hugged her figure as if made for it, a truly spectacular suit of armour the likes of which Phoenix did not know even existed in the Waste. It even had a plated starry halo rising up behind her collar and over her head, which itself was encased in a star-shaped full-face helmet.

She screamed.

He screamed.

They all screamed for ice cream.

And blood.

* * *

"Tornado! Tornado!"

Something was coming, and it was something big. Very few were in a position to see what it actually was, and the rest just had to listen and try to discern what threat loomed on the horizon this time. It came on a wave of beeps and bops, some type of brass instrument played with the enthusiasm of a life-long dreamer, but the skill of a pile of steaming shit - with lips. Additionally, the ground started to tremble, reverberating with the drumming of many feet pounding closer and closer and closer. The wind howled and screeched all around, whistling past people's ears and pushing, always pushing, to topple them over. Dust kicked up large coughs, splashing dust, tiny stones and unsuspecting insects into the eyes of the equally unsuspecting humans. Then came the voices: the taunts and battle cries bounding over the undulating landscape at the head of what many could now see to be a vast horde of weaponised cultists.

"Burn the Unworthy!"

"Slay them all!"

"Eat their hearts and step on their kidneys!"

Ripples of worry moved through the ranks. Bandits on the Farm side shuffled their feet uneasily, not sure whether to turn around and face this new threat or to remain facing forwards, a bulwark against Bert's Battalion. All eyes, as they so often do in these situations, fell to their superiors for support.

Bert was locked in a furious internal debate when she heard the tell-tale bugle sounds of an incoming Starry surprise. She was on the verge of taking Farmer Brown into the bar and having a proper, reasonable debate, a conversation where the outcome genuinely wasn't anything to do with mutilation - not even a little bit. It was something she hadn't expected, but yet, here she was all the same. But she still didn't know whether she could trust him. In fact, she was damn sure she couldn't. But she couldn't trust anyone.

Adapt.

Help Brown, cut a deal to minimise her Tax rate, reap the financial benefits, then deal with it at the time if he ends up getting too powerful.

For crying out loud, Bert thought to herself as the bugle grew louder, and the wailing battle cries of violence and stars only got more disturbing. Of all the times for Phoenix to arrive...

Brown noticed at much the same time, but he had no prior experience with this particular genre of crazy, and quite frankly, didn't really know what to do. Pivoting on the column of granite he called a body, the big lord turned back towards his people. He craned his head upwards, towering over the bandit army like a human periscope. Over their bobbing heads, he watched as the entire Starmy crossed over the top of a shallow hill, spears in the air, mouths screaming. It was an entire sea of black figures, a crashing steel-tipped wave rolling straight for the bandit line. And to make matters worse, behind *them* was the roiling, thrashing wall of a dust storm eagerly bounding after it.

In a flash, Brown was looking back over his shoulder at Bert, his look so twisted with rage it made her skin crawl. His lips curled into a snarl and spittle hung out of his mouth, clinging on as the soundwaves of a deep growl exploded out of his jaws.

"What th' hell is this, woman?" he roared. "You tryin' t' trick me into peace while yer friends come an' hit my flank?"

Bert scowled and shook her head, offended that he would accuse her of such underhanded tactics regardless of whether or not it may or may not have been, technically, true. "You angry son of a bitch, how about you keep your head on, alright? You're right, that's my second army over there – and yeah, I have a second army, I told you I was gonna kick your ass outta my place, didn't I? But I can stop it just as easily so cool your shit and move aside."

Bert stormed past his big form, making sure to bump into his arm on the way past (even though she couldn't possibly push him aside. It was a principle kind of thing). Next she ploughed into the Farm bandits, violently grabbing at them with her human hand and manhandling them out of the way. Some of them tried to resist, understanding on some instinctual level that she shouldn't be amid their ranks, but a swift punch across the face from her locked left hand showed them a better way. She had to properly kick her way through the last few bandits, who weren't paying enough attention to avoid being hammered – understandable, considering the circumstances. She finally struggled and punched through a couple of final burly figures – who turned out to be two figures conjoined somewhere at the face and whom Bert realised, a bit late, that she couldn't pass through between – before stepping out into the open Waste and staring down Phoenix's approaching lines.

She smirked slightly at the edge of her face, proud of what Phoenix had rallied together. It truly was a magnificent sight. Phoenix ran ahead of the crowd, weapon out, screaming at the top of his lungs until he ran out of breath, had to stop, and then started screaming again, while all around him were more cultists than she thought even existed. Their one army vastly outnumbered Farmer Brown's, and might have even outnumbered Brown's and Bert's Battalion combined into one. And they were all here, unless Phoenix had fucked up, to save Smack-dab. It was almost ironic, being rescued by the very same group she shot at mere days earlier, but then, that was the Waste for you. You really did have to prepare for anything.

Anyway, standing ahead, or rather, behind, the Farm forces, Bert glared out at Phoenix and raised her hands for him to stop. She yelled much the same, trying to throw her voice over the din of the wind and stampede combined, not to mention the clamour for arms behind her.

Miraculously, the army stopped. Indeed, Phoenix and the other pack leader skidded to a halt first, followed rank by rank of cultist soldiers. Dust rose in surprised wisps at their feet, trailing off into the smog as confused Starry faces looked to each other, then their leaders.

Then Bert noticed the strip of brown grease coming closer. It looked like, after a certain distance, the Waste vanished - was gobbled up, even - by a huge sepia wall. The strip towered so high into the sky that it was even attacking the smog.

Oh crap, she thought. That's just perfect.

Anybody trying to fight in that mess was going to be in for a hell of a time, especially if they didn't have adequate eye and mouth protection. Basically anything uncovered was going to be in for a bad day. Waste storms were not known for being gentle on skin.

Bert spun to go and warn the other leaders and...

...face planted straight into the monolith of Farmer Brown.

"Ya got 'em t' stop, eh?" he stated, his rib cage vibrating like a loudspeaker in Bert's face. He lashed out next, gripping her collar and lifting her into the air once more. But Bert was done being lifted this week. This time she had her weapon in hand and jammed into his cheek before she was even fully off her toes, attempting to keep her expression stern and confident despite the strain of hanging from one's collar.

Brown seemed to ignore the weapon, allowing it only the briefest of reactions. He stared deep into her eyes, his teeth visible beneath chunky lips. "Now tell 'em t' walk real close an' put their weapons down," he ordered.

"They won't attack, you giant sack of meat," Bert retorted. "I just ordered them to stop. Now put me down before I pull the trigger and we see what constitutes for a brain inside that thick skull of yours."

He grunted under his breath, and it sounded like a frustrated swear. Bert wondered if she was finally getting under his skin. He frowned, a loud gesture considering the size of his features, and then placed her back on the ground. Bert, in response, withdrew her weapon and returned it to its holster.

"There, that wasn't so bad, huh?" she said. "Now let's go inside and talk - *talk* - about this plan of yours to make me rich, OK? We'll see what we can do about this obsession with Tax you have."

Now, all of this was all and good and well and nice, but it's not what Phoenix saw...

* * *

Moments before...

Phoenix, riding a wave of adrenalin he hadn't felt since his last battle with a rogue pine tree, was about ready to start taking shots at the bandit line. His rifle, even at such a range, would have no issue knocking a few heads off a few necks. Plus, the adventurer didn't really have to aim, just sort-of point at the mass of necks and pull the trigger. He was bound to hit a few. Secretly, he especially desired that damned robot's head, with its beady little bulb-face-eye-thing and, and it's stupid antenna.

But then he saw Bert. She was struggling with a freaky conjoined twin monster, pushing at him - them, rather - and slapping them with her robo-fist. It was nice to see her still alive and being Bert, that is, hitting people with her robo-fist, but something seemed wrong. Why was she amid the Farmers? Unless...

...unless she had been captured! Oh it was a disaster, Phoenix panicked. She was trying to fight through the crowd to get to the safety of his manly arms, but had been grabbed at the last minute by the four-armed, one-faced thingamabob. She was even waving at him and yelling his name, and boy did she look terrible.

Correction, Phoenix thought. She looked amazing, because she always did. But she looked a more terrible version of it. Her arms were all bruised, her clothes were filthy, and her neck looked like it might have been glowing red - but it was hard to tell at this distance. She seemed to be avoiding using her left hand, too. Either that or she was just keeping it in a fist for some weird reason. No, it was definitely being avoided. It must have broken in the scuffle.

Phoenix scrunched his face in anger. Those dungarees-wearing bastards must have disabled it to prevent her from being a bad-ass threat. Those mother fu–

The Constellator stopped. Phoenix skidded to a halt next to her. Then the entire Starmy clattered to an ungainly stop a few seconds later.

Phoenix, exasperated, ran in front of his companion and looked between her and the enemy. "Why the hell did you stop?!" he cried, growing panicky.

She cocked her head back at him, resting her sword on her shoulder. "Isn't she asking us to cease, Oh Bringer of Dreams?"

"*What?*" Phoenix replied. "Look at her!"

Affirming his greatest fears, the nightmarish monster of Farmer Brown ambled through the line of bandits, stared out with his meaty, square face at Phoenix's proud and mighty army, and then gripped Bert by the collar, lifting her into the air. She held her pistol to his head, but he couldn't make out what they were saying.

"You call that asking us to stop? We have to charge before it's too late!" Phoenix could hardly contain himself. He kept running a few paces forwards, turning desperately back to the Constellator, and then running back.

The Constellator herself stared at the scene, humming with thought. "It ... doth look quite unfriendly. But she was definitely asking us to cease before. The Constellations be'th witness, she was asking us to cease."

Phoenix was in disbelief. Bert could be killed at any moment, and here he was standing having a bloody debate about it. What would Sandra Bulletface do in a situation like this? Why she'd, she'd just bloody run in there with bullets, and, and her face.

"Mighty Const– Mighty leader of the Starry people, I *demand* that you start charging again. I am the Bringer of Dreams! I have spoken!"

"But–"

"No! Every second we waste is another that this shitshow steps closer to being more shit and less show. We need to strike hard and fast. And that means striking now! While the enemy is in disarray."

The Constellator remained silent a moment, staring at the exchange between Brown and Bert.

Phoenix stepped in to block her gaze, his eyebrows sailing at the top of his forehead.

She met his eyes, then sighed. "Alright ... for the Dreams."

Phoenix let out a breath of relief. "For the Dreams."

The Starry people looked anxious, breathing hard on the spot after their lengthy march and partial charge. They all awaited the word to come down, their weapons hungry for hearts and kidneys and various other organs. The Constellator turned to face them, casting an eye across all of them. Then, she lifted her sword high in the air (aloft) and bellowed at the top of her lungs. "For the Dreams!"

Their faces brightened instantly. "FOR THE DREAMS!"

And then they started sprinting.

* * *

Farmer Brown roared louder than Bert had heard before, so loud she thought her ear drums might rupture. "Ooh ya tricked me again, ya lyin', two-faced bitch!" he screamed. Then he lashed out with two hammy fists to grasp her clothing, hefting her high into the air (also aloft) and tossing her away like a toy doll he had lost an argument to.

Bert soared through the air, not sure what the hell was going on. In a heap of limbs and curses, she slammed hard into the dust, rolling a few times before coming to a halt somewhere between the two bandit lines. She felt the ground vibrate once again as not only an army approached at full speed, but Brown stomped with heavy feet, bellowing orders at his troops.

"Kill them all!" he cried, face almost bursting from the blood. "Drown th' dust in their blood an' wipe this pathetic bar from the Waste!"

Bert quickly scrambled to her feet, muttering all the while. She glanced up to see Sir Robert coming to her flank, Toddrick and Doris on the other side. Their weapons were out, ready and gripped tight.

"What the devil is happening, Berty? It looked like peace for a moment there," said Sir Robert, now having to shout over the noise of the Farm army (Farmy) reshuffling into a battle group capable of fighting on two fronts.

Bert, truthfully, didn't have the answer to that question, but she knew deep down that it ended with the name "Phoenix". She drew her pistol once more, clutching it tight to her breast. "We're going to do what we came here to do, Sir Robert," she said, voice going cold.

He paled.

"We're going to kick some Farmers outta my bar."

By Duncan P. Pacey

Part Ten

Anger During the Storm

In the old Waste region of Can't Be Buried, outside a particularly slanty bar by the name of Smack-dab...

...chaos ensued.

The ear-pounding rattle of machine gun fire ripped through Can't Be Buried as a small fortune of bullets deposited itself into the fleshy Starmy bank. A veritable torrent of steel and lead ploughed into their screaming number, bursting through limbs, heads and unsuspecting internal gibbly bits, vast pools of blood flowing readily into the dusty ground beneath stampeding feet. But the horde of starry warriors closed the last distance between it and madness, spears and other weapons tipped forwards, mouths equally lost in the wailing cries of bloodlust and the sudden screams of pain. The sea of white-speckled, black-robed figures crashed into Farmer Brown's bandits like a tsunami, blasting apart the Farmy's pitiful front line. Spears drove through dungarees. Axes fell on heads.

The Battle of Smack-dab had officially begun.

And then the storm hit.

It rose above the landscape like a vertical ocean, roiling and crashing, a swirling maelstrom of dirt and shit that tore through the landscape on an unstoppable path of destruction, straight into the battling bandits of Smack-dab. In its wild frenzy it swallowed the bar and all who dared stand in its path, whipping up vast tendrils of dirt and weeds from the ground and throwing them into the air before crashing them back down. Currents of tiny rocks and particles of dust swam at deadly speeds, sweeping with them debris, blood, and the weapons of those who didn't hold on tight enough. It bit with millions of tiny fangs into any skin it could find, and raked at clothing and armour to taste that which it could not. Anyone whose eyes were unprotected found their sight scrubbed into oblivion, their mouths packed full of crap and their ears sawed off. Only those quick enough to don goggles and face masks would survive the full brunt of this awful Waste storm.

Somewhere within the chaos, Bert staggered. She was one smart enough to pull out her emergency goggles and mask, but the thick air bit into her many wounds and pounded at the exposed parts of her face not covered by a mask. Fighting shadows morphed in and out of view all around her, the sounds of weapons clashing and throats crying out in horror barely making it to her drowning ears. A bloodied scalp drifted past her and rolled immediately out of view. But she carried on, searching for the biggest shadow she could find.

Sir Robert was close behind, but neither he nor Bert knew that. His elegant face scrunched tight, peering through the disaster of a scene three hundred and sixty degrees around through well-cared-for goggles - one lens bigger than the other, giving the appearance of a monocle. Doris, Toddrick, and the rest of Bert's Battalion were also close by, but again, not that anybody knew that. The Polite leader cocked his weapon and shot at the nearest shadow, suspecting it to be wearing dungarees. It wasn't. Meanwhile, Doris was having a wonderful time with her machete, beginning what would soon be a glorious collection of bloodied scalps, so long as they stopped blowing away before she could bag them

Jeb and another trader heaved one of Smack-dab's tables in front of the broken doorway while Orsen watched on, dancing from one foot to the other. Their tired old muscles strained as they wedged the wooden table into the open frame, blocking the wild storm from pushing its way into the bar so that they could go back to drinking and enjoying the show. But Orsen wasn't so happy.

"We've got to go help them!" Orsen cried, frantic at the scene unfolding somewhere out in the wild. He couldn't see said scene even if he tried, but he knew it had an Orsen-shaped hole somewhere in the middle of that storm.

"An' what are ya gonna go do, lad? Yer'll get killed out there!" Jeb replied, leaning his back against the table-turned-door.

"But so will our friends!"

"It's not our business, Orsen. Stay out o' trouble!"

"We can't, Jeb! Didn't you used t' be a hero? We need old Jeb."

"I didn't used t' be a hero, lad, I was a sheriff - an' look where it got me."

"A successful an' happy life on th' road with an adopted son whom you love?"

Jeb paused for a moment. "Err, aye, that. But if I had stayed a cop, I'd be dead."

"But you'd be a hero."

"A dead hero is still dead, lad. Stay out o' trouble, wadda I keep tellin' ya? I lost a lot o' good friends savin' you from the commune. We're not ruinin' it by throwin' our lives away for some bar."

Orsen's eyes glistened, a thin film of wetness dribbling over them and pooling at the corners. "Not even the best bar, Jeb?"

Jeb gritted his teeth together and forced down the eggy lump in his throat. "Aye, lad. Not even th' best bar. It's not worth death. Let's get another drink an' just watch. Meatsack! ...Meatsack?"

But Meatsack was no longer there. In fact, he was wearing his goggles and face mask just like Berty Bert had shown him, and had snuck out the back door, weapon in hand. It was a knobbly club, with the appearance more of the tree itself than any tree branch. He gripped it tight and swam through the dust, frightening thoughts of Berty Bert Bert getting hurty hurt hurt swirling around in his head like a little internal storm made entirely of anxiety. Tears brimmed in his eyes as he desperately sought Bert. He knew he was going to get in trouble, for being out here, for unlocking the bar, for accidentally letting the giant spider back in without anybody realising it yet, but those didn't seem nearly as important as the thought of losing Bert. And so he sniffled, sucked in whatever breath he could in the terrifying weather, and kept looking.

Phoenix and the Constellator were like ballet masters, but ones who killed bad guys instead of dancing about swans or their lakes. She would twirl and slash with her glittering sword, him leaping around, pulling a dramatic hero facial expression and shooting bandits with an automatic rifle. They made a beautiful murdery partnership, pirouetting around a farmer's axe, lopping his head off at the neck with one clean swoosh, the other partner twirling in from behind to fire off one bullet, two, three, and down goes another enemy. It was a perfect unison, until it literally all went wrong.

OK, so maybe it didn't literally *all* go wrong, but literally a few things went wrong more or less at the same time, which close enough. Firstly, two bandits conjoined somewhere in the middle stepped between the Constellator and her Bringer of Dreams, successfully cutting them off from each other. The storm then moved in, a particularly chewy whorl of dust spluttering across the scene and reducing visibility from "I can't see a bloody thing" to the same, but less of a hyperbole. Phoenix fired off a few shots at the two-man band(it), but very quickly lost sight of the body – he couldn't tell if it was a kill or not. But he had, most assuredly, lost the Constellator.

Then another bandit, whose dungarees were made of stuck-together metal mugs that jingled and jangled as he moved, clobbered Phoenix from behind with a wooden bat. It struck him on his already sensitive skull, which had been clobbered more than enough recently for his liking. Phoenix heard himself croak as he went down into the dust. His rifle clattered to the ground a few feet away and promptly vanished. Phoenix was alone, dizzy, and now weaponless. Well, not *weaponless*, but without his favourite one...

Farmer Brown growled loudly in his throat, his goggles strapped tightly to his skull. They were made from more than one pair of goggles, for no singular strap could fit his vast, meteoroid head. With muscles bulging out of his sleeves, he hefted his giant anvilhammer into the air, thick globules of blood clinging between it and the smooshed corpse now blended with the landscape. He could hear fighting all around him – weapons clashing, guns crashing, and his truck still letting loose on its unfortunate victims. He had no idea if he was winning or not, but he knew that his lads would fight to the bitter end no matter what, and they'd make damn sure it was as bitter as can be if they weren't to be the victors. It truly was a sad affair, though. For some reason, he couldn't just improve people's lives for them – he always had to kill a whole bunch, first. What did that say about society?

Well, it said it needed improving.

Terrance Leeland's pistol had jammed almost instantly when the storm hit, on account of its many poorly attached upgrades letting too much dust in. Sheer ferocity was his weapon of choice, now, aided by a metal pipe he found in a corpse (not on, *in*) that at one stage had been painted with a naked lady. Now she flaked and peeled, looking like a naked zom-bee. Each bloody kill with the pipe splashed Terrance's black leather coat with more crimson ichor, and his boots were splattered with the contents of some intestines he had stamped on a few minutes earlier. He didn't give two shits about some nobody bandits, though. They were just meat, and he didn't want the meat. He wanted the butcher. His dark eyes scanned all around, searching for any silhouette that could be one of Smack-dab's staff members. And he was not disappointed, for what appeared before him but the awkward, lop-sided shadow of Bert's disgusting grey mutant. He smiled grimly to himself and stalked after it, metal pipe gripped tightly in his fingers.

H2-149 did something. And that something, specifically, was to tear out a star-cultist's spine via his neck, all the while lecturing him about the futility of organic life, and how having his spine removed was actually the kindest thing someone had ever done for him. Needless to say, the man did neither agree nor disagree. He didn't put up much of a fight at all, really, just sort-of tried to flee, fell on his face, cried to his gods and his mother, then died. Spineless, some might have called him.

Randolf the Conqueror, Ruiner of Worlds, Bringer of Shadows and Lord of Rabbit-Like Kind folded his paper hat away into his stomach pouch and marched, resolute, through the choking storm. He hunched as tightly as he could within the folds of his matted grey fur, his black marble eyes as narrow as can be without being closed. The dust ravaged his tiny, rabbit-like body, but onwards he marched all the very same.

Behind him strode The Many Sons and Daughters of the Grentuputron Moon, a nasty, war-loving mercenary group he had hired from the great rabbit-like capital, The Burrow of Lords and other Reputable Sorts. Most of the Many Sons and Daughters of the Grentuputron Moon were rabbit-like in nature, although it would seem that they had recently hired some additional muscle in the form of a bird-like creature, dog-like creature, and some kind of giant insect - Helga Who Eats Your Internal Organs, who turned out to be Randolf the Conqueror, Ruiner of Worlds, Bringer of Shadows and Lord of Rabbit-Like Kind's favourite.

Humans seemed to be fighting all around the warband, but over what did not matter to the small creatures who marched at their feet. Randolf the Conqueror, Ruiner of Worlds, Bringer of Shadows and Lord of Rabbit-Like Kind was here to enact his swift and merciless vengeance against the spiked beast; that which would not only destroy his predecessor (which, admittedly, was not such an issue), but would dare insult Randolf the

Conqueror, Ruiner of Worlds, Bringer of Shadows and Lord of Rabbit-Like Kind. To his face, no less.

His vengeance would be complete, of this he was certain.

* * *

Bert continued to storm through the, well, the storm, her human hand locked on the holster of her beloved pistol. She would only draw it out when necessary, for fear that exposure to the crazed, manic winds would clog up the weapon and render it useless. She wasn't wrong to worry, either, for not too far from where she marched, three separate bandits lay dead because their guns had jammed awkwardly at the last minute. One of them had even asked for a brief pause to the fighting so that she could quickly clean it out, and you know what? Her opponent had kindly obliged, taking the opportunity to attempt rolling a smoke. Needless to say, the bandit with the jammed weapon was killed by an axe that someone had carelessly let go of up-wind, while the other bandit died from inhaling too much dust from a cigarette made mostly of dust, that was promptly inhaled.

A figure fell suddenly out of the haze, landing at Bert's feet and quickly scrabbling to get back to his. It was a skinny stick-figure of a man, heavily scarred and wearing a set of stained denim dungarees beneath armour made from two old car doors. The spiked stick in his hand was coated with dust, glued to the metal by fresh blood. When he finally noticed Bert, he glared through his filthy goggles and then leapt with a battle cry to swing his spiky blood-stick at her face. Bert stepped back quickly, bringing herself just outside the arc of the man's heavy swing. He travelled past her, the force of his attack accidentally stripping the bandana from his mouth and revealing it to the world around.

And oh how the world was ready for it.

The moment his lips were in sight, dirt rushed in at lightning speed and pelted him in the teeth. Tiny stones and clumps of dust bore through his best attempts at keeping them out, barging through his fingers and into his throat. The man fell to his knees, clutching his throat, gagging and choking. But the dust swept in as fast as he cleared it out. It filled his lungs, coating them in filth and grit. The bandit looked up at Bert, tears in his eyes, his face pleading with her to do something. He tried to suck in a breath but started coughing uncontrollably. Blood specks gathered at his knees.

Bert gritted her teeth and walked on, trying not to hear the man's final screams. She pushed through the whirling winds that howled and roared in her ears, that unrelentingly attacked her exposed skin, her sapphire eyes scanning all the time for any sign of Farmer fucking Brown. She was terrified of the scene hidden all around her, and of what might be happening, or already *have* happened, to her bar. And being terrified made Bert angry. Very angry.

And to think that all of this had escalated from what was a budding peace treaty. Ain't that just the way, she thought. You can't have nice things in the Waste, like peace and quiet, or living to an old age. Because Farmer Brown was a bastard, and a genuine turd. She couldn't trust him as far as she could throw him, and she doubted she could so much as push him over, let alone give him any air. But his theory on Can't Be Buried, his thoughts on how to improve the local economy, were interesting. They sounded damn well plausible, even though she disagreed strongly with his methods. But methods could be changed, couldn't they? With sufficient negotiating, and bullets. Negotiating with bullets, maybe.

But looking around, it seemed that the only options that hadn't been blown off the table by the storm were to find Farmer Brown and broker a new peace, or find Farmer Brown and kill the bastard - which would at least create a temporary peace, in the sense that there'd be nobody left to fight that day. It was possible, now that she was considering it, that she might be able to convince Sir Robert - who would logically be the next lord of the fort - to follow in similar footsteps to Farmer Brown, but without all the violence and Taxation. Even slight improvements to the economy could bring in a better class of customer for Smack-dab, not to mention a better class of adventurer - unlike the Phoenixes and Terrances of the world. But that would require removing Brown from the picture, and of Sir Robert surviving the battle.

Well, it seemed that no matter what, she needed to find Farmer Brown. He was key to ending all of this madness one way or another. And she had a more than a few strong words for the hulking great bastard, and plenty of bullets if it was to come to that. So it's convenient, then, that at this moment, as her raging thoughts twirled back into images of violence, that she felt the ground shake.

If a mug was resting on a table, its liquid would have rippled. Then, after a short moment, it would have rippled a second time. Bert guessed that it might be the weighty attacks of Farmer Brown and his stupid weapon. Hell, it could even have just been the titan taking a few steps. She paused, waiting for the ground shock a third time. She followed back to its source, right hand closed tight around the handle of her pistol.

And she saw him. Or, rather, she saw the silhouette of him. It was obvious who it belonged to. Nobody else in Can't Be Buried would have a silhouette such as his. It rose from the ground like a statue of truly biblical proportions, great stony muscles clearly defined even through the shifting haze of the dust storm. Gripped in the arms of this behemoth was a long, thick pole with some kind of anvil strapped precariously to one end, large shadowy chunks dripping from it as it lifted from the ground.

Bert swallowed hard and clutched her weapon a little tighter, her Bertrage wavering for a moment. If she could barely kill Hurl, what were her chances of fighting a Being like Farmer Brown? And with one hand completely non-functioning, too. She let out a slow, nervous breath, focusing her attention on the silhouette before her, trying to clear her head of the whistling winds, and the screams that they bore. She didn't have a choice. It was either talk to Farmer Brown now and risk getting into a one-on-one gladiatorial death match that was gratuitously rigged in favour of her opponent, or let the Battle for Smack-dab play out and risk the ultimate destruction of everything she knew and loved in this stupid Waste.

The choice was at least clear, if not easy.

She marched forwards, into the maw of the beast, to talk to a man-god who hated her, and potentially, to shoot the man-god who hated her in the head. And for some reason, all she could think about was just how fucking hard it was going to be to clean up all of this mess after the storm moved on and the battle ended. That, and the annoying sound of

Phoenix's voice singing a stupidly catchy Waste tune by the name of "*Sliced up in heaven*".

Brains are weird.

* * *

Somewhere on the other side of Smack-dab, Phoenix ducked clumsily under the wide swing of an axe made from glued-together kitchen knives. He had lost count of the number of dungarees-wearing assholes he'd had to fight off since the storm hit, but quite frankly, he was losing everything. His hat was long gone, as was his beloved rifle. He was fairly certain he also had more grenades at the start of the fight, and an extra throwing knife. But he still had his wits, at least, and plenty of grenades in case those failed.

The she-bandit with the knife-axe swung at him again, screaming a high-pitched banshee wail of a cry. It was a garbled mess of clichés, pertaining to Phoenix's soul, blood, heart, eyeballs, and with particular detail, his testicles. Deciding that he was happy with how intact each of these items currently were, he continued to avoid the attacks, looking for an opening in the bandit's defences so that he could slip his Waste Beast tooth knife somewhere inside and jiggle it about.

Phoenix had no idea where his starry brethren were, nor Bert, nor even Smack-dab itself. He could barely see a few feet in front of him before the boiling dust snatched away his vision, and it was beginning to make him feel slightly ill. Was he still in his starry line, or had he strayed completely into the Farmy forces? It would certainly explain why he was encountering so many enemies and so few pals. But then, how was he ever supposed to go back to the front line? He didn't even know where it was, let alone which direction was currently considered 'front'.

The bandit came in again, determined this time to dismember his member so that he would remember her, if he lived through it. Which it didn't sound like she wanted him to do, so really, Phoenix felt she just liked saying "member". Anyway, she was attacking.

Phoenix stepped inside her swing and grabbed the shaft of the knife-axe, pulling it in close to his body so she couldn't do any harm with it. At the same time, he brought his Waste Beast tooth knife up and drove it through her dungarees, feeling the sharp tip slice through bone and flesh as though it were only the flesh part.

"Lautilda!" a voice cried somewhere in the storm. "Lautilda! I need to talk to you!"

Phoenix cocked his head, listening. Who was Lautilda?

The woman in his arms (and knife), not quite dead, croaked some kind of response through the blood pooling in her mouth.

Then a figure materialised directly behind Lautilda. He was a pudgy little bald man with a very recognisable rifle clutched in his fat little greasy, dirty bandit fingers.

"Lautilda, thank goodness I found you," he said, apparently unaware of Phoenix standing behind the woman whilst, and this could not be stated enough, holding a knife in her belly. "We need to talk about ... us. I know it's a bad time but I just, I just can't hold my tongue any longer. I want to get married, Lautilda. I want to get married and run away together."

Lautilda gargled on her own blood.

Phoenix could see the life fading from Lautilda's eyes, and the tears brimming at the edge of them. Uh oh.

"Lautilda, I know your father doesn't approve of our union, but I say to hell with him!" the pudgy man continued, walking closer so he didn't have to yell as loudly. "Who is he to stand in the way of true love?"

Phoenix felt Lautilda's weight begin to shift as her body lost its strength. He bent his knees slightly and tensed his back muscles, desperate to hold her up. He felt the knife cut slightly higher into her stomach as her body slipped down an inch. Everything was spiralling so very quickly out of control. What are you meant to do when the bad guys have a good guys moment? Especially if one of them is about to die. Namely, because of you.

"Lautilda, my darling of darlings, light of my life, let's forget being bandits. Neither of us want this awful life. We can run to Second Edin, start a new life. Maybe open that cafe we always talked about."

Lautilda slipped slightly more, and Phoenix felt blood creep its way beneath the fingers currently holding her from collapsing entirely. He was losing grip, fast.

"What do you say, my love? Will you marry a poor soul such as me?"

The pudgy bald man was close, now, getting down to one knee, the rifle still clutched in his thieving fingers. But Phoenix's grip was slipping faster than his concept of reality after taking too many bonkerberries. Soon, she finally gave way. Phoenix's fingers slipped off her clothing and gravity took hold of her paling, limp figure. She fell to the ground at an incredibly slow, almost comedically awkward rate, the impossibly sharp edge of the Waste Beast tooth knife slicing her from belly up to her neck. It caught for a moment on her chin, forcing the knife out to the left and opening the side of her skull to the world. The dead figure of Lautilda then split very slowly in half before her lover's eyes, with the sound of someone pulling two sticky sponges apart, and fell finally to the ground in two distinct halves. Phoenix was left standing over her corpse, her fresh blood on his clothing, and his knife and hand smothered with red.

"Err..." Phoenix said dumbly, glancing at the butterfly steak that was Lautilda the bandit.

The bald man froze in place, face as white as snow.

"So ... if it makes you feel any better, she told me before she died how much she loved you."

He stared at Phoenix, body beginning to tremble.

"I'm so sorry, that was a lie. I just lied to you. She just threatened to cut of my balls and then I impaled her with this knife." He waved the knife, as if it made anything any better.

The man's eyes began to fill with tears. He was trembling quite visibly, now, his hands vibrating at an alarming rate.

Phoenix tried to smile, but it just came out awkwardly. "Um," he said slowly, "don't suppose I could, you know, have my rifle back...?"

And the bald man, whose name Phoenix didn't know, nor would ever know was Arnold, aimed the rifle at his chest and pulled the trigger.

* * *

The Constellator, in all her glittering metal splendour, watched as yet another one of her faithful servant warriors was slain by a heathenous bandit. That made four in the past minute alone, and these were only the ones she could see. Screams and shouts came from all direction, and she recognised many of the voices to be that of her mighty horde.

The great Stars above had certainly unleashed all hell on the Waste, as could be predicted when the Starry Place goes to war. But, the Constellator wondered, could they have perhaps toned it down just a little bit? So it wasn't so damned hard to see. Or fight. Or breathe.

She bounced to her left, driving her sword through the eye socket of the bandit that slayed'th the nearby faithful servant warrior. The slim metal blade drilled easily through the man's skull and into his brain, poking out the other side to point straight at another bandit, who was to be the Constellator's next victim. But before she could so much as pounce, a hail of machine gun fire burst through the storm and poured over the area in front of the Constellator. She threw herself backwards in panic, narrowly avoiding the worst of the stream as it raked across the landscape, unsure of its target. A sharp pain sung in her leg, and she looked down to see her magnificent black armour punctured on two sides, blood seeping out the bottom as dust crowded into the top.

The Constellator winced with pain, dragging herself backwards away from the bandit she had sworn to destroy, but was now not quite as confident about.

The battle did not go well.

* * *

Meatsack couldn't find anyone he knew, and it was beginning to stress him out. He half-walked, half-ran through the seemingly infinite dusty shroud, deafened in his sensitive ears by its constant, grinding howl, and of the shouting and fighting that seemed to be happening everywhere. He fought down tears in his eyes and a lump in his big throat, determined to find Berty Bert and protect her from whatever the bad people might try to do.

His cowardly legs threatened to carry him back the way he came, to his room, safe at the back of Smack-dab, where he could lock the door, curl up on his bed, and pretend nothing was happening. He so desperately wanted to run, but he couldn't just leave Bert.

Plus, he didn't know where Smack-dab was anymore.

A figure ran out of nowhere and slammed into Meatsack's side, knocking itself to the ground. Meatsack, completely unmoved by the knock, flinched wildly with his club in fright. He felt it collide with the figure's skull and watched as it exploded into a large mist of red and purple goo, scattering into the winds. The decapitated figure fell to the floor, lifeless, but Meatsack didn't hang around to check the body.

He turned immediately away and ran off in a random direction, hoping that the figure he hit was wearing dungarees, but too scared to actually confirm it.

He sniffled as the tears broke free in his eyes, and snot bubbled in his nose.

* * *

Terrance Leeland, clothes covered in blood and dust, stalked through the storm after the silhouette he was certain to be Bert's grey mutant. He had watched as the thing swung its club at someone, and then that someone promptly fell to the floor as limp as an empty sack. He snarled beneath his mask, thinking that the giant beast should be kept on a leash like the animal that it was.

The creature darted out of sight somewhere ahead, and Terrance was forced to move a little quicker so not to lose it in the turbulent weather all around. He gritted his teeth in frustration, scanning the horizon constantly with his dark eyes, curses forming on his chapped lips at the fucking storm that currently chewed up Smack-dab. He stepped over a bloodied corpse, its head all but evaporated, the rest of its body slowly disappearing beneath trails of dust.

He ran faster, desperate not to lose the disgusting creature. And his efforts were rewarded. Soon he spied its silhouette, closer than ever before, and standing still ahead of him looking left and right, clearly wondering which direction to go next. Well, Terrance knew exactly which direction he intended for it to go.

Down.

By Duncan P. Pacey

* * *

Randolf the Conqueror, Ruiner of Worlds, Bringer of Shadows and Lord of Rabbit-Like Kind smiled grimly to himself, his band of ferocious warriors gathered in a cluster at his tail. Before them lay his prize, his prey – the great spiked grentuputron beast, in all its scaly glory.

Humans sat atop it among its great back spikes, using some kind of chunky sticks to spew noise and fire into the blustering winds. The sound shook Randolf the Conqueror, Ruiner of Worlds, Bringer of Shadows and Lord of Rabbit-Like Kind to his very bones, the sheer force of the strange sticks rattling his rib cage and threatening doom on all who dared oppose the great beast. But he would not be undone by trepidation, for an insult had been made and an insult was to be met with the most ferocious of vengeances.

He turned to Helga Who Eats Your Internal Organs and gestured an order towards the beast. She nodded slightly, her sharp pincers bowing down and up, before getting down on all eights and scuttling on her belly towards the truck. Helga Who Eats Your Internal Organs would go in and scout first, for the beast looked to be at ease right now, its glaring yellow eyes closed. They would need to test the waters before blindly rushing in. A wild attack with no intelligence would be the undoing of those reckless enough to charge. Randolf the Conqueror, Ruiner of Worlds, Bringer of Shadows and Lord of Rabbit-Like Kind was not so foolish - not like his predecessor.

Many humans fought nearby, some getting a little too close for the group's comfort. Humans, tall and pink and hairless (most of them), were highly disrespectful of rabbit-like kind, and all its many cousins of other species. Perhaps, whilst he was here, Randolf the Conqueror, Ruiner of Worlds, Bringer of Shadows and Lord of Rabbit-Like Kind, along with his mercenary band The Many Sons and Daughters of the Grentuputron Moon, could teach some of them a painful lesson, so that they might think twice before pulling a rabbit-like creature's ears in the future.

Yes, he thought. This would be a day of reckoning.

* * *

"Brown, you bastard!" Bert yelled into the winds. She watched, eyes narrow, brow furrowed, as the monstrous shape of Farmer Brown, lord of the Farm, stood upright and listened. Something gooey continued to drip from his anvilhammer, and also from his hands. His shape appeared to turn, facing towards Bert, then it hunched slightly, as if peering into the thick air to see what might peer back. Next, the shape took a step forwards, and then another, and soon the mighty figure of Farmer Brown appeared through the rolling currents like a carnivorous blue whale crashing through the waves of a stormy ocean. His armour was scratched, dented, or just plain missing, his body covered densely in filth. Bert could now see that the ichor dripping from his hammer was the meat of ... somebody, still clinging to the end of the weapon and falling off in slimy chunks.

And when he spoke, the ground trembled. "Woman," he said, the anger clear in the gravel of his voice, "it's 'bout time I found ya."

Bert clutched at the revolver holstered by her side, keeping her feet apart in case she needed sudden and immediate balance. She glared at the towering creature before her, not sure whether to berate him for his twisted rage earlier, shoot him straight away and save the conversation, or attempt renewed peace talks. At the look of his bruised face, a little pixie voice on her shoulder suggested that, perhaps, peace talks were not going to be an option. So that left two...

"You lumbering great troll," Bert shouted, "look what you've done to my bar!"

"Me!?" Brown roared back, his voice far louder and scarier than whatever the wind could throw around. "*I* almost gave ya peace, ya two-faced bitch! But noooo, ya had t' bite th' hand feedin' ya, eh? Well, now yer gonna learn that I bite back."

Bert stood her ground, determined not to be the villain of the story. She had done her best to halt the battle and talk with this asshole, despite what he'd done to her precious bar. And here he was, taking the high road. Well fuck his high road, Bert thought. She was gonna kick the foundations out from under it and see it crumble down to her level. "I was trying to accept your peace, you lumbering great- oh bloody hell," she yelled, cutting herself off and diving to the side. An atomic hammer strike struck the ground just where she had been standing.

Bert staggered to the side, drawing her pistol and hammering it back in the same motion. She didn't wait for Brown to regain himself, pulling the trigger immediately and aiming straight for his skull.

Click.

Her weapon didn't fire. *Again!* Why did this keep happening?

Click, click.

Brown was back to full height, hefting his ludicrous weapon for a new assault. Bert, meanwhile, was learning very rapidly that her weapon had jammed in the storm. She took a deep, calming breath, holstered the pistol and bent down to grab a discarded axe at her feet. It seemed to be an old axe shaft that someone had lost the blade from, and to repair it had duct-taped a second, shorter axe to the end of the shaft, rather than just use the shorter axe by itself. She realised, of course, how useless her new weapon must have looked against Brown's needlessly huge hammer, but there was something distinctly psychological about having at least a small thing with which to stab and slice when facing your nemesis.

And so, axe-axe in hand, feet apart, and face set to Full Glare, Bert readied herself for the final battle.

* * *

Phoenix opened his eyes and decided that he wasn't dead. He came to this conclusion primarily because he could still feel, and what he felt was horrible, horrible pain.

Smack-dab's adventurer rose to a sitting position, finding himself lying in the dust somewhere near where he was previously standing in the dust. His chest cried out at him to stop moving, and begged for him to just lay down and die. He glanced down to see what the sensation was, only to find a crumpled bullet stuck to his body armour. It looked sad, like it had deflated when it failed its one and only purpose in life. On the bright side, though, Phoenix's armour had now been properly tested and he could conclude without the shadow of a doubt that, yes, it *was* bulletproof. It felt good not to have been scammed.

Ahead of him a few feet stood a small, pudgy bald bandit clutching an automatic rifle in his hands. He was staring in shock at the quite noticeably still-alive figure of Phoenix, but occasionally hazarded a look down at the rifle that failed to kill the adventurer. Phoenix watched the little man pull the weapon's trigger a few more times, but nothing came out but disappointment and regret, although arguably those came from the wielder, not the weapon.

Phoenix sighed. "You jammed it up, mate," he said, glad to not be dying from his own weapon but also sad that he was going to have to completely clean it out.

The bandit looked back at him, his previously red face returning to its sheet-white ghostliness.

"Yeah, see when ya fired the first shot without being careful, that flap there will have opened up and now dust'll be all up in its mechanisms. You know, that's gonna be a real pain in the ass for me to clean."

Phoenix glanced quickly around the dust to find his Waste Beast tooth knife, feeling satisfied that it was jutting out of the dirt patiently waiting to be picked up again. He did so, and tossed it casually from one hand to the other to intimidate his foe. Then, when the wind tried snatching it mid-flight, he hastily grabbed the knife before it toppled away, cut himself on the finger, and decided to stop throwing it.

Plumpy McStealsyourgun flipped the aforementioned automatic rifle around in his hands, now holding the barrel like the shaft of a club. Phoenix tensed his leg muscles, lowered his torso and dropped a shoulder, about to spring towards Baldasaurus and tackle him to the ground with a shoulder plate, before stabbing him a few times while he presented a lecture on the disrespectful nature of stealing somebody's personal belongings.

But...

Four more bandits dissolved into view. They looked around for a moment, clearly disoriented from the storm, before identifying both Phoenix and his rotund opponent. Each of the newcomers was wearing dungarees, splattered with runny globules of blood. They brought their various stabby, slicey or choppy weapons to bear and faced Phoenix with their angry, bandity faces.

Five bandits, eh? Phoenix thought. He took a step back, ready to adjust his battle plan – he could do it.

Then five more farmers appeared, stumbling, coughing and screaming into the immediate vicinity in a messy arc around Phoenix. They too scoped out the players, coming to the conclusion that there were ten of them and only one of him.

So, ten bandits. Well, Phoenix had talked the big talk, so now he supposed it was time to walk the walk – preferably all over these wise-asses.

He lowered his body and carefully removed a couple of throwing knives from a bandolier, gripping them both in his left hand while he clutched the Waste Beast tooth with his right. He eyed up the ten bandits surrounding him, and they eyed him right back again.

And charged in all at once.

Part Eleven

Tornadoes Left, Right, and Centre

The dust storm wasn't through with Smack-dab yet. It howled and howled, crashing and smashing into the bar and its garden, hammering everything and everyone. It boiled and toiled, swirled and whirled, and quite frankly, made a bloody great racket.

And the Battle of Smack-Dab raged on.

* * *

Bert breathed hard and held up her axe-axe, now an ex-axe-axe due to an unfortunate failure of duct tape and the subsequent falling off of her shorter blade. Now it was just a stick, and not a particularly effective one at that.

Meanwhile, Brown was also breathing heavily, large droplets of sweat falling from his thick brow. He had suffered a few extra minor cuts, and his chunky left arm was now a little bit less chunky, on account of Bert having sliced out a chunk of it. The wound had bled at a steady rate at first, but the dust was clogging it up and although it would likely cause a horrible infection one day soon (should Brown even survive the battle), it was unfortunately acting as an effective coagulant. The stream had trickled to an absolute minimum, and Bert's plan to weaken Brown until he collapsed was trickling with it. But she was still alive, and she was still quicker than him. So long as she stayed in control of her Bertrage and kept moving, she'd hopefully remain both of those things for a good few years longer.

Bert watched as Farmer Brown grunted loudly to the storm and threw his hammer to the ground, feeling the shockwave in her boots as it struck dirt. He then flexed both of his arms, although his left one somewhat understandably less so, and stalked towards her. Bert figured he must be freeing himself up for speed over strength. From the sluggish start to their fight, she reckoned he hadn't come across someone as nimble as her before.

But the bastard was smartening up.

Bert pounced first, hoping to steal the initiative. She needed to get to the other side of him and pick up the short axe, which was loitering by itself on the ground with some ripped duct tape flapping loosely in the wind attached to it. She ran fast, but was careful where and how she planted each step. She needed to be able to move at a moment's notice. Brown stopped stalking and remained where he was, lowering his hands and widening his grasping fingers. But Bert wasn't stupid enough to just charge head-on without a weapon better than a blunt stick. She stepped to the right as she approached the bandit lord, making him flinch in that direction. Then, with a quick back-step, she pirouetted to the left and took herself right out of his lashing arms and arcing around his opposite side.

On the way past, she swung her stick with all her might and brought it down across Brown's cheek. She felt his face contort from the blow, and a bone-shattering shock vibrated up her arm. The pain in her muscles caused her to stumble the landing, but the blow forced Brown staggering in the other direction, holding his face.

He took two clumsy steps forwards and spat loudly, a mixture of spittle, blood and yellow shards cascading out of his gaping mouth. Bert, behind him, massaged her arm as much as she could with a non-functioning metal hand, trying to ignore the horrible pain in her skeleton from both the Hurl fight and now this one. Her small frame really couldn't take much more action. Just one or two hits from Brown and she was done for - but Bert reckoned Brown could still take plenty more himself.

Not good.

Brown looked back over his shoulder, his big face twisted in an ugly, red rage. His eyes flamed, nostrils flaring. "Ya knocked a tooth loose, bitch," he seethed, more spit and blood dribbling from his gargantuan lips.

Bert sneered back. "Only one? Damn, I missed."

Brown howled like a wounded Waste Beast. He was losing control of his anger, allowing it to pump his decisions full of gunpowder and sparks. The big lord flung himself at his tiny opponent, but Bert was already side-stepping out of the way, making a run for the axe as he sailed past harmlessly.

Excellent, she thought to herself mid-flight. If she could just keep him angry, he would be out of control and she'd be fine. All she had to do was keep jabbing him until he made a mistake, then she could start lashing out at some of his softer spots, like his throat, or his balls.

By Duncan P. Pacey

The axe was nearby, rattling in the wind as if about to take flight. While Brown was a few feet away and still turning his rhinoceros body around to charge again, Bert took the opening and dived for the weapon, sliding past it in the dust, grabbing it, and coming to a halt up against something solid as hell. She glanced up and met The Woman's firm gaze, her eyes challenging all of Smack-dab's opponents, but reminding the world of what had been lost to pointless battles beforehand, like that time...

...like the time The Woman's body had-

-hang on a second, Bert thought. Something was wrong. Resting at The Woman's feet was the distinct shape of her arm, clutching a replica of the pistol that now lay jammed in Bert's side holster. The arm had been broken off, and it looked like someone had dropped it in the dirt a few times for good measure. Who the fu-

"He he he," she heard behind her, a mischievous cackle from a mouth so large it could swallow most mischievous cacklers whole. "Sorry 'bout yer statue, woman. Looks like I broke it."

Bert spun to see Farmer Brown standing close, a smug look on his battered face. He grinned wide beneath his mask. The pipes in Bert's head were already burst from earlier. There was nothing the mechanics of her brain could do anymore. Her rationalism and common sense exploded into black curls of smoke with rib-shattering bangs. The mechanics were caught in the blasts, torn to oblivion by the heat and force alone. Any of them that somehow survived were then struck by the flinging shards and shredded on the steaming concrete floors of Bert's mind. Smoke billowed through her brain and rushed out of her ears, pushing the blood capacity of her face to its absolute load limit.

"You son of a bitch," she hissed quietly, her voice overwhelmed by the emotion coursing freely through her veins.

"What?" Brown replied, grinning wide with that canyon mouth of his. "Ya feel all sad about yer itty-bitty statue? Well, how 'bout ya come say what yer feel to me face?"

And Bert fully intended to, whether she intended to intend to or not. Rage wormed its way into her every limb, casting away the oppressive shackles of self-control and nestling its red ass into the driver's seat. It hijacked each of her nerves, jammed them up to full blast, pumped some heavy metal music, put on a pair of dark sunglasses and a spiked leather jacket, and cracked its knuckles. Bertrage was here, and it was finally in control.

Bert lunged, short-axe in hand, straight for Farmer Brown's bulky, waiting figure. He ran, too, pounding the dirt with his heavy boots as he brought himself up to full speed. They ran for each other, closing the small gap between them, and then something happened that Bert wasn't prepared for, but that she should have been.

Brown stepped to one side, which Bert twirled left to avoid. But, mid-twirl, Brown pulled the very same manoeuvre that she had done to him mere moments before, pushing his weight off his front foot and throwing himself in the other direction. She was caught completely off guard, expecting to be able to sail past the giant and axe his ears off. But instead, a rock-hard shoulder the size of at least three rock-hard shoulders struck her in the ribs, picking her straight off her feet and tossing her through the roiling storm, a mere feather on the wind compared to Brown's powerful strength.

You could have thrown a building at Bert and it would have hurt less. But no sooner was she on the ground and trying to catch the breath pumping out of her lungs than Brown was above her, grasping her by the neck and leg tightly in huge hands and lifting her to the sky once more.

Again Bert flew, this time in a daze, before colliding with The Woman's statue. The stony figure rocked on its platform as Bert's small body wrapped around it the wrong way. Something inside her cracked loudly, or maybe it was many things all cracking in unison. She couldn't tell. Blood seeped from her lips and nose as she came to a rest at the feet of her one-time saviour and mentor. Blackness curled in thick tendrils across her vision, spots forming in front of her eyes. Noise dulled into a distant thrum. Sensations numbed to a tingling cold.

Not far away, a monster of a silhouette towered into the sky, hefting an anvil onto its shoulder and taking the first steps towards its prone opponent.

The ground shook with every ponderous, angry step.

And so did Bert.

* * *

Jeb stared at the large table he and the other traders had erected over Smack's front door when the storm hit. Something was behind it, coming closer. They could hear the porch creak, but barely. It was hard to tell how many folks were there, or what their intentions were. The wailing storm covered too much up.

"Wadda we do, Jeb?" squeaked Orsen in a hushed whisper. They were both on the other side of the room from the door, huddled at a table near the other traders and wandering folk.

"Jus' stay outta trouble, Orsen. That's all we gotta do," Jeb whispered back, feeling his body starting to shake from the adrenalin his heart pumped into his limbs.

From their vantage point in Smack-dab, they had watched all kinds of violence today. People shot each other with whatever guns still worked, then beat each other over the head with the same guns when they stopped. There was axe murder, machete slashing, hammer bashing, and straight-up fist fights. Orsen swore he had seen someone bite another man's fingers off, but Jeb had missed it, instead watching a small band of fuzzy creatures running between people's feet towards where the truck still sat, spewing lead and steel at random into the fray. It was impossible to tell who was winning the battle when all they saw were tiny snapshots, but the farmers were fighting with extraordinary ferocity despite having fewer numbers. Jeb couldn't imagine them losing a battle.

And as if the farmer's ears were burning (which, to be fair, they could well have been out in that storm), the Smack-dab doortable burst inwards with a mighty wooden bang, flying away from the entrance to land in two near the bar counter. The manic storm blasted into the room after, screaming at the top of its windy lungs as great torrents of dust swirled through the door frame. Two figures stood in the entrance, one holding a bloodied home-made morning star (home-made from a tree branch, old brass globe, and a *lot* of nails), and the other a green metal crate. The one with the crate was an older wiry fellow with messy hair, no eyebrows and a bandana over his mouth, while the man with the heavy weapon had a decent set of muscles, but a dim-witted stare to suggest nothing decent going on anywhere else. Quite frankly, Jeb reckoned they looked like an alternate-universe version of himself and Or-

-Hey! he thought. He'd encounter these guys before. It was Gob and Job, or was it Lob and Tob? Or maybe Rob and Bob...

Yeah, that sounded right. But he'd be buggered if he could remember who was which.

"Keep th' customers back there, Maddison," said the older one, who would now be known as Bob. "I'm gon' put the bomb in th' kitchen. Then we blow this sucker."

Maddison, henceforth known as Rob, nodded dumbly and flexed his impressive muscular system, waving his nail-globe at Jeb and the band to threaten them into submission. Behind him, Bob scurried on his stick legs towards the kitchen, heaving a crate that was clearly too heavy for him to hold comfortably.

"A bomb!" whispered Orsen nervously. "Did he say bomb?"

"Aye, lad," replied Jeb, sweat forming on his frightened old face.

"What are we gonna do? We can't let Smacks get blowed up!"

Rob scowled at the duo. "Stop talking!"

Orsen scowled right back. "You stop talking!"

Rob looked stunned, then took a quiet step back. "OK, sorry."

"We gotta stay outta trouble, lad," whispered Jeb, who stared wide-eyed at the old man disappearing into the kitchen.

The other traders and wanderers around Smack-dab muttered quickly to each other. They descended into a tense ambience of hurried and hushed tones barely audible over the roaring wind that poured through the open doorway. Jeb coiled and uncoiled his fingers, playing with pieces of his clothing and staring all the while at the older invader, who had just disappeared into the kitchen. Orsen, meanwhile, was practically pressing his face his mentor's ear, grasping with his youthful fingers at the puffs of Jeb's puffy jacket.

"If we stay outta trouble we're gonna get blowed up, Jeb. And Smacks, too!"

Jeb could feel his whole body petrify with tension. Oh, maybe this is what being petrified felt like, he wondered as an afterthought. But he couldn't move, for moving was getting into trouble, and getting into trouble was the quickest way to getting killed, or getting the boy killed. He'd dedicated years to Orsen, and many had given their lives. He couldn't let that be in vain. He had to be safe. He had to *stay* safe.

But a bomb...? And Smack-dab...

Orsen cursed under his breath. "If you won't move, Jeb, I'm sorry. I gotta do this."

Jeb's bubble popped. "Wait, what?"

But Orsen was already moving. He sprang to his feet away from his older mentor, grabbing the nearest mug and lifting it like a mighty warhammer. He screamed at the top of his lungs and charged mug-first towards Rob, who had a clear picture of all of this happening and had more than enough time to prepare. The young bandit buck put two calloused hands on his morning star and wound it back like a sports bat.

"Orsen!" cried Jeb.

"FOR SMACK-DAAAAAB!" shouted the boy, closing in on his target.

And so Jeb made a decision, though he wasn't left with much choice. He rose to his tired old feet as fast as his tired old body would allow, which, given the nitro-glycerine-like adrenalin in his system, was surprisingly quick (but would be regrettable by the morning). His wiry fingers wrapped themselves around the nearest plate and he spun it like a discus towards Rob, who had more than enough time to prepare and avoid, but was too dim-witted to focus on two things at once. Rob took the plate square in the nose and it shattered on his baby face, slicing open tiny little cuts all over him and, more importantly, distracting him from the impending Orsen assault. Orsen then hammered his mug over the top of Rob's skull and it too shattered, showering the man in pieces of dirty glass and left-over grog and backwash. He howled with pain and staggered away from Orsen, still clutching his morning star.

Jeb was running forwards to intervene before Rob could recover and smash open Orsen's globe with his own, when he saw the older guy, Bob, reappearing from the kitchen door on the other side of the room. He looked confused as hell, and about twice as annoyed.

"RUN, LAD, RUN!" screamed Orsen, who promptly grabbed a chair and charged towards Bob.

"Wait, Orsen! Don't run, DON'T RUN!" screamed Jeb. He had just spotted what was in Bob's hand now that he didn't have a crate to lug about. It was a small semi-automatic pistol known as a Clock, which wasn't too common up in the Orcklands, but was an incredibly reliable and effective weapon - even long after the Old World has passed on. Orsen ran chair-first towards Bob, either not seeing the gun or not caring about it. He screamed his battle cry at the older bandit and lifted his chair for a hammering smash.

And Bob pointed his pistol and squeezed the trigger twice.

Two booming shots rattled the floorboards and shook dust from nearby surfaces, although more dust immediately piled back on. The shots roared over the noise of the storm, and Orsen was struck down by the gunfire: once in the thigh, the other in the torso, both bullets ploughing through his slender body and popping out the other side in a spray of blood.

And Jeb screamed.

* * *

Phoenix was bent over, hands on his knees, trying to find the air somewhere in his lungs. So far he was struggling, and so he just stood, doubled over, rasping on the spot, wishing he wasn't so unfit. His bandit tackling shoulder was so buckled that the plating would need replaced before it was of any use again, and the bruises beneath would last for weeks. His head felt like a little irradiated pixie with a hammer was pounding on his amygdala, and the side of his neck bled from where a bandit with a machete got a lucky hit mere seconds before.

Something in the dust at Phoenix's feet groaned quietly, and twitched a small puff of dust into the raging air. Phoenix eyed up the thing, inspecting his handiwork as he caught his breath. Plumpy the bald-headed thief was foetal in the dirt, his clothes torn apart by the Merciless and Supremely Painful Castigation of Seven Million Phoenixes. A throwing knife lay embedded in his ear. All around were nine other bodies in a neat circle, slashed, broken, stabbed or beaten. One was also inside out, but Phoenix wasn't sure he did that. A little rabbit-like creature with a scar over its eye was battling for at least some of the ten-on-one frenzy, and didn't have quite the same mercy as Phoenix.

But, killing nine out of ten bandits by himself still counted as the whole ten, because who would believe that a small, fuzzy creature would appear and obliterate the poor inside-out man? Phoenix smiled as he ladled breaths into his tired lungs.

And as for the gun-thief dying in the dirt, Phoenix crouched down clumsily, woozy from the pain in his brain, and shuffled almost drunkenly to the bald thief's face. His beautiful automatic rifle, Phoenix's pride and indeed joy, was mangled, buried in multiple pieces around the battlefield. All because of this asshole's poor handling.

He pulled himself on top of the man, poking him in the cheek. "See ... you bastard," he puffed, poke poke poking all the time. "This ... this is what happens when you steal."

The figure groaned and curled up tighter, looking away so as to die in peace, rather than pieces. Phoenix scowled and crawled further on top of him, trying to catch his eye line. "Hey, don't you look away from me. Stealing..." poke poke poke "...is wrong."

No more groans.

"Did you die?" Poke poke.

Nothing.

"Oh, how rude."

Then, from somewhere close by, a voice that made Phoenix's hairs all stand up wafted in on the torrents of dust and stones and bits of human organs.

"PLEASE STAND STILL, FLESHY SCARED HUMAN. THIS WILL BE FASTER IF YOU REMAIN STATIONARY."

Phoenix gazed in the direction he reckoned he heard the voice from, squinting into the maelstrom. The noise sounded suspiciously like one particularly dastardly robot, whom Phoenix had developed a distaste for...

"LOOK AT WHAT YOU HAVE DONE NOW. BY MOVING, I HAVE CLAWED YOUR ARM OFF, NOT YOUR HEAD. THIS PAIN YOU FEEL IS YOUR FAULT. PLEASE STAND STILL."

Oh ho ho, thought Phoenix. An Overlord – a very special bastard of an Overlord – was somewhere close and, by the sounds of the horrible squishy noises, quite distracted.

Aside from being violent, bossy, and creepy-looking, the robotic race of Overlords that lauded over mankind were Phoenix's single biggest nemesis, even greater than Dr. Nemesis, whom he had a brief but explosive exchange with in his earlier career. You see, for as many successful adventures that Phoenix and his various adventuring buddies had completed, there was almost an equal number foiled by these pesky, meddling robots. Particularly the H-models like H2-149, who were notoriously common, aggressive and, unfortunately, accurate.

Phoenix, still resting on top of the now-deceased Arnold, inspected his row of grenades with the anticipation one might feel as a child on Christmas day – Christmas being the day when most of the Orcks in the Orcklands left weaponised gifts for all the little boys and girls, hoping to turn them into psychopathic killers and, one day, employees. Phoenix's reddened, cut-up fingers delicately caressed a high-explosive grenade, then an inferno grenade. Such beauties, they were. So shiny and quiet, yet so rough and loud. He quietly unhooked the explosive number, looking into the eyes of the smiley face painted on one side of the cylindrical object. He held this alongside his Waste Beast tooth knife and a sly grin spread beneath his bloodied dust mask. This was way too good an opportunity; a chance to let out some stress.

H2-149 was dead meat. Dead parts, anyway.

Phoenix rose to his feet, or more accurately, *eventually* rose to his feet (he was not in the greatest of health). Then he started jogging lightly, towards the sounds of excruciating death being dealt by a particular robot apparently not too far away. Next he was sprinting, charging at full speed with a dangerous grenade in one hand and a less-dangerous, but still rather deadly Waste Beast tooth knife in the other. He pounced, hurtling through the air with a battle cry on his lips that he was far too light-headed to realise was escaping his lips. His battered body flew through the air, a majestic Devil Terror diving on its tiny rabbit-like prey, preparing to land on the robot's back and immediately cave a new hole into its skull. Then he'd hit the button on his grenade, pop it in the new hole, dive off in an amazing feat of acrobatics, and stare away from the explosion as it tore apart his metallic rival – because every adventurer knows that you should be facing the other way when an explosion happens, just in case someone is watching and sees how cool it looks.

And so Phoenix flew, visions of grandeur sweeping across his imagination, straight for H2-149's back.

And then he landed on H2-149's front.

Phoenix yelped squeakily and clanged off its skeletal body, landing on his ass in the dirt. He immediately scuffled back a few feet to put some distance between himself and the robot, but it took steps equal to his shuffling and loomed over him like some personification of death (which, if the bodies were anything to go by, it had been more than once this afternoon).

"HELLO, NOT-TRADER. PLEASE REMAIN STATIONARY WHILE I KILL YOU."

Phoenix yelped a second time, higher-pitched than the first, and rolled to the side as a metal heel thumped down where his skull used to be. He rolled again, and again, moving constantly so as to avoid the barrage of metal heels bombarding him from above.

"I APOLOGISE IF YOU DID NOT HEAR ME, NOT-TRADER. I REQUESTED THAT YOU REMAIN STILL. YOU ARE MAKING THIS DIFFICULT."

Phoenix scrabbled quickly in the dust and moved himself farther away, this time creating some actual distance between him and the robot, if only a miniscule amount. It was enough, though, for him to spring deftly to his feet and turn to fight back face to bulb. But the bulb of H2-149 was closer than Phoenix anticipated, and next he was ducking and weaving, once again barely avoiding the robot's swift attacks. It lashed out with claw after claw of sharpened metal fingers, each aiming straight for the adventurer's throat.

"ACCEPT DEATH, FLESHY NOT-TRADER. LIFE IS INCONVENIENT FOR ORGANIC BEINGS. PLEASE ALLOW ME TO ASSIST YOU."

Phoenix ducked again, H2's pinky claw nicking his scalp and cutting a tidy little line into his head. Blood bubbled out and dribbled through his hair, clogging instantly with eager particles of dust. Phoenix winced. Why was it always the tiny cuts that hurt so bad?

He began to run in big circles, hoping to confuse the robot's eye sensor at least a little. For all their advanced technology, the Overlord's eyesight still wasn't as accurate as a human's during a storm. Or rather, it was *too* accurate for a storm, in that its many imaging scanners had trouble determining quick movement amid such a tumultuous backdrop. Granted, the chances of Phoenix moving quick enough for that to be relevant were next to nothing in his current state, but it felt better to be trying.

On his third lap, Phoenix was ready to close in and stabby stab stab the robot when he noticed its cannon lying lifeless in the dust. Ahah! he thought hungrily, swooping over and grasping it in his hands, momentarily stowing away his grenade and knife. He hooked an excited finger around its bulky trigger and swung the huge weapon around, resting it partly on his knee. He smiled at H2-149, which stalked straight towards him without so much as an emotion.

"Overlord? I'm over you," he stated loudly, and squeezed the trigger.

The big weapon hummed to life, a mechanism somewhere inside suddenly whirring up to full speed. Blue lights lit up all along the gun down towards the barrel and then ... nothing. No bullets came out.

"THE RG-003 THAT YOU HOLD, NOT-TRADER, RAN OUT OF AMMO AT B30 dash 29 dash 19585. IT HAS ELIMINATED APPROXIMATLY FORTY-EIGHT SKINBAGS."

Phoenix lowered the weapon. "Forty-eight, are you serious?" And here was Phoenix thinking ten was heaps.

"PLEASE DIE NOW, NOT-TRADER."

H2-149 leapt suddenly forwards before Phoenix could react, bounding across the final few feet to tackle Smack's adventurer with its metal face. He let out an audible yelp as the blow connected, sending him reeling backwards. The cannon clattered away from his fingers, useless.

He tried to sit up and run away, realising at least on some instinctual level that the fight was going entirely not his way, but a clawed hand reached out and grasped him by the collar.

Oh butts, Phoenix thought.

Next, another razor-tipped set of claws raked across his back, screeching awfully as it scored great gouges in his armour. Phoenix started to roll away but a second claw came thundering in, striking him in the back a second time and knocking him to the side.

He landed, once more out of breath, but far woozier than before, not far from the Overlord. It towered above him, a shadowy figure against the glowing brown rage of the storm, with one pulsating red eye gazing down at him, devoid of any readable expression except 'red'. Phoenix reached for his knife, but caught a heel to the hand for his troubles. So instead he scurried backwards, hoping to get away again - but H2 was learning his tricks. It jumped forwards instead of stepping, landing with a metallic thud next to Phoenix's retreating form. He turned to look at its shiny legs, giving him a front-row seat to the foot that swung for his face.

Blood streaming from his mouth, Phoenix recoiled backwards from the blow, landing starfish on his back as dust, blood, and air all fled his weakened body. He wheezed loudly, blood pooling in his mouth, wishing the world would stop spinning so that he could stand up and do something useful.

Above him, H2-149 stepped towards him to finish the job.

* * *

They found Ernest covered in the blood of some one-armed cultist, and the internal organs of his bugle-wielding sister. His clipboard was broken into three pieces, and it looked like he'd been using them as daggers - successfully, even. His eyes were wide with fear, but alight with blood. He'd seen and done things he'd never seen or done before, and would likely never see nor do again. He told them that he felt sick, disgusted with himself, but some suspected he felt sick because, against all expectation, he had enjoyed being the strong one - the one with power. The one to dish death, not count it.

He had asked if they were winning, and they told him yes. But nobody knew for sure. What else would you tell a man who still had a piece of kidney clinging to his dungarees?

* * *

A figure darted behind Meatsack and he spun. Nobody was there.

Then there was a flash behind him. He turned. Nobody there.

Meatsack shuffled anxiously on his big feet, his tiny arm held worriedly to his face mask. He couldn't find anyone he knew, and he didn't know where to go. He wanted frightfully to ask Windy's father, Stormy, for assistance finding his way, but he didn't have much of a relationship with Stormy, and he was very afraid of him. He was loud and violent, and cared little for Smack-dab. Stormy was mean. Meatsack needed Berty - Berty would know what to do.

A silhouette flew through the air somewhere ahead of him, and it looked like it had the chunky hand of Berty Bert! Meatsack's face lit up in a big grin and he started running for her.

Then something landed on his back.

* * *

Terrance Leeland yelled loudly as he tightened his metal pipe around the grey mutant's neck. He wrapped his legs either side of the giant's disgusting body and squeezed tightly, using as much power in his lower body as possible so as to not fall off the bucking creature. At the same time, he pulled on the pipe and used his stub hand to hold it in place, trying to starve the thing's brain - or whatever it had as a replacement - of oxygen. Then it would fall down to ground level and he'd have all the time in the world to do as he pleased.

"Hold still, you ugly grey bastard," he growled, squeezing even tighter.

It whimpered loudly and dropped its heavy wooden club, staggering in big circles as its arms, both large and small, flailed outwards in panic. Terrance felt an immense satisfaction at being on the other side of the strangling, his neck still coloured by the bruising of Phoenix's attack the other day. He decided to pump the pipe a few times to add more panic, and for a little flare. In quick bursts he'd yank the pipe inwards, then again and again. The creature whimpered and whimpered, stumbling and staggering all the while waving its arms around in every direction. Terrance didn't bother ducking out their way, for he was confident that the muscles in its big arm were too gratuitous for it to reach behind itself

299

and grasp at the adventurer. But, just to be safe, he kept one eye on the monstrosity all the same.

After a minute of squeezing, the giant mutant's movements began to ebb. Its staggering slowed, arms held lower than previously. Terrance Leeland grinned evilly, snickering confidently to himself. He always felt such ecstasy when he was winning, like he could hold an erection for days on the pure pleasure of the thing. He pumped the pipe again, forcing the creature to gag and choke so that it would wear itself out even faster.

And it did. Gargled coughing noises escaped out from under its big mask, and soon it fell to its knees, strangled moans of pain wheezing out from its closed throat. Terrance let go of its torso and stood firmly with two feet on the ground, the monster now low enough that he could comfortably stand whilst still holding his pipe in place. For good measure, he put one of his black boots on the small of its back and pushed, all the while pulling with his pipe.

It had a great effect, too. The stupid creature let out a particularly pathetic gag and its body went almost limp. But, just before it was dead, Terrance released his pressure. He didn't want it to die just yet. He needed it alive so that it could see and feel every ounce of vengeance he had planned for its ugly face.

He'd drag this out as long as he could.

* * *

The great grentuputron beast spewed its fire and noise down onto the ground, and Randolf the Conqueror, Ruiner of Worlds, Bringer of Shadows and Lord of Rabbit-Like kind saw human after human explode into bloodied pieces as its rivers of hellfire struck them down. Helga Who Eats Your Internal Organs had never returned, and so The Many Sons and Daughters of the Grentuputron Moon were charging in blind, as foolish as it may be. But the great beast might awaken at any moment, and it could not be allowed to escape.

Together they weaved their way through the legs of the clashing humans, fighting their way through the angered storm as it drove dust and stones in their fur and eyes. One of The Many Sons and Daughters of the Grentuputron Moon, a rabbit-like fellow by the name of Hondor the Strong and Mighty and Sometimes Wise, had been struck by a falling weapon and cleaved in half by the thing, which did not go down well with his scar-faced life-partner, Filder the Fast and Sly and Always Wise. She did something to the human's internal organs Randolf the Conqueror, Ruiner of Worlds, Bringer of Shadows and Lord of Rabbit-Like kind had never seen before, was highly impressed by, and would never forget.

The group had slain four humans by the time they finally managed to break through the throng and reach the spiked, scaly hide of the great beast. It towered above them, a veritable titan of a creature, that rocked and shook violently as its humans unleashed their devastation on other humans. Without needing further prompting, The Many Sons and Daughters of the Grentuputron Moon started climbing the thing, finding easy footholds between its scales and its spikes. Strangely, its head seemed hollow, with great cushioned padding and many human things inside it. Randolf the Conqueror, Ruiner of Worlds, Bringer of Shadows and Lord of Rabbit-Like Kind could only guess as to the symbiotic nature of the beast and its humans, but he knew that he wanted nothing of the sort for him and his people. The humans ate rabbit-like creatures, and in kind, the rabbit-like creatures ate humans. That was symbiosis enough.

"Mawp mawp, mawp mawp mawp mawp!" came a noise somewhere over their shoulders.

A human had spotted The Many Sons and Daughters of the Grentuputron Moon clambering up the beast, and was pointing at them and yelling with its bizarrely complex mouth noises. Another human appeared, both armed with close-quarters weapons, and they started chopping at the beast to shake off Randolf the Conqueror, Ruiner of Worlds, Bringer of Shadows and Lord of Rabbit-Like Kind's mercenary group. Nervous of this unfortunate turn of events, he beckoned for Filder the Fast and Sly and Always Wise, and Barolf, Wielder of Many Strengths, to leap from their footholds and attack the humans. They did so with skill and bravery, landing on the human's faces and slashing into them with claws and teeth and more claws.

The rest of the group continued to climb the great scaled cliff of the beast, but the humans atop it were alerted to their presence.

"Mawp! Mawp mawp!" one shouted.

"Mawping Mawp!" shouted the other.

One of them brought forth a small shiny block with a handle at one end and a hole at the other, aiming it towards The Many Sons and Daughters of the Grentuputron Moon. It erupted with noise and smoke and flame, its powerful magic tearing a hole through the slender torso of the bird-like Harhar'a'keet. Her blood splashed across her dog-like friend, Woof, who growled loudly and bared his fangs in response. His eyes changed at that moment, from determination to blood-lust. He howled to the storm and changed climbing direction, heading straight for the human with the magical block. She unleashed her fire on Woof, and his head burst open, body falling limp to the dust below.

"Mawp mawp!" screamed the human with no magic, for the only remaining mercenary, Brinhold the Undoer of Life, was almost upon him. There was a brief scuffle at the top of the beast, and then Brinhold the Undoer of Life fell from his lofty position, his life undone. Randolf the Conqueror, Ruiner of Worlds, Bringer of Shadows and Lord of Rabbit-Like Kind suddenly found himself entirely alone on the great scaled hide of the grentuputron beast, its two humans both staring straight at him.

* * *

All around Smack-dab's garden, the battle raged. The Starry Place soldiers had no idea, but their numbers dwindled with each passing second, Farmer Brown's mighty truck carving great swathes of death among their ranks, even amid the tumult of the dust storm.

On the other side of the battlefield, Bert's Battalion fought bravely against the farmers, clashing with axes, clubs, and many an impolite word. But try as they might, they struggled to break through the Farm's front line, unable to coordinate any semblance of a coordinated strike in the midst of the howling winds and raging filth.

The Battle of Smack-dab turned ever closer in the favour of Farmer Brown.

Part Twelve

The Big Finale

Randolf the Conqueror, Ruiner of Worlds, Bringer of Shadows and Lord of Rabbit-Like Kind stared down the barrel of the female human's magical block and snarled. He saw the face of his father gazing at him from the distant past, remembering the days when he was just a young thing. His father, the Uniter of Rabbit-Like Kind, hated failure, and despised weakness even more so. His love was tougher than the meat of an aged human, but its fiery pressure moulded Randolf into a Conqueror, Ruiner of Worlds, Bringer of Shadows and Lord of Rabbit-Like Kind.

And so he stared into the shadowy hole of death and dared it to spit fire, to spew its magical orange streak, and to just try knock him from the side of the great beast.

But it never did.

From behind the female human arose Filder the Fast and Sly and Always Wise, drenched ears to tail in dust-coated blood, with a blazing fire dancing in her wild black eyes. She bounded onto the arm of the female human and bit deep, slashing down on her wrist with a clawed paw.

Next, Barolf, Wielder of Many Strengths, was beside Randolf the Conqueror, Ruiner of Worlds, Bringer of Shadows and Lord of Rabbit-Like Kind, nodding at him slowly to speak the thousand unneeded words that said the deed was done, and it was time to deed some more.

In perfect synchronicity, the two rabbit-like warriors forced themselves up the last remaining distance to the top of the great beast and dove for the male human and his hellfire stick, before he could turn it on them. He squealed pathetically, a high-pitched cowardly bawl, as tiny little fangs and tiny little claws dug into his skin, clawed at his clothes and bit into his eyeballs. In those same moments, the female human had dropped her magical block and was trying desperately to clamber from her scaled nest and flee down the side of the beast, but Filder the Fast and Sly and Always Wise was fast, sly and wise, not allowing her the opportunity. When the female human put her hand on the beast's hide to climb over, fangs were there to tear away her fingers. When she tried putting a foot over instead, claws were there to sneak up her trouser leg and slash at her calves. And, finally, when she tried to dive head-first off the side, she was allowed to - and she broke her neck by the beast's round, black feet.

Randolf the Conqueror, Ruiner of Worlds, Bringer of Shadows and Lord of Rabbit-Like Kind plunged his bloodied fist into the human's last remaining eyeball, feeling it burst around his claws. Meanwhile, Barolf, wielding many strengths, dragged a sharp claw along the wailing throat of the human, prying it open so that blood could flow freely. He dug into the crimson meat below until he felt windpipe, and that too he opened.

Soon the human was drowning in his own blood, gargling and spitting and coughing and spluttering, collapsing into his nest while his stick of death lay dormant. Randolf the Conqueror, Ruiner of Worlds, Bringer of Shadows and Lord of Rabbit-Like Kind rose his fist in triumph, his companions doing the same. He smiled wide, proud in their great victory, but the day was not through. The beast's humans had been eradicated, but the grentuputron monster itself remained.

But how to destroy such a mighty, armoured creature? Randolf the Conqueror, Ruiner of Worlds, Bringer of Shadows and Lord of Rabbit-Like Kind thought then, of the hollow skull this strange creature had. How its very brain seemed designed to be viewed by humans, to be touched and prodded and manipulated.

Maybe it wouldn't be so difficult after all...

* * *

The storm was losing enthusiasm, but the bad man hitting Meatsack wasn't. All around him, Stormy's winds slowed their ferocious energy, dulled their manic howling, and Windy's father seemed to be coming to the end of his untamed mad destruction. But Meatsack could take no joy in such simple pleasures, for the bad man wouldn't let him go.

He felt weak and tired, his neck pulsating with an awful, hideous pain the likes of which Meatsack hadn't felt since he was a child. He would try to run, wobbling to his feet and making it a few steps before the bad man would catch him up and trip him, or strike him in the back of the head with his pipe. And Meatsack would fall back to the ground, tears welling in his wide eyes, feeling helpless and mewing for Berty to come save him. But she never appeared, and the bad man was always there.

Meatsack swung his thick arm out in defence, wildly missing and upsetting his balance. He felt so woozy and sick, like he'd drunk too much of Bert's happy grog, but also like someone was stomping on his head, probably because someone was. He saw spots over his eyes and tried to rub them, but couldn't because of his goggles. In an almost delirious state, he thought of removing the lenses so he could get at them, but Berty said to never take them off in a bad storm and he felt fearful for breaking her rules.

So Meatsack shook his head and placed his big arm on the ground, pushing, trying to get up again. He was a few inches up when a muddy boot swung in from the left and caught him in the side of the head, sending him back to the dirt again.

Everything was sore.

Everything was sad.

He sniffled, and the bad man kicked again.

Now came the sound of laughter, finally audible over the waning orchestra of the storm. It was low, long and completely sinister. It rolled out of the mouth dripping with poison, a laughter less of fun, but more of satisfaction. Of a hideous job well done, a desperate need being fulfilled. It circled Meatsack like a wolfcat waiting to strike. It relished in every second of the hunt, taking no hurry in the miserable art of what it was doing. It was a laugh of pure evil, in Meatsack's ears.

But to Meatsack, laughter was for fun. It was for nice thing. It was when two people were happy. When two people enjoyed what they were doing together, like hugging, dancing, or mopping blood off the floor. It was fo–

–a boot came down on the back of Meatsack's head and pushed his face painfully into the dust and rocks below. Pain swept through his large body greater than before. The big giant felt his heartbeat pulsing in his brain, each pump causing him to wince and whimper.

Then the laughter wafted through the air again.

It wasn't right.

Meatsack wasn't having fun.

The bad man shouldn't be laughing.

Laughter was for nice people.

This wasn't nice.

This wasn't fun.

No.

No it wasn't.

Not for Meatsack.

The angry bad man with the dark face and black clothes crouched down near Meatsack, smiling. This wasn't right. He shouldn't be smiling. Smiling was for happy occasions, like when you help people, not hurt them.

Meatsack ... felt mad.

"Time to die, you ugly monster," came the bad man's darkened voice.

Meatsack couldn't take anymore. A dam burst somewhere in his innocent mind and out flooded the red mists of chaos. Meatsack lashed out with his massive arm, smacking it into the bad man's chest and flinging him across the dirt as though he were a trivial little bitefly. The bad man groaned loudly as he crashed into the ground far from where he started, rolling a couple of times before coming to a messy stop.

Breathing hard, now, Meatsack rose slowly to his feet, swaying as his balance threatened to collapse. Both of his eyes fell sharply on the bad man, aiming the same direction for the first time in years. Meatsack stomped slowly towards him, sweat pouring from his bruised grey skin, his breath coming out in heavy, untamed sighs. His fingers, both large and small, curled into tight fists, digging their nails into his palms. Every muscle in Meatsack's giant body bulged as though inflated like balloons, thick blue veins popping on his big arm and on his forehead.

This man was evil.

He hurt people.

He laughed at it.

Evil. Evil. Evil.

The bad man roared something at Meatsack, but he no longer processed the words. He lashed out with his big hand just in time to catch the bad man's sudden attack. Meatsack's thick fingers curled around both the pipe and the man's hand, crushing them with all his immense strength. The bad man screamed loudly, hurting Meatsack's ears, but he didn't let go. He felt hard things snapping in the palm of his hand, heard the crying of metal as it bent under the pressure. Little bits of something moved and cracked and shrunk in the hand of the bad man. He tried to beat Meatsack over the head with his stump hand, but compared with the beatings from earlier, the grey giant barely so much as noticed it.

The man screamed louder.

Meatsack gripped tighter.

More hard things snapped. He heard little cracks and pops; the same grotesque, meaty sounds that came from the kitchen when Phoenix had caught an animal to serve. He thought of Phoenix, humming his happy tunes as he worked, Bert hovering by the passover window chatting lightly to him. He thought of them smiling and laughing together, enjoying their daily work. They were like parents to Meatsack. One the loving mother, one the hard but fair father. He loved them both so much it hurt his big heart.

Meatsack suddenly let go, realising how much he was hurting another person. He recoiled away as the bad man pinged in the other direction, staring at the blood and cuts covering his wide hand as one of his eyes rolled lazily in the other direction, no longer focused. The bad man fell to the ground in a ball and cried loudly, clutching his broken hand by his breast, the pipe now jammed into it at multiple horrible angles. He scuffled his boots on the ground, pushing himself away from Meatsack as blood poured from his hand.

Meatsack held his small arm to his face, big tears welling once more in his eyes. He'd gotten mad. He wasn't meant to get mad. He'd hurt someone just like Berty said not to. He whimpered softly, wishing Berty were here, not knowing what to do. He watched in panicked indecision as the bad man kept crawling away, his face twisted in a way a face shouldn't be twisted, his hand a mangled mess of flesh and bone.

A woman's voice cried out nearby, and it sounded like Bert. It sounded like she was in pain. Like the bad man. Meatsack looked desperately between him and from where he heard the sound. It sounded like Berty might need Meatsack's help, but Meatsack had hurt someone. He should fix his mistake, make it better. He needed bandages. He needed all the bandages.

But what if Berty needed him?

Meatsack sobbed loudly and once again looked between the bad man and where he heard Bert.

He felt so sad.

But Berty might need him.

Meatsack closed his eyes, squeezing big droplets of tears down into the bottom of his goggles, and ran.

* * *

"Orsen!" Jeb screamed.

The lad took the bullets dead on and toppled immediately forwards, the chair flying out of his young hands. His blood hit the floorboards moments before his body, but the chair carried forwards at the speed of Orsen's sprinting. It collided into old Bob and knocked him back, his finger twitching on the trigger and shooting himself in the foot.

Jeb ran forwards as Bob yelped with pain and surprise, shouldering past Rob to knock him to the floor as he charged for Orsen. Behind him, a grunty, drunk voice yelled "Get 'em!" and Jeb heard the pounding of many footsteps as the long-suffering traders and wanderers of Can't Be Buried saw an opportunity to deal a little bit of suffering back.

Soon the whole bar was filled with the shouting of a brawl, now far louder than the waning wind outside. Jeb got to Orsen seconds after, sliding to his knees next to the lad and slipping a withered old hand beneath his skull. The boy had landed on his front, but rolled to his back. His blood pooled on the floorboards, mixing with the dust that was still swarming in from the storm.

"Orsen, can you hear me?" Jeb cried, checking the boy's eyes.

"Blah," Orsen replied, frowning. "I think I bin shot, Jeb."

"Yeah lad, you bin shot. Twice, like an idiot."

"Sorry, Jeb," he croaked. "I'm tryin' t' save Smacks. We gots t' save it, Jeb."

"I know, lad, I know. We'll save it, OK? We'll save it. I'm sorry I didn't help sooner - I didn't want anythin' bad t' happen to ya, lad."

Orsen reached up and put his young hand on Jeb's, smiling up at the old man's face. "I know, Jeb, ya always got my best interests at heart, I know ya do..."

Jeb watched as Orsen's eyes swam in and out of focus. His heart thudded loudly in his ears, his fingers trembling on the boy's. Somewhere nearby, Bob was being swarmed with more wanderers, fighting them while his toes flopped freely around his boot, sliced away from the foot. Rob was already somewhere in a pile of bodies, unable to reach his morning star, not smart enough to be able to fight off multiple drunk opponents. The air buzzed with the slams of a good beating.

"Orsen?" Jeb said, seeing the boy become particularly dazed. "Orsen?! Don't you die on me, lad."

The boy's eyes shot open wide. "Oh shit, Jeb, do ya think that's gonna happen?

"Wait, I didn't mean-"

"Oh man, I thought I was gonna be fine!"

"Orsen, wait, you'll be-"

"Oh no, oh no, oh no, I'm gonna die. Oh no, oh crap, oh no."

Jeb squeezed his hand tight, staring into Orsen's eyes. "Shut up for once in yer life, lad. You'll be fine."

Orsen stared back, a watery film across his glittering pupils. "Is it jus' a flesh wound, Jeb?"

"Aye lad," he replied, briefly pulling back some clothing to check the wound. He almost recoiled at the sight, feeling a significant amount of vomit bubbling like a cauldron in his stomach. "Aye ... lad. The flesh is definitely wounded, there."

"Alright, Jeb," he croaked. "Ya gotta go stop the bomb. Save Smack-dab, Jeb. I'll be fine lyin' here. I feel alright, I do."

"Yer've been shot twice, Orsen. Ya don't feel fine."

"Naw, I feel great. Just horrible pain is all. It's nice t' lie down for a bit. One o' the other traders can help me out."

"No they can't, lad, I gotta stay with you until I can patch ya up."

"Yes I can," said a deep woman's voice somewhere behind. A trader was moving in next to the pair, a haggard old woman with blood on her knuckles and a toothless grin spread on her face. Her breath stank of rancid gums and grog. "You go deal with th' bomb. I'll stay here and patch up th' boy."

Jeb looked between her and Orsen. "No, I need to stay with him. You can deal with the bomb."

She shook her head. "Hell naw, old timer. I ain't dealin' with a bomb, but I know how t' patch up a bleedin' lad. Go, piss off an' save the day or whatever."

"Go on, Jeb," said Orsen weakly. "I'll be alright."

Jeb looked once more between the two and then groaned loudly. He stood up slowly and stepped away from Orsen's prone figure while the drunk old woman moved in. He almost sat back down again, but she glared up at him and made a shooing motion with her hands.

Finally, Jeb gave up. He ran for the kitchen entrance as he heard the old woman mutter, "Now lad, this is gonna hurt a shit load, so buckle up yer boots," before Orsen screamed at the top of his lungs. It almost shattered Jeb's resolve and brought him running back, but he steadied himself, steeled his nerves, and marched through the kitchen door to find a bomb and defuse it.

Something he had never done before in his life.

The kitchen was a mess. Pots and pans lay scattered about, and most of the knife racks were emptied of their knives. But there, on a metal bench in the middle of the room, was the green crate, its lid open. Jeb scurried up to it and peered nervously inside, spying a large mess of wires and chipboards, with a clock smack in the middle. It counted down, but Jeb couldn't tell from what because the left-most numbers had been damaged and were displaying weird shapes. All he knew is that he either had thirty seconds, or an undefined amount of minutes *and* thirty seconds. OK, actually twenty-nine. No, twenty-eight. Oh bloody heck, Jeb thought, his mind a whirlwind of panic.

He moved around the room as quick as he could, checking every drawer and cupboard and surface for anything that might help him somehow defuse the bomb he had no idea how to defuse. He thought about maybe cutting the wires like he'd heard on Lord Ash's radio plays, but all the cutting utensils were gone - being field tested, most likely. But he did find a mouldy, rotten wooden crate labelled Bits 'n' Bobs. Inside was all manner of horrid-smelling organic material (undefined), and plenty of glass jars with 'contents' in them. To determine what those contents were would be impossible. But one particular jar stuck out in Jeb's eyes. It had a kind of black liquid inside, a sort of tarry substance, but a bit more watery. Scrawled on the side of the jar was:

DO NOT USE

May contain traces of freezing people in place

Jeb looked it, then at the bomb, then back at it. What if he could ... you know, freeze the bomb? The heroes in Lord Ash's old plays had never tried something like that, but plenty of them had splashed liquids on defective Old World security drones and made them short-circuit. What was a bomb but just a series of circuits designed to explode instead of come to life? There were plenty of exposed circuits, certainly...

Jeb quickly examined the time counter again to see that it now said there were forty-two seconds remaining. But was that forty-two seconds, or over a minute? Sweat started to form on Jeb's brow again, and he could feel the panic rising. He was about to bloody vomit into the thing at this rate.

Well, it was do or die. If this was the Orcklands, he wouldn't have thought twice about chucking an unknown substance into a strange electrical device. It was just how things were done back in the day. But he had a lad to look after, now, and everything seemed so much scarier. But, there would be nobody to protect if a bomb went off.

Not quite resolute but at least still trying his best, Jeb grasped the DO NOT USE jar, tore open its lid and splashed it into the bomb. The black liquid sloshed out with minimal enthusiasm, and Jeb had to hit his palm against the bottom of the jar to try and encourage it out and onto the circuit boards. Eventually enough of it came out to have any kind of effect, and soon the whole circuit board was crackling and buzzing with strange noises. The clock was going wild, too, displaying whatever time it felt like. It counted up, then down, then shut off, then turned on and displayed random numbers at random intervals.

Next the circuits themselves started to spark, drifts of smoke rising up from somewhere beneath the tangled nest of wires. The crackling got louder, the sparks grew larger, and Jeb honestly had no idea if he had saved the day or doomed Smack-dab to immediate and rather sudden oblivion.

Finally, a huge fountain of sparks burst up from inside the green crate and showered Jeb in hot embers. He staggered back, patting his coat as a cloud of smoke wafted out of the crate and up into the ceiling. The box sparked and crackled, embers cascading out in all directions.

Jeb shut his eyes.

But then, that was it. Only smoke came from the crate. The other noises died out.

Jeb dared to peer back into the box, through the smoke, to at least know if he was going to die or not. It obviously wouldn't matter in the end whether he was aware of its coming or not, but Jeb still wanted to know. While he was still alive.

Inside the box, the clock and circuits smouldered, great black streaks smudged across them with smoke coming from the surface. But importantly, the clock was no longer functioning. And nor, would it seem, was the bomb itself. That is, provided the clock truly wasn't functioning, rather than simply not displaying. But, Jeb felt that a small victory had been won today, and that deserved at least some recognition.

He spied a dusty bottle of cooking grog sitting on a shelf and figured, well, hadn't he earned a reward? And so he popped the top, took a swig, and staggered back to go see how Orsen was doing.

* * *

H2-149 was spouting more of its gibberish about the inadequacies of human life, but Phoenix paid it no attention. He needed a plan, and a plan he needed. Preferably a good one. And fast. A good fast plan was needed.

But there were some issues.

Issue number one was the robot's proximity. It loomed, and that was never a good thing for your opponent to do, let alone a robotic one with a glowing red face. But the proximity meant that Phoenix would have to sacrifice his own life if he was going to grenade the stupid thing, which was something he really didn't want to do. Sacrifice himself, that is - not grenade the stupid thing (he was dead set on that).

Issue number two was the horrible crippling pain that his body suffered. Phoenix was sure that not *everything* hurt, but was quietly confident that about eighty per cent of his body was blaring out pain alerts, and that was a little bit too high on the ol' pain percentage chart for his tastes. But more to the point, horrible crippling pain hindered his super speedy movements, and a lack of super speedy movements would make it more difficult for Phoenix to do anything that might get the robot to back off. He'd already tried drawing his knife at lightning speed, but the robot was quicker than that. It was quicker than lightning.

What's a guy gotta do to get an easier opponent around here? he wondered.

"THANK YOU FOR REMAINING STILL, NOT-TRADER. YOU WILL MAKE THIS EASIER FOR ME. <lord and protector of the Farm, Farmer Brown, long may he reign> WILL APPRECIATE YOUR DEATH."

Phoenix was barely listening to it speak. He wasn't going to die in some shitty garden in the middle of nowhere. He had everything in life right where he wanted it. A horde of mad cultists loved and adored him. He had a stable job away from the trials and excessive debts of adventuring life. He spent large amounts of time alone (sort of) with a gorgeous woman whom he was absolutely certain would fall deeply in love with him after the battle was finished and he had saved the day.

Oh yeah, life was perfect. And some dumb Overlord wasn't going to ruin it. It couldn't ruin it. No way.

And then it struck him.

A foot, that is. Metal, to be specific. The robot kicked him one more time, probably to make sure he truly was going to stay still. H-units could be real bastards like that. But secondly, a memory struck him. Once upon a time in Phoenixland, he was out adventuring with a guy called Rad-man the Third, famous for his totally radical close-quarters ability and also his life-threatening radiation poisoning. Rad-man and Phoenix were pinned down once by a machine-gun-toting G-unit Overlord, a much heavier soldier than the H-unit, whilst a couple of other Overlords moved in to flank. Rad-man knew they couldn't escape just by squealing and fleeing, and the classic "What's that behind you?!" had already failed miserably. *But,* Radsy did figure out a way to get the robots to stop firing so that they could make a break for it with the ammo they stole.

He threw a grenade.

Now, Rad-man was well aware that a fizzy grenade (a deadly acid that also makes an exciting popping sound, fun for the whole family) would do little harm to the Overlords, but when threatened by explosives, they curl up into little armoured balls for protection. Then they stand up in place, unharmed, and murder you. However, the moment they curled up and protected themselves from the acid, Phoenix and Rad-man the Third bolted it backwards and disappeared into the sewers, never to be seen again. Except a bit later when they had another firefight, but they weaselled out of that one, too.

And so Phoenix had a tasty little morsel of an idea forming in his head. And also, potentially, a blood clot. He was getting beaten in the head a lot.

The Overlord known as H2-149 stood tall and pulled back its claws, about to strike down and finish Phoenix off once and for all. But, Phoenix had his plan - and a man can do anything with a plan. So long as it works...

"GRENADE, SUCKA!" he screamed, lobbing the high-explosive canister at the Overlord's light bulb. The robot immediately stepped backwards and folded in on itself, shrinking down with a number of clanks and whirring noises until it was an armoured egg, barely waist high.

"FOOLISH UNINTELLIGENT SKIN-BAG. A GRENADE WILL ONLY KILL YOURSELF."

But Phoenix was already stumbling away, and his plan was going perfectly.

"Who's the unintelligent one, now, tin-man?" he called back, after a reasonable safe distance. "That grenade isn't even turned on!" He flipped the Overlord off, just to be safe.

A red glow leeched out through the cracks of the egg and it promptly hissed open, unfolding dangerously quick into the full, skeletal height of the robotic unit. Its light was brighter than ever, locked on Phoenix's gesturing form.

"THIS RUDE POSTURING WILL ONLY MAKE YOUR SUFFERING WORSE, SKIN-BAG," it said, synthetic vocal chords unable to show frustration. But Phoenix imagined it, because he reckoned it was still true.

"Sure," he said, smiling widely. "And that inferno grenade *next* to the explosive one is certain to make yours worse, too. Asshole."

The robot looked down.

The inferno grenade exploded.

The high-explosive grenade also exploded.

A massive eruption flared up at H2-149's feet, sending a brilliantly bright, hammer-like shockwave in a huge circle all around. A dazzling inferno twirled up into the sky and spread out, blasted in all directions by the powerful shock. H2 vanished into the blinding light, as did a number of other nearby bandits of undetermined loyalties. The flames swallowed everything indiscriminately.

Of course, as physics would have it, the blast also swept towards Phoenix himself, who had not put nearly enough distance between him and the blast zone. Squeaking a curse, he dove into a not-quite-armoured ball on the ground and cowered beneath the force of the wave, feeling an immense heat lather his body and singe his hairs. But, on a little side note in his brain, he wrote down that mixing a high-explosive grenade with its inferno counterpart made for a truly wonderful experience. For him, that is. Not the robot.

He decided to remember it for later.

After he lived.

* * *

Farmer Brown stood staring down at his opponent, his face coated in dust that clung needily to the sweat and blood. Bert could vaguely make out his shape through the dizziness, a sort-of titan-sized blur that occupied a darker, larger smudge than most of the other smudges that were both dark and large and somewhere smudging in front of her. She almost didn't care that he stood so close, and that he had dragged his heavy weapon through the dust towards her. Her body felt broken, as if literally snapped in two, or three or four or...

"Ya coulda had it great, bitch," she heard a deep voice mumble, the sounds coming from a throat as gravel and reaching her ears as mud. Bert closed her eyes, wracking her brain, trying to focus on the situation. A subconscious instinct told her that now was an appropriate time to speak, and to do so quickly. A little smooth talking could extend her life, or at least let her go down saying something cool. But all she could think about was her body, how much it ached, how tired it felt. And, also, "Was that a rabbit tearing a man inside out...?"

The blur that was presumably Farmer Brown changed shape, crouching lower to grasp its weapon with both hands. It grunted loudly as its muscles flexed. But it seemed to be ignoring the chunk missing from its arm, for with a mighty breath and another loud grunt, it hefted the weapon high into the air.

Then the explosion happened.

Riding on the ribs-shattering sound blast of a devastating explosion somewhere close, a powerful shockwave tackled Brown in the side, sending him growling head over heels somewhere out of sight. His hammer thudded loudly as it fell just a second later. Then came a roaring inferno, a torrent of fire that swept across Smack's garden, singing all in its path. Bert jammed her eyes shut on instinct and cringed as the blaze washed over her. She felt her face burn, her eyebrows and lashes sizzle, and then it retreated almost as fast as it arrived. Had she been closer or standing up, she could have melted into a tiny puddle. The Woman's statue behind her was coated on its front face with a sooty black layer. The weeds and dry shrubs of Smack's garden had vanished, and the dust that remained was grilled crispy, like a layer of volcanic ash. That is, until the blackened ash disappeared under a new layer of proper, raw stuff, carried in by the waning storm on a fresh wave.

Bert curled up in on herself. How could she have let things get so bad? Bandits invaded her home, and bandits risked their lives to protect it. Bandits bloody everywhere. There hadn't been so many at Smack-dab since ... since...

Since Mayor Barns had arrived seeking revenge for the theft of his goods (he didn't really care about Hurl's face – that was comedy gold). When The Woman went down, Bert lost herself. It was the first true Bertrage of her life, and she had

317

By Duncan P. Pacey

no way of controlling it. She spent every bullet she could find, even pressing one into someone's eyeball when she had lost the gun to shoot it with. She was deep in a sea of red, a blood-curdling berserker rage that drove her to do things that she'd never forget, and not to mention plenty that she had since completely repressed.

Barns himself was one of the last to fall. Bert found him cowering in the kitchen area behind some debris, two of his personal guards lying dead on the floor. He pleaded for his life, begged and sobbed, but Bert could still feel The Woman's blood crusting on her face, could still taste the coppery tang in her mouth. She grasped him by the collar and sunk into the Bertrage, only emerging when a figure scuffed a shard of wood behind her. The Mayor's face was almost concave when Bert spun around, seeing a Barns bandit leaping towards her, hands outstretched.

He had nearly choked her to death, and it was The Woman that saved her life. Apparently not fully dead, she had pulled her dying body inch by inch through Smack-dab until she arrived at the kitchen, her blood streaking all the way back to the hall in which she got shot. It took all the last reserves of strength The Woman had to stab her vicious hunting knife into the bandit's thigh and distract him from Bert. When Bert had regained consciousness, she stabbed the bandit in the spine with a wooden splinter, but The Woman's wounds had been exacerbated by the conflict. She was well and truly dead the second time. And it was Bert's fault.

In that moment, soaked in blood, beaten all to hell, and having just survived almost certain death, Bert vowed never to let her anger take control again. It could sit there in her brain, pump her full of adrenalin, make her mad at people, even violent, but never, ever, would it control her. She couldn't allow herself to drown in that sea of red. It killed The Woman who saved her life, who protected her. It had turned Bert into an isolationist, with few friends but plenty of enemies. The pain had soured into years of anger, of repressed emotions.

And now, so many years on and in the very same place, it had happened again.

But this time it would not be her undoing, and it would not take her family from her. Bert blinked hard, trying to get her eyes to focus. She scrunched her face tight, squeezing every ounce of sensation back into her ears and eyes, forcing her brain to overcome its obvious concussion through sheer force of will. She could make out blurred shapes morphing in and out all around her, still fighting. She could vaguely identify the truck, its gunners both torn to shreds in their metal cups. She could see bodies all around and in various states of being intact, wearing dungarees, white-speckled robes, and the mish-mash armour of her Battalion. And finally, she could see Brown, staggering to his feet after being rocked by the explosion.

His entire left side was singed black. He looked like a demon straight from one of Lord Ash's radio plays, a blackened figure, smouldering smoke rising in wisps from his clothing, staggering to his feet as though climbing out of the pits of Freckle. His eyes, red-tainted jewels in the midst of a darkened face, stared at her as much as she stared at him. His chest rose and fell in heavy, emotional breaths, his thick fingers curled into thicker fists. The beast that was Farmer Brown rose unsteadily to its feet, and took the first wobbling step in a resolute if unsteady march straight for Bert - who was still, most assuredly, lying down.

She rolled onto her stomach and slowly slid her arms under her body, needing to get up. Trembling and feeling close to vomiting, she pushed herself up and nearly passed out straight away. She stopped, lowered herself down, puffing out her cheeks with every breath, hyping herself up for another try. A quick glance told her that Brown was stumbling hard, giving her precious moments to become fighting fit. Hah, fighting fit, what a joke. She was aiming for "upright". Baby steps.

But he wasn't too far away. She could probably spit the distance between them. So she tried again, pushing down with her arms and concentrating only on not passing out. Vomiting she could handle, but unconsciousness now meant unconsciousness for the rest of her life - which would not be very long indeed. Bert managed to ease herself up high enough to slip a knee under her stomach, propping her body up as she rested for a third attempt. She felt the ground thud from close, monstrous footsteps, and then a mighty foot placed itself on her ribcage and pushed her over. It didn't even take any effort, for she could not offer any. She just fell sideways, back into the dirt, a lump of uselessness at the confident feet of The Woman's memorial statue.

"Stop gettin' saved at th' last minute, woman" rumbled a voice, "an' just die already."

She looked up from the ground into the solar system of Brown's face. "After you," she hissed.

Bert saw him reaching once again for his hammer. No, Bert would not be killed – not here, not now. A small moan escaped between her chapped lips as she rolled once again to her stomach, her world seeming a little black around the edges as consciousness threatened to abandon ship. She could feel Brown moving, feel him picking his monstrous weapon from the ground. It meant her time had run out, and here she was barely even mobile. She reached out with her human hand and felt the cool stony trench coat of The Woman, felt its rough texture and billowing waves. No, this was not her time to die.

Bert gripped the coat folds tight and started pulling herself up, using The Woman for support. Half-way up she stole a glance towards Brown, and saw him fully upright, hammer in the sky. Oh shit, she thought.

"Die, bitch! Jus' die already!"

But Bert was right – 'twas not her time to die, for who ran into the scene at the last possible moment than the trembling, sobbing figure of Meatsack, and all his muscular glory. Bert saw his grey form blur into view and tackle Brown in the rib cage, and for the second time in barely as many minutes, the big lord went down. She saw Brown easily wrestle Meatsack off and toss him aside, but then Phoenix sauntered into the scene with a beautifully carved tewhatewha, two gloved hands gripping together at the base of the handle, swinging in a wild arc towards Brown's face. He missed completely – really quite badly actually – but it made the lord jump a retreating few steps backwards all the same. Phoenix then pressed in with what appeared to be zero strategy or consideration. He just launched himself like a madman and swung his weapon like a club, looking more like a drunkard after a night at Smack-dab than a warrior who just outsmarted an Overlord H-unit.

Meatsack bounced back slower, taking a few moments to find his two feet. He seemed dizzy, but Brown wouldn't let him stand there doing nothing. The lord of the Farm swung a hammy fist at the grey giant, sending him reeling away clutching his face with a small hand, blood seeping between the fingers. Phoenix was there to assist, bringing his tewhatewha down in a heavy swing right on Brown's scalp. Bert could hear the cracking of bone all the way from The Woman's statue, and the roar of pain and anger that followed.

And half way between them and Bert lay her one-time short axe (the ex-axe-axe). She gritted her teeth and tried clenching her robotic fist, only remembering afterwards that it was already clenched. Meatsack and Phoenix looked beaten all to hell, and she didn't even know why Meatsack was out here, let alone how he had so many bruises. But she did know one thing, and she knew it very well.

Nobody hurt her family. Nobody except her, and even then only if it was Phoenix.

The ground may as well have been made of ooze monsters for all its help stabilising Bert, but she couldn't let Meatsack and Phoenix fight alone. She had to finish this once and for all. Standing up to Brown had failed. Talking to him had failed. Talking to him *again*, which most folks wouldn't attempt twice, had failed. That left just one option.

Bert took a first staggering step and stopped, feeling her stomach lurch and the sounds around her fade briefly to a muddy drone. She reached back again and held on to The Woman for support before taking another step. Again she had to stop, but this time it didn't feel so horrible.

Ahead, Meatsack was tossed over Brown's head and onto the ground, the poor giant's weight bringing him down harder than most. Brown moved to stomp on him, but Phoenix tackled his leg to prevent it, pushing Brown backwards. Farmer Brown then retaliated by grasping Phoenix's clothing with a thick hand and throwing him away like a dirty piece of cloth.

Bert felt the familiar sensation of Bertrage bubbling in the lava chamber of her mind, a warmth spreading through her as a new course of adrenalin pumped into her limbs. Concentrating on the next steps, she made it to the short axe and stopped to pick it up. Doubling over brought the dizziness back in full force and she had to hold still for a few seconds, but she would not be undone by a mere severe injury. She scowled hard, glared at the dirt and swore at herself to toughen the hell up, forcing another foot in front of the other.

Brown wasn't far now, barely a few feet. His attention was torn between Phoenix and Meatsack, and who to stomp first. Both of them writhed on the ground, their fightiness all but spent. Brown cursed and spat and swore, his face as red from the blood inside it as the blood outside it.

Bert took another step.

And another.

And then a quicker one.

She was moving faster, using her legs more to keep her torso afloat than to actually run. She let gravity draw her forwards, towards Brown, getting faster and faster. She bounded towards him, knuckles white around the axe handle, her face folded tight in a determined frown. Bert saw her opponent catch her eye and see her incoming, but it was too late to react. She pushed with the last of her energy and flung her entire body, however small, at the dungarees-loving beast, bringing the axe down in a quick arc towards his monolithic chest. She didn't care what she hit, so long as it was something important.

And something she most certainly struck.

Her axe carved itself into Brown's chest cavity and stuck fast. He thundered with agony, falling backwards with hands flailing at the axe handle, and at Bert who fell forwards next to him. Blood burst out of his chest as the skyscraper that was Farmer Brown toppled to the ground. A huge wisp of dust blasted out all around him as he hit the floor, a small tremor fleeing through the earth. Bert landed next to the man, lacking in the energy required to do anything other than face-plant. She felt her body slam down, but that was it for Bert. She shut her eyes and just focused on breathing.

In first.

Then out.

In. Out.

No dying today, Roberta. There's a bar to run.

Don't die.

Part Thirteen

Is Anyone Even Still Alive?

Sir Robert wiped the blood off his hands as Doris and Toddrick finally found him again in the storm. He was impressed but not necessarily surprised to see that not only was Doris' belt full of fresh scalps, but she'd stolen someone's backpack and it looked jam-packed with all sorts of human trophies. Toddrick, on the other hand, seemed like he had fewer eyes than before. Poor bastard.

The Constellator swung her sword, lopping the hand off a farm bandit who prayed for mercy. He had prayed to some being known as Gachook, which sounded more like a sneeze than a god. Pathetic.

Jeb sat with his bottle of cooking grog and stared at Orsen, who was now fast asleep. The old woman had done a good job sewing him up, he had to admit that. But the whole situation only solidified his determination to keep the boy out of trouble - if that were even possible. He wondered if travelling was no longer the right decision, and considered the possibility of opening a store somewhere nearby. A little cafe, perhaps. Everybody loved cafes, right? He shook his tired old head and drank until he finished the bottle (which was not even remotely close to being finished when he first grabbed it).

All around, the storm waned further. The crying, howling winds lost their bluster, fading into angry blasts, then frustrated gusts, then finally, little more than slightly disgruntled breezes. Visibility stretched out from "I can't see a bloody thing" all the way to "Hey, is that man inside out over there?", and people began to realise how obliterated the Farm's forces were - particularly the last remaining bandits from said Farm, who were arguably the most concerned with the fact. And when people saw the toppled tree of Farmer Brown, axe still jutting from the trunk, they knew that it was over.

The Star Gazers were the most numerous group standing, and had coalesced together near the bullet-riddled bandit truck to regale each other with war stories of mostly truth. Mostly. Like, a solid sixty per cent truth. OK, call it forty-five.

The Polite Bandits had taken some serious losses, but together they still held a formidable force. They exchanged words now with each other, expressing concern where appropriate and politely offering to help.

"Oh, you lost an arm? I am ever so sorry."

"That head wound really is bleeding hard. Here are some bandages."

"Goodness me, is that your intestines on the ground? Why let me help you pick them up."

And Bert's Battalion? Currently leaderless, they milled about in a confused group, figuring out who was still alive and who was now the highest rank. Considering there were previously very few ranks other than "Hurl", this was a difficult undertaking, and Sawface knew it would likely require further bloodshed to fully sort out.

Blood and worse littered Smack-dab's garden as scavenger birds meandered over in the sky to have a look. The battle was over, the points were tallied, and would you look at that folks, it was a victory for the underdogs.

The Battle for Smack-dab had been won.

Well, maybe not "won", per se. But it was over, at any rate.

* * *

Bert lay motionless next to Farmer Brown. Blood pooled beneath his big chest and his arm leaked worse than Smack-dab's plumbing, no longer clogged by the constant pounding of flying dirt. The axe that protruded from his chest rose and fell with the heavy rhythm of his laboured breaths. Bert, meanwhile, felt paralysed. Everything right down to her skeleton ached and groaned. She could feel pain in parts of her body she didn't even realise were parts of her body. Half of her brain wished angrily that Brown had just cut her up so that she could bleed to death already, rather than suffer all of this infernal internal stuff. The other half of her brain sobbed quietly in a corner.

After a long, silent moment of nothingness, Bert could hear the scuffle of feet on dust as something approached. She winced in pain as it rolled her onto her back, revealing Meatsack's trembling, worried form standing above her. She squinted up at him, seeing only a blurry mess as though the pixie in her eyes that painted the world for her brain to see had gotten blindingly drunk, then high, then vomited on the canvas. The big friendly giant knelt low and fretted about Bert's body, checking every inch of her, then hugging her tight, then checking her again.

"Med ... kit," she croaked, weakly putting her human fingers on one of his hands.

He nodded quickly and sprinted away, leaving Bert alone with Brown again.

To her left, she could still hear the heavy, hoarse rattling sound of Brown's breathing. It sounded like one of his lungs might have been punctured by her axe, if that were even possible. His lungs must have been like bagpipes, but made of steel. Bert rolled her head to the left to see him, feeling her vision swim for a moment with the movement. She eventually saw his chiselled, gigantic head, eyes wide open, staring up at the sky, his gaze distant and unfocused. If she couldn't see her axe riding his chest like a rickety old boat on an ocean that didn't want it there, she'd have thought he was dead.

Bert thought again about everything they had talked about prior to him, you know, yelling and screaming and trying to kill her with his big-ass hammer (which she was *definitely* going to keep as a trophy after this). She thought again about how close they had come to peace, and about whether or not it was even real. Was it just a foolish dream - her business owner's greed made manifest by the manipulations of a murderer? Or was it *the* dream? She had to find out.

"Hey ... asshole," she said, her voice barely squeaking out through the rubble of her organs.

Brown's boulderous head rolled to the right, a little trickle of blood finding a way out of his valley mouth.

"That stuff you said ... about making the Waste better. Was it true?"

He stared, emotionless, for a long moment, gazing into her eyes. Then his chest convulsed, his throat shuddering with the effort to find where its voice had run off to. Eventually it managed to find the words: "Aye, true ... th' lot o' it."

Bert felt her vision start to cloud again but growled at it internally, willing herself to stay awake. She needed this conversation, for her own sanity if nothing else. She concentrated on every syllable, just one at a time. "So why ... why all the violence, man?"

Something happened to Brown's chest that may have been a laugh. At the same time, it may also have been a small seizure, or an internal organ exploding. But Brown managed to speak, regardless. "T' go from bein' ... a farmer, t' bein' a bandit lord, ya gotta be violent. Ya gotta be th' man who ... who walks on oth'rs, or else yer'll be the ... th' man who gets walked on."

Bert frowned, or at least tried. She sent the message from her brain to her brow and hoped it would cooperate. "That's a messed up view of the world."

The beast rolled his head back the way it came, staring up at the smog with a serious gaze. Blood still pumped from his wounds, and occasionally the big man coughed harshly, little splatters shooting up from his lips. "Sometimes," he said, recovering from a particularly bad cough, "sometimes, if things are bad, ya gotta be worse. Ya gotta dig up th' bad soil t' ... t' plant new crops."

Bert stared at him for a few moments longer, waiting to hear him say something more. But the big man had fallen silent, just staring endlessly up into the sky, the axe in his chest rising and falling, rising and falling. It was almost hypnotic, in a gruesome sort of way. She debated internally all the things she had seen, heard and, perhaps worse, felt, over the past few days. Farmer Brown's words and actions just didn't connect, and it made him hard to trust. So what do you do when you want to believe someone, but what you truly believe is that if there wasn't an axe jammed somewhere into their squishy parts, they'd be pulling yours out through your chest cavity (now with extra cavity)? It made Bert's head hurt all the more just thinking about it.

"Are you..." she started, giving her words one final check in her brain before releasing them to the world. This was probably dumb, but Bert hadn't survived this long by turning down seemingly good opportunities – she'd just need to follow The Woman's advice and be prepared. "Are you gonna survive those wounds? I wanna ... talk again."

Bert noticed Brown's fist clench and his jaw grow tense, then he finally turned to look at her, slowly. The hand on the far side of Bert moved towards his leg. "Aye," he said, "I wanna talk to you t-"

–his words were cut off by his head exploding, which tends to make words difficult.

"WOOO!" screamed Phoenix somewhere nearby. "Oh yeah, baby!"

Bert craned her neck to find his shape and saw the adventurer-turned-chef fist pumping near the corpse, a hunting rifle in hand. Little wisps still crept out the barrel as he waved it around, a big, stupid grin on his face. She felt her heart start pumping faster, felt her brain releasing more Bertrage hormones into her system. Her vision started to cloud even more. Blood bubbled in her veins.

"Quick, quick," Phoenix yelled, limping over to Brown's body and placing one foot on his chest, "somebody paint a portrait or something." He wrapped his fingers around the handle of the axe. "I wanna remember the moment Phoenix saved the day."

The adventurer then yanked the axe from Brown's deflating chest and a veritable geyser of blood shot up with it, splashing over Phoenix's face and getting into his nose and mouth. He fell away from the corpse, dropping both his axe and rifle, clawing with dirty fingers at his mouth to get it out. He spat and blew, swearing loudly as he stumbled backwards.

Bert finally passed out.

Part Fourteen

A Bird in Hand is Worth Two in the Ground

Dawn rose over a new Waste day like a lazy teenager ambling out of bed, or a senior citizen who just doesn't give a crap anymore. Light crept along the undulating, barren landscape to illuminate the disaster that it was, and remind all those present that they lived in a nightmare, and no, they hadn't finally died in their sleep. The dust storm from the day before had moved north for a while and then finally given up, and now, all things considered (which they invariably must be in this setting), it was a relatively calm day.

The wind whistled a gentle tune through the shallow hills all around Smack-dab, where numerous bodies – too many for Things to get them in a single night – still lay bloating in the dawn's dewy air. A truck, painted red and covered with armoured plating and nasty spikes, remained dormant next to the scene. Its internal organs – what was left of the patchwork technology that kept it running – were spilled across the landscape, bitten and slashed where biteable and slashable, or just haphazardly discarded where not. Two corpses rotted in metal gun emplacements atop the ancient shipping container attached to this dead vehicle, hidden from the sights of whatever might come to take them in the night. It would be a while before anybody discovered their bodies.

Far away, the last remnants of Farmer Brown's once-mighty horde encountered a scouting party sent to see where they had gotten to. What few had fled from Smack-dab had barely made it through the night, and those that had, wished they hadn't. The survivors tried to explain how their leader – a god of a man, to some – was slain by a tiny, angry woman at a rickety wooden bar, but the scout captain wasn't interested in what he perceived to be their lies. The survivors were all cuffed and taken back to the Farm, to be shot for cowardice. The captain stared at the execution as he eagerly awaited the valiant return of his powerful, undefeatable lord.

To the north, a shadowy figure stumbled into the town of Second Thought. He was covered in blood, dust, and numerous substances that anyone passing by quite instantly knew they didn't want to know more about. His face was contorted in a deadly grimace, a twisted mess of furrowed brow, bared teeth and dark eyes that spoke the word of death (which was just "death" repeated). He limped visibly on a damaged leg, with one boot missing as well as two toes. His coat looked like it had been clawed apart by Things, his trousers shredded with holes, and if the man once had a backpack, he did not anymore. Both of his hands were bandaged stumps, and nobody would ever find out how he managed to bandage them both by himself. Nobody wanted to know more about this man. They tried very specifically to know as little as possible, actually. It was like he had a bubble six feet all around him that nobody wanted to step into, even in some of the more crowded Second Thought markets.

An occasional trader recognised this black figure, and for a second, there was a glimmer of something other than hatred within the man's heart. "Wasn't he the man who single-handedly toppled the Sandcastle?"

"I thought he was the man who quelled the Bank Island riots with only a spoon and a piece of chalk?"

"No, it was a fork and a small rock."

"No you damn fools, it was a knife and two amputated fingers."

"Actually ... it can't be him. That man had two good fingers and a fine set of toes. This guy's just a nobody."

A nobody.

Nobody.

The bloodied man would clench his fists if he could, and the fact that he couldn't made him want to clench all the more. He stared at a store down the street, a single-storey workshop with the sign "Harry's Robo-Limbs in a Hurry" scrawled on the front next to cartoon figures of a happy family all holding robotic hands with one another. He gritted his teeth together and marched for the entrance.

* * *

Bert woke up - so she was off to a good start.

To be more accurate, though, Bert woke up over a period of time. Her brain required a number of run-ups to get fully started. Her various receptors all flickered on limb by limb, and each one came with the disappointed feeling of wanting to go to sleep again. The forever sleep, preferably. It really felt like she needn't have woken up at all, for all the aches and pains. And that was lying still - she couldn't even imagine moving.

But, regardless, wake up she still did.

"Morning, sunshine," said a voice.

She opened her eyes groggily, her heavy lids demanding that they be left alone. Bert was in her bedroom, by the looks of things. Someone had carried her to bed, tucked her in, and - by the looks of a nearby bucket filled with something awful - tried to clean her as well. They hadn't removed her clothing, though. Her pigcow vest was gone, as was her gun belt, but the important covers-the-private-bits accoutrement were still stuck to her skin with blood. The top few buttons of her shirt were undone, but it appeared that whoever had started chickened out at the last minute - which was fine, in Bert's mind.

The room itself was small, designed for function rather than comfort. Bert had a small, hand-made single bed on one side, a squat chest of drawers on the other and a rough desk in the middle, where a leather-bound accounting book sat gathering dust. And sitting next to her on the bed was the smiling figure of Phoenix, all cleaned up and dressed in fresh clothing (or as fresh as clothing can be in the Waste, anyway). He even had his apron on.

"How ya feeling?" he asked, smiling gently at her.

"Bliaehgia" Bert replied, realising her throat was too dry to form real words.

Phoenix quickly grabbed a short glass of liquid (to call it 'water' would be a lie) and held it near Bert's face, where she could sit up slightly and drink it down. She did so, groaning loudly with the pain of movement before forcing her lips onto the tumbler. Bert hadn't really realised how dry and inflamed her throat was until the cool liquid sloshed over it, and it felt like heaven in her mouth. That is, until, she swallowed.

"Throat a little sore, huh?" Phoenix asked, putting the glass back down. "You took a fair walloping yesterday, that's for sure."

Yesterday...

So it had only been one day since Bert passed out. Her thoughts wound lazily back to the day before, to the chaos of the storm, the blood and screams and violence. And Farmer Brown, the monstrosity of a man, the type of man lesser men would make cults out of, and that giant hammer of his.

"Brown...?" she croaked weakly, the images of what happened to him a foggy blur in her memory.

"Oh don't worry about him. We tried burying the corpse, but nobody was strong enough to push him into the hole. Also, nobody wanted to dig a hole. We just left him outside and made sure the floodlights weren't on him. Half the body is already gone."

So, Brown was dead. That made vague sense in her recollection of events, but she couldn't quite put her finger on the details...

"Meatsack is fine, too," Phoenix continued. "He's just out serving drinks. He wouldn't leave your side, but a bunch of bandits are still here so I needed him out there helping me while I cooked. Jeb is helping out, too, while we look after Orsen. Do you remember Jeb and Orsen? I like those guys - they're weird."

Bert frowned. "There are bandits ... inside Smack-dab?"

Phoenix's face froze, then he shuffled noticeably further away from Bert - just out of punch range. "Err, yeah. Um, about that. We felt bad kicking them out, you know? After they helped us and all... Sorry, Bert, I know your stance on bandits in Smack-dab, I just, I couldn't ... you know?"

Bert continued to frown, mulling over the thought. Before yesterday, she would have pinned bandits in Smack-dab as the worst thing that could happen to Smack-dab, at least in her mind. They were like a stubborn weed: Once you let them get into your garden, they just hung about, multiplied, and ruined everything. But yet, for some reason she didn't feel so disgusted by the thought. Her trigger finger didn't even twitch (although, to be fair, she hadn't checked to see if it still worked at all).

"No, it's OK," she said, almost surprised by her own words. "Let them stay for a bit longer, then kick them out. We owe them the grog."

Phoenix nodded and smiled, moving a little closer again.

Bert thought for a moment longer about Farmer Brown and the circumstances surrounding his death. She stared up at Phoenix, into his big eyes, and tried to piece together the utter madness of the day before. Phoenix looked like he was inching closer as she thought.

"Don't you fucking dare," she growled at him.

He cowered backwards. "Damn," he said, "I really thought that one was a proper *moment* moment. What on account of me saving the day and all yesterday."

"You saved the day?" Bert asked, ignoring the obvious guilt trip that lay in his humble brag. She often wondered if men realised how obvious their deceptions were, or if they were just stupid. ...probably the latter.

"You don't remember?" Phoenix replied, smiling widely. Beaming, you might even call it. "You and Brown were lying on the ground together and when he moved towards you, I shot him in the head."

"Woah, woah, woah," Bert suddenly snapped, glaring up at Phoenix. "Stop right there a moment."

"Stopping here."

"Rewind a second."

"Rewinding..."

"You did *what*?!"

Phoenix scratched at his scraggly beard. "I ... shot Farmer Brown in the head?"

"Argh! No, Phoenix," Bert wailed, slapping her face with her human hand and holding it there. "Fuuuuuuuuuuck," she growled through her palm.

"Is there, err, something wrong?"

"Do you know how close I was to negotiating peace with that guy? Peace that would have made us rich!"

"Oh, err, um, err, really?" Phoenix grinned nervously and his eyes darted about the room looking anywhere but Bert.

"He was unarmed, lying in the dirt and badly wounded," Bert continued, her face going red. "Why the hell would you shoot him in the head?!"

Phoenix shrunk away to the foot of the bed, a puppy being rebuked for what it thought was an exciting triumph, but turns out was just a shit on the floor. "He wasn't unarmed," he mumbled.

"What do you mean he wasn't unarmed? I axed him in his fucking chest and watched him fall to the dirt."

The chef nodded quickly. "Yeah, sure, but he had a knife stashed away on the other side from you. I was watching, Bert, I swear. He tried to grab it when you were talking, so I blew his head off. Err ... at least I think it was a knife. It could have been something else. But I'm pretty certain it was knife-like, at the very least. Almost a hundred per cent certain. Maybe eighty. But higher than fifty, that's for sure."

Bert stared at him wide-eyed and red-faced. A knife? Bloody hell, why did everything have to be so complicated all the time? First she couldn't believe that Farmer Brown was telling the truth, now she couldn't believe Phoenix was saying he wasn't. Bert seethed, hating the mad farmer for ever having come to Can't Be Buried.

"...Bert?" Phoenix mumbled quietly, gazing at her. He was pale. "Are we, err, you know, umm ... good?"

Bert stared at him for a number of tense seconds, then sighed loudly, allowing herself to be defeated. "Yeah," she finally said, "we're good, I think. Just, I dunno, go clean something. I don't have the energy to yell at you right now."

And as if on cue, a sweaty-faced trader burst into the room, panting loudly from what looked like sheer bloody panic. "Bert, Phoenix!" he cried, voice high-pitched and scared.

Bert frowned at the man. "What's up, Regis?"

Regis babbled for a second, then formed the sentence: "One of the bandit folk went to the toilet and he dun' come out, so's we go to investigate an' there's a bloody huge spider in there!" He held his hands apart to indicate size, at least three feet.

Bert processed this for a moment, then sighed again.

"Phoenix, you wanna take this one?" she asked.

The adventurer looked at her as though she were mad. "Do I have to?"

"Oh yeah, big time."

He mewled sadly and heaved himself off the bed, forcing each step to thud loudly in protest as he trudged towards the door.

"Phoenix," Bert called after him.

He turned.

"Try not to ruin the corpse, alright? We'll serve it as a special today."

...and that was how Smack-dab returned to normal.

More or less.

The Post-Credits Scene

Sir Robert stood with one hand on the sling of his rifle and the other twiddling the wiry strands of his lush moustache. He smiled widely beneath the thick fur, staring up at what, to him, was the most beautiful sight in the world.

The Ash Fort, in all its magnificence and glory, rose before him. Its walls towered into the cloudy grey sky, and stretched on into the horizon. Its famous ramparts lay near-empty, Sir Robert only able to see a small skeleton crew patrolling the many mile's worth of perimeter. There were even a couple of literal skeletons duct-taped into vague standing positions.

Magnificent, he thought to himself. Absolutely bloody magnificent.

Sir Robert turned around to look the other direction, soaking in the splendour of his new bandit horde. The Polite Bandits stood alongside their Bert's Battalion brethren, and even a few disenfranchised starry teenagers had joined up, looking for a life of excitement and daring and dashingness, not realising that banditing was mostly drinking and standing around waiting for traders to walk past, with only a small amount of excitement and daring, and very little dashingness. But they didn't need to know that just yet.

He smiled again, feeling the wind splash on his face with icy little fingers. Soon, he thought, soon he and the others would be resting inside the fort's mansion, sleeping in actual beds, eating food that wasn't rotten. It was a dream come true. He just had to reach out and snatch it.

"Alright, lads!" he cried. "Shall we tally ho and take back the fort?"

A chorus of cheers blasted past him in response.

"Perfect. Well then, I'll jolly well start us off then, eh?"

And so Sir Robert discharged his weapon at the nearest Farm guard and started sprinting for the gates, hearing the roar of his forces behind him as they did the same.

And the bandits above looked down in horror, for they knew their end was near.

IF YOU ENJOYED THIS BOOK

If you thought this dumb novel was worth your time, please leave a review on Amazon, Goodreads, social media or frigging anywhere, I don't know – I'd just really appreciate your thoughts.

And tell your friends! They won't think your reading taste is dumb, I swear. They'll like Smack-dab too, right? Maybe they will. Hopefully. Let's assume.

Oh, and hit me up on social media on your way out. I'd love to hear from you. You read my book, so that makes you pretty awesome.

Facebook.com/dppacey
Twitter.com/dppacey

Thanks!

Duncan

By Duncan P. Pacey

THE
CRUMBLE BULLETIN

Find more stories from the Waste by visiting the Crumble Bulletin, a fictional newspaper-thing set in the same world as Smack-dab, which is sometimes funny and also often not.

www.crumblebulletin.com

75615283R00202

Made in the USA
Columbia, SC
18 September 2019